# Contents

THE GATEKEEPERS

# Through the Green Glass Door

KATIE ZELIGER

Meraki Press

To the girls who are still trying to find their purpose,
there's a world beyond that has a place where you belong.

Paperback ISBN: 979-8-9991650-7-7
eBook ISBN: 979-8-9991650-8-4

Book Cover and Chapter Headings Designed by Kathryn Jordan
Formatting by Katie Zeliger
Editing by Leah Taylor and Shira Rodriguez

Library of Congress Control Number: 2025927623
Publisher's Cataloging-in-Publication Data
Names: Zeliger, Katie, author.
Title: Through the green glass door / Katie Zeliger.
Series: The Gatekeepers
Description: Monroe, LA: Meraki Press, 2026.
Identifiers: LCCN: 2025927623 | ISBN: 979-8-9991650-7-7 (paperback) | 979-8-9991650-8-4 (epub)
Subjects: LCSH Coming-of-age--Fiction. | Romance fiction. | Fantasy fiction. | BISAC YOUNG ADULT FICTION / Coming of Age | YOUNG ADULT FICTION / Fantasy / Romance | YOUNG ADULT FICTION / Religious / Christian / Fantasy
Classification: LCC PS3626 .E55 T47 2026 | DDC 813.6--dc23

First edition, 2026
Printed in the United States of America.

# Glossary of Terms

**Fates:** The three sisters who created everything. The Sisters: Darkness, Justice, and Mercy. Also referred to as "The Creators" or "The Creator".

**Twins:** Descendants of The Fates. The Twins: Destiny and Free Will. Destiny created Stewards, and Free Will created Humans.

**Gates/Portals:** What separates the Humans and Stewards, guarded by Gatekeepers.

**Gatekeepers:** Human guardians of the gates/portals between our world and the other realm: Landow.

**Stewards:** Descendants of the Fates/Twins. They are born into one faction of energy: earth, wind, fire, water. They have the ability to steward the energy of their faction.

**Hybrids:** A steward who possesses two factions of energy. It is very rare.

**Manters:** One of the original and most ancient earth-bound energy stewards. They possess heightened, matured abilities and primarily steward healing energy. They also act as guardians of the energy storehouses in Ruack Valley.

**Inaras:** One of the original and most ancient wind-bound energy stewards. They possess heightened, matured abilities and primarily steward knowledge and wisdom. They act as guardians of the observation temple in Prentiss.

**Tembis:** Non-corporeal orbs, often enlisted as spies for Kilburne. They have the ability to expand into large siphoning orbs and drain stewards.

**Imprint:** A soul bond formed between two stewards. It can be platonic, romantic, or traumatic. An imprint leaves the mark of a fingerprint on a steward.

**Channeler:** A steward who can pull energy from any source: earth, wind, fire, water, human, steward, etc. Has no limit and no reserve. They can be very dangerous.

Places

**Landow:** The fantasy land home to the stewards. Also referred to as "The Mirrored Kingdom" or "The Land Beyond the Veil".

**Kilburne:** The land where the fire-bound energy stewards settled.

**Ruack Valley:** The land where the earth-bound energy stewards settled. Also, a sanctuary for other stewards looking for refuge.

**Prentiss:** The land where the wind-bound energy stewards settled.

**Solmere:** The land where the water-bound energy stewards settled.

**The In-Between:** A prison realm between our world and Landow.

**Whispering Winds:** A sentient forest with mind-altering winds. Can cause paranoia, madness, and anxiety.

**Mountains of Anguish:** A sentient mountain range with mind-altering trails. Can cause melancholy, lethargy, and depression.

# Scout

I barged through the front door of our sixth house in four years and leaned back against the frame, letting my book bag fall to my Converse-clad feet. On the stand in the foyer, in a basket full of mail, lay a stack of large envelopes. *The* large envelopes that every senior in my year was still hoping to see slide through their mail slot.

I winced and trodded over to shuffle through them.

Three new acceptance letters. I wanted to throw them in the trash right along with the others I received. *How can you know what you want to do for the rest of your life at seventeen?*

"Scout, honey, was that you? Did I hear you come in?"

"Yeah, Mom, it's just me."

From the kitchen, cupboard doors banged open and closed. Followed by the fridge doors beeping open and my Mom's muttering as she stood in front of them.

*Mom is stress-baking. Great.*

My phone vibrated several times in my pocket. I slid it out to see my friend's group chat had an obnoxious amount of messages.

**Macy: OMG!! did u hear??**

**Danny: hear about what?**

**Macy: the Navitas are playing at the Last Blast Summer Fling!!**

**London: No way!! We have to get VIP tix, I've been dyinngggg to meet them!!**

Macy was the first friend I made when we moved to this coastal town in South Carolina halfway through my junior year. Macy took me in when we both realized we had the same birthday, June 28th. She introduced me to her friend group and Danny. The boy I had been secretly crushing on since he complimented my green eyes. Macy and Danny had been friends since kindergarten, growing up in the same class since Pickins County only had one small school.

Sometimes, I was jealous that they had each other's lifelong friendship. And sometimes, I liked to imagine that I grew up with them. That I met them the summer before we all started kindergarten. In my fantasy, our parents would bump into each other in the local park just down the street from the swimming beach. They would meet, laugh, and gush over the fact that they were all raising kids the same age. It would be perfect.

But that's not how it happened. Nothing like that, *nothing so kismet*, had ever happened to me. Mom's job made sure of it as it dragged her coast to coast, Dad—with his work-from-home counseling practice—and me in tow. She was a marine biologist, specializing in some kind of aggressive, invasive algae that made all kinds of organizations need her help. Don't get me wrong, I loved my mom, and seeing her dreams come true was amazing. But it had a cost. I just didn't realize it until this year. Being a senior with eight previous transcripts made me stand out in a way I'd always wanted to avoid.

My mom swore Pickins County, South Carolina was the last place. This was "the dreamiest of all dream jobs," she'd said. We were close to hers and Dad's alma mater, and my soon-to-be alma mater, Duke.

I glanced back at my phone as another text came in, this time from outside of the group text.

**Macy: when can we go shopping for our birthday dresses?**

The moment Macy and I found out we shared a birthday, she flung her hair over her shoulder and deemed us birthday twins. And so last year we threw a big party—*nay, a birthday bash*, she said. My parents were thrilled to see me being so "well-adjusted" despite the move halfway through my junior year. The party had fallen the week before the town's Last Blast, a community event that celebrated the graduating seniors the month after graduation and before they went off to college.

This year, our birthday fell on the same day as the event, a few short weeks after graduation, and everyone would be leaving shortly after. Macy to New York City for fashion school, and Danny to the local community college to study finance, like his father, so he could take over his accounting office in the next ten years.

Everyone had plans. Dreams. Aspirations. Ten-year goals. It felt worse than moving, losing my friends as they raced towards their dreams while I stalled out waiting for one to find me.

I had the acceptance letter from Duke, a stack of wait-list acceptances still rolling in, and no desire to pursue any of them. Mom and Dad had waited months for "the big one": my acceptance—or rejection, I'd had my fingers crossed—to Duke.

To go where they went had been *their* dream. Even before we lived so close to it, they pushed me to take every advanced science course possible, attend every STEM camp, and be a part of all the scholastic challenges available.

My acceptance to Duke came a month ago, in April. My parents shopped the school catalog and had my three years planned out already, because, of course, they'd already made me complete a year of dual enrollment. They had fast-tracked my life for a career of scientific breakthroughs like my mom. I was going to be the next Nobel Prize winner, whether I liked it or not.

And I did not like it.

I didn't know what I wanted to be, but I knew it wasn't a scientist. I didn't know where I wanted to end up, but I knew it wasn't Duke. Following my parents' coursework plan through high school was all I could bear. It gave me something to do, an outlet, something to distract myself from making friends and having to inevitably end those friendships when we moved. I appeased my mother, and it has been enough until now. Even though the acceptance already came, and they had sorted my schedule for the first semester, I was still hoping for a miracle.

Could I really go to Duke, the last place I ever wanted to go? Could I really forfeit myself for my parents' dreams? I had this summer to come up with a plan or have fun trying.

My phone vibrated in my hand again, and I sighed. Macy.

**Macy: helllllooooooooo**

**Macy: I see you typing, I know you're thereeee**

**Me: Sorry, just got home. Stack of envelopes waiting. Insert eye roll here. Idk, soon.**

"Did you hear me? I asked you to come in here for a moment," Mom said, appearing in the hallway. She wrung her hands in a dish towel before throwing it over her shoulder.

I sighed and gave the most nuanced eye roll ever, so I didn't get a tongue lashing.

I locked my phone and slid it back into my pocket to follow my mom to the kitchen. The window over the sink was open, and a breeze puffed the linen curtains into billows before sucking them back against the screen. The scent of apple pie swirled around the room.

My dad sat at the breakfast nook adjacent to the kitchen, reading the paper. When he saw me come in, he set the paper down and took off his reading glasses. My father had a kind face and the sort of eyes that crinkled even when he wasn't laughing, like he was anticipating a joke to be told at all times. The mossy green of his eyes made me smile. I had a matching pair, and I loved that we had this trait in common.

He gave me a little smile, eyes alight, and scooted further into the breakfast nook. Tapping the seat next to him, he said, "Have a seat, Poppet. Mom and I want to share something with you."

I hesitated and glanced at Mom.

She was bent over, scowling at the pie in the oven. She always loved creating exquisite pie crusts. Unfortunately, they would be so decadent that she couldn't figure out how to get a grip on the pie to remove it from the oven. Inevitably, she would burn it, bust it, or end up getting burnt herself. Thus perpetuating the stress-baking cycle.

Whatever it was they wanted to talk about must have been big. My mom hadn't baked a pie since our last family Christmas in Maine, which was a certified disaster. Over the counter, I watched as Mom decided to crack the lip of the crust, preventing what she spent all afternoon working on from being charred to the point of destruction. She muttered to herself through frustrated huffs, and I laughed.

I slid my gaze back to my dad and eyed him suspiciously, but he just patted the cushion next to him again and motioned dramatically for me to join him. His over-the-top motion got a snort out of me, and I slipped in beside him.

"How was school, Poppet?" There was a faded accent in his voice, what was left of his English mother, Grandma Claire. She was born in England but fell in love with an American, much to her family's dismay. Sometimes, I would try to ask Dad what it was like growing up in England, but he'd always change the subject. Grandma died when he was little, and the accident was still a sore point for him.

"Fine," I said, scrutinizing him for a clue as to what this sit-down meeting was about.

"Tell us more. It was the last week of class, wasn't it? Must be exciting. It's your last 'last day' of school before college!" Ah, *college,* the looming shadow in the room. It found a way to seep into every conversation these days.

"Not really. Quite the opposite, actually. Everyone's ready to be done, and honestly, most of the senior class skips the last few days of school, so the halls are a ghost town. And this heat wave hasn't helped. It's been miserable since the AC broke in half of the school." Mom deposited a glass of ice water in front of me and plopped a dish of clean grapes between us as she seated herself across from me with a tuckered-out sigh.

"I think we have an idea to help with that, don't we, hon?" She looked at my dad like she was asking for backup or a steely nerve. It forced my eyes to narrow even more. "How would you feel about a little vacation this summer? Maybe a bit of time to relax before enrollment this fall?"

I brightened considerably. "Is that what you're being shady about? A surprise vacation?" I considered what that might mean... no science summer camp. "Count me in!" I plucked a grape from the dish and popped it in my mouth with a smile. Mom and Dad shared a look that unsettled me. "Why am I sensing there's a catch?" My stomach began a slow descent to the pit of panic.

My father was the one to speak first, eyes still on Mom. "Well, honey," he brushed a hand over his mouth, "Your mother has received a very prestigious invitation to collaborate on a research dive in the Faroe Islands." A small alarm bell went off in my head. *The what?*

"It's really the trip of a lifetime," my mother rushed to cut in. "I've waited my whole career for an opportunity like this. The discoveries we make could change the trajectory of marine biology as we know it. Not to mention, we could write for journals, publish articles about our findings..." She trailed off as she searched my father's eyes again for what seemed like approval. His eyes crinkled in response, and she settled a bit.

"Okay... so let me get this straight. We're going to the Faroe Islands this summer? Wherever that is." I threw a questioning look between my parents, as I tucked my mousy hair behind an ear.

"Not quite. It's a work trip, and there won't be room on the boat for all of us." My father looked as close to sorry as he could manage with an involuntary twinkle in his eye.

My breathing sped up just a bit, though there was no reason to be nervous. I could stay home alone for a while. It wasn't a big deal. I took a sip of water to disguise my mild freak-out at the news. Mom worked hard at her job, and after all these moves, some recognition was well-deserved. I wanted to be excited for her, but something in my gut told me there was more.

"So…" I tried to process what this meant for me. *They said vacation, though, didn't they?*

Dad continued, "So we've made arrangements for you to stay with my mom's sisters: Aunts Efrata and Griselda. They're already expecting you and couldn't be more thrilled." My mom reached across the table to squeeze my father's hand with a tight smile. He patted hers in response.

That's when things started clicking into place in my mind. "You're sending me to *England*? But," I sputtered, "but I had plans for this summer." I nearly toppled the water glass as I pushed up from the table. The glass rattled, and my mother winced. I glanced around, looking for an excuse, a way out of it. "What about summer camp?"

It's not what I meant. What I really meant was: *I am not ready to confront the fate of college; I need more time!*

"You can't just ship me across the ocean to stay with complete strangers!" My voice climbed higher. I had a plan. I was going to find a way out of attending Duke this summer. Silently, I had followed my parents around the country, and I obeyed every demand and expectation they put on me. This summer was going to be my last chance… but now it was slipping away. What if I never found a way out of Duke? *Dr. Scout Larsson, Ph.D. in Biomedical Engineering…* Oh, that sounded dreadful.

My mother's fingertips settled at her temple, and now her stress-baking made sense. My reaction was exactly what she was anticipating. Even knowing it, I couldn't stop the fluttering in my chest.

"Darling, it isn't the *whole* summer. Just a few weeks," my father began, ever the diplomat. "Besides, we're long overdue for a visit."

"*We?*" I squeaked out.

They guffawed at one another like *this* was the preposterous part of the whole conversation. "You don't think we would let you travel alone to a foreign country, do you?"

"I don't know what to think. I didn't think you'd send me to a foreign country to begin with, so it looks like we're all out of our depths here," I fired back as I began to pace, feeling trapped.

Dad tried hard to make it sound appealing. "We'll all fly into London together. Effie and Zelda will meet us at the airport to get you, and your mother and I will catch a connecting flight to the island. We'll be there to make sure everything is taken care of, don't worry." He nudged me with a brilliant smile, trying to get me to rally. But I wouldn't budge. "And after the trip, we'll return for a short visit."

How could this be happening? I groaned, letting my head fall into my hands right there in the middle of the kitchen. The overwhelming feeling of losing any hope I had for this summer eclipsed the embarrassment of losing my cool in front of them.

My father appeared at my side, gently rubbing my arm. "Cheer up, Poppet. It'll be the adventure of a lifetime. For all of us," he said brightly, reaching for my mom and drawing us all close.

"God, I hope so," I mumbled into his shoulder.

"But don't worry," Mom added before diving into the hug, "We'll be home with plenty of time for us to get you ready for Duke in the fall!"

*Oh, great.*

# Scout

The three of us spent the afternoon huddled together, hovering over my mother's cooled pie, passing a fork back and forth as we ate it from the pan. They explained the trip's details, and I understood things would happen very quickly. Pickins County graduation was tomorrow, but the research crew needed to be on the Faroe fjords as soon as possible. If the tides shifted, they would lose the window of time needed to collect samples. Mom negotiated from leaving tomorrow, during my graduation ceremony, to Sunday night. It was the latest they'd allow, or they'd have to select another biologist.

My parents saved the biggest bomb for last: This was no quick trip abroad. This was a month-long stay at a virtual stranger's house in a foreign country.

This whirlwind of a trip had me caught somewhere between shock and denial. With a final forlorn lick of the fork, I trudged upstairs to pack.

Once in my room, I called Macy to lament. She was devastated to learn our birthday bash was off. But I couldn't tell if she was more upset that I wouldn't be here or if it was because I was going to Europe without her. At least her jealousy had given me a laugh. I tried to see it from her perspective; England *was* Europe. But my aunties were ancient and lived as far from London as you could get. I doubted there would be any parties or cute guys to speak of, despite Macy's delusional British fantasies.

Realizing there was nothing more we could do, we grumbled until a knock sounded at my door.

Mom peered in and, seeing my tear-streaked face, crossed the floor to perch on the corner of my bed. "Oh, honey," Mom tutted, "I know this must seem like the end of the world for you, but I promise it's just the beginning." She gave my feet a quick squeeze and leaned over to speak into the phone. "Macy, can you help her rally? Maybe get her packing? Thanks!" Mom headed toward the door.

"Remind me again why I can't stay with Macy?" I whined.

"Honey, your dad went to a lot of trouble to arrange this with his aunts." She pursed her lips before pulling the door closed behind her.

"Besides," Macy said to me, "I have to leave for fashion camp in two weeks. Sorry!"

With a groan, we said goodbye, and I got to packing.

I gathered my favorite jeans, some nice tops, and a bunch of plain tees and comfy shorts. Thinking I might need a nice outfit, I surveyed what I had on hand in the closet and grabbed a couple of options.

I folded everything and rolled it into my suitcase. Before zipping it up, I took another look at the closet. There, on the top shelf, sat an old white gift box. A smile ghosted across my face as I remembered the Christmas I got it. I must have been ten or so.

I pulled the box down and opened it. A gift from my great aunts.

Shimmying the lid off, I tugged the old wool material free from the tissue paper. Objectively, it was a hideous brown sweater.

A small white card sat at the bottom of the gift box with an elegant handwritten note: "*Something suitable to warm you this holiday.*" I still kept it in the box, tucked on the shelf above my clothes rack in the closet.

Despite never knowing my aunts, they seemed kind. Their cards never got "lost in the mail," and they sent birthday and Christmas gifts until I was ten. Despite the gesture, they felt oddly nonexistent in my life. Except for now. I hugged the sweater to my chest and buried my nose in it. I expected it to be musty, but it smelled like sweet cardboard and pine.

The only reason I kept it at the time was that it would've hurt my Dad's feelings to throw it away. But holding it up now, I realized I liked having it there, neatly folded and wrapped in tissue paper in the white box in my closet. It linked me to a place far away.

And I thought, if I didn't open it, I could hold that link frozen in time and space. It could be whatever I needed it to be.

Opening the box reminded me that, as much as I wished I could pause and relish the idea of some rich and mysterious old aunties doting on me, time had slipped away. And without any further communication between us, the gifts had dried up. The letters had stopped coming. The link was pretty much gone. Except for there, in my closet, with the lid on the box firmly shut tight.

My thoughts grew sour as I realized I had a tendency to hold on to everything like that, thinking I could freeze and keep it the same forever. But inevitably, time moved on, even if I didn't.

A new knock sounded at my door, heavier than the first. Dad.

"How's it coming along, kiddo?" Entering my room, his eyes trailed to the white box at my feet and the sweater on my lap. "What have we here?"

"It's the sweater the aunties got me when I was little."

Dad sat on the bed next to me. Slinging an arm over my shoulder, he tugged me close. "You know, Effie knit that for you." I shook my head, my hair catching on the stubble of his chin. I ignored it, nuzzling closer as I breathed in the minty scent of his deodorant. There had been many times when Mom was traveling for work that it felt like just Dad and me against the world. I guess now was another of those times.

"Will you tell me about England?"

Dad pulled back and bit his lip. "Oh, there's not much to say."

"Dad. Seriously. You grew up in a foreign country, and you're about to send me there. Why are you being so weird about it?"

Dad looked off wistfully, his head bobbing left and right on his shoulders, considering what to share.

"How about this, I'll tell you one thing, and then you come down for dinner with me, and you get to pick the movie tonight?"

I laughed, but agreed.

"I thought I would spend my whole life at the seaside in that cottage with my aunties. But when I turned eighteen, it changed. I moved here, met your mother, and we created a life together. I just don't like to look back at the what-ifs when our world is full of promise here and now. Okay?" He patted the bed and eased up. "Let's go."

A small thought niggled at the back of my mind, telling me that my father was not being totally honest with me. That *"something changed"* bit felt like a redacted report. A new need was growing in my mind. If I couldn't get out of going, I would go. And I would find out what he wasn't telling me.

# Scout

Forty-eight hours later, our redeye touched down in London. I peered through the double-paned window into the cloudy blue sky. My mother gave me the consolation prize of a window seat to make up for yet another move that changed my plans. You'd think I'd have gotten used to it by now, but it seemed like each time her career dictated a move, it was like yet another axe mark in the tree of my heart: destined to fall. *Oof, even I cringed at myself that time. I've gotten way too dramatic for my own good.*

The flight attendant's voice crackled through the speakers, announcing that local time was six a.m., and the temperature was thirteen degrees Celsius. My body shuddered at the oddity. I felt exhausted, knowing it was only midnight back home.

I squinted as the lights flickered on and the commotion began around me. Not wanting to get off the plane, I braced myself with a breath before my mother reached over to squeeze my shoulder, prompting me into the aisle.

Twenty-four hours ago, I was celebrating graduation. Tossing my cap in the air alongside Macy and Danny hadn't felt as good as I thought it would. With so much unknown still in my future, graduating felt like a trap. Embarking into the unknown was horrifying. I'd either be moving into Duke in the fall... or, well, there wasn't another option. Yet.

"Scout, are you coming?" Mom called from a few steps ahead. I snapped to attention, shaking off the feelings.

We trickled off the plane and passed through customs and border control before finally exiting the airport. The morning air greeted us with a gusty hello, sending a chill down my legs that started them quaking. Whether from the wind or the emotional exhaustion, I couldn't quite tell. We waited under the large terminal sign for the aunties.

"I'm actually really excited to see Aunt *Zelfa*... and Aunt... *Helen*?" I tried to remember the aunties' names, but judging by the amusement on my dad's face, I made a blunder.

"You mean Aunt Zelda and Effie, don't you?" He just chuckled and pulled me, completely deflated, into his arms for a hug. "This trip is going to change things for you, you know that, don't you? Even though we can't be there with you, it's going to be amazing." He gave me another good squeeze before releasing me. "Listen. Being here now reminds me of when I lived here as a boy. England may seem frumpy from the movies and whatnot, but I promise, it's a magical place. Just give it a chance, love, hm?" He did that very British thing where he sucked in his lips and raised his eyebrows, folding them like an accordion.

"Yeah, okay."

While we waited, we converted our phone plans to international, and Dad exchanged our US dollars. When Dad returned with some money for me, I stashed it expertly between my varying luggage pieces and in my socks as the travel blogs Macy sent me told me to do.

Twenty minutes later, a nondescript, black sedan rolled up to the curb. A severe woman, with silver hair pulled back so tight it gave her a facelift, stepped out of the driver's seat and scrutinized me up and down slowly. Her cheekbones protruded like knuckles, and the sallowness of her cheeks made her look gaunt and vicious. A shiver raced over my spine and lingered while she glared at the luggage in my hands.

My dad greeted her as Aunt Zelda with a brisk handshake before turning to hug and kiss the cheek of the petite woman next to her. She was a flash of yellow, bold and bright against the backdrop of her sister's all-black get-up.

Aunt Effie had matching silver hair, worn long, tied neatly in a braid. Her eyes twinkled like my Dad's, and I saw the resemblance immediately. She smiled warmly at me and gestured me into a hug with her.

"Oh, Scout! You're so grown!" She crushed me into the fabric of her brightly colored dress. The moment she embraced me, my father whisked the luggage away and into their trunk.

She pulled back from the hug with her hands firmly gripped on my upper arms. "Let me get a good look at you. Dear gods, are they feeding you?" She twirled me side-to-side and poked at my ribs. "We'll fix that, won't we, Zel? Come on, I've got a crock of soup on at home for you."

"Now, Efrata, please don't overdo yourself," my dad said. "Scout is almost an adult, and she can more than care for herself. We are so grateful you are letting her stay during Evalyn's trip, but please don't put yourself out for us. We'll be back in three weeks to collect her." My father was so gracious. So kind. I hoped to be like him when I grew up.

"Speaking of putting ourselves out, I believe we came to an *arrangement*?" Aunt Zelda sidled along Aunt Effie, nudging her out of the way in a smooth motion.

My mother audibly balked, but recovered by feigning a yawn, throwing wide eyes at my father. He apologized while digging in his pocket for his wallet. He pulled out a thick envelope, and I could barely stop my jaw from dropping on the ground. He had to *pay* them to take me in? He *bribed* them and lied to me. I shot daggers at the back of his head as he crossed in front of me to hand Aunt Zelda the wad.

She opened it and peered in, "That should suffice. It's time to go."

Aunt Zelda turned and slid into the driver's seat, shutting the door to us. I was astounded. *Aren't British people supposed to be classy? That was so uncouth!*

"Well," Aunt Effie clasped her hands and smiled brightly as though the most awkward greeting hadn't just occurred. "It'll be a long trip, so we'd best get on with it." She hugged and kissed my parents again before turning to squeeze my hand. "We'll give you a moment to say your goodbyes."

Once I heard Aunt Effie's door slamming shut, I whirled on my parents.

"You totally lied to me! They don't want me here! You had to *pay* them to let me stay! Ughhhh!"

"Shhhh," Dad looks over my shoulder at the car. "They'll hear you, and that's not a great foot to start off on."

"Oh, you want to talk about getting off on the wrong foot?" I asked, crossing my arms over my chest. "Aunt Zelda didn't even say hello to me, let alone two words to Mom! She's awful."

"Watch it, Scout." My mother chimed in. "Your father went to great lengths to make this trip possible for me. The least you could do is give it a chance."

"A chance? Are *they* gonna give me a chance?" I huffed as my cheeks burned with embarrassment. There was nothing worse than being the new kid and getting rejected on the first day. *Trust me, I know.*

"I promise it's going to be okay. We love you, and we'll see you in three weeks." Dad gave me a good squeeze and traded me off to my mom's arms.

I grumbled as Mom rubbed circles on my back. "I really appreciate your willingness to get to know your Dad's side of the family, hon." She said in that pointed way mothers do. It wasn't true, but she hoped that by saying it, it would become true.

"Yeah, yeah..." I pulled back, and for a moment, I was tempted to cry. Getting in the car meant leaving safety, leaving comfort and familiarity behind. I almost wish I were going to be stuffed on a boat in the Faroe Islands this summer. It would be a lot cozier than time with Aunt Zelda, that's for sure.

"Alright?" Aunt Effie asked, a lilting question in her voice.

"Yep," Dad answered. "Be good, Scout." He kissed my forehead, then opened the door for me.

As he shut me in, an immediate pang of regret struck me. I twisted in my seat to wave goodbye to my parents. Why hadn't I fought them harder? I would rather go to every science summer camp and do all the summer reading for the fall semester than be stuck in this overcrowded small car, driving away from the only source of home I had in a new country.

Every so often, Aunt Effie twisted in the front passenger seat, crinkling her bright yellow cotton dress, to sneak a peek at me. I tried to hide my contempt behind a tired smile, but her full-lipped smile faltered seeing mine. I sighed heavily.

"When we get back, we'll need to go to the *shops*," Aunt Zelda said in a low whisper, which piqued my interest.

Aunt Effie nodded and pulled out a small scratch pad and a pair of red reading glasses from her purse. "What do we need?" She began jotting things down before Aunt Zelda responded.

"Can I come?" I asked, leaning forward. I was not ready to be cooped up in an old maids' house all summer, and the idea of exploring something local seemed not so bad.

Aunt Zelda's piercing blue eyes flashed sharply at me in the rearview mirror. "It wouldn't serve you well to do so. You aren't to pay any mind to the *others*."

A chill blossomed through me at what felt like a warning, and my brow furrowed in response. Before I could open my mouth in retort, Aunt Effie spun around with an overly pleasant expression, her eyes bright through big, round red glasses, "What she means, pet, was not this time. Let's get you settled in first, then we'll see about going to town together. Alright?"

I watched the interaction between Aunt Effie and Zelda. The way Aunt Effie toyed with her long gray braid while looking over Aunt Zelda seemed so submissive—like walking on eggshells. I didn't like it. I stilled, watching their interaction. Aunt Zelda would make a strong statement, and Aunt Effie's eyes would roam for a moment before settling. I had a warning in the pit of my stomach. Something felt off about Aunt Zelda.

I sat back in a huff and crossed my arms. Watching out the window, the city turned from sky-scraping buildings to rolling hills and small cottages with stone fences. Even the sun seemed to warm as the trip went on.

Aunt Effie noticed me craning my neck to see the sun and bright blue sky. "The southern coast of England is the sunniest place in the UK. You should have plenty of lovely days to go for walks and such."

The rest of the three-hour trip passed mostly in silence, broken up by small murmurings between the aunties. Leaning forward slightly, I tried as hard as I could to seem uninterested while eavesdropping, but every so often, Aunt Zelda caught me and unleashed her deep blue gaze on me.

My Dad wouldn't tell me about his time here. Was Aunt Zelda the cause of this? I fixed her with an unyielding glare. If she bullied my dad like an emotional terrorist and expected to do the same to me, she had another thing coming.

I yanked my luggage across the gravel driveway that was all give. Rather than helping, Aunt Zelda threw a disapproving look over her shoulder and *tsked* at the sound and the deep grooves my luggage was making.

"Welcome to Biddenmore, our home on the Southern Shore! Let us give you a tour," Aunt Effie sang, pausing at the edge of the grass to turn and open her arms, a display of her affection for her home.

Aunt Zelda brushed past her, ignoring all sense of propriety. Zelda zipped across the grass and around the back of the house, moving so fast I was surprised she didn't burn a streak in the lawn. Aunt Effie only looked at me and laughed, waving away her sister as though this were her usual antics.

Standing in front of the house was surreal. It was a sweet two-story cottage made of river stone and pine with a stone chimney carved out of the top. The front porch was decked out in plants; I mean, they were *everywhere*. Large overflowing hanging plants were draped on either side of the entry, just above railings that were also obscured by flourishing plants in window boxes. All along the stone path leading to the house was expertly manicured landscaping.

To the left of the main door was an addition made entirely of river stone, with a panel of windows cut out. The window boxes matched those of the porch and spewed forth with dangling greens. More plants hung from the corners of the house, and little shrubs and flowers popped forth from the landscaper's mulch.

"Wow, this place is beautiful!" I breathed. Our cookie-cutter ranch-style home in North Carolina paled in comparison.

"Come, let me show you around." Aunt Effie took my hand and led me down the stony path through the front door.

Inside was a mix of rich, decadent colors that I expected to see in a proper British home, and airy open windows. What I didn't expect to find were the little potted plants and herbs of various colors and sizes crowding every flat surface and windowsill I could see.

"Your room is upstairs," Aunt Effie said, taking my bag from me and hauling it up worn and discolored wooden stairs. As we climbed, I peered at the tall, floor-to-ceiling shelves carved into the walls. They were littered with beautiful old cloth-bound books. At the landing, Aunt Effie turned and climbed the last two steps and dropped my luggage.

"Here we are," she ushered me into the guest room, the floorboards creaking in protest. She set my suitcase just inside the door and dusted her hands off. "This was the best we could do on short notice. I hope it'll be okay."

The bedroom was small, but the peaked ceiling with exposed beams gave it a warm and cozy feeling. Across from the door was a large double-paned window that let in plenty of bright afternoon sun. Just below the window sat a faded dresser with lots of little plants dotting the top. And there, in the midst of the room, was a tall and tufted-up bed. The sheets and quilt were a stark white that added to the airy vibe in the space. Straight across from the bed was a compact wardrobe. But as a terrible unpacker, we'd have to see how long before my clothes ended up in there.

"Take a few minutes to get settled in, then meet me downstairs." She eased the door closed behind me so quietly, it was only the *swish-swish* of her dress floating down the hall that alerted me to her absence.

I edged towards the bed, and the floorboards groaned deeply, as though the house was chiding me for even existing. I ignored the feeling and jumped up on the bed, my feet dangling a good four inches from the floor. The bed was lumpy under me, so I reached back and pulled down the sheets. There was a little stuffed elephant, squished beneath me.

When I was little, I had one exactly like this. I never knew where it went; I figured I'd lost it somewhere between playing at the park and falling asleep on car rides home.

Mine was unique, though. I remember scribbling my initials on the tag: SNL. I spun the elephant upside down and felt for the tag. There, in violet faded marker, were my initials. Scout Novaleigh Larsson. My heart leaped into my throat. What was this doing here? *How* did it get here? My dad said I visited when I was little, but why don't I remember anything from that trip?

A rap at the door startled me, and the stuffed animal slipped through my fingers with a soft *thud* on the wooden floor. A small yelp exited my mouth as I whirled toward the door.

"Scout?" Aunt Effie leaned in through the cracked door with an eager look. "It's tea time. Come on down, love." Her eyes followed my gaze to the elephant at my feet. She looked back up at me and winked. The door closed so softly I didn't even hear it. *Is everything she does so silent?* Then again, with my heart hammering in my ears, I couldn't hear myself think.

# Scout

Effie led me through the downstairs into the kitchen, but continued out the side door. We paused in the mudroom so Aunt Effie could gather her shoes, bright yellow Muck boots that matched her dress, before leading me out. She must have noticed my confusion, because she added, "We have a few minutes while the tea steeps. Let me show you outside, then we'll warm up with a nice cuppa."

"Biddenmore has been here for more than a century. Our mother's grandfather built the estate when they moved here from Wales. Story goes that our great-grandfather was a jailer who heard mysterious rumors about this land and the treasures left behind by the Vikings in the early days." She wiggled her brows in mischief.

"Really?" I asked as we crossed the patio. It was a sweet space enclosed by matching river stone retaining walls. Posts in the grass around the pavement acted as light poles, connected by strands of fairy lights and lantern globes. I imagined what it would look like at night and made a note to peer out later this evening to see it.

"Can you tell me more?" I asked, genuinely curious. I mean, who doesn't love a good treasure hunting story? "Did he ever find anything?"

"Well, our great-grandfather tried to search for the treasure, but all he ever found were these old books. I guess they were full of some Norse poetry and writings. One of them he called 'The King's Book'. Our Mother told us he was obsessed with it. That he would read it by candlelight every night after they'd all gone to bed, and in the morning, the kids would find him sound asleep at the kitchen table where they left him. It was like his Bible. He eventually went mad, claiming the book was magical and could open our eyes to things unseen." She paused to make a gesture with her fingers to indicate *crazy*.

"Yeah," I chuckled, "crazy."

"I always wondered what would have happened if he had just let it go?" She mused out loud, but in such a wistful way, as if it wasn't for me to hear. Effie snapped her focus back to me and breezed onward.

Beyond the patio sat a decrepit greenhouse. Effie didn't stop or gesture to it as we walked past, but the green glass door intrigued me. I stopped to take it in. The shabby little wood and glass structure was warped and leaning slightly to the left. The paint was peeling and cracked, the window panes were covered in a remarkably disgusting sheen of green mold and dead plant spores. *This place should be condemned*, I thought, peering through the cracked windows. Pieces of the ceiling had fallen in, brown mud puddles dotted the tile floors within, and the distinct odor of decomposition radiated from the greenhouse.

Peering over my shoulder, I looked for Aunt Effie. She was several paces away now. I knew I needed to jog to catch up with her, but there was something about this space that was hauntingly beautiful and had completely captured my attention. I leaned forward again to get a better look inside and placed a hand on the door frame to brace myself. Paint chips colored my hands. I grimaced and dusted them off. Everything inside was dry, dead, and cracked. But how was *this* space so dead and obviously abandoned when their home looks like an honorary greenhouse?

"Scout?" Aunt Effie called and waved at me from the seashore, beckoning me on.

I jogged across the wispy grass and down the small sandy path towards the shore. The view was breathtaking. I couldn't see the ocean stretch out behind the house from the driveway, but now that I'd seen it, I knew where I would be spending my entire summer: where I could see this view.

"What a beaut," Aunt Effie beamed, hands on her hips, stopping to take in the view.

"Do you ever get tired of it?" I asked, a genuine smile playing at my lips.

"Never." And the look she gave me was so profound. Her light blue-green eyes had a depth I'd never seen before. Pain, grief, and hope stirred in the bottomless pit of her ocean eyes. She blinked, and the moment was gone.

"What's with the greenhouse? It looks like you don't use it much anymore."

Sorrow bobbed to the surface of her eyes, and she sighed, "Yes, it's true. It was my mother's pride and joy, and ever since she's been gone, it just hasn't been the same. We tried to keep it going, but it seems that without her, nothing will grow. Not even the English Ivy."

"But your house is full of plants. I don't understand why they wouldn't grow in the greenhouse?"

Aunt Effie shifted her weight uncomfortably and looked at her watch. "You know, I bet our tea is ready. Best get back before it gets bitter!"

) ) ) ● ( ( (

I entered the living room after using the *washroom* to find the aunties whispering to one another. The fact that they stopped abruptly when I plopped down on the couch across from them wasn't the least bit concerning at all.

"Since you'll be here for a month, I suppose we'd better get a few things clear," Aunt Zelda said while Aunt Effie settled in next to her on the evergreen velvet couch across from me.

"Just a minute, Zel, this conversation would be better if we all had a teacup and a biscuit in hand. Help yourself, Scout." Effie leaned forward, gesturing to the tea service laid out on the low table between us..

*It's a cookie,* I wanted to say, *not a biscuit.*

I poured a bit of cream into my steaming cup of black tea and dropped three sugar cubes in before picking up a small spoon to stir it. Muffling a yawn, I glanced between Aunt Effie's cheerful face and Aunt Zelda's rather stern one. I noticed how dissimilar their features were. Where Aunt Effie's features were dainty and feminine, with round, supple cheeks that looked puffed into a smile all the time, a thin, pointed chin, and slightly upturned eyes, Aunt Zelda was ever her opposite. Zelda was all angles; sharp cheekbones, with carved sunken cheeks as though she was always sucking on something sour. A square chin with a harsh, prominent jaw line caught my attention before I cast a final sweep over her eyes. Downturned in an ever disapproving gaze. They were both beautiful and striking in their own way.

Zelda cleared her throat to regain my attention. I nodded tiredly and picked up the dainty teacup. The jet lag was beginning to dawn on me, and I silently begged the tea to give me energy. The floral hand-painted porcelain was weightless in my hands and felt like a toy. Zelda exuded nothing but class as she held her own cup with such grace that her fingertips barely grazed the porcelain. Judging by Zelda's expert care of it, I'd guess this set was a priceless heirloom.

Aunt Zelda continued. "The pantry is off limits, and the greenhouse is forbidden unless we give you explicit instructions to enter. Do you understand?" She held my gaze a beat longer than was pleasant and sipped her tea before beginning again. "While you're here, you will be a productive member of society, picking up around the house, helping when needed, et cetera. I don't know what your father said about this visit, but it *isn't* a vacation." Her eyes narrowed on me.

It took all I had not to drop my jaw open in indignation. The audacity of this woman supplied me with the spike in energy I so desperately needed. This was my summer vacation, my *last* summer vacation before writing my life off to my parents' whims. She had another thing coming if she thought I was going to be her little slave while I stayed here. I'd hitchhike to town and stay in a rental if I needed to.

Her thin lips tightened as she took notice of my barely bottled eruption and waited for spillage. I organized my face in a blank slate, and bit down on the insides of my cheeks to keep from saying something nasty. I held her gaze until she tutted and reached for a biscuit.

I glanced around the sitting room to escape her imperious stare. *Oh, sorry, the drawing room.* It was a spacious room with two long, low couches separated by a coffee table in the center of the room. On the far end of the room, opposite the entry, stood floor-to-ceiling windows that looked out over a field that dropped down to the sea. The crimson curtains on either side looked weightless as they billowed in the ocean breeze.

My eyes caught on something behind them while I nodded along to Effie, tutting over the *delicious biscuits*. Behind the couch the aunties sat on was a metal and stone fireplace. Gold glass sliding windows were charred with black smoke from forgotten winter nights. The mantle above was decorated with a large copper vase full of fragrance-less green plants and lit taper candles. The walls around the room were a dark green with floor-to-ceiling bookshelves built in, much like the ones in the stairway.

My attention flicked back to Aunt Zelda. Her fine silver hair was full and swept up and over to one side with a slight upwards curl at the tip. I noticed that it was prettier than what she had earlier at the airport. The tight bun gave her a shark-like appearance, but here she looked regal, especially compared to Aunt Effie's long hair tied back in a loose and disheveled braid.

"As I was saying," Aunt Zelda leaned forward now, balancing her teacup on her crossed knee. "You are not to disturb us while we are working, especially if we are working in the pantry. The pantry is to remain locked at all times and is strictly off-limits. Dinner will be served each evening at six p.m. sharp. We eat together as a family, and you are expected to be washed up and dressed. Do not be late. You will be respectful of our private rooms, especially, but of the great rooms as well, leaving things as you found them. Keep in mind, you are a guest in *our* home, and it is a privilege for you to stay here. And lastly," she leaned back with an almost pleasant smile dancing on those thin lips, "you will not question or ridicule our beliefs or traditions."

*Weird, but okay?* I didn't even mask my confusion as I returned my teacup to the table and grabbed a cookie. I didn't care what they said; snickerdoodles were *cookies*, not biscuits.

Aunt Effie chatted with Zelda about the upcoming farmer's market. She needed more mint and basil. I couldn't help but notice how her accent on the word *basil* made my ears cringe, pulling me back to the conversation.

"I would love it if you'd come with me. You can see our little hamlet and maybe find a trinket or two as a souvenir. What do you think, love?"

Effie's head bobbed in excitement. It took me a moment to realize she was talking to me and waiting for my answer. Much to my dismay, I caught myself checking out Aunt Zelda to gauge a reaction. Didn't Zelda say not to go to town? What changed? But not seeing any signs of disallowance, I replied.

"Sure, that would be nice." I tried to smile, but a yawn escaped. Maybe a walk about the *hamlet* would help shake off the jet lag.

"It will be wonderful, just you wait and see. The farmer's market is different; it isn't full of close-minded people like the town is." She reached across the coffee table to the couch where I sat to squeeze my hand. *How can I tell her that doubling her smile's brightness won't make up for the lack of my own?* I sighed. It's nice she was making an effort.

As we stood, Aunt Zelda ushered us out of the drawing room to the kitchen. She bent below the kitchen island and took out a box. Holding it out to me, she asked in a way that didn't give room for anything that wasn't a *yes*. "Be a dear and run this out to the greenhouse for me."

I was about to argue, perhaps mentioning that she had forbidden me from going out there, and *obviously, I can see why...* But she held a finger up to me for extra measure, and shook her head once. No room for arguments.

$$) \; ) \; ) \; \bullet \; ( \; ( \; ($$

Just before I reached the greenhouse, my phone rang. I set the box of clay potters and cleaning supplies on the ground to reach into my pocket. Seeing my Mom's face splash across the screen picked at my heart, flooding me with relief, frustration, and finally... homesickness.

"Hi, Mom! How are you? Did you make it? Where's Dad?" Cradling the phone between my ear and shoulder, I leaned down to gather the box up.

"Hi, honey! Yes, we made it. We just got on the research ship. Your father's in the bathroom, turns out I didn't marry him for his sea legs." She laughed, and I groaned. *Gross.*

Crossing the rest of the yard to the greenhouse in a few short strides, I paused in front of the weathered green glass door so I could balance the box against my hip.

"I just wanted to call and make sure you remember to be on your best behavior for the aunties. This trip means a lot to your father."

"Yes, Mom, I know. I won't forget." I shuffled the phone from one ear to the other and heaved a sigh.

"Oh, honey, I just miss you so much. Are you sure you'll be alright there without us?"

Even though I knew goodbyes had always been hard for my mom, it was still uncomfortable to suffer through them with her. "It's only a few weeks, Mom. And then I'll see you and Dad."

"I know, Scout, but we've never been apart for this long. I hope you know your father and I adore you!" She sniffled a little on the other end, and I just nodded as she shared her love profusely.

"I love you, too, Mom. Good luck finding that prehistoric goop or whatever it was you're looking for! Tell Dad I'm rooting for him!" A few seconds later, I slipped the phone into my back pocket and pushed the greenhouse door open.

The smell hit me first, hard and fast. Earlier, from outside, it was just a dull scent of rotten, wet wood. But now with the door open wide, it reeked of putrefaction.

I scanned the interior, looking for a place to deposit the box. "Rubbish," I muttered. Some of the ceramic pots were cracked and chipped, while others had dirt or residue caked to them. The bottles of solution were half empty and covered in grime. I shrugged to myself and strode down the narrow corridor in the center, crossing over fallen beams and dodging mud puddles, towards the back, where a few shelves hosted a litany of botanical materials. I set the box under the workstation desk and brushed off my hands.

I turned back toward the door, but walked slowly so as to take in every bit of the place. The raised beds that lined the narrow corridor were filled with dried and cracked soil, broken up with the occasional dead plant poking through. A shudder of wind racketed against the old warped beams above my head, sending dust particles and bits of hay into my hair. I cringed and roughly finger-combed my hair. Glaring up at the splitting beams, I spied a forgotten sparrow's nest that was the culprit. The weathered beams, streaked green with mold and mildew, groaned and swayed unpredictably. *Ew, this was definitely a safety hazard.*

A muffled bang came from the direction of the main house, and I peered through the distorted glass windows to see ripples of the world outside. It looked like Aunts Zelda and Effie were standing outside the mud room looking this way. I got dizzy just trying to train my eyes on anything. Blinking hard to reset my eyes, I spun on my heels to head back to the house, but my hip bumped into the decaying raised bed behind me. It knocked me off balance, and I stepped back only to crunch a tray of wilted seed sprouts underfoot. I put a hand out to steady myself, and cobwebs consumed my fingers. My skin immediately began crawling as I swatted at the invisible spiders covering my body.

In my frenzy, I clawed at the air wildly, and the sound of pitter-patter rain filled my ears. I whirled around even more, looking for the source of the sound. My blood rushed through me as fight or flight took over. When the sound suddenly quieted, I froze. My eyes darted around the stagnant room and found the corridor between beds littered with dead leaves. The frenetic movement of my body must have made ripples of wind that sent rotted, brown leaves tumbling to the ground. I shrank back against the raised bed, cautiously looking where I placed my hands this time, and closed my eyes to take a deep breath.

"Hello, dearie." The sharp tone of Aunt Zelda's voice came at the worst possible time.

I screamed bloody murder. Like, seriously, I should get paid to scream in horror films. But alas, this was not a horror film. And my life was not a movie. I was just a teenager with an overactive imagination and a mild anxiety disorder.

As I collected my breath and let my heart rattle to a normal pace, I looked up into my Aunt Zelda's piercing blue eyes. She stepped up beside me, peering at something over my shoulder before looking me up and down appraisingly.

"What are you doing?" She harrumphed, in what I assume was a most British way, before flitting around me to look at some of the plants. She touched a few dead leaves and *tsked* before promptly spinning on her green Muck Boots. Shoving her hands into her oversized mustard canvas jacket, she folded her face into a scowl that looked practiced.

"You brought the pots out, did you?"

I cleared my throat to rid myself of the panic I was just experiencing and pointed under the workstation desk. "Yes, just over there."

"Perfect." Her eyes crinkled. I could see the resemblance between her and my father that must have been inherited from her mother. The same as I saw in Effie at the airport. Although that felt like days ago now, instead of only hours.

As I turned to go, I looked over the lifeless greenhouse. A tiny glimmer of light caught my eye. Hanging above the workstation at the back was a metal mobile that spun ever so slightly, throwing small bits of light around the still space. The dainty tinkling of the metal was close to a chime, but softer.

My eye was drawn just above the workstation, where rugged beams kissed wavy glass. There were vines and ivy coverings that seemed woven right into the structure. A tiny movement caught my eye. I blinked, and it was gone. It must have just been the light and shadows in this place.

Aunt Zelda followed my gaze and surprised me by firmly linking her arm in mine and steering me back toward the house.

"Maybe you'll be of some use to us after all." She muttered with an uncharacteristically optimistic note.

I slowed my feet just a moment to look back over my shoulder. *What did that mean? Did she see something I missed?*

She gave me a tug and trudged back to the house. It was just as we pushed through the back door and shed our outerwear in the mudroom that it dawned on me. Those vines and ivy plants I saw... They were the only living thing in the whole greenhouse.

I waited for Aunt Zelda as she straightened after removing her shoes and jacket, thinking back to earlier. Aunt Effie said nothing had grown in there since her mother had been gone... There shouldn't have been any living vines then.

# Alaric

The images flashed quickly behind my closed eyes. A girl at the base of a tree, crying as a storm raged around her.

Another image, her eyes locked on mine—fierce and full of fear and confusion. The wind whipped her fair hair into green eyes, obscuring the emotion for a moment. But the fire between us remained. I had never seen her before in my waking life, but there must be some reason the Creators had thrust her into my dreams.

Then, another image blurred into sight. Her lips slowly pressed into mine. A soft and gentle caress. The kiss was so light I barely felt anything. I tossed and turned onto my side; the image blurring at the edges and fading into a more gruesome scene. Blood on my hands. Her blood pooled on the floor around me.

There was a deep familiarity that stilled within me from the dream, like a memory or deja vu. This girl, her pain, her kiss, felt too real and visceral to be a meaningless dream. It dawned on me.

I had seen her before. I've known her before, loved her before.

*Where?* This line of inquiry roused me from my mild dream state.

This must not be the first dream I've had of her.

I forced myself up into a sitting position on the threadbare cot and racked my brain for a dream memory that included her. I tried to reach for my energy, to seek it out, invite it to find a space within me, as King Khalon instructed us to do here in Ruack Valley. It's not a technique my people ever taught me. In Kilburne, Queen Soleil ruled the fire territory with a very different ideology around energy. Energy was a gift given to us by the Creators, and thus we could do with it whatever we wanted; it was ours for the taking, breaking, and manipulating.

I waited and felt no tingle of energy creep upon me, and I groaned. Trying to access my dream memories was futile until I'd gotten recharged.

"You still dreaming, sleeping beauty?" Rhydian jested as he pinned back the opening flap of our tent.

I grunted in response as I shoved off the cot and out of the tent. It would be better for me to leave now than to take out my anger on a nice kid like Rhydian. The weakness of energy depletion taunted me. I never used to have this issue when I lived in Kilburne. But here, in the valley, my body wasn't used to the elements or the lack of fire. It was an exchange I had to make: safety and peace of mind in the woods for weakened energy levels.

As I stalked off from camp towards the river, I caught the first glimpse of light peeking through the trees. My skin tingled with anticipation. I needed the heat, the rays upon my skin. I tried to make it to the river before first light each morning. All the better to avoid the others. The river was *their* space to recharge, and not many of the stewards were happy to share it with me, a rival fire-steward who crashed their safe haven.

Decades had blown by in a blink, hundreds of years captured in a breath, but still, their trust was lacking. I glanced sidelong as I emerged from the tree-tunneled path to the bank of the river. A few earth-bound and water-bound energy stewards were already present, basking and recharging in the daybreak. No one looked at me.

When it first began this way, I gave them the benefit of the doubt. Perhaps they hadn't seen me, hadn't heard me, or known of my arrival. But as time wore on, it became increasingly obvious that they were going out of their way to not see me. The rejection was nothing compared to my experiences in Queen Soleil's court.

As I had topped the ranks of the fire army and became her commander of the guard, I had become well-acquainted with the mental warfare of interpersonal dynamics. Manipulation, deceit, selfish ambition—those were all daily tactics I'd seen the fire-bound energy stewards use for their benefit. We'd always heard that Khalon ruled differently:

"A new generation of stewards." They also whispered, *weak, pathetic, and easy to destroy,* as synonyms to his campaign slogan. But here Khalon's camp continued to stand, a millennium behind him, a testament to his new way of thinking.

Standing along the riverbank today, as I had done every day before, being ignored and whispered about, reminded me that there was no such thing as a pure energy steward, only hypocrites and lesser hypocrites.

I stripped my tunic off and sat back in the grass, absorbing the sun. As I closed my eyes and sought out the energy that made me feel whole, I found it. It wrapped around my lungs, and I breathed it in deeply. Filling me as the moments went by. I tried once more to access my dream memory bank for any remnants of this girl. The dreams of fire stewards weren't like the dreams of other stewards. They were providence. They provided direction and guidance. If one could only figure them out before they came to be.

The dream memories flashed through my mind at high speed, all the way up to last night's dreams replaying. The red stains on my hands, the pools of warm sticky blood... A new scene bloomed in the center of my imagination. A weathered door, creaking floorboards, a faded room. It was an old ache, hundreds of years old. The cold, stale air tinged with the metallic scent of blood hit me. The scream suffocated in my chest and brought me to my knees. There was no undoing what had been done, and there was no way to unsee the massacre of ripped flesh before me.

I forced my eyes open with a jerk, trying to get away from the scene. I hadn't seen Queen Soleil's vengeful handiwork in a lifetime. Even if I'd lived a hundred lifetimes, it would be too soon to see her again.

Running a hand over my face, I wiped away the images and memories. *They're just dreams,* I wanted to tell myself. But they weren't, not really. Not the last image. I had to live with myself knowing that Samirah was gone and it was all my fault.

The memories haunted me with increasing frequency. What were they trying to show me? Surely our Creators weren't masochists hoping to exploit the worst moments of my life. My brow dipped in thought. Although *Soleil* was certain they were masochists.

I refused the memory of Samirah and shuffled through the dreams from last night again, letting the face of an angry girl resurface. As my energy charged, I sought it for wisdom, invited it to reveal its insight to me. The images of the girl blurred into one another as I watched them over and over again, looking for significance. I was no stranger to people's anger and hatred. Her rage didn't affect me.

I kept my eyes closed tight, though the sun was brightening, threatening to make me see stars if I stayed put much longer. My energy pulsed, reviving, but wasn't up to par yet. I lingered longer, breathing in the strength this moment could afford me. A sliver of peace in an otherwise unlivable new reality.

The longer I flipped through the images, avoiding the last two scenes, I found that the intense emotion I saw in my dreams ignited me. Finally, I allowed my mind to recover the final images of this girl and me. The kiss and what it elicited in me had me reaching up to graze my fingertips across my lips. The blood on my hands, too much to survive... I hadn't felt that way since—

No, *no*. I refused to think about Samirah, about what happened. That life was over, and I refused to return to it, even in memory. Twigs snapped behind me, and soft chatter cracked the quiet stillness I was enjoying. A few more earth stewards joined the growing crowd along the river, and their proximity prompted a restlessness in me, unsettled by my own untamed emotions.

Shoving up from the ground, I thrust my tunic back on and stalked back to camp. When I stepped through the path into the clearing, I heard various gruff shouts as men passed in a slow jog. It looked like the guards were changing positions; the night team who ran the perimeter must have returned to rest as the next shift was heading out. Khalon liked to keep a constant rotation, which was a kinder approach than Soleil's. A glance at the climbing sun told me I wasted more time than usual at the river. Those memories. I shook my head to clear them out again. I usually worked the second or third shift, depending on what kind of mood Airian, Khalon's commander, found himself in.

One of the guys clapped me on the back in passing. Maël. His dark, emerald eyes were often brooding, like mine. It made him feel more akin, like I was not the only one who had suffered at both ends of a sword.

"A word, Alaric?" he said in our MirVis dialect, his voice gruff.

I nodded and jutted out my chin to the left. We took a few paces away where we couldn't be overheard.

"The guys got back from running the perimeter last night, and there's something off out there. Be warned. King Khalon's holding a meeting at the Manter's later today about it." He quirked an eyebrow.

I blew out a breath and thanked him. We clasped each other at the elbow and departed as simply as we came. I didn't think anyone could call Maël friendly, but he was the only one who hadn't gone out of his way to avoid my existence here in camp. For that, I was grateful.

The morning breezed by in a mix of hunting, drying meat, and chopping wood. I waited to see if anyone else would alert me to the meeting, namely Airian. Airian was a fine commander, despite being what he was. A rare earth and wind-bound hybrid steward. The factions were fated; only the Creators knew who we were meant to be. Every once in a while, I suppose even they couldn't tell what faction or gift we were meant to steward. Of course, in Kilburne, no one called the fire-stewards *gifted*.

I stacked wood by the fire and cursed my mind as it wandered back to the days I was Soleil's commander in the northern region. I would never lead like Airian. He was cocky and dominating, controlling and untrusting. He ran his warriors ragged and never trained them for the right things. I couldn't help but shake my head at the thought. I would have to table these thoughts, or my fire would kindle. Probably not the best to do standing next to the firewood.

It was hard enough needing to take a lower rank than I was qualified for, but it was another thing to be at the mercy of a hybrid. Soleil had a special distaste for hybrids; if the Creators couldn't sufficiently place them, why should she? Her unfortunate views had rubbed off. Even a hundred years later, as I've worked to rid myself of her ways, they still lingered.

"Ahem," a throat cleared behind me. I was so lost in my thoughts, about to be overtaken in my anger, that I didn't see the king approach me.

I stopped what I was doing immediately and bowed to him.

"My lord."

Khalon just smiled widely and gestured for me to stand.

"I told you, you needn't bow, my boy. And quit calling me that, it's Khalon."

Having been a man under authority for a long time, I knew there was a right way to behave with royalty. But somehow, for some reason, Khalon denied all facets of his royalty and demanded friendship instead of respect. It was the most peculiar way to lead. I was not convinced it was a very good long-term strategy, but with the mild-mannered energy stewards he led here, I suppose he'd proven it could work.

He roped his arm through mine and led me around the fire pit to the upright logs to sit. We sat next to each other, and I wondered why he pulled me away. This was the one thing the territories had in common—everyone mattered, everyone's work was a load only they could carry, and was thus integral to the success of the whole. It undermined the instinct to compare or compete.

"You must be wondering why I asked you to talk with me." He leaned forward, forearms resting on his thighs.

I didn't respond since it wasn't a question. *You don't speak unless spoken to,* I was taught long ago.

"Some of the guards found something interesting in the woods last night. Just beyond the perimeter. You wouldn't happen to know anything about this, would you?"

*Is he suggesting what I think he's suggesting?* A flash of outrage caught in my throat and curled the words back into my mouth. I knew most of the earth and water stewards didn't want me here and were often suspicious of my presence in the camp, but when Khalon offered me sanctuary after what Queen Soleil did... I thought we had an understanding after he granted me clearance. It wasn't common to let a fire steward into another territory after Queen Soleil started the war that left our lands torn apart.

The sudden accusation fired me up, and heat prickled in my fingers. I latched onto it with all my strength, willing my face into neutrality. What's more, a small seed of betrayal unfurled in my gut. I shut it down, unwilling to yield to the thought that must follow it.

"What are you suggesting?" I tried to keep the edge out of my voice, but by the softening in Khalon's gaze, he heard it anyway.

"Oh, Alaric, I didn't—" He reached for me to pat my hand. "I'm not insinuating you have anything to do with it. I actually came to ask you because I know your gifts; you have dreams." His gaze was unyielding, searching mine.

Heat withdrew from my fingertips, and the breath slowly released from my puffed-up chest. I pursed my lips.

"I also know," he said, leaning close and lowering his voice, "that you are unlike the others. You know things they perhaps aren't privy to, things you may have seen in the North that we do not have here?" When he pulled back, he was looking at me with a deviously cocked eyebrow and a knowing smirk.

And then I understood.

"Yes," I said slowly, not quite meeting his gaze. "I believe something is coming, but I'm not sure what yet." The image of the kiss flashed to mind, and I forced it at arm's length so he couldn't discern even the hint of emotion in my words.

"When you find out, you'll come to me?" he asked with a smile.

I nodded reluctantly. He wasn't just asking for intel, he was asking for trust. An alliance. These things were currency where I came from, bartering coins and nothing more. I learned a long time ago that trust was an illusion, a glamour to be broken.

# 6

# Scout

An hour later, we strode down the gravel driveway and turned in the opposite direction from town. Aunt Effie bustled down the dirt road towards the elusive "market" she kept referring to. But since all I'd seen so far was tree, tree, bush, wild berry bush, tree, I thought she was delusional. Surprisingly lithe for a sixty-something-year-old woman, but definitely delusional.

"I just have a quick errand to run, but you can take your time and visit all the vendors." She told me about the market now and how it had been going on for a hundred years. She told me about the friends she made: nomads, artisans, and people with *perspective*, whatever that meant. She called it a "coalition of the common people." I think she even uttered a *huzzah*. It all seemed extremely bizarre, given their reclusive behavior and animosity towards the townsfolk. *Must be some coalition.*

I was working double time to keep up. Even though I was taller than her by at least a good four inches, the slight incline and the force of jet lag in my legs had me out of breath.

"It's all in the hips," she said when I commented on how speedy she was. "Keeps me from arthritis." She winked.

Aunt Effie was sunshine incarnate. To be near her, even at this breakneck speed, was soothing. She filled the immediate vicinity with a sense of belonging and wanting. I could see traces of my grandmother's kindness in her. It would be my guess that for my dad growing up, Aunt Effie was the "cool" aunt. She had never married, and my dad said she was quite the adventurer, always traveling as if to a whole new world.

I watched her now, jolly as ever, not even breaking a sweat. And I couldn't help wondering how she and Aunt Zelda were so different. She caught my eye and gave me a sideways glance.

"You know your Aunt Zelda is happy you're here again, don't you?"

I scoffed. "Yeah, right."

She halted, hand on my forearm, stopping my wildly swinging arms. "Oh, Scout." Her eyes searched mine.

I wheezed as we came to a stop. Blinking away from her gaze, I tried to catch my breath and shuddered, feeling wholly vulnerable under her attention. I kicked at some gravel with the toe of my tennis shoes.

"But seriously, like what's her problem? I didn't ask to be dumped on your doorstep. Why was she taking it out on me?"

"Oh, pet, is that what you think? That she's cross because you're here? No, no." She looked me squarely in the eye with her hands on my shoulders. "We all have our strengths, Scout." Her gaze was piercing, and the weight with which she spoke felt intense for the moment. "Even your Aunt Zelda. Warm welcomes might not be her thing, but family loyalty is. Trust that everything will make sense eventually."

And just like that, the moment was over as she turned on her heel and returned to her spritely jog. "C'mon, Poppet!" she called over her shoulder.

I scurried to catch up and focused on her walking to match her stride. "How much longer until we get there?"

"It's just up ahead." She pointed at the bend in the road.

The forest showed no sign of human life, and I wondered what I had gotten myself into by agreeing to come on this errand. The longer we walked, the denser the forest became. I didn't remember driving in through these woods to get to their house. The journey to their house was an open road, along the countryside and then along the shoreline. I looked back down the way we came, but it didn't seem familiar. I shook my head and wondered if it was the jet lag. I wouldn't feel so confused if there hadn't been only one road leading away from their house.

Glancing back up as we crested the small hill and began around the bend, I heard it. A high-pitched, tinny song was playing lightly through the air. It sounded mechanical, like the ballerina jewelry box I had as a kid. I used to shut it and open it and shut it and open it, over and over again, until my mom would hide it from me. I would giggle, not even mad at her for taking it away. She always gave it back. But I could never tire of it.

The familiarity of the music filled me with a wave of warm nostalgia, and I wanted to get closer to the sound. Aunt Effie grinned at me.

"Can you hear it? We're almost there now," she said.

The dense forest grew closer now as the path narrowed. A warm overcast glow dipped through the trees, the shadows playing peek-a-boo. I felt safe here, where the forest wrapped me in a hug and smelled just like the pine candle my mom would burn when she had had a tough day. A tingle of excitement pulsed at the base of my spine and ricocheted off each vertebra on its way up my neck. I breathed in the forest air, letting its life flood through my veins. If this was even a fraction of what Effie felt, now I knew why she practically ran to get here.

As the trees opened into a clearing, the gravel road came to an end, and a looming rock wall faced us. The tingling of excitement still coursed through me as the music grew louder, but I was utterly dumbstruck. She brought me to a *mountain*? Where are the vendors, the people milling about, the vegetables? I came to a halt, gaping up at the rough rock face towering over me. I turned to question Aunt Effie when I realized she hadn't slowed down when I stopped. Ahead, I saw her walk right up to the mountain and disappear into the cleft.

My heart started to pound at the fear of losing her, of being lost in the woods. My mind started spiraling. *Is this a joke? Did she bring me out here to ditch me? Was this all just some elaborate ruse to put me in my place?* I ran up to the rock wall where she disappeared, and two large, disjointed boulders came into view. Up close, the smaller boulder sat in front of another larger rock, obscuring the pathway that led into a gulley. *It was just an illusion,* I told myself. My brain was always scouting out the worst-case scenario and bullying me into believing it. I put a steadying hand on the boulder and took a deep breath.

Aunt Effie popped back around the boulder. "What are you doing standing there? The market is in here."

$$) \; ) \; \mathbf{)} \; \bullet \; \mathbf{(} \; ( \; ($$

I couldn't close my mouth. Every time I did, it dropped back open. Nothing said "farmer's market" like a caravan of vendors in a rock glen.

*Not.*

Aunt Effie had graciously slowed her pace to a stroll so I could take in the sights around me. It looked like a mountain was sliced down the middle and pushed apart. A waterfall flowed down at the far end where the mountain must have first begun eroding, and it gave way to a stream that flowed through the center of the opposing mountains before changing directions and disappearing into another ravine out of sight. The grooves were deep and spoke of the many years the water coursed through. The vendors filled every inch where the water was not, packed closely together, and backed right up against the rock wall. I had never seen anything like it.

We took our time visiting each stall, but no amount of fruit or knit handbags could tear my eyes away from the sheer beauty of this place. I almost wished I could come back when no one was here to take it all in. History was clearly folded into each stratum of the rock layers. I wanted to reach out to touch it and see what it felt like against my fingertips. I turned, searching for Aunt Effie, but she had already moved on and waved for me to catch up.

She stopped at a vendor, running her hands over the white linen tabletop, and turned to me, holding up a jar of fresh honey. "Can you believe it? It's elderberry honey!"

I raised my eyebrows in response and looked back at the rocks where vines and moss clung to the spots jutting out. At the very top were thin trees with dainty leaves. If I tilted my head all the way back until my neck crinkled, I could see them. But the sunshine splintered into dancing rays and caught arcs of rainbow light around the glen.

Up ahead, vendors bartered and called to passersby on the other side of the stream, and I looked to see how they got there. Not too far away was a little makeshift footbridge of stepping stones in a shallow spot. Eager to explore, I completely forgot to look for Effie. I turned to where I last left her and saw a new woman perusing the fresh honey.

The buzz of music and light chatter kept me grounded. Instead of freaking out when I didn't immediately see her, I moved on to the next vendor. Following the most likely path she would have taken, I was sure I would find her shortly.

The next vendor had beautifully made scarves. When I ran my fingers through the soft fabric, I heard a rhythmic *shhh, shhh, click*. I stepped closer to the vendor's table and looked over the other side to see an older woman sitting at a loom. She had a pile of shorn wool in her lap, and her fingers spun carefully. One foot was planted on the ground, and the other was on the pedal below, tapping in rhythm to keep the spool spinning.

"Hi, my name's Scout." I gave her a little wave.

She spared a glance from the wool still moving through her hands. "Meryl," she said.

"These are really beautiful. Did you make them yourself?"

She gave me an "mhm."

Her reticence didn't deter my wonder one bit. I imagined I wouldn't be able to speak either if I tried to take one of those wooden spinning spools for a whirl. I moved on quietly with a true smile and a little wave goodbye.

The next vendor booth was less cluttered than the others, and the tent had one small table and nothing else. Metal chimes hung from the rails lining the canopy, and their melodic tings rang long after the wind hit them. Beside the small table, sheltered from the wind, was a jewelry tree stand. Hanging from it, on an invisible fishing line, were dozens of tiny hummingbirds. Painted wood and vibrant feathers were crafted into a flock of birds. I picked one from the tree and looked at it, mesmerized. It was delicate and perfect. I needed it.

"Those were hand-crafted in Spain," The vendor finished a transaction and came to stand by me, pointing out the small bird. "They contain the essence of the salt from the Balearic sea." She swept her graying hair over her shoulder and winked at me.

I turned the one in my hands, "How much?"

"They're three for ten pounds, love."

"It's a deal," I smiled.

She reached across the table for tissue paper and wrapped the one in my hands while I fussed over the lot to choose two more.

I carefully picked a turquoise one for Mom and a black and gold-spotted one for Dad.

She finished wrapping them up for me while I played with the delicate chimes and dancing, swirling wind gadgets. I thanked her and exited her booth.

The sweetest smell wafted up to me, like fried dough and spices. I let my nose lead me and found a small man behind a big griddle. He was flipping what looked like mini pancakes that smelled delicious. I realized I hadn't eaten any breakfast, and since I barely deigned to eat a "biscuit" at tea, my stomach protested. I reached into my pocket, only to find a few coins that I didn't recognize.

The man behind the griddle must have seen me counting the coins because he called to me before I stuffed them back into my pocket. He waved me over with a wide gesture. He flipped a few more fried dough bits as I closed the distance and took a big whiff.

"They smell so good. What are they?"

"Ginger crumpets. Old family recipe. No one makes 'em like Ninny." He waved the spatula over them and wiggled his eyebrows as if to say, *You know you want them.*

My mouth watered just looking at them, "No, that's okay, thanks anyway," I said with a wave.

"BAH!" he bellowed, and he slid three fluffy discs on a paper plate and sprinkled them with spices and confectioners' sugar. He shoved the plate into my hands and practically pushed me out of his stall.

A chuckle escaped my lips as I stumbled back. He reminded me of Macy's Italian father with that aggressive hospitality. He was a big Italian Catholic man and was gonna take care of you whether you liked it or not. The memory made me smile.

I was tempted to be sad, but when a breeze sent a new tantalizing waft of the fried dough and ginger spice right up my nose, I couldn't help but fall face-first into the plate. As I happily shoved a pound of fried dough down my throat, dainty jingling bells filled the vicinity around me. I turned to see a small woman pushing a cart. She had cards in the wheels that flicked with each rotation, and bells of all sizes decked out around the cart.

I moved out of her way when I saw her coming, but she stopped just in front of me. Peering into her cart, I saw all kinds of dreamcatchers and crocheted and macraméd items. People continued to press in around us. We were clearly in the way. But I felt so drawn to her and her goods in the moment, I was stuck in place.

"Oh! These are so beautiful," I said, reaching into the cart to pull out a dreamcatcher. I didn't usually feel enchanted by these things—by spiritual stuff—but this was undoubtedly cool.

I turned it over in my hands; its weavings were unique. Black string criss-crossed the center, forming the shape of an eye at the center. Turquoise beads dotted the inner circle, followed by dark marbled crystals. Long strands of soft, night black feathers glided through my fingers. Holding the delicate piece in my hands warmed something in my belly.

"I can see you have a keen eye," the old woman winked at me. "That dream catcher is special. It's not for everyone, only... *certain types* of dreamers."

Looking up at the old woman now, I saw she looked both ancient and young at the same time. The wrinkles and sun-worn skin told of the years she'd worked, but the fire crackling in her gaze and quick movement belied her age.

"I only have coins, I don't know how much this is," I said, holding it back out for her to grab, but she made no movement. Old knobby hands held fast to the cart's handlebars.

"Did I ask for your money?" The flames in her gaze startled me with their intensity. Her voice was warm but edged with something sharp. An icy thrill ran down my spine, and I felt irrationally uneasy.

"Take it. It has chosen you." And with that, she pushed her cart onward. The bells and flickering cards in the wheel spokes made a racket but slowly faded into the background as the hum of people overtook it.

Sliding the dreamcatcher into my bag from an earlier booth, I resumed munching on my dough bites. As I was coming up for air, I spied Aunt Effie up ahead. I squeezed through those milling about and reached for her elbow. She turned and spied the lone crumpet on my plate.

"Ahhh, I see you met Bertie." She gave me a knowing look with those sparkling eyes.

"Small man? Aggressive with a spatula?"

"That's the one," she chuckled. "What do you think so far?"

I looked around again, eyes wide and taking in as much as I possibly could. "I already can't wait to come back again."

"I knew you'd love it here. This was your father's favorite place to come as a kid, too! The people here aren't like the townsfolk."

My brow furrowed in reply.

"Did your father ever tell you about this place?"

My eyes flicked from the vendors to my great-aunt and back again as I tried to gauge whether to throw Dad under the bus or if it would hurt her feelings to know the truth. It took me too long to guess, and tactfulness took too much energy, so I went for the truth. It was easier to remember anyway.

"Dad never told me about this place. He didn't even share much about you guys." I tucked a strand of hair behind my ear. I watched Effie to see how she took that last bit. She didn't miss a step.

"Well, I guess we have a lot of catching up to do, then. When we get home, I am breaking out your father's baby book." She gripped my hand in a tight squeeze, and we both burst out laughing.

"That sounds perfect, Aunt Effie." I beamed at her.

"What else you got there?" She pointed to my bag. I pulled out one of the little hummingbirds with turquoise wings to show her, then the dark dream catcher.

"I don't know why, but the lady who was selling these just gave it to me. Weird, right?" I shrugged, then hesitated when I saw the look on Aunt Effie's face.

"She gave you *this*? Did she say anything else?" The intensity pulled her face taut, resembling Zelda. I didn't like it.

"Not really, is something wrong?"

"No." The smile didn't reach her eyes, "but before we go, I want to introduce you to someone." Her words had a chilling effect, and I shuddered as she turned, leading the way.

I followed Effie along the stream but hesitated when she skipped across the makeshift bridge to the other side without breaking stride. Ah, the movements of a woman who had done this before. While I, on the other hand, lived landlocked in a city. There were no skipping streams where I came from. So I navigated the stream at a slug's pace. Once I made it to the other side, I skipped to catch up to Effie. She drew nearer to the waterfall but checked over her shoulder to make sure I was still with her. I gave her a thumbs up, considering I could have died back there. And she forged ahead.

I looked up all around me. Tree roots dangled off the edge of the plateaus they sprouted from, small plants and flowers blossomed all around us—a result of the dew and water droplets that filled the air this close to the waterfall. The mist wetted my skin as we got close, and my chest opened up and breathed deeper than I have before. I let all the stress drown under the roar of this beautiful waterfall. I let the disappointment of plans changed and memories lost get pulled under the gushing water as it pooled below us. I reached out to feel for the tree roots, and it was like they were reaching back for me, too.

We trekked up stairs carved into the rock wall, and Effie walked even closer to the water. Just when I thought she was going to walk right into it, a small path came into view, leading behind the curtain of water. I squealed inwardly. Even I had to admit that this was actually pretty cool. We took the slippery path behind the waterfall, and I cursed my shoes for not having more traction. Effie moved on ahead, on the other side of the horseshoe curve was another set of steep steps. We climbed them quietly. *Who could we possibly see this far out?* But at the top, I saw where we were. We were at *the* top. I looked around and listened for the faint music. The chatter fell away, and the music moved with the wind.

Warmth surged in my heart. The moment was everything I didn't know I needed. The trees I had tilted my head to gaze at on the way weren't so thin now that I was parallel to them. They were tall and ancestral with boughs reaching out wide. The shadows they cast loomed over us. Effie turned, and I saw behind us a humble camp. I would have said house, but it was more like a shed. Either way, it didn't appear to be a vendor.

"What are we here for?"

"Something special, child." That's the only answer she gave me. "Wait here."

Effie walked around the small lean-to and disappeared inside. Moments later, she came out with a small cloth bag draped over her shoulder and across her chest. She began to walk down the steps we had just come up. I was still catching my breath from our race up the mountain, only to find it was all for nothing. No way.

"Wait, I thought you wanted me to meet someone?"

She shook her head. "It isn't time yet."

"What's that supposed to mean?" I pressed.

"They're not ready." She didn't look concussed. But somehow, my very able-bodied aunt had lost her mind. She didn't even know she wasn't making any sense.

"Who is '*they*'?"

She smiled and trotted down the stairs, whistling.

# Scout

On the walk back, Aunt Effie was acting differently. She didn't have quite the same brightness. She slowed her pace a fraction and kept looking at me as we walked, as if she were waiting for me to be the latest rare case of human combustion. I wanted to jump at her and scare her back to normal, but I refrained.

I had such a good day with Effie that I didn't want to let the weirdness taint my first positive memories in England.

We got back to the seaside cottage just a bit before dinner, and jet lag hit me hard. The house was quiet when we entered, and Aunt Effie told me Zelda was in the greenhouse if I wanted to go say hello. I considered it, but Zelda's warning to steer clear resounded in my head. Besides, the idea of relaxing in my room for a few minutes before dinner sounded better.

As I started up the steps, Effie darted into the pantry. The lock slid into place after she closed the door. How strange. I sighed, their weirdness was becoming normal.

Now upstairs, I deposited my goodies on the dresser, clicked the fan on, and turned down the quilt so I could wiggle under it. *How much sleep is too much sleep when fighting jet lag?*

I turned onto my side to plug my phone into the charger and set a timer for dinner. I didn't want to ruin any progress I'd made. As I lay back down, I looked at the stuffed elephant again. I had forgotten to ask about it. But Aunt Zelda didn't seem wholly approachable yet. And Aunt Effie, while open, was still a touch too mysterious to trust.

Just as I was about to drift off, I remembered the dreamcatcher. Crossing the room to the dresser, I pulled it from the small bag. I admired it in the afternoon light until a yawn pulled me back to bed. I placed the dreamcatcher atop the headboard and snuggled down in the covers.

Closing my eyes, I savored the day again. I imagined the moment at the top of the waterfall overlooking the glen. In my mind's eye, I focused on all the fine details I hadn't had time to revel in. From the rock's crannies to the gentle rise and fall of the burbling stream, it lulled me right to sleep. I stood on that mountain ledge and let it whisk me away.

But in that moment, between asleep and awake, standing atop the mountain, I heard it. A quick jostle through leaves, a twig snapping. Glancing over my shoulder towards the humble, mysterious shed, a breeze kicked up around me.

"They're coming." A haunting whisper came to me on the wind.

I looked around frantically, trying to find where it originated from. But as I searched back and forth, I missed a step as hands grabbed and shoved me.

I was falling.

Falling, falling, falling, and the heat of anticipation threatened to overwhelm me.

I was falling to my death.

I flailed around to grab onto something, but there was only the wind. The sharp *caw* of a bird echoed off the stones around me on my way down, the sound of my execution. When I hit the ground, it launched me into another dream.

A dark dirt road, barely illuminated by moonlight blurred past in the car's dim headlights. I sat in the driver's seat, squinting into the dark, when a snake launched from the middle of the road. Gripping the wheel, I pumped the brakes and tried to swerve. The snake reared up like a proud viper, coils fanning out from either side of his fanged face. It lashed out, striking at the car, and I flinched behind the wheel as it cracked the windshield.

It was going to kill me.

I screamed and screamed, but no one heard me. No one was coming. I banged against the windows, but I was trapped inside with no escape. When I turned back to look at the snake, its obsidian-slitted eyes locked with mine. They glinted with vengeance, and I knew it wanted me dead. It sprung toward me with murderous intent.

I expected a swift death, but the viper pulled back as the scream still echoed in my ears. The shadow of a raven's wing flickered in the headlights as it picked up the now small reptile, and slipped it down its gullet before flying away.

I shot out of bed, drenched in sweat and mildly vibrating from shock. I sat up and rubbed my eyes. Reaching to check the time on my phone, the alarm I set before napping went off. Perfect timing. I paused for a moment, letting the images from the dream ebb back into my unconsciousness. It was just a dream, nothing to get worked up about. Rolling my neck, a prickling sensation crept up my back into my hair. I ignored the eerie sense that someone was watching me and slipped out of bed. *Just a dream*, I reminded myself.

On my way to the bathroom, I knocked my pinky toe against the hard luggage on the floor. Growling under my breath, I hopped on one foot and rubbed the stupid little toe. I glared at the luggage, newly determined to put it all away today in the wardrobe.

From the corner of my eye, I saw movement and whipped around, expecting to find someone there. But what stared back at me was just my reflection in the mirror above the sink. *Get it together, Scout.* Jet lag just messed up my sleep schedule, that was all.

After washing my face, I trudged downstairs to find the aunties. Hearing no one in any of the downstairs common areas, I slipped on my tennis shoes from the mudroom and pushed through the back door towards the greenhouse.

"Hello? Aunt Zelda? Aunt Effie?" I called.

"We're in here, love," Effie chirped from the greenhouse. *That's odd... I thought it was abandoned?*

The greenhouse door was slightly ajar, so I crossed the twenty paces or so and hesitated before pushing it open. The aunties were inside, tutting over the fallen beams and broken windows.

"What are you guys up to?" I grimaced, expecting Aunt Zelda to berate me for breaking one of her rules so quickly. *The greenhouse is forbidden unless we give you explicit instructions to enter...* Perhaps Effie's beckoning counted as explicit instructions?

Without looking up, they replied together.

"Isn't it obvious?" From Aunt Zelda.

"Sprucing up the old place," from Aunt Effie. I smiled, learning to expect the contrast between the sisters. Something reliable.

As I stepped up to the threshold, I watched them pull dead roots from the raised beds. Okay, so what changed? Earlier today, this place was abandoned and forbidden. Now, there's some commotion over the place? My phone pinged, tugging my thoughts from the aunties' oddities, and I rocked back on my heels to check the message.

**We Miss You! xx Mom & Dad**

**See Attachment Here**

She sent a photo of them in wetsuits on the back of a boat. The dark blue waters stretched out behind them. They both smiled and squinted at the camera so much that their eyes disappeared. I wanted to crawl through the photo and hug them.

I wrote back quickly, surprised they had service.

**I miss you too! xoxo**

"I thought dinner was soon?" I asked, noticing the time on my phone screen.

**6:04 p.m.**

The expression on Aunt Zelda's face was one I never expected to see. She finally looked up at me, wide-eyed and crazed. Her hair was disheveled, and her sweater's sleeves were mussed up and covered in filth. She had completely lost track of time, and it wasn't a good look for her. She spotted my knowing gaze and quickly schooled her face into the usual mask of contempt she'd been sporting.

"Some things have come up, and we have some pressing matters to tend to. Why don't you run along, and we'll call you when dinner is ready?"

*Wow, what happened to that 'Always Prompt' rule? Maybe they were fickle as well as eccentric...*

"Why not check the beach for sea glass? Bring me back some!" Effie called before digging back into the mess. I glanced between them. *What's come over them?* I watched Zelda dig frantically in the decomposed filth. Something clearly happened; what else would have her acting so strangely? They were oblivious to my open stares, so I fell back, turning towards the ocean, following Effie's advice.

The path down to the shoreline was a short walk, but the view invited me to walk slowly, taking it all in. The water was various blues and greens, with small white capped waves breaking in the distance. Once I reached the rough sand, I began scanning slowly, looking for shiny bits among the opaque pebbles. I spotted something deep green and pushed back some of the obscuring sand and pebbles to get a better look.

I held it in my hand, brushing off some of the dirt. It felt smooth under my fingers along all the edges, though cloudy like a pastry chef had dusted it with sugar. I pocketed it and kept going.

When I straightened up from my squat by the water, I'd collected several pieces of sea glass. From tiny fragments to large chunks of bottles. Looking back, the cottage was barely visible. Up ahead, I spotted homes and what could be the makings of a small town.

I made a mental note to check it out soon: to see if my aunts were as wacky as I thought, or worse, if they're the normal ones here.

Several minutes later, I returned to the cottage. Twilight had set in, and the patio lights sparkled like stars. The crackle of music and the low hum of a crooner filled the air. A small smile crawled onto my face. I stepped onto the patio to see Aunt Effie swaying on her own to the sound, her arms raised and lost in the moment. My smile grew as I watched her; she was uninhibited, and while it was quite the opposite scene from earlier, I loved it. I envied the easy way about her; she adapted so quickly to her sister's ever-changing moods. I took a deep breath and cleared my throat.

Her eyes sprang open.

"Oh, Poppet, you must dance with me. Let the music carry you away." She reached for my hands, pulling me to the center of the patio. She began swaying again, nudging me to join. I just chuckled.

"Aunt Effie, I brought you some sea glass. Look." I held out the teal piece and a few mint ones as well.

Her eyes sparkled up at me as she took them greedily. "They're perfect. How did you know this was my favorite color?"

"I just had a feeling." I resisted her pursuits and escaped through the open mudroom door. The music was louder here. I slipped out of my shoes and coat, grabbing the glass from my pocket first.

Aunt Zelda moved between the rooms, and I caught up with her.

"Aunt Zelda," I called into the hallway.

Her head popped out of the pantry. "What is it, child?"

I stepped up to the doorway, and she stepped out, easing the door closed behind her. Odd. But whatever.

"I got you some sea glass, too." I had picked out the amber and yellowing opaque glass for her. "Here you go." I smiled, lifting my hand to show her. I hoped this was the start of a peace treaty.

She didn't look at me or even seem to acknowledge the offering. So I took her hand and placed the pieces gingerly in her palm. She nodded at last.

"Wash up for dinner. We'll eat on the patio." She turned back into the pantry but gave me a sliding gaze over her shoulder to add, "since Effie is determined to soak up every bit of summer."

# Scout

Aunt Zelda placed the finishing touches on the beautiful wooden and iron table. A porcelain serving tray and a matching Dutch oven. She lifted the lid off, and out wafted the most glorious-smelling roast and Irish potatoes. My mouth watered in response, and my stomach weakened.

"Oh my gosh, I'm starving." I reached forward to grab the serving utensil for the potatoes.

"Ah, ah," Aunt Zelda chided. I froze. "We must give thanks for the harvest first."

*Ooh, Dad didn't tell me the aunties were religious.* I should have guessed with the talk of their traditions and all. I whispered a quick apology as I snatched my hand back into my lap. I didn't know whether to bow my head or fold my hands, so I held still, peeking up through lowered lashes.

"Let us have a moment of silence to show our gratitude for the harvest."

Both aunties bowed their heads and murmured softly to themselves. I stared at my lap and waited a moment for them to finish. The heat of embarrassment crept up my neck, and I swore to never grab a serving utensil first again.

Aunt Effie breathed a relieved sigh, and I picked my head up. She smiled at me, though she looked rather tired. Aunt Zelda also straightened but didn't look at me. She simply plated her roast and passed the dish to Effie.

"Thanks again for taking me to the market today," I said to Aunt Effie. "I appreciate you letting me go," I said to Aunt Zelda.

Zelda's only response was the pursing of her lips as she placed a spoonful of potatoes on her plate.

"You should show her the little gift you got," Aunt Effie offered kindly to keep the conversation from dying.

"Yeah!" I brightened, remembering those little feathery birds of flight. "They're the cutest little painted wooden hummingbirds. They have the most brilliant colors. I'll show you after dinner, Zelda."

Again, she responded with a lack of candor, the only sound escaping her side of the table being the clanging of silverware from serving tray to dinner plate.

"They're beautiful, just like the ones you had when you were little," Effie responded, fork lifted to her lips.

"Really?" I asked.

"Mhm." Effie nodded while chewing. "I took you when you were little. What was it," she counted on her fingers, "about thirteen years ago?"

I didn't have any memory of it... But my stuffed elephant was here, that had to mean something. I wondered briefly if they had any pictures. *Maybe then I could know for sure that I was really here. I mean, they have no reason to make this up, but why don't I remember it? And why didn't Dad mention it before leaving?*

I tried again. "So Aunt Effie was telling me Dad used to come here when he was younger," I ventured as Effie passed me the roast after taking some.

"Did she now?" Aunt Zelda was clearly responding to me, but she was zeroed in on Aunt Effie. Finally, a response. *Why do I get the feeling Aunt Effie wasn't supposed to tell me?* I thought she'd give me a piercing look for telling on her, but she didn't.

"She should know about her history." Aunt Effie shrugged as she spooned heaping potatoes on her plate.

It fell quiet, and I realized Aunt Zelda didn't plan to share more.

"Dad's never told me about this place before. Have you guys always lived here?"

"Yes, it's part of our *traditions*." Aunt Zelda kept her eyes firmly on her plate, neatly stacking potatoes with her fork.

"What tradition is that? Are you guys religious?" I asked.

"Something like that," Zelda said through gritted teeth, taking another bite.

Aunt Effie watched Zelda and then glanced back at me. She gave me her tired-eyed smile again, then went back to eating.

"When was the last time Dad was here?"

"Aside from when you were little, I think it was his eighteenth birthday, if I'm not mistaken. Right, Zel?" Effie's eyes lay on Zelda.

"Mhm."

That intrigued me, considering I would be here for my eighteenth birthday as well. Was it just a coincidence? I pushed for more information, "Was there anyone else here then? You know, since it was his *birthday*?"

Zelda's eyes flicked up to mine at last, and her deep blue eyes slanted at me. I mentally retraced my steps, but didn't see how I triggered this reaction.

"No. If we could have a quiet supper, that would be lovely." Spoken like a proper, pissed Brit.

"Sorry for wanting to know more about my family," I grumbled, goading her. But the only thing she bit on was the forkful of roast. She cleared her plate in seconds and rose from the table to head back inside, leaving Effie and me alone.

When I thought she was out of earshot, I whispered to Aunt Effie, "Psst."

Her gaze slid slowly to mine.

"Remember when you said you'd get out Dad's baby pictures? Could we do that after dinner?"

Her face contorted in a pained expression, like she was about to break a promise. "Scout," she whispered back, "I don't think it's a good idea." Her eyes flicked to the doorway that opened into the mudroom, where Zelda disappeared.

I knew she was worried about Zelda. But I didn't care. They're being so mysterious for no reason. Probably some old family drama, but I had a right to know my own family's drama.

"Come on, pleeeease?" I flipped my lip inside out and pouted as hard as I could. My eyes even sprang to life, watering to play the part.

"Oh, good Lord, Scout. Don't you make me cry. Fine, after dinner." She pushed back from the table, too, heading inside.

) ) ) ● ( ( (

"He was always such a chubby lil' lad." Aunt Effie sat next to me in the drawing room with the photo album arching over our laps. She pointed at a picture of my dad as a baby in a bright yellow onesie sitting on my grandmother's lap.

We flipped through several pages, stopping occasionally so I could ask questions about people I didn't recognize. Aunt Effie slid different photos out from behind the film and flipped them over. She read me the old cursive annotations and then told the story she remembered. It was a nice back-and-forth we had going on.

"Oh my gosh, and look at this one. He's so cute! " I pointed excitedly to a photo of my dad at three years old in a swing seat with a red knit hat on his head. Two women were behind him as he swung.

"Who's that?" I asked.

The women wore a-line dresses with thin belts and block heels. I cringed. I couldn't imagine living in a time when *that* was the fashion.

"Awe, sweetheart, that's your Grandma Claire and our mother Josephine." She said as she slipped the photo out from its sleeve.

"Oh! great-grandma Jo? I've heard Dad mention her." I scooted closer to look at the photo with her.

She traced a finger along great-grandma Jo's face, and I did a double-take. Her light hair was tucked behind her ears, pinned in loose curls. Her lips were turned up in a smile, pushing her full cheeks even higher. *Is it just me, or do we share an uncanny resemblance?*

"What did your father tell you about her?" she asked without looking up.

"Nothing really, just that she died before he could form memories with her."

"Hm," she tutted softly and gazed out the window, taken away by grief. I continued to flip through the cellophane sheets, but she was unmoved. The faraway look in her eyes pooled a mixture of melancholy and dread in my belly.

"Dad doesn't really talk a lot about his time here, just that it happened. I really wish I knew more about our family."

"I'm not really all that surprised, love. There aren't any happy endings to share when it comes to the Larsson family. We're cursed." Her voice fell, and I trailed her gaze to where it was glued to a spot beyond the sea.

The way the word rolled off her tongue, like she was telling me the time, made me stumble over my thoughts. Cursed? She must have more of a dramatic flair than I thought...

"I'd still like to know... if it's not too much trouble, Aunt Effie," I spoke slowly and hushed, respectful of the depth of emotion she was experiencing.

"Well," she stirred a bit now, refocusing her gaze on the fireplace. "The Larsson family hails from Norway. But somewhere along the line, we moved to Wales, and as I explained earlier, our great-grandfather brought us here." She looked down at her hands gathered in her lap, picking at her nails. "I was only two when we all moved here. But it wasn't good. With Emrys going mad, and all the deaths... Granddad Bertram, Amelia, and then our dear, sweet Mother..." She took the photo from me now, tears glistening at the edge of her lashes. She outlined her mother's face with a heart.

"Ahem," a throat cleared in my periphery.

I jumped and shut the book. Caught off guard and totally red-handed.

"What are you doing?" Aunt Zelda's tone was sharp enough without having to raise her voice.

"I... We..." My eyes pleaded with Aunt Effie, but she was still caught up in her thoughts, leaving me to fend for us both.

I started again with more resolve, "I wanted to know more about the family and Dad's time here. Aunt Effie was showing me his baby pictures."

Aunt Zelda held out a hand for me to give her the photo album, but I was about to do no such thing.

She tired quickly and shook her outstretched hand. "Give that to me."

I clutched it against my chest. "I don't understand. Why can't I see?"

Just then, Effie stood up and floated out wordlessly, leaving the photo on the seat in her wake. It was completely uncharacteristic of her, and both Aunt Zelda and I were stunned by what had just happened. Zelda's hand went limp against her side, and I relaxed the album on my knees.

"Well, now look what you did," Aunt Zelda snapped and whirled around to follow Aunt Effie.

I stared down at the photo in my hands. I had no idea there was so much tragedy in the family. Considering Aunt Effie's near catatonic state, and how Dad goes mute every time the subject of England comes up, I'd wager something really bad happened.

And I was going to get to the bottom of it.

The mudroom door creaked open and shut, followed by the rubber *thwack* of mud boots on the tile. Then the outer screen door banged. Listening for any more sounds, I found myself encased in a hushed silence. Had the aunties gone off into the night, or just out to the patio for fresh air?

The image in my hands told a story, but I wish I knew more. I checked to make sure nobody could see me before I quickly slipped the photo into my pocket and shut the album. I tiptoed to the bookshelf to return the album, making sure I went unnoticed. But as I settled it back in its place on the shelf, I thought better of it.

I grabbed the album and made a mad dash up to my room.

Throwing open the bedroom door, I tossed the album on the bed and pushed the luggage up against the door. Leaning against it, I retrieved the photo from my pocket. It was faded, but vibrant enough that I could practically hear the infectious giggle bubbling up from my dad's chubby cheeks. Grandma Claire was directly behind him, hands outstretched like she'd just given him a big push. Off to the side was great-grandma Jo. Small build and sharp features—like a stick of dynamite. And that face... I strode to the bathroom and looked in the mirror. Holding up the photo next to my reflection, the resemblance between us was uncanny. I turned it over in my hands. Scribbled on the back of the old white film was a tear-stained label: *Jo's last summer.*

As I ran my finger over the old cursive annotation, a shiver rushed down my spine, fanning out across my arms and chest. I rubbed the little bumps dotting my arms.

*What happened to Jo?*

Curiosity built in my chest, and I fed it resolve like kindling.

*I will find out what happened one way or another.*

I tucked the picture back behind my pillow for safekeeping and snuggled down in bed.

Once I was under the covers, I opened the album back up and turned to where we left off. I moved slowly through the photos, pausing to take them out of the sleeve and flip them over. Hungry to find a trace of information tucked in a neat, cursive receipt on the back.

A few pages later, I found a picture of a little girl in a hospital bed. *Our Dear, sweet Amelia (Aug. 9, 1959-1967)*. I paused to consider what it meant, but tucked behind the photo was a newspaper clipping: the obituary. Scanning it quickly, I found the cause of death immediately. Polio. My heart sank. Amelia was Effie and Zelda's sister; that had to be so hard on the family to lose her so young. I could hardly imagine growing up with a sister, let alone surviving the heartbreaking tragedy. I blinked away the wetness in my eyes.

As I reached the back of the album, my pace slowed. Letting my fingers trace the faces of relatives I'd never meet, or even know the names of, if Zelda had her way. The last page was particularly thick, and I felt behind the picture to produce two worn letters.

*Dear Efrata Darling,*

*I don't have much time now, but I must go. Things are spiraling out of control in Kilburne, and Khalon needs my help. I know you won't know what this means until you're older, but promise me you will look over the greenhouse for me? I have hidden Granddad's special book for you in the pantry. I can't explain it now, but it's all connected. When it's time, you'll know how to find it. If you have questions, the Dream Catcher in the glen can answer them. Whatever you do, don't give him my Granddad Emrys's book; he is ancient and wise, but cannot be trusted.*

*My darling, look after your sisters. They don't see things the way you do, and I fear the curse will claim them.*

*Mama*

My mind jumped from question to question. I needed to know what was in that second letter. I folded the letter and tucked it under my thigh, so I could open the next. On the outside fold, it read: "*To Effie on your 18th birthday.*" I slipped it from the envelope, then paused, thinking better of it. This was personal; maybe I shouldn't read it. I thought back over all Aunt Zelda's dismissive comments about the family and how Aunt Effie seemed to avoid the topic like an acrobat, and made a decision. If they didn't want to tell me about my family, I'd learn about it on my own. I opened the letter with sure fingers.

*Dearest Effie, my love,*

*Today is your eighteenth birthday, and if everything went according to plan, then today will be a normal day. There will not be a mega moon, there will not be blossoming ivy in the greenhouse, it will just be another normal day.*

*All I've ever wanted for you was a full and satisfying life. If I had known what consequences would come of Granddad Emrys's doing, I never would have helped him. I hope someday you can forgive me.*

*If I am not there to hug you today on this most ordinary eighteenth birthday, something went wrong. Please watch over Zelda, she isn't as strong as you. Give my love to your father and your sisters. I hope to return to you soon.*

*All my love,*

*J*

My jaw hung open. By the sound of these letters, Josephine didn't die, she *left*. What would be worse, thinking your mother had died while she was still alive, or finding out she had left you?

A tension headache began radiating up the sides of my neck into my head. *Release your shoulders, unclench your jaw,* my Dad would say. I did both, but neither alleviated the terrible sense of dread building within my ribs.

A gust of wind blew against the house, whistling through the cracks in the window. The panes vibrated with an eerie ache, the dainty hummingbirds clattering in response. Above me, the dreamcatcher fluttered, and an icy chill ran through me. The same one I felt when the peddler gave it to me.

*Dream Catcher in the glen...* Wait, it couldn't be the same person great-grandma Josephine wrote about; they'd be long dead by now.

Throwing back the covers, I twisted around to get the woven creation from the headboard. Pulling it into my lap, I let the feather tickle my crossed legs. What did the dreamcatcher, book, and greenhouse have to do with one another?

I flipped it over, and, remembering the bad dream from earlier in vivid detail, flicked the eye in the middle. "So much for nothing."

Great-grandma Jo said the Dream Catcher wasn't to be trusted. But I'd say no dreamcatcher should be trusted. I tossed the hoop of weaves and feathers onto the dresser as the headache returned full force.

Sliding under the covers, I was ready for a full night's sleep, one that would be as tranquil and dreamless as usual.

# Alaric

The fire crackled as the Manter fed it more kindling. Mireille was always *doing* something; it didn't matter how many times I offered to help her, she would refuse. *Just because I'm older than the dirt you're standing on doesn't mean I can't serve my community.* She had a point, but in Kilburne, leaders were respected and feared to the point that our lives were a sacrifice for theirs.

I stood and gestured for her to give me the kindling so I could feed the fire for her, but she swatted me away with a friendly *tsk*.

Around the campfire, the guards were huddled close to Airian, their idol. His dark skin absorbed the sun's beams from above, and his platinum eyes flicked around the group, taking in their admiration. I scoffed and dug the fire poker in my hand deeper into the dirt.

Next to me on either side, the upright logs were empty. It didn't bother me; this was just how every meeting went. As if I could singe their eyebrows by sheer proximity. I felt a pair of eyes on me. As usual, they belonged to Airian; his gaze on me was unfaltering.

He maintained eye contact even as he took a bite of the stew Mireille made for our meeting tonight. Anytime we met, food was involved.

"It's good, but... needs a little more salt, Mir," Airian said playfully with a wink as he scooped the soup up. She laughed and stepped around him, spooning more stew into Khalon's bowl.

I sat statue-still, holding my bowl, letting the stew cool. I couldn't help the boiling resentment that bubbled below the glare. How dare he speak to Mireille that way? He demanded respect, but couldn't even offer it to one of his own elders.

I cleared my throat. "I love it, Mireille," I said with a tight smile for Airian. "I wouldn't change a thing." She sidled up to me, rubbing wide circles on my back. Her fingers grazed over the imprint there. Small and dainty, just like her fingers, a rigid scar sat just at the edge of my shoulder blade. A perfect replica of her fingerprint.

Bonding among stewards was rare; it was the most altruistic form of love that existed. Immature stewards always assumed it was romantic or sexual in nature, but it was deeper than that. A bond that connected two people at a soul-deep level, having nothing to do with romance. I remembered the moment I received Mireille's bond.

A little over a hundred years ago, Soleil had only been a woman in the fire army. Until she staged a coup d'état. Soleil's idea of a takeover was violent and controlling. She committed many dark acts in her quest for vengeance and steamrolled every essence of morality in order to conquer, including but not limited to mind control. I had barely survived escaping the fire territory in one piece. When I made it to the edge of Khalon's territory, Ruack Valley, this kind woman, whom I later came to know as Mireille the Manter, was out assessing the protector poles they had installed for their invisibility from neighboring enemies. She was checking on the very thing meant to hide herself from me. If it weren't for her, I'd have been dead.

When I saw her, I barely made it two steps before collapsing from the journey. I had managed hiking the Mountains of Anguish and through the Whispering Winds Forest, and I could not go one more step.

When I awoke, I was in her small hut, lying on the table in her kitchen. My tunic, sliced and torn, hung in strips around my chest. The elder expertly separated shorn bits of fabric to get to my wounds. I lifted my head to see what her hands were doing, applying salve and poultices to my chest and abdomen. I tried to sit up, but my broken body protested louder than the woman's "Ah, ah, ah!"

She tended my wounds day in and day out for weeks. The horrendous war I'd pried myself from stole my humanity and left me a shell. The despicable things I had done crushed my heart to dust, and though I was unable to speak, it was like she could tell. She sat with me in silence, fed me, and cared for me in a way no one in the fire territory ever had. After a few days, she let Khalon know about my arrival.

I expected a quick expulsion. If Soleil had found anything but a fire-bound energy steward in her territory, she would cry '*spy*' and have a stake driven through their head. The violence I'd become accustomed to had completely numbed the small part of my conscience led by a sense of justice.

Khalon graciously offered asylum to anyone seeking refuge from Soleil's reign of terror. He welcomed me into their southern territory, offering the richness of a sanctuary I didn't deserve. I knew I was the monster their legends were made of. I wasn't dense. But over the years, between Mireille's care and Khalon's willingness to offer me a second chance, I began to hate myself less. I learned to make room for the humanity I'd once lost.

Mireille bonded me to her through this experience and brought a part of me to life that I never knew existed. Or if it did, I'd long forgotten it. She was the purest form of energy, and she'd cultivated in me the closest thing I'd ever had to love.

She *tsked* at me now, and a reluctant boyish grin faded across my face. I knew she saw through this petty back and forth, but she cared enough about me to not shame me in front of my commander and peers.

When she moved on, I squinted across the fire. The others didn't know about our bond, and I preferred to keep it that way. When they saw the scar, they assumed it was someone from Kilburne. Airian's gaze found mine and narrowed. My already rigid shoulders tightened as a reflex. My left eyebrow danced up a notch without my permission. A challenge.

He sent out a low vibration that shook the log I was sitting on. Not enough to make me fall, but just enough to make everyone aware that he would always have the last word.

When we finished eating, Khalon called the meeting to order.

"As you all know, the portals between our world and the human world have been closed for a millennium. Until now. We have had our first signs of the portal opening outside our woods."

The full guard quirked up at this; their chatter took on a hushed and urgent tone. Khalon gave us a knowing look and motioned to quiet down so he could continue. "It occurred to me that the portals have been closed long enough now that some of you may not know what life was like with them. These portals have been open as long as most of us have been around; even though they fade from place to place at various times, they've always existed. The connection between our worlds has always been present since the Twins' creation. Until the last millennium. We can pinpoint almost exactly when they were closed, but it's been a confounding mystery to us, as well as our allies in other territories, as to *how* they closed."

"Maybe we ought to be asking *who* closed them," Coen snarked from across the fire.

The dig was aimed at me. It took all my self-control to maintain my cool.

*Don't let their mistrust produce mistrust in you.*

My jaw flickered in response to the voice inside my head. Mireille had worked tirelessly to teach me the ways of peace, but unlearning a century of savagery took time. Even so, her voice was a guide, warring against my flesh.

Khalon cleared his throat, dissolving the tension. "Coen, what an interesting comment you bring forth. We have been considering who could have enough power or resources to cause this breakdown, but at present, we feel it's best not to commence a manhunt, hurling unnecessary accusations at our kin. We trust that the truth will win out. However, until then, we must remain on high alert regarding what, *or who,* may come next."

"Khalon, pardon my interruption, but we know it's gotta be Soleil. It can't be a coincidence that her coup happened within days of the portals closing." Thane, a young steward, spoke up brazenly. He was referring to the Great Blackout. Shortly after Soleil's coup, the portals between the human world and ours began to fizzle out, one by one, like stars erased from the night sky. *Good riddance*, I had thought. Humans hadn't added to our world in any way.

"One can never know, but it's best not to assume." He turned now to the rest of the guard. "You are not to discuss this with anyone, for we mustn't raise fear in our people.

"Airian and I have discussed our next steps at length, and we have decided how to move forward. We will be ramping up security and rotations around our perimeter and in the specific realm of the portal's opening. Airian will help you with your routes. Your shifts will now be four hours in length to prevent burnout. Please rest up appropriately between your shifts. We cannot be caught off guard. And no matter what happens, no matter who comes through the portal, you are to bring them to me. Immediately. Do I make myself clear?"

The silence hung heavy, leeching down into my bones, making space for the reality of what he'd spoken. When Khalon approached me earlier, my first instinct was suspicion.

I thought he was accusing me of dark energy work or worse, collaborating with Queen Soleil behind his back. I was nothing if not loyal. *Loyal to a fault*, Mireille said. But my loyalty to Soleil ended the moment she began using mind control.

I felt foolish for jumping to conclusions about my conversation with Khalon. This was what he was worried about: the signs of a portal opening. In the fire territory, we had quite a few portals, and Soleil constantly worked on new ways to open more. She was obsessed with revenge and power.

Airian called for a response from his tired crew. This was as rested as we were going to get. With this news knocking around in our heads, I mentally prepared for the sleepless nights. Who could slumber when danger lurked around the corner?

A chorus of "aye" and "yes, sir," went around the fire. I nodded solemnly, and when I looked up, Khalon's eyes were waiting for me.

"Alaric, I want you to lead the perimeter run this evening. If you come across anything out of the ordinary, you are to bring it to my attention immediately."

"Are you sure that someone will try to access the portal so soon?" I asked without thinking.

He smiled kindly, not at all put off by my genuine inquiry. "We can never be too sure, but I am waiting for a dear friend to return. I can only hope she will be among the first to come back to us."

The hush broke, and the chatter rose again. I hadn't been here long enough to know this story, so I waited, listening. But all that spoke to me were the kind eyes of Mireille and the crackles of fire licking wood.

# Scout

Sleep came slowly. I fought the tangle of my sheets to get comfortable and an eerie silence full of dread before a restless slumber claimed me.

At once, I was in a dream. All around me, sweaty bodies moved and gyrated under the influence of strobe lights and electronic music. The surround sound speakers thumped and rattled, the vibrations pierced my chest and shot pain through my head. *Water, I need water. And some peace and quiet.*

The space around me rippled, and I was on the grand staircase, ascending to the darker, and hopefully quieter, second floor.

The thick carpet absorbed my steps, embracing me in sudden hush. I felt a whole world away from the noise. I passed by two closed doors and saw the next was slightly ajar. Hoping it was a bathroom, I nudged the door inward and grappled for the light switch.

With the light illuminating the spacious room, it was clear this wasn't a bathroom. In the center of the far wall sat a king-sized bed cloaked in black satin, framed by tall wardrobes on either side. To the side of the bed was an en suite bathroom. With both the bedroom and bathroom doors shut, I savored the quiet and tried to coax the headache away by rummaging through their medicine cabinet. With two Tylenols down the hatch, I roved about the luxurious room, hand trailing the satin sheets.

The bedroom door ricocheted open just then as a leggy, scantily clad woman backed into the room, dragging a man glued to her face in with her. They stumbled backwards, heading for the bed... and me.

I squeezed my eyes shut, willing myself to be anywhere but here. When I dared to look, I was squinting through the slight crack in the wardrobe doors. The guy was nearly passed out on the bed, head cocked towards the wardrobe, dark hair mussed over his face. The girl hovered over him, propped up on one elbow, her fire-red hair cascading over him. She traced a finger gently across his cheek and chin, then grabbed him roughly, yanking his face toward her. He groaned sleepily.

"You worthless piece of..." she scoffed, "no wonder your daddy didn't love you, it's a miracle I even take pity on you. You would be dead without me." Pulling her knees up under her, she straddled the guy in a domineering way. "Are you listening to me, Eric, baby?"

A soft snore escaped the man's lips. He was beyond drunk, a total goner. I expected her to take the hint and leave, but as she eased off the bed, she stopped and looked over her shoulder. Right at me. I clasped a hand over my mouth to silence my breathing. She squinted, then turned back to *Eric, baby*. She leaned towards his face like she was going to kiss him.

But instead she slapped him.

"Just checking, you know how I hate when you play dead as foreplay..." she cackled as he lay perfectly motionless. "Fine, but you'll regret this tomorrow. You owe me."

I waited three excruciatingly long minutes after the bedroom door opened and closed before I extricated myself from the wardrobe. As silently as possible, I inched toward the door. I was nearly home free when a throat cleared behind me. I spun to find *Eric, baby* sitting on the edge of the bed, looking quite sober with a red handprint on his face.

Enjoy the show, did you?" He chuckled in a self-deprecating way, eyes not meeting mine. I must have looked like a deer caught in the headlights because after a few moments, he murmured, "It's fine, just go."

I swung around and scurried those last few feet to the door when I heard him clearing his throat again, but not for attention. It sounded like when Dad tried to clear the choked emotion away. I froze. If I were in his situation, it would be a case of abuse, and I'd want someone to... *to what?* At the very least, say something.

Steeling my nerves, I slowly spun back around. But he was no longer on the bed; he was standing in front of the bathroom mirror eyeing the mark she left. His chestnut gaze slid to mine, and the heat that trailed after it surprised me.

"What she did, what she said... it wasn't..." *Wasn't what, Scout? You don't even know this guy.* "It wasn't right. No one deserves to be treated that way." I finished, finding my resolve.

She didn't always used to be this way." He sighed, stooping to run his hands under the faucet before splashing the water over his face..

"Who? That girl—er—your girlfriend?"

"Lei-Lei isn't my girlfriend, it's complicated..."

"Well, whatever she is, you should leave her. Why do you stick around when she abuses you like that?"

He gritted his teeth, jaw flexing, and my eyes followed the ripple of muscle from his cheek down his neck and arms, finding his fists gripped tight, knuckles white. A small shiver ran down my arms.

"You wouldn't understand." He muttered before flicking off the light switch and striding from the bathroom. Crossing the bedroom floor in three long strides, he opened the door and peeked down the hallway. "You should go while the coast is clear. If she finds out you were in here, it'll be bad for us both."

The music downstairs was no longer muted, but shrill in my ears. "I think my head will explode... I'd rather take my chances here, thanks." He nodded, shutting the door with a soft click. The stillness in the room was an instant and welcome reprieve.

"Try me." I challenged his earlier comment.

"Let's just say she has powerful friends, and I have made the mistake of caring about people she hates. If I don't do what she says, when she says it, *they* pay the price."

Dude, that is so messed up."

"It is." He was solemn as he perched on the edge of the bed next to me.

"Can't you and your friends get out of it? Whatever she has against them can't be worth signing your life away to torture." I urged him. He turned, and for only the second time, our eyes met. The intensity in his swirling brown eyes was warm; it anchored me to this moment. Something like a fire kindled in my gut as a strange instinct to protect this man overwhelmed me.

His gaze dropped from mine, "It doesn't matter, it's too late for me."

It was as if a bucket of ice water had doused me, shutting me out. Taking the hint, *unlike Lei-Lei*, I headed for the door. "I should let you rest."

I'm not drunk, if that's what you're thinking. When we come to these parties, I take a Benadryl beforehand so she thinks I'm getting drunker. It usually gets me out of whatever she has in mind for the evening."

"Do you need a ride home?" I asked, fingers closing around the doorknob.

"Nah. This is my buddy's house. I'm crashing here for the night. Could you do me a favor, though? Lock the door on your way out?"

"I would be happy to."

As the door clicked closed, another door nearby slammed shut, startling me. When I blinked, taking in my surroundings, I was in the aunties' upstairs guest room. The faint sound of shuffling in the hallway must have been an auntie going to the bathroom.

With a groan, I rolled over to check my phone.

**3:14 a.m.**

Waiting for sleep to find me, I watched the shadows of the tree branches outside dance across the ceiling. After fifteen minutes, it became clear that sleep was not coming for me. So I hurled the covers over and stumbled out of bed. A glass of ice water usually did the trick at home.

I ambled to the kitchen and procured the water. The house was unmoving, like it was holding in a breath, waiting for something. It was hard to imagine that this place was cursed, like Aunt Effie said. A small light glinted from the drawing room. With glass in hand, I peered in to find a candle flickering in the window. Aunt Zelda must have lit it before going to bed. I settled onto the couch near the window and placed the glass on the tea table.

Across from me stood the proudly adorned shelves where Aunt Effie got the picture albums. A curiosity built up in me, and the urge to snoop was irresistible. I ran my finger along the spines of the old books until I reached the wider spines of the albums. The spot where the album I took was the only clean spot among the dusty ledge, I made a mental note to return it in the morning before I got in any more trouble. Continuing past the spot, I read the names, but they were all boring old lady things. *Embroidery for Beginners, Bird Watching in the UK, Travel Guide to France.*

I was really hoping they just happened to have that special book out on the shelves. But of course they wouldn't. If it was as crazy as Aunt Effie said it was, it was probably under lock and key.

*Wait! That's it...*

I raced from the drawing room down the main hallway towards the pantry that they kept locked. Josephine's letters said that the book would be waiting in here for Effie. What were the odds it was still in there waiting to be found?

I reached up and gave the padlock a fruitless tug. Gazing around the hallway, I quickly ruled out the plants, the knick-knacks, and the catch-all mail basket as useful tools for breaking a padlock. But maybe... I crossed the hall to the mail basket and rifled through it. "Aha!" I whispered in victory as my hand closed around a letter opener.

Quickly and heartily, I dug the letter opener into the key slot and jimmied it around. In the distance, I heard a faucet turn on. *Oh no, oh no.* I tossed the letter opener into the basket and raced up the steps and into bed as silently as possible. Then shuddered under the covers, waiting to get caught. But after another long beat of stillness, a door snicked closed.

I was safe. For now.

# Scout

"Scout?" The rap sounded on the bedroom door, startling me awake. I groaned and turned over, grabbing my phone to check the time.

**6:50 a.m.**

"Meet me in the greenhouse in ten minutes."

I couldn't mistake that stern, proper British accent if I tried. What did Aunt Zelda want me in the greenhouse for? Did she know about the letters in the album? Did she know I was snooping?

The exhaustion of a sleepless night weighed me down and made me paranoid. I considered rolling over and going back to sleep, but the image of an angry Brit throwing a bucket of cold water on me got me out of bed in a jiffy.

While I flipped through the clothes I hung in the wardrobe yesterday, I thought about last night. I was so close to finding that book! I just had a feeling it was the key to getting some answers.

Settling on jeans and a faded camp shirt for the day, I jogged down the stairs, pausing to take in the morning light as it filtered through the windows. In the kitchen, I grabbed a slice of bread from the loaf on the counter and looked for the peanut butter I brought from home and stashed in the cupboard.

The mudroom door to the kitchen creaked open, and Aunt Effie flitted in. She had on worn overalls with a black-and-white polka-dot linen shirt underneath. Her gorgeous white hair was pulled up into voluminous space buns that bobbed atop her head as she swooped around the kitchen island. She went to the cupboard by the sink and pulled out a teacup.

"Would you like some tea?" She smiled over her shoulder at me.

I bit my tongue. Should I tell Aunt Effie about the letters I found? I checked the time on my phone.

**7:16 am.**

"I'd better not. I think I'm technically late." I rolled my eyes with exaggeration and tried to make a break for it. I was not a good liar, and if Aunt Effie started to poke, I would cave.

Aunt Effie just chuckled, set a second cup in front of me, and gestured for me to sit on the barstool by the island. She flicked on the electric kettle and pulled out some loose-leaf tea and two infusers. She moved with ease, and less than two minutes later, my cup steamed with fresh black tea. She turned to the fridge and pulled out the little cream pitcher. We took turns adding cream and sugar in silence, only the sound of metal spoons against glass cups between us.

My nerves started to tingle with anxiety. Could she tell just by looking at me? Was I stirring weird? Did she know I knew something she didn't—

"How did you sleep?" Aunt Effie broke the quiet with a soft question.

I held my mug to my face and breathed in the tea. Warm notes of bergamot and orange calmed me down. My dad always kept orange essential oil in his office for his patients; he said the scent of orange relieved stress and often diffused it during therapy sessions.

"Alright, I guess. The jet lag is worse than I expected." I said after a sip. *Keep it short, Scout,* I chastened myself.

"Any dreams?" She spoke over the cup cozied in her hands, not quite meeting my gaze.

"Hm, I don't think so." I didn't usually have dreams back home, but since she asked, there was something I couldn't recall. Like a word stuck on the tip of my tongue. "I think I had a crazy one the other day," I answered honestly.

"Really?" she asked with piqued interest. "Tell me about it?"

"Oh, I don't remember now. I think I was falling. Yeah, at the glen." I dismissed it with a wave and nibbled on the peanut butter bread.

"Some believe dreams come from the gods and give us direct... or indirect messages about our destiny." She scrutinized me with her sparkling, hazy eyes.

I laughed. "I don't know about *that*. Dad and I have talked about all the theories of dreaming, from Freud to Jung. Dreams are nothing more than a chemical reaction. I don't believe any of that *woo-woo* stuff."

She arched her eyebrow at me, giving me a mock serious look. "Well, all right, Dr. Larsson."

We finished our tea and headed out to the greenhouse, where the door was propped open with a cement block. A wheelbarrow stacked with soil bags lingered nearby.

"Well, I see you decided to take your good, sweet time and let an old lady do all the heavy lifting," Aunt Zelda grunted as she hauled a bag of soil from the wheelbarrow into the greenhouse.

"You could have waited for us," I said.

"Grab a bag. We've got work to do." She breezed by me, ignoring my comment.

"What are you doing?" I pouted a little at the order.

"*We* are reviving the greenhouse," she came back through the door and pulled another bag from the wheelbarrow. "Now grab a bag, please." *I guess that rule about it being off limits is void now.*

I started to tug one of the bags off the pile in the wheelbarrow and realized it was like a hundred pounds. I grunted, straining to pull it off the pile, but I had no idea how Zelda was doing this.

"Uh, a little help here, please?" I asked over my shoulder, to which Zelda just scoffed.

"Here." Effie was at my elbow, taking the other half of the bag. We waddled together into the greenhouse and set the bag down just inside the door. I was breathless already and looking for a glass of water. Meanwhile, Zelda was lapping us.

"Guess I should have left you in bed," she passed me, carrying a bag over her shoulder.

My jaw dropped, and I stared at the back of her head, willing it to pop. I gritted my teeth and turned back to the wheelbarrow, determined to show her.

I yanked, but the bag barely moved. I cursed my flimsy nonathletic arms and kicked the front wheel of the wheelbarrow in frustration.

"Scout!" Zelda hollered from the greenhouse. "Get in here."

I turned and crossed my arms over my chest. I stepped up to the threshold and whined. "Why are we even doing this now? I thought nothing would grow in here."

Zelda shot a frantic look at Effie, who was contentedly gazing at the blooming ivy above us. It had spread and created a lattice work any gardener would envy. Zelda's eyes snatched back on me and withered me where I stood.

"Oh, and you're suddenly the expert, are you?" Zelda ripped the tops off the bags with scorn and poured them into the empty garden beds.

The dead plants and the dry soil that once filled the raised bed were nowhere to be found. The fallen beams were removed, and the impromptu skylight had been patched. The work shelves at the back that once displayed random pots and bottles were now empty. It made me wonder how long Zelda had been out here this morning to get this all ready. She was a surprising old woman. I made a mental note to stop underestimating her.

"You wanna do something useful, or you just wanna stand there?"

She made me want to scream. She was so pushy and abrasive. It took all my self-control to bite my tongue and walk over to where she was putting soil in the beds.

Effie followed and hip-bumped me. "What do you say we make this place beautiful?" She leaned into me like a friend would. I appreciated what she was trying to do, but it didn't lessen the fury Zelda brought out in me.

"Just imagine the blooms we could grow with your help, Scout." She lifted her arms over her head like a ballerina, and twirled around, stopping in front of me with her eyes watery and full of fragile hope. My jaw loosened seeing the emotion in her eyes.

"Please help us, Scout?" Effie's face shone with fresh perspiration and buoyancy. "It's been so long since we've had life here. Won't you help us revive it again?"

And now I was melting. How could I not when she asked like that? I wanted to turn to Zelda and shove Effie in her face. Why couldn't she be more like her sister? And then a pang hit me in the gut. It wasn't nice to compare them. I took a deep breath and wrestled this feeling down deep.

"All right, let's make this place beautiful," I beamed back at Aunt Effie.

"Keep dumping the soil in the beds, and we'll run to the garden center to pick up some sprouts after lunch," Zelda said, dusting the soil off her hands and heading out.

"Wait, where are you going?" I leaned back from the bed and peered around Effie, trying to keep the glimmer of relief out of my voice.

"I have an errand to run. I'll be back before lunch. Think you can manage on your own for a bit?" She asked a question, but it seeped with sarcasm. "Oh, and try not to leave your things all over. It's not my job to pick up after you." She leveled me with a glare, but I couldn't remember what I had left lying out.

Without replying, I spun, ripped the top off the next bag, and began scooping soil out of it. A little while later, the car's engine roared to life, and the tires displaced the gravel in the driveway with a loud crunch. I snorted as I imagined Zelda correcting me, "It's the *car park*, dearest."

Aunt Effie and I worked quietly together. She hummed and whistled while I let the frustration wick off me and focused on the garden. We bumped into each other a few times and chuckled. It was a calm, peaceful sort of work, but I truly had no idea what I was doing.

"Am I doing this right?"

She was behind me at the raised bed parallel to mine. "Oh, Scout, it's perfect!" She clasped her hands in front of her with a big smile, sending flecks of dirt flying off her soil-crusted hands.

I gave her a bemused look. All I was doing was emptying bags into empty beds; I would have settled for an affirmative grunt.

As she stood next to me, hands spreading out the soil with mine, a series of pictures floated to mind. Around us, little girls danced and twirled through a vibrant and lively greenhouse. In the next picture, they snuggled close under quilts, camping out beneath the glass sky, warmed by the day's captured heat. And in the last picture, an older man kicked the door and stormed away, while the smallest girl peered through the window. Where it was once rich in flora, there were now rows of wilted flowers and cracked, dry soil beds. Her tears fogged the glass until the pictures vanished from my mind.

*What was that?* The reverie was gone, as though it never were. I rarely had dreams or random fantasies. What was going on?

"You really have no idea how much this means to me, Scout," Effie spoke, pulling me from my thoughts. She gazed out the greenhouse door to somewhere beyond.

"Hey, what's the matter?"

"Oh, it's nothing. It's just this greenhouse..."

She was silent for a long moment. I paused my work and waited for her to go on.

"This greenhouse has been in our family for generations. It was our mother's favorite spot. When she died, something happened. It's like it knew she was gone, and it refused to grow without her."

My mind flashed back to those letters. *If all goes well, nothing will happen, there won't be any blossoming ivy...* What did Josephine do that made things quit growing here? The guilt of having read her personal letters gnawed on me. Even more so, knowing that Effie must not have seen them. Would *I* want to know that my mother left, alive and well? I chewed on my lip. The knowledge was a thousand-pound burden on my chest.

"Wow, that's so sad," I said, turning back to the raised beds to hide the dilemma I was facing. She was silent again for a long time and eventually slumped back against the wooden frame of the bed. I studied her, taking in her sudden state of grief.

She had mist in her eyes, and it was like she couldn't hear me. "It didn't matter what we did. No amount of tending to the garden would bring it back to life. Zelda tried everything. She studied the pH of the soil, and she concocted herbal remedies to nourish the plants." She looked around at the empty line above the beds and reached up like she was touching phantom plants. Then she looked back at me with a small smile, "When we were little, we would sleep over here. All five of us, until Amelie..."

The picture I saw in my head... it was just a weird coincidence. I put it out of mind and rubbed her arm gently. It was the first time I had seen Effie sad; it was also the first time she had spoken about great-grandma Jo and her siblings. I didn't know what to say, but I remembered that sometimes the best things can't be said. Instead, I pulled her into me and held her close. It made me miss my mom, too. I couldn't imagine the sorrow of losing your mom and then losing a piece of her.

"I'll help you restore this place to its old glory, I promise," I said, pulling back from her.

"Scout, you still don't understand," she said, reverting to her feisty self. She gripped my arms and looked into my eyes. "Nothing would *ever* grow in here after she died. Until you came. And now that you're here, the English ivy is back, and it's flourishing! It's a sign, I am sure of it." She pointed up at the green vines now taking up the whole corner, stretching out to claim more territory.

*A sign? Of what?* I frowned momentarily, and an eerie shudder emanated from my center. No, Effie was caught in a wave of nostalgia and that thought softened my suspicion.

I seriously doubted that I had anything to do with the ivy growing, but I also knew that people sometimes looked for meaning in insignificant things, especially people who were grieving. Dad did a lot of counseling with grieving patients in his home office and would share snippets over dinner. I'd often seen people leaving his office with sniffles and Kleenex. When I was little, I would ask him why he made the people cry, and he would chuckle and explain that sometimes the tears are healing.

So instead of finding empty words, I offered Effie my most compassionate smile.

When Zelda returned, Effie went out to the car to help her, leaving me to tut about the greenhouse on my own. I took this moment to check out the workstation. The tabletop was rough-hewn with scrapes and gouges from the years of work it had witnessed. I ran my hand over the top, feeling the bumps but careful not to get a splinter.

And that was when I saw it. The letters CAL carved into a knot in the grain. *Christopher Alexander Larsson.* My dad's initials. I instantly felt closer to him. Even though he never told me about his time here, this little breach of time and space told me I was right where I was meant to be. For the first time in a long time, I didn't feel like I was being pushed in someone else's direction. Being here, meeting my family, and finding out about our heritage felt right. It felt important.

$$) \; ) \; ) \; \bullet \; ( \; ( \; ($$

We paused for lunch, and I ran upstairs to change out of my grimy jeans and tee. As I slipped a clean shirt over my head, my phone rang.

Macy's face popped up on the screen.

"What are you doing up so early?" I asked in place of a hello. A quick glance at the wall clock told me it was seven a.m. where she was.

"Well, hello to you, too, I guess," She scoffed, but I could hear her car engine muffled in the background.

"Ha ha. But, like, for real, what are you doing up so early?" I sat back on the bed.

"Ugh, it's summer volunteer hours. You know, gotta pad that resume." I could practically hear Macy's eyes roll out loud. "My parents have been up my butt about all these extracurricular things, 'just in case' my school in NYC doesn't happen to work out. But, I'm sure you know what I mean, with you being a legacy and all."

My heart stopped and twinged before beating again. I was so conflicted; if I were home now, I would be doing the same thing as Macy… per our parents' command. A part of me was relieved to be free of it for a bit, even if it meant being here in Snoresville with my aunties. The anxiety that came from thinking about going to college and following in my parents' footsteps was nauseating. But an even bigger part of me was seized with fear— how was I going to tell my parents that it was the last thing I wanted to do? It would break their hearts.

"Anyway, I miss you! What the heck am I supposed to do without my birthday twin?" Her voice edged into a pitchy whine, drawing me back into our conversation.

"This sucks." I flopped back on the bed, holding the phone to my head.

A rap at the door preceded Effie's head popping in, "Ready to head to town?"

I sat up and nodded, covering the phone, "I'll be right down." Then said into the phone, "Macy, I gotta go, I'll call you later."

She groaned in response before clicking off.

My head sank into my hands for a moment, my heart aching a bit. I missed home and my friends so much, but my life was racing forward to a projected destination I never signed up for. In a way, I was realizing my being here was like dodging a bullet, or at least delaying its impact.

At the end of my bed sat my backpack with the old brown sweater stretched atop it. I left it out when unpacking in case the house got cold at night. The wool was itchy and ugly in my hands, but it reminded me that I had roots here and a story of my own to explore. Before I went home and returned to the predetermined path set before me, I was committed to finding out who I was and where I came from.

# Scout

After lunch, we got ready to go to the garden center to pick up sprouts, as Zelda had promised. We piled into her car and drove in silence. Now that I was no longer mind-boggled by jet lag, I realized, rather consciously, how it felt to drive on the left side of the road. I didn't know where to look or lean. The signs weren't where they usually were, and the traffic lights didn't hang overhead like they did back home.

The car groaned to a stop in front of a small, red brick, single-story building. The emerald green awning out front said "Dobbie's Garden Centre." As we walked in, the smell of freshly watered soil and blossoming flowers greeted us. I started sneezing instant-ly.

"Good heavens." Zelda shushed me as if I could help it. "You can wait in the car if you can't stand it in here."

I just shot her daggers; I was not going anywhere. I trailed behind the aunties as Zelda pushed a cart and Effie glided down aisle after aisle, touching petals and leaves as she went. Grumpiness aside, things seemed back to normal after the wild dinner we had last night. I was not sure what spurred them on to decide now was the best time to replant the garden. I was pretty sure June and July weren't sowing seasons, no matter where you were.

I stopped to look at some pothos plants. They were small potted green plants with leafy vines hanging over the lip of the basket. My mom said they were the only ones she could ever keep alive long enough to appreciate. For a biologist, she sure lacked a green thumb.

"Can I help you find anything?" A round woman with an emerald green vest asked me. Her name tag said *Hi, I'm Connie.*

"Scout, keep up," Zelda ordered from a few aisles over near the blooming hibiscus plants. The store clerk looked from me to Zelda, and I watched it dawn on her that I was with her. She raised her hands and backed away slowly.

"Sorry, ma'am, I didn't mean to disturb you." Her eyes lowered, and she made a quick escape to the back of the store.

"No, it's fine—" I said, but it was too late; she was already gone.

*What the heck was that about?* I knew Zelda's scowl was enough to make my skin crawl, but I didn't think she actually carried that sort of matriarchal authority out in public. Maybe there was more to Zelda than I realized.

"Coming," I said to no one in particular and kicked my way over to their cart.

Effie danced in the aisle with a bright pink pot of tulips, swaying in her white linen button-down dress to music only she could hear. I giggled.

The cart was full of a variety of starter sprouts and flower bulbs. Zelda scanned her list and checked each item off after inventorying the cart. I peered in the cart as she tutted in something closer to pleasure than her usual disdain.

"...Calabrese, French beans, and aubergines for the vegetables. And"—she flipped her list over—"verbena, marigold, cornflower, tulips, and muscari."

I looked around the garden center and realized everyone was giving us a wide berth. A small child dawdled down our aisle toward us until the young mother saw and rushed over to grab the boy's hand and tugged him back toward her. She bent over him in what almost looked like a curtsy and breathed an apology under her breath, eyes just barely meeting our presence a few feet away.

Zelda waved a hand dismissively, in what I was learning was her signature move. This was officially getting weird. People were acting like she was royalty or worse.

"We'll take these to the car now if you're quite finished gawking," Zelda said to me, pulling me from my thoughts.

"Aren't you going to check out?" I looked to the back of the store, where two clerks leaned languorously by their registers.

She gave me a piercing look before she spat, "We have an arrangement." Her vicious remark took me aback, and I jolted from the affront.

"I wasn't finished yet," I stammered, looking around. Something about Zelda made me defensive. My pride could only let her win so many rounds before it would truly cost me.

Her eyes narrowed on me as if she could smell my bluff.

I spotted the pothos a few rows to my left that reminded me of my mom.

"I wanted to get a pothos before we left."

She sighed most exasperatedly but allowed it. "Fine, I'll add it to my order, and we'll go."

"No," I stopped her. When she turned to look at me, one sliver of her silver bangs fell into her eyes. It looked like a scar for only a moment.

"I mean, I have money. I'll get it myself. You guys can load up the car, and I'll be right out." I headed to grab the pothos before either aunt could object.

Effie looped her arm through Zelda's, pulling her out the double doors into the sunshine. I silently thanked my sweet aunt for the rescue and grabbed a plant. I surveyed it closely as I carried it to the register. The heart-shaped leaves stuck up in tufts like bed-head. Each leaf had unique marbled green markings. I hugged it close to me. Now I had a piece of mom and dad here with me.

I set it on the register and waited for one of the clerks to check me out. When neither made a move, I considered just walking out and letting Zelda put it on her tab. But I was determined to prove a point. Although I was not sure exactly what point that was. Maybe simply that I was not an ignorant and compliant sheep.

A young guy, about my age, came bustling out of the back, pushing through two heavy plastic flaps. He fitted his vest and adjusted his watch like he was late for work. He came right up to the desk to check me out.

"All right?" he asked me quickly.

I paused. How was I supposed to answer that? Was that even a question? I hedged a bet and just nodded.

"That'll be eight quid," he said after punching a few buttons into the antique machine.

I pulled out a few bills from my pocket and unfolded them. He must have seen me second-guessing because he tapped the twenty-pound note. I slid it across the table.

I folded my lips in and muttered, "Thanks, I'm not used to using *quids*."

"Blimey, that accent! Where are you from?" He gave me a smirk as he counted my change.

"The States." I slid the change back into my pocket.

"Oh, you must be knackered, eh? On holiday, are ya?" he asked, leaning his elbows on the counter.

"I'm visiting my aunts. They live just out on Willow Road?"

He straightened up immediately, suddenly fascinated with his badge and reordering his vest.

I took a deep breath and realized that this conversation was probably already over, just like all the others. Too bad. He was cute.

"Blake." A lengthy older man stepped through the double-flap doors and beckoned to the guy with a wave.

Blake, the cashier, shook out his hair with one hand, a nervous tic I'd seen guys at school do, and turned back to the man. The thin older man stood tall with his light green plaid shirt tucked into worn brown jeans. His matching brown belt cinched his pants high above his waist in granddad fashion. He appraised me over his thin glasses as he spoke to Blake. There was something very soft about the man, very endearing. He leaned down and whispered into Blake's ear.

When Blake returned, he barely made eye contact. "I'm sorry. I have to ask you to bugger off. A shame, innit?" He scratched the back of his neck.

I didn't know what exactly that meant, but I understood the sentiment. It was time to go.

I picked up my plant, whose leaves drooped as sadly as my shoulders. Pushing away from the counter, Blake cleared his throat and followed me to the exit.

When I got to the doors, the weight of his eyes bored into me, and I turned to him. "It's because of my aunts, isn't it?"

He didn't respond. He just shoved his hands in his pockets and twisted his lips up to the side in a wince.

Zelda pulled up to the curb, anticipating me. I hopped in the backseat with my plant when she turned to look over her shoulder at me.

"Couldn't make friends, could you?" She turned back around, muttering under her breath, "Load of cowards, they are."

"What's that supposed to mean?" I asked, setting the plant between my tennis shoes while I buckled.

"Nothing, Poppet. Brits just aren't as friendly as Americans, is all," Effie said, rolling down the window to let her fingers dance on the breeze. The lie left a metallic taste in my mouth.

) ) ) ● ( ( (

We spent the afternoon in the greenhouse getting all the new blooms and bulbs situated in their rightful places. Zelda and Effie bickered about which raised bed should contain which plants, as I lingered at the back. I set the potted pothos on the workstation and dreamily traced my dad's initials until they settled on a decision.

"All right?" Effie appeared at my side.

"What's that mean?" I asked her.

"It means *how are you*, dear," she said with a smile.

"Oh, when we say it, it usually means like it's time to go or we're done," I explained.

"Innit something?" She cocked her head sideways like she was amused with me. What a temperate woman.

"Anyway, I'm just feeling homesick today." I traced Dad's initials again.

"Have you heard from your parents today?"

"No, have you?"

She shook her head. "You should give them a ring before dinner!"

"Yeah, I guess."

"Is there something else?"

I heaved a sigh. The homesickness was like a bubble building in my chest. The more space it took up, the more it ached within me.

"It's just," I chewed my lip, succumbing to the fact I was about to sound like a whiny baby, "My friend Macy and I have this special tradition. We share a birthday, and we always throw a big party together. This year, our birthday would have fallen on the same day as our town's Last Blast, so it was a big deal. I don't know, but missing it this year is just somehow worse."

She pulled me into a hug, "Oh, child, I understand the ache of disappointing birthdays."

"You do?" I brightened at this confession.

"Yes, when I turned eighteen, nothing happened. There was no celebration like I thought there would be; none of our traditions were honored. It was a bit of a let-down, honestly. I was gutted."

I pulled back from the hug and looked into Aunt Effie's eyes. They were the color of faded sea glass today, blues and greens mixing and glazed with memory. Great-grandma Jo's letter popped into mind. She had written as much, hadn't she? That if everything played out the way she intended, Effie's eighteenth birthday would be ordinary? I still couldn't understand what any of it meant. It felt like it was just *right there*, right within reach, yet the pieces weren't connecting.

"But don't worry, dear, that won't happen to you. Your birthday falls on a very special day this year, and we'll make sure you get a proper celebration. It's the first mega moon in a hundred years!" Effie dropped her arms from mine, and a stab of betrayal rushed through me. I was withholding things from Effie that she deserved to know, and it made me feel awful.

She mistook my remorse for doubt, and quickly added, "Trust me, dear, I have a feeling this will be a birthday to remember."

# 13

# Scout

The days working in the greenhouse melted and blended together like the sunset on the water's horizon. My time with the aunties was already more than halfway through, and my birthday was this weekend. Feelings of homesickness and disappointment played in my mind as I watched the sun settle onto the ocean.

It had become my nightly routine after dinner. I'd find my way outside to watch the sun say goodbye. It gave me time to think. Between pitching in around the house and greenhouse, my aunties and I were warming up to each other. We developed a cadence to our movements and it wasn't as unfamiliar as I would have thought. I could see my Dad in them from time to time, and when we laughed at the same time, I realized theirs had the same lilt as mine. All this time, I thought I would be losing so much by coming here; it didn't occur to me I might find something good.

Lost in thought, I didn't notice the person lying in the grass until I almost tripped over him.

"Eh, mind yourself!" a voice cried from below, and I screeched to a halt.

I looked down to find a guy in jeans and a zip-up, lying with one elbow over his eyes, dozing in the fading light.

"Are you lost?" I asked.

"Do I look lost, lady?" he asked grumpily without budging.

His abrasiveness made me frown in response. What's a girl to do? This wasn't my land and I didn't think he was technically on my Aunties' land either. I looked up and back to the shore to see how far I'd wandered and I realized I must have mused my way at least a mile or so from their house. I wasn't too far from town now. I looked down at him again. *Should I shoo him? Just step over him?*

He finally sat up on his elbows to get a look at me, realizing I wasn't leaving until he did. He shook his brown hair back and I recognized him. It was the guy from earlier, the clerk from the garden center.

"Hey, I know you. Blake, right?" I backed up so he could stand.

"Ehhh, I gotta go." He brushed off his back, clapped the dirt from his hands, and turned to hike up the knoll to the town.

"Hey, wait, I want to talk to you!" I called after him. He didn't slow, so I kept after him.

"Look, I don't know what you want, but I can't." He turned slightly and gestured to back off.

"Your name is Blake, isn't it? From Dobbie's?" I was sure it was him, but maybe he had a twin?

He picked up the pace with a nervous chuckle. I dodged clumps of sea grass and rodent holes, skipping to close the gap.

"Listen, I seriously don't know what you're on about, but I can't talk to you." It was his emphasis on *can't* that really bothered me.

"What do you mean *can't*?" I threw my arm out to slow him down, but he wiggled away like I had cooties.

"You almost got me fired that day, you know," he said over his shoulder, bustling through a sparse patch of thin trees.

"What? What did I do?" I exclaimed.

"You know the rules. You're not supposed to talk to us when you come to town."

"Whoa." I pulled up short. "What are you talking about? I don't know about any rules."

I didn't know if it was the fact that I stopped pursuing him or the disheartened tone my voice took on that got him to stop, but he paused. Long enough to look at me and reconsider.

"I could get in serious trouble for talking to you."

My eyes went wide and I held up my hands in surrender, a gesture to say *don't let me stop you.* My eyes fell as my heart thrummed. Mostly from the aerobics I did to keep up with him, but also maybe a little bit because what he said stung.

Turning to head back to the aunts, I planned to resume my isolation now that I knew how little the local townsfolk wanted to do with us.

"Wait, you seriously don't know about the rules?" I didn't even bother to look at him. This was already more pathetic than I hoped to be. "*Bloody*, this is gonna make me sound like a proper wanker."

I looked up at him now. He sounded more stressed than I did. He scratched the back of his neck and looked around.

"Well, we can't really be seen together, so let's get out of view." He passed me, heading back to the seaside, and I followed. We paced carefully back down the grass knoll and found a spot right after the hill dipped. He explained that if we leaned back a bit no one could see us unless they were standing right above us.

"My favorite hiding spot when I was little, hiding from my mum during chores." He looked a little sheepish and I couldn't help but appreciate him more for sharing this bit of information about himself. Even though he was using it as metrics to prove we'd be out of sight, I think I learned a bit about him.

"Right, well, best just dive in I s'pose," he said, leaning up on one elbow reclined. I'd say he looked relaxed if not for his pained expression that made it clear this was not about to be an easy conversation.

"Right," I said. "So why are you not allowed to talk to me?"

"I don't know whether to just say it or give you the history." His amber eyes drilled into me. "It's probably not my place to tell you this. This really seems like the type of thing your own family should tell you. Maybe if they didn't tell you, there's a reason."

I cut him off. "You're rambling. Just say it."

He took a breath to steady himself. Beside him, I faced the sea, watching the remnants of light disappear from the sky.

"Your family is cursed." He blurted.

*I'm sorry, what?* I threw my head back and cackled. He sounded as dramatic as Aunt Effie.

But Blake lurched forward cupping his hand over my mouth, shushing me. He peeked his head over the knoll to see if anyone heard us and was coming for us. He was acting absolutely ridiculous.

I sat forward, pushing him off me. "Seriously? That's what you're going with?" I chuckled again, and his eyes widened, ready to shut me up if I got too loud, but I stifled my laugh at his warning.

"I'm serious. It's true." And he did look serious—I'll give him that—he looked scared to death.

"All right, all right. Say, *hypothetically*, I believe you. What is this curse?"

He paled and wiped his hands on his jeans.

"So, those are your *aunts*?" he asked.

"Great aunts," I corrected.

"All right, then that would make Arden your... great-grandfather." He looked off to the side like he was recounting the details before beginning again. "So your great-grandfather was the mayor here back in the 40s, him and Josephine had five girls. Things with Josephine were always a little... *mad*," he said, making the finger gesture for crazy at his temple. "I guess they had five little girls who had strange talents that made people nervous. They always knew when it would rain, they'd dance and play along the seaside during a storm and the townspeople would holler for them to get inside. When they did, the storm would stop.

"Over and over again, strange things would happen, and everyone started whispering about magic. 'Perhaps they were women of the moon,' they'd say. But rumors died down and eventually, one of the poor girls got sick." He cleared his throat. "Amelia. Arden spent all of his time and money trying to find a doctor who could properly diagnose her or a cure for her. But no luck, Amelia died a child. It was a tragedy.

"Then it seemed like Josephine went off the rails. She was disappearing for days and weeks on end. At times, strange people would be seen entering and exiting the greenhouse. When people would ask, Arden would say she was doing research to help sick children, and that the guests were holistic physicians. But no one really believed him. She wasn't the driven-to-heal and make-a-difference type. Apparently, she was more the type to seek revenge or destroy herself trying.

"This continued until one day when all the girls were grown, Josephine never came back. She was just... gone. And she never came back. By now, Arden was still mayor, but he was slipping away more and more. Stopped hosting town meetings and accepting office visits. He started drinking and eventually was convinced Jo died. Thought maybe she couldn't bear the loss of her child and threw herself off the point by the lighthouse."

I watched Blake closely as he told this story, and he winced as though he really cared and believed it all. Glancing away, my eyes settled on the periwinkle ripples on the sea. They blended into a gray and heathered navy blue. I thought about that picture under my pillow. *Jo's last summer.* That must be what it meant, why Aunt Effie couldn't bear to look at it, and why Zelda practically ripped the book from my hands. The wound was still bleeding for them.

My head sunk into my hands. Why did I have to be so nosy and selfish? I never once even considered that maybe they were in pain and just didn't want to relive a traumatic past.

I groaned.

"So, Jo is gone and Arden is rapidly declining. And the town is falling to pieces, he forgot important paperwork, let permits run lapse, and ultimately drove the town into poverty."

I gasped and looked over my shoulder towards the town, imagining what it would have looked like back then. I guess eighty years made a huge difference in commerce.

"That's not all," He lowered his voice like he hadn't gotten to the worst of it yet. What could be worse than child morbidity and a family covering up suicide?

"In Arden's drunken state, he started hosting seances, obsessed with finding his wife and child whether dead or alive. It was Arden who corrupted the moral standing of the community and invited witches, necromancers, and every kind of dark arts into the community. None of them could help though, and they never reached Amelia or Josephine.

"Since then, everyone believed the daughters were witches. The rumors of the curse didn't start until another decade or so later when the daughters began dating and taking husbands–from out of town of course. No one in town was willing to marry them after hearing the stories. But one by one, the daughters' husbands suffered tragic ends. Something happened to every one of them: one died the victim of a mugging, another in a car accident, and the other..." He trailed off. Something even more gruesome must have happened.

I thought about what Dad said about Grandpa–he died in a car accident when Dad was in college. I never got to meet him. Was he a victim of this supposed curse?

"They say the point is haunted." He pointed off in the distance to where a lighthouse on a jut of land dotted the horizon. "That's where he fell to his death. Well, some say fell, others say pushed. And yet others say jumped. No one knows but Zelda. She was the only one there that night." He let the implication linger between us, but I dismissed it. Zelda was cold and abrasive, but she wasn't a murderer.

"What about Effie?" I asked.

His face scrunched. "As far as I know, she never took a husband and so the curse never claimed her. But they say anyone who talks to one of Arden's girls or their descendants gets cursed."

The pieces began clicking into place. "Earlier when we were at the garden center, Zelda didn't check out. She said there was some kind of arrangement?"

"Yeah, I'm pretty sure she just gets her things and mails them a check. No one even double-checks. They don't want to have to correspond with them if they don't have to."

"That is so sad." I couldn't fathom the pain Zelda must be shouldering. She was the oldest of the five girls, and to think she had to carry all that when her mom left? Who took care of her sick sister? Probably Zelda. It gave me a new perspective on her dour affect. I wanted to run all the way home and hug her now, even if she bristled at my touch. What she went through wasn't fair, and here I was making it harder for her.

"Yeah, pretty beastly."

"Well, after living with them for a few weeks, I can assure you of one thing."

"What's that?" He looked at me.

"The only thing witchy about Aunt Zelda is her bad attitude."

He let a small laugh escape, and it broke up the moment of heaviness that fell with the dusk.

"I should probably get back before they wonder where I am," I said, standing up.

"Want me to walk you back?"

"Yeah, actually, that would be great. I've only been out here once before looking for sea glass."

"Oh, that's ace."

He was describing the same scene I saw in my head! At first, I was tickled thinking we were sharing a secret, but then common sense got the best of me. I must have heard someone explain that to me and visualized it like a movies. That's all it was.

We walked under a sliver of a moon, more stars popping out now, chatting a bit about Dobbie's, and I apologized for almost getting him fired. He accepted my apology, and when he stopped at the path up from the sea to my Aunties' house, he put his number in my phone. I smiled and waved goodbye.

When he was gone, I looked down at his contact: **Blake, your cursed friend.**

And something like butterflies released in my stomach.

# 14

# Scout

The next morning I awoke to an empty house and a note on the kitchen island. Aunt Zelda and Effie were running an errand, and I found I could breathe a little easier without Zelda's piercing glare following me from room to room. I sighed, tapping the note, reminding myself what Blake told me last night. I needed to be gentler with Zelda now that I understood what she was going through.

A glance through the empty space sent my mind spinning with ideas... Now would be a perfect time to try to figure out what was in the locked pantry—and if the book was still in there.

Sliding open a few kitchen drawers, I quickly found the staple of every kitchen: the junk drawer. Rubber bands, pens, and batteries cluttered the small space. Then my eyes settled on some tacks, paperclips, and staples. Perfect.

I snatched a couple paperclips in different sizes and hip bumped the drawer closed. On the way to the pantry, I glanced around listening to make sure I was truly alone. *As if the note was a setup*, I rolled my eyes at my own trepidation.

With the paperclips unbound, I leveraged them into the padlock and tried to wiggle them around. In the movies they made this look so easy. It couldn't be that hard could it? I focused intently, sure I would hear locks and pins clicking into place. I visualized the padlock sprinting open and bowing for the invisible crowd at their applause. But no such luck. The silence washed over me as nothing was happening.

Then a shrill ring ruptured the stillness of the moment. I dropped the paperclips with a yelp, then pulled my phone out of my pocket and saw an incoming FaceTime from my Mom. Frantically I shoved the paperclips in my pocket, and fled the scene of the attempted crime before hitting accept.

The image was pixelated and moved slowly as it configured, but there they were. Mom and Dad sitting on a bench in front of some Plexiglas. I could see the bobbing horizon and knew they were on a boat.

"Hi, hon!" They said in unison.

"Hi, Mom! Dad!" My smile widened. I couldn't believe how happy I was to see them. "How's your trip?"

"Oh, it's amazing! You wouldn't believe the sights out here. The whales swim so close to the boat that it's unreal."

"Your mom is a natural!" Dad leaned into the camera, voice competing with the wind. Mom blushed but accepted the compliment with glowing vibrance.

"I'm so happy for you guys. It sounds amazing!"

"Oh, it is, and the research we're conducting is absolutely riveting. Did you know that because of global warming the Arctic Circle is melting and those pockets of what used to be ice are now creating a higher carbon export?"

"Dad, is any of this making sense, or has mom fallen overboard?" I joked. Even though Dad had on black Ray-Bans, I could see his eyes crinkle as he laughed.

"She has absolutely fallen overboard... a couple of times."

I watched as Mom elbowed him and laughed too. Mom was glowing, absolutely in her element. She deserved this.

"What's the matter, sweetie?" Mom said, leaning into the screen so her forehead took up my whole view.

I chuckled, realizing tears were forming at the corners of my eyes. "It's nothing. I just miss you guys! I'm so glad you're getting to do what you love, Mom. It somehow makes this whole trip worth it."

"Oh, honey, it's not that bad, is it?" she said to me, then turned to Dad. "Chris, you said your aunts would be happy to have her." Then back to me. "They're treating you all right, aren't they, honey?" Her brow furrowed as she turned to Dad, "Maybe you should fly back and stay with her until—"

"Whoa! Mom, relax!" I held a hand up to back her down. "Everything is good. It's just not the same as being home with you and everyone else." I watched her face fall and felt like the biggest jerk robbing her of her moment, her once-in-a-lifetime discovery trip. I could rein it in for my mom, to let her have this one thing.

"It's only for a little while longer," she said, looking at Dad who opened his mouth to say something, then closed it.

They were acting strange all of a sudden. "I know. I can't wait to see you guys. Next week right?"

Dad sucked his cheeks in and Mom avoided looking at me; instead, she stared at a spot over Dad's head.

"About that... The team hasn't gotten the data they need because of a recent storm and they've extended the trip another couple of weeks."

"*Weeks?*" I cried. "What do you mean another couple of *weeks*?!"

"Honey, lower your voice. You sound like the seagulls out here," my mother chided. "The Faroe Bank shelf we've been studying is more than a hundred miles off shore. It takes a lot of time to travel roundtrip, and we can only collect so many samples before it's time to head back. And besides, considering what our new data is indicating, we're looking at expanding the field of study and taking a few day trips into the sea surrounding Iceland."

I whimpered in response.

"I know this isn't ideal, but really, this is never going to happen again." My father so lovingly put it into perspective for me.

"Okay," I said, resigning. "What's a few more weeks?"

"Oh, thank you, thank you! You have no idea what this means to me!" And the tension was gone.

We spent the rest of the phone call chatting about the whales and the greenhouse and my reading list for Duke. Much to my dismay, they were still pushing for a heavy class load and for me to join the biology challenge team, just like my mom did when she was there.

Two days later, I nudged open the wobbly antique door to the greenhouse with my foot, two watering cans in hand. I was on greenhouse maintenance duty per Zelda's request, with no break, despite it being my birthday. But I guess I didn't mind. It gave me an excuse to see how things were going out here.

The pothos was always my first stop. I watered it just like Effie showed me, lifting up the leaves and watering around the roots slowly enough for the soil to drink it in.

Next, I liked to water the vegetables. No blooms had shown up yet, so we'd have a while before seeing anything to eat come off the vines. It was marvelous to watch them grow day by day though.

I continued watering, finishing off the hanging plants now and slowing down. Emptying the first watering can, I set it down by the door. I hauled up the second and began pouring into the flowers when I noticed the vines. The English Ivy had completely taken over the place, crawling along the raised garden beds and threatening to move in with the flowers. It didn't seem right.

*Must need pruning*, I thought.

Grabbing some shears from the workbench, I trotted back over and started pruning them back. I wasn't sure if Ivy's invasive or not, but something was wrong. As I pruned, a strange warmth pooled in my tennis shoes. But I chalked it up to the heat of midday. I finished pruning the ivy around the garden bed and stumbled as my vision began to tunnel. Blood sloshed in my head slowly, the sound plugging my ears and throwing me off balance.

"Effie? Zelda?" I raised my voice as I trudged to the greenhouse door, the morning sun bright through the glass. Effie was filling the bird feeder on the patio, musing and humming about.

"Effie, I don't feel so..." And that's when I looked down and saw red pooling beneath me.

"I think she's ready."

"No, no." A shush came from Zelda, followed by metal tinkling on porcelain.

"It's time, Zel," Effie's hushed voice roused me from my stupor.

My eyes fluttered open and I took inventory of my body. My hands, heavy like lead, struggled to obey. But, groggily, I used them to pat around my body. All parts accounted for.

"It's too soon. She's not eighteen yet—"

"She will be in a few hours, Zel," Effie whispered, cutting in.

"—Besides, she doesn't know the traditions." Zelda's tone sounded final.

My eyes fought against the heaviness of sleep to look around the room. I turned my head slowly and took in my surroundings. From where I was lying on the couch, I watched the afternoon sun pool on the rug in the center of the room.

"We don't have a choice. It's obviously chosen her." A cupboard opened and closed. A drawer opened and the contents shifted inside.

"Guys?" I croaked with a sleepy voice. "Guys?" I tried a bit louder.

They came bustling in, Zelda first with a tray of tea and biscuits. Effie trickled in behind, her arms full of gauze, bandages, and bottles of what I can only assume are medicinal things. They set everything out on the coffee table as I tried to sit up.

"Whoa, now, Poppet, you just stay put," Effie said, kneeling beside me, looking me over. "Gosh, what a way to spend your birthday, hmm? What's the last thing you remember?"

"I was in the garden pruning the ivy." Zelda and Effie shared a serious look that gave me pause. "And I must have fainted from the heat or dehydration. That's all." I attempted to push up on my elbow again but Effie blocked me.

Zelda sat at the end of the couch, and it was only then it registered that my feet were wrapped in gauze. She fussed about with the bandages, opening them, applying salve, and rewrapping them.

"What happened?" I asked.

Effie and Zelda looked at each other. Effie pushed up to stand and turned away to make me a cup of tea.

Zelda squared up to me. "You stepped on broken glass," she said.

That didn't seem right. "I don't remember that."

"You were dehydrated and about to have a heat stroke. You managed to make it inside for a glass of water but you dropped it and stepped on it before fainting. Thankfully, Effie was there and she caught you before you could fall." She patted the top of my foot, satisfied it had been tended to, and began to leave. "It'll heal up before you know it."

"Wait, how is that possible? I never made it out of the greenhouse." I pressed.

"I don't know what to tell you besides what I just did. That's how it happened." Her voice was clipped. She turned back to me with exhaustion in her eyes. "Scout, why would I make this up?" And she returned to the kitchen.

Aunt Effie placed a kiss on my forehead. "We'll have a special dinner for you tonight, and a special treat outside under the mega-moon like I told you." Effie followed in Zelda's wake, but turned before pressing through the door. "If you need anything, just holler. I'll be in the pantry or kitchen."

I wiggled my toes as she left, checking for pain, but there was none. Something didn't add up. I pushed up to sit and unravel my bandage; under the top layers revealed bloody ones so I prepared myself for a gruesome scene, but once I got it unwrapped, there was nothing there.

I held my foot out in front of me, wiggled it, and brought it back across my other knee to get a closer look. No scratches, no puncture wounds, no bleeding, no scars. Just dried blood. Evidence that something did indeed happen, but now there was no telling what.

I pulled my phone from my pocket to check the day and time, and my heart sank. It was 3 o'clock on Friday. My whole day was wasted. In eight hours, all of my friends would be gathered together for the Last Blast Summer Fling dance. Macy and whoever else she corralled into the group date. Not only was it Friday and the day of the dance, it was Friday—our eighteenth birthday.

**No New Messages.**

I couldn't help but pout. No one remembered it was my birthday. I chucked my phone at the end of the couch. How much worse could this day get?

# Alaric

The night's perimeter run was more demanding than every night before it combined. Every broken twig carried the intensity of an ambush. The whisper on the wind let us know they were coming. As we passed by the opening in the woods for Colling's Cavern, I heard one of our men stumble. My focus was sharp, on high alert and I scanned the men's thoughts for danger.

What I found instead was a haunting memory in the mind of an earth-bound steward, who was quiet but scrappy. Elys was lit with fear, as an image pressed into the forefront of his mind. Not far from the cavern's entrance was a hollowed tree, burned from the inside out. I tried to remember if I'd heard of anything happening near there, but came up blank. I pressed into his mind following passing thoughts and fleeting feelings to find a long lost memory. A woman, youthful with flowing brown hair and piercing white eyes stood, palm to trunk with the tree. She pulled the energy from it as she chanted. When she turned around, his memory fizzled out and was replaced with men from Ruack Valley sitting around a fire with Khalon telling stories.

One of the elders held court, and as he spoke, the fire gleamed in his green eyes, *"Just hanging out near the channeler's tree could deplete an energy steward. You had better behave and stay to the marked path."*

Elys shut down the memory at that, trying to stave off the creeping fear of folklore. Channelers weren't real, they were a character in the oral stories passed down of old. Even if they did exist, they weren't all powerful as our elders led us to believe. I rolled my eyes and refocused on my breathing as we completed the circuit.

We ran the inside perimeter every quarter-hour for the first evening shift, but when the shift changed, Airian and I stayed near the portal and surveilled. A set of carved stones laid just beyond the Manter's protector poles. Khalon had them made when the portal first formed and opened a way into the human world. Now, we braced a few yards from the marking.

Crawling up a tall tree, I used low-hanging boughs as my shield, and waited. The sun set and the moon began its lazy crawl through the sky. Every few minutes, I looked around to check on the others. First to my left was Maël, then Tieran, Kallias, and Zanthria. Even though I'd only been with them for a short while, we connected as a unit. In our day to day, we felt tension. But here, under the cover of night during patrol, we acted as one. They felt my eyes on them—a certain stillness from my tree—and each man nodded and blinked slowly in response to my silent check-in.

All good.

It went on like this for a while. Nearing the end of the shift, Airian ran a solo circuit and his return was soft as a breeze through the trees. His stealth was unparalleled as a wind-bound energy steward. I wouldn't call his movement flying, more like gliding or hovering across the earth's magnetic fields. I envied his smooth movements.

Airian's eyes found mine, glowing and pulsing toward him in orange and golden hues. He nodded and scaled a tree several yards away.

The night wound down, and though we were all still alert, the calm of the warm midnight air washed over us. The hush of the forest at night soothed my senses. All that stirring and working and toiling the animals did all day came to a stop.

Though the night was calm and I welcomed the end of another day, in the silence, my mind became my enemy and I fought a futile battle to keep my regrets at bay.

Images of the queen of the fire kingdom seeped into my mind. I breathed hard against them—harder to stop them at night with less to distract from it.

"You'll pay for this mistake," she had screeched at me one night when I came back from patrolling the palace grounds.

I knew better than to respond, so I bowed low, my face parallel to the obsidian stone floor.

Her heels clacked viciously against the shiny ground, and she approached me so fast that I didn't have but a moment to react. She grabbed the scruffy hair at the back of my head and wrenched me up to face her.

Soleil's eyes were a deep crimson, so dark in places that it looked like the pupil had leaked into her iris.

She bared her teeth at me in a low growl. Everywhere her skin touched mine radiated with heat, the burn becoming intolerable.

I willed my face into a mask of stone.

"If those rebel warriors make it into our territory because you left a portal unattended, I will remove your head from your body and enchant it to do my bidding." She spat in my face and released me.

If I were anyone but her top commander and bedchamber slave, it would have already been done.

I hadn't left the portal unattended. One of my men did. He stepped out for a moment, and when I found him derelict, I handled it quietly. But word got back to Soleil.

Those days she only had my life to threaten. I cringed, thinking of Samirah. She never asked to be a bargaining chip.

"Get out of my sight before I change my mind and skin you alive." She had turned on her heel and threw open the doors, exiting the throne room. The heavy wooden doors slammed back against the wall so hard that they ricocheted and the sound hit me viscerally. She had always been one to make a dramatic exit.

My core shook with the memory. It was so real, bending my grip on reality here and now. I latched onto the tree to steady myself. *I'm safe here. Soleil has no idea where I am.*

The vibration in me grew stronger. With one hand on the tree trunk and the other on my abdomen, I breathed to center myself. But it wasn't just me. The branch trembled under my hand. Everything shook.

The portal.

# 16

# Scout

"Bath time!" Aunt Effie announced an hour later, strolling into the room. She crossed her arms and looked me over. "Are you quite finished sulking in here? Zelda whipped up the most excellent remedy for what ails you, child, and it's waiting for you upstairs."

"Nooo," I moaned. "Just leave me here to rot. Have them carve open the floorboards and place my headstone outside the window." I rolled over, shoving my face into the couch pillows.

"Up, up, up! Zelda assures me that your wounds should be healed by now and that you can walk."

*Sure, cause there was no wound to begin with...*

I hobbled up to my room with Effie's support, lopsided from the bulky bandages and a numb leg. She showed me to the master bath where a large jacuzzi nestled in the corner of the bathroom, opposite the door. The ceiling slanted down, making the large room feel smaller, cozy even. Around the tub were cream tiles littered with small house plants. Tall pillar candles flickered all around the room, alight but without fragrance. It was surprisingly arresting. I assumed it was Effie's touch, as Zelda struck me as someone who'd rather function over form.

I unwrapped my feet, which still looked fine, and undressed to slide into the tub. The warm water felt heavenly on my aching, nonexistent biceps. I leaned my head back against the lip of the tub and soaked in the moment. The bath was filled with sparkling bubbles that, as they fizzed and popped around me, wafted a warm, earthy smell to my nose, something like lavender mixed with sandalwood.

The waters rejuvenated me and filled me up where I was lacking, just like Effie said they would.

"Knock, knock," Effie said, popping her head in. "Dinner will be ready in twenty minutes. Do you need any help getting out?"

"No, I should be fine, thanks." I shrugged deeper under the water, wanting to absorb every last good feeling I could.

"Brilliant. Towel's on the hook over there." She pointed to the shelves above the toilet before continuing, "I got you something special for tonight. It's waiting for you in your room." She disappeared with a wink before I could ask for more details.

I groaned, dreading the moment the cold air would inevitably hit my skin when I crawled from this luscious bath. Giving myself a count down, I hauled my body out of the fragrant waters and pulled the towel from the shelf.

After wrapping my hair up in a towel, I trod down the hall to my room in the plush robe Effie left out for me. There, lying stretched across the bed, was a stunning, crimson satin dress. I let my hand graze down the beading on the front. The small crystal beads shimmered in the setting sun leaking in from my bedroom window. So intricate and detailed that it pulled a murmur of awe from my throat. There were no words.

I was so excited to try it on that I quickly ditched the robe and stepped into the dress. It slid perfectly in place. I thumbed the thin straps over my shoulders so they lay flat over my collar bones, and did a little jig to work it over my hips. It hugged me in the right ways while still being loose enough to sit and move about. I stood in front of the mirror and swished the dress. The beading weighed it down just enough to give it some real movement. Smoothing a hand down the front of it, I couldn't help but feel beautiful. Cherished.

I finished getting ready and dried my hair. I put on some mascara and lip gloss to add a little something. Before I headed downstairs, my phone chimed.

**Mom: Happy Birthday, my sweet girl. Promise to celebrate you extra hard when we're all together again! xx**

**Me: Thanks, mom. Love and miss you!**

I fired back quickly, dropping my phone on the bed, then remembering something. I picked it back up and sent a text to Macy.

**Me: Happy Birthday, birthday twin! Hope tonight is magical!**

Just because Macy was caught up in her own stuff didn't mean I needed to be. I slid the phone into a silver wristlet and brought it downstairs with me. A little too fancy for dinner at home, but so was the dress.

"Dinner's ready," Zelda said, stepping out from the dining room into the hall just as I hit the bottom step.

Effie popped up behind her, whistling and clapping slowly. "Now don't you look like a million quid!"

Her words deepened the blush creeping over my cheeks. I brushed my hair back, overcome by the fullness of her attention. I nervously touched the dress. "How did you know?"

Aunt Zelda frowned and looked away in appalled fashion. She *tsks* at me.

"We would know when our own kin's birthday is, even if you hadn't whined and complained about it," Aunt Zelda said with her signature wave.

Though Zelda's face was perfectly arranged to show no emotion, the affection was there, just below the surface. I melted. Her thoughtfulness made up for her lack of showy displays.

I thought of what Aunt Effie told me when we were walking to the market in the glen. *We all have our strengths, even your Aunt Zelda.* She was right. I couldn't see it before, not when I hadn't known what she'd been through. But now I saw it. Zelda was responsible, attentive, and thoughtful. Nothing made it past her. She had eyes on everything, and she took good care of all that was in her charge. Including me.

"Well, what are we standing around here for? Chicken roast and Yorkshire pudding is on the table getting cold." And just like that, the moment was over. I smiled. At least this felt normal.

Apparently, fainting makes a girl ravenous, because no sooner had we plopped our bottoms in the dining chairs than I began gathering my feast. I nearly forgot my Aunties' traditional dinner prayers, two bites into the mashed potatoes. Zelda cleared her throat gruffly and got my attention.

My fork clattered on the fancy dinnerware, and I apologized with a simper. My stomach growled during my Zelda's blessing, and her closing remark was the only green light I needed to dive back in.

"My, what an appetite you have!" Effie commented as I devoured the chicken and parsnips. She pushed a dish toward me and urged me to try the eggy bread she calls pudding. It wasn't as bad as I expected. Effie and Zelda shared some low chatter about local news and a fundraiser for a new bridge in the city park.

These domestic sounds of dinnerware scraping and conversations lapping reminded me of home and I smiled.

When Zelda finished her plate, I expected her to get up and head to the kitchen, but instead, she leaned back and interlocked her fingers, watching me.

Okay... That was weird. I finished my last few bites and cleaned my fingers on the cloth napkin draped over my lap. My cheeks began to warm under her gaze and I slid my dress straps back in place, even though they hadn't shifted, and patted the neckline. Everything seemed in its place. So, why was she staring at me?

"Do you remember when I told you the house rules when you first arrived?" Zelda finally said.

"Yes." I nodded while dabbing my lips with the cloth napkin I'd draped across my lap.

"Good. We have special birthday traditions, and it's important that you indulge us old women in the joy of celebrating your eighteenth birthday with you." She shared a kindred look with Effie.

I gulped. *More weird traditions? Great.*

Aunt Zelda continued. "So do you agree to allow us to celebrate you according to our traditions?" She waited for me to answer.

"Sure," I said with a squint and tentative smile, "it's really nice that you guys are willing to go to such great measures for me... but what do these traditions entail?"

Effie looked at Zelda, whose gaze never wavered from my own. "Never you mind, child. Just enjoy."

Effie and Zelda rose from the table and led me through the kitchen to the mudroom. They donned boots and Effie covered my eyes with her hands. She deftly maneuvered me out of the mudroom and across the patio to stand in front of the greenhouse, I was guessing, but I hadn't the slightest clue why.

"Okay, no peeking!" Aunt Effie said over my shoulder as if her hands over my eyes weren't enough to tell me so. I didn't even try to mask my widening grin.

"I'm not, I'm not, I swear!" I giggled.

The fact that my aunties went out of their way to plan a special surprise for my eighteenth birthday—which was in fact the last thing I expected them to do—filled my little heart up to near bursting.

"Are you peeking? No peeking!" Effie squawked, but the trill in her voice let me know she was having at least as much fun as I was with this. "When I count to three, you can open your eyes."

"Ready?" Aunt Effie asked me as we crowded around the door.

"One..." She kept one hand squished over my eyes and reached around me with the other to turn the knob. Its brassy rusted handle squealed in protest.

"Two..." She pushed the door open with a creak, and it caught with a thud on the warped flooring. Leading me over the threshold, I stumbled over the old spot where the floorboards buckled.

"Three!" She dropped her hand and I opened my eyes. It took a moment for my pupils to adjust. It was evening now, and the sun had finally given way for the stars to light the sky in turn. A few glints above the glass greenhouse ceiling. Moon beams warped and reflected off the old glass windows and bounced around the enclosed space.

I noticed the usual damp smell of the greenhouse was gone. The air was warmer and smelled like freshly struck matches and fermenting fruit. Effie stepped up beside me, her skin warm to the touch against my chilled arms. Zelda huffed behind me, bringing up the rear.

It looked completely different than it did even a few hours ago. The raised beds were now pushed back against the paned window walls to make the center of the greenhouse spacious enough for a table. Candles dappled every surface. Tall, white tapers sat in tarnished and worn gold cups, offering a soft glow to displace the darkness. There must have been at least forty votives in this small space—it was ablaze and warm with hope.

While my heart broke finding out I would be away from friends and family during my eighteenth birthday, this gesture made the pain ache a little less. With a smile and wide eyes, I stepped into the space between the raised beds to take in the most ornate table spread I'd ever seen.

The rectangular table had four chairs seated at it, one at each side, with carved backs and satin purple seat coverings. Gold chargers sat atop a shimmering table runner decorated with bowls and serving dishes of varying heights. On one serving platter was a large copper goblet overflowing with deep purple grapes and plums with small orange flowers placed among them.

Down the middle of the table was a thin, gold-dipped serving boat, and within it were three large pillar candles, equidistant and unlit. Filling in the space around them were a smattering of fruits—figs, pomegranates, and mixed berries. Among the display, sweet-smelling yellow, gold, and red flowers with ruffled middles wove themselves through the display. Around the outside of the serving tray were herbs and freshly cut vines draped with dainty posies. Several small jewels and gemstones gleamed in the light.

It was the most beautiful and intoxicating display I've ever seen.

A candelabra lit up the table from the workbench. Below the display, I spied some paper, a black bowl, and pencils. At the other end of the work table was a crystal punch bowl. The way the candles illuminated the purple liquid reminded me of the berries littered on the table. The same delicate flowers displayed among the fruit floated in the punch bowl. Next to it were antique, painted teacups; they had vibrant colors, but I couldn't make out the design from here. There was also a small tin pitcher of water just behind the punch bowl.

Effie stood by my side in silence, allowing me to take it all in. She beamed in pride, eyeing the displays with me. She looked back at me, checking for my approval. I beamed right back at her. No one had ever gone to such lengths to care for and surprise me. I was overcome, and my smile slipped. My eyes prickled with tears that blurred my vision ever so slightly. She quieted me with a soothing rub on my arms, and I reached out for her, enveloping her in a hug. She gripped tightly in a way only a seemingly frail, but fit lady can. I tucked my head down in her hair and breathed deeply. She smelled like eucalyptus and mint with something spicy. Not quite the old lady smell of roses and death I expected.

Zelda shifted behind me, and I pulled away, stashing my tears for later when I could be alone upstairs.

Zelda reached out to me and placed a cold hand on my arm. "There, there, dear." She withdrew and moved to the far side of the table before saying, "Let's begin."

I breathed out a snort and chanced a peek at Effie to see if she was offended, but with eyes fixed ahead on the beauty she had created, she didn't even register Zelda's lack of awe for her work. She was content in herself, without needing her approval. I appreciated that about her. I logged that in the back of my mind as something to aspire to.

We followed Zelda's prompting and moved to the table where a large gold rimmed tome was lying open. I was surprised I didn't notice it when we first came in. I looked to Zelda for instructions.

"An eighteenth birthday is no small thing. Before the 1900s, a long life was not guaranteed. Each passing year was considered a miracle. And so we developed traditions to honor the gift of life and measure the passing of years in tangible ways. These traditions have been passed down for many, many generations. It is no coincidence that you are here now to celebrate with us this very auspicious occasion. I believe there are things at work around us greater and more divine than we can dream of."

Zelda motioned for us to come closer. She pulled out the chair at the head of the table for me to sit. She stood at my right and Effie at my left. Zelda lifted the unlit pillar candle from the serving boat in the middle of the table.

"As the firstborn, it has always been my duty to look after those around me. I take this charge with utmost respect and diligence. This is the blessing I possess and pass on to you," she said without a flourish. Holding the unlit candle, she leaned in towards one that was lit and borrowed its flame.

Effie took the next unlit candle from the left. "As the last born, it has been my joy to take up space, push boundaries, and challenge the status quo." With this, she winked at Zelda. "This is the blessing I possess and pass on to you." Each word eked out through her effervescent smile, the polar opposite of her sister. She tilted her candle toward Zelda and allowed her flame to consume the wick.

"As the oldest and youngest of our lineage, we represent wisdom and experience. We hold the harmony of balance and grace. We have been the keepers and repairers of the breach, and tonight we pull back the veil and usher you into the next chapter."

She nodded for me to take the last unlit candle from the serving tray. But based on the heaviness in the air, this wasn't just a luxurious birthday treat. I hesitated, and looked between them. This was a little mystical and I was not sure I was into it. I opened my mouth to protest as Zelda cleared her throat and gave me a warning look. And I remembered her rule: respect the traditions. I didn't know why. But now wasn't the time to ask, I supposed.

I reached across the table for the candle and sat back with it in my hands. I gave Zelda a *Now what?* look. Zelda closed her eyes and murmured something quietly. I glanced up at Effie to see what was happening, but she was doing the same. So I pursed my lips and gazed around awkwardly. I sighed. This was going sideways fast, a nervous churn in my gut urged me to make it stop before it was too late.

I waited until they finished, then glanced between them again. Their eyes opened, and it almost looked like Zelda was smiling. She leaned in first, and a half second later, Effie leaned in too; together they lit my candle. The moment mine flickered to life, they breathed a sigh of relief and Zelda nearly chuckled.

I wanted to ask what was so funny, but I let it go. They sat down, and I couldn't help but notice how loose Zelda was, her rigid posture rounded and even her austere frown lines disappeared into the resting smile she sported. It was so nice to see her eyes sparkle with wonder. I didn't want to make the stern look reappear by asking about it. It also had me wondering about the traditions and what more was to come if that was only the first part.

I reached for some fruit to snack on, something to fidget with, but Zelda slapped my hand so hard it stung. I dropped the plum. So much for getting over herself.

"Not yet." She got up and fetched the water pitcher and two medium-sized gold bowls. "You must wash and be cleansed under the mega moon before you can partake."

I lifted my eyebrows, tempted to protest, but the look she gave me had me slumping back in my chair. I resigned myself to participate and be grateful, even if the beautiful party came at the cost of being a little weird. I took a breath and reminded myself that I was surrounded by family. Even though I didn't always know them, they always knew me, and that should count for something. But there was something familiar in her speech. Glancing up, the candlelight illuminated the blossoming ivy, and it tickled something in my memory. Something I couldn't put my finger on.

Zelda took the pitcher and filled her bowl with water then handed them to Effie who did the same. They looked up, nodded, and, at the same time, they both took one of my hands and dipped it in the bowl of water. They each gathered up a handful of gemstones from around the golden boat at the center of the table. In a practiced rhythm, they placed gems and jewels along the tops of my arm spaced out proportionately. I was one haunting "oooooh" from losing my dinner, which prompted a squeak out of me.

I could see why the townspeople steered clear of her.

"So wait, are you guys, like *witches*?" I shrank into myself and braced for a storm. The idea of my aunties being witches felt nauseatingly on point, and could easily explain the weirdness.

Zelda froze, her fingertips just grazing my forearm.

"What do you mean *witches*?" She reared back from me. "Who said we were witches, Scout?" Warning laced her voice.

"No one," I hurried to say, "it's just, you guys are being a little weird and *voodoo-y*, you know? All this talk about generations and the full moon and then there's whatever you did to my foot? But the weirdest bit is..." I couldn't bring myself to meet her unwavering fury-filled gaze as I said this next part. "How everyone in town was afraid of you..."

I snuck a peek at Aunt Zelda, who looked as horrified as if I'd slapped her. I gulped. The moment was ruined.

"Did someone say something to you? It was those insipid townspeople, wasn't it?" She jumped to her feet, pacing at once. "I don't care what they told you. It isn't true. None of what they said is true." Now she was coming unhinged. I shrugged out of the stones, letting them fall onto the table, and wrapped my arms around myself.

"No? I don't have any idea what you're talking—"

She continued as though she didn't hear me, "They like to make up stories. They're just bored with their pathetic, little lives so they decide to try and ruin ours. But I'll tell you what, Scout. They don't care about you. They don't care about us. They only want to exploit our story for their entertainment." She stopped and sneered at me, lips curled back and teeth bared.

"Our family has endured so much pain because of this place. And yet we're bound to it. Why, if I had half a mind, I'd—" She stops abruptly.

Silence enveloped us, filling in the heavy pockets of pain. Her side eye pierced me. Like she was asking me where my loyalty lies, accusing me of betraying her. But I didn't, did I? I just asked a question.

"All right," Effie stepped in. "Why don't we cool it down? Zelda, come along. Scout, stay here just a minute." Effie led the way out the door and turned to snap at Zelda. "*Now*, Zelda." And they were gone.

The quiet that filled in their absence wasn't quite peaceful, but it was far less fraught with dynamite. I pull my phone out of my wristlet.

**NO SERVICE.**

I slid it back in and slumped in the chair. I didn't know what to believe now. If they weren't witches, then what did all this mean? What were these traditions? What was the "sort-of religion" they practiced? I really hoped to get some answers soon because I didn't think my little heart could take much more of this.

The door to the greenhouse creaked open on a breeze and the evening air ushered them in, this time Effie in the lead. "Let's have a proper birthday. Shall we?" She resumed her chipper nature in the wake of a natural disaster. It felt a bit out of touch, but if Zelda could be pushed over the edge by a small storm, I didn't want to know how easily Effie could be ruined.

She gave Zelda and me a pointed look. I shrunk down in the chair, reserved to be quiet the rest of the evening, and Zelda lifted her chin with a tut.

"I suppose we owe you an explanation." Effie extended a hand to Zelda. Zelda crossed over to stand at the opposite end of the table.

"It's time. Tell her everything." It wasn't the words that surprised me as much as who said them. Zelda deferred to Effie.

Effie sat down at the head of the table and Zelda hovered behind with her hands perched on the back of the chair.

The hair on the back of my neck bristled as I braced myself for answers.

# Scout

"What we tell you now must never leave this room," Effie said sternly.

I couldn't believe it—I didn't think I would ever see the day when Zelda let Effie take the wheel.

"Scout?" Effie's eyes softened, and she turned her head to murmur to Zelda, "I think she's in shock." The hand she raised to buffer her voice did nothing to block the side comment.

"I'm fine." I shook my head to break my gaze on Zelda. I flicked my eyes down to Aunt Effie. "Go ahead."

"Are you sure, Poppet? I don't know, maybe this isn't such a good idea." She darted her eyes back to Zelda. *This* was the Effie I expected. Soft and ever so slightly unsure.

I reached across the table to her. "Aunt Effie, I need to know what's happening. Please, tell me."

"All right, dear, let me think where to begin." She clasped her hands in front of her and bowed her head for a moment. Was *she praying?*

When she picked her head up, she slid her gaze to the large book on the table.

"Do you remember your first day here? When I told you about our great-grandfather who moved here from Wales?" Zelda's knuckles turned white on the chair behind Effie's head, like this was news to her.

"Oh, the guy who was looking for Viking treasure? Yeah..." *The one who Josephine mentioned in her letters as connected to the greenhouse...* I added silently.

"Well, he found it. I didn't mention the cost of his escapades or what happened. Our great-grandfather was looking for riches, a way to take care of his family, but what he found instead was an ancient relic. Because Emrys uncovered the secrets of the book, he unlocked the curse and shackled our family lineage to it."

She patted the open book before us. The temperature around me plummeted. *They were going to use that on me tonight?* My insides turned to liquid fear.

"Now, Scout, we would never hurt you," Effie responded to my obnoxiously loud facial expressions. "As long as each successor in our family line honors their role, the curse is averted."

Zelda cut in. "Scout, this is very serious. I need your word that you will listen to Effie and consider the weight of what's being offered to you." Zelda shifted her weight uncertainly.

Alarm bells began a serenade in my head. *Offered?* Seeing the grim look on Zelda's face by candlelight accompanied by her hesitation gave me pause. A frisson of anxiety spanned out across my chest. The candlelight flickered in her glassy eyes as she waited for my response.

My heart ticked faster in my throat, keeping me from speaking. I bobbed my head in response.

Effie leaned onto her elbows, drawing nearer to me. "Scout, there is more to this world than meets the eye. For thousands of years, our reality has been separated from another place only by a thin, shimmering veil."

I blinked carefully. It sounded like the start of a *Star Wars* movie or a fantasy book; not the real world. Here, there was only *this,* what we could see and touch.

"There are special places in the world where the veil is thinner, and another world bleeds through. These places have ancient gates that allow us to either pass through or receive others who pass through. These gates require gatekeepers, and a gate cannot be left unattended. Someone must attend the gate at all times during the season of its appearance.

If they refuse their role, the curse will claim them. I admit, we don't know everything since the gate has been closed for so long, but that much we do know."

She hesitated and surveyed me for a moment. I inhaled a sharp bit of stale air and locked it inside my chest as she spoke. I focused on the candle's flame before me, dancing as it dodged my long exhale.

"When I told you that our great-grandfather went crazy believing the strange things this book taught him—I lied. Everything he found out was true. This book opened our family to a whole new world—"

"And when I told you we were bound to this place," Zelda cut in, "that we would leave if we could, but we *can't...*" she trailed off, looking down at her sister. "This book may have opened us up to one new world, but if sufficiently cut us off from our own and cursed us to this wretched place."

I didn't move, sensing what came next. A chill spider-walked across my arms, leaving goosebumps.

"Scout, the greenhouse we are sitting in is an ancient gate. And we have been the gatekeepers since our mother Josephine died."

None of this was computing. I heard the words coming out of their mouths, I knew it was English, but—

"There's more," Effie said, watching Zelda. She gave a solemn nod. The way both aunties moved—almost rehearsed—pulled the air from my lungs. Their intent gaze told me something big was coming.

"You've been chosen as the next gatekeeper."

Words were too good for my lips. My mouth formed and reformed around incoherent squeaks. A dull ache knocked at my temples, frustrating my ability to focus. I held my hands up for a time out.

"What?" I finally spat out. I had expected some religious coming-of-age blessing or talk of this generic family curse, but this revelation, if you could call it that, was too much.

"I know this is a lot to take in, but if you would let Effie finish—" Zelda's voice overlapped mine.

"No! What is this? What are you guys?"

"Scout." Effie sat back in her chair, one hand fluttering to her chest as her lashes bat away pin pricks of tears.

They shared a long look across the table.

"Our roles were always to be protectors of the gate, to seal it from discovery. The Others consider the gates like we think of ports, numerous place to pop in and out of their world and into ours. But something happened. When Mom died, the greenhouse's gate closed. We checked the other gatekeepers, all the gates had disappeared or withered."

"Until," Zelda said, eyes trained on the serving boat of lavish fruit before us.

"Until... you got here," Effie finished.

"The greenhouse revived in your time here, a sign of the portal reopening." Zelda raised a hand to the creeping ivy. "It has claimed you. We weren't sure at first, but this afternoon solidified our curiosity."

"What do you mean?"

Another look fraught with meaning passed between the aunties.

"I'm sorry, Scout." Effie looked ashamed. "We lied to you earlier."

"There was no broken glass that you stepped on." Zelda sighed her remorse. "When you were in the greenhouse earlier, pruning the ivy, the damage you did was reflected in your body. Cut for cut."

I reached down and pulled back the red skirt around my legs, slipping my feet out of the sandals to look at them. There were still no scars or evidence it happened. But I remembered the sensation of blood pooling in my sneakers and feeling woozy from something. I didn't know what to believe. They already lied to me a few times. Who was to say they weren't lying now?

Zelda continued, "When we were claimed as gatekeepers, we never tried to break the bond or cut ties. So we never experienced it before. Although we did have one relative who tried to light the greenhouse on fire, but ended up with severe burns all across his body. We can only assume the greenhouse perceived your act, as innocent as it was, as a threat and linked itself to you irreparably so that you couldn't leave or kill it. That's part of the curse."

"Incredible defense mechanism," Effie mused as she toyed with the vines on the table.

"Uh, no, this is straight out of *A Little Shop of Horrors*, actually."

Zelda's brow furrowed in a disdainful response. "Really, Scout."

"What? I'm trying to listen and process this, but this is a lot. You're telling me because I pruned a plant, the greenhouse attacked me?"

"Good heavens, Scout," Zelda said. "That isn't at all what we're trying to say. You have become rooted here. Your lifeblood has intermingled with the life force of the greenhouse and the energy of the world beyond it. We have to finish the traditions in order to complete the bond acceptance ritual or else the curse will claim you."

"Wait, bond acceptance ritual? Curse?"

"Yes, the ceremony to become the gatekeeper of the ancient gate must happen on a full moon, the night of the protector's eighteenth birthday. I told you it was no mistake that you were here, especially now. It all makes perfect sense." Effie tried for an endearing smile, but it didn't reach her sad eyes.

"And if you run, the curse will seek you out and destroy what you love," Zelda said sharply. "Be it a man, a job, or life itself. And if you try to destroy the greenhouse, or any other gate, it will destroy you." Effie looked up at Zelda with a shared sorrow. Zelda knew from experience.

"So what, you weren't even going to tell me all this first? Make me promise to respect your traditions without question? Do the ceremony and sell my soul to this "Other" world to be its protector, bound forever? 'Or else'?" I asked, my eyes wide and voice shivering with contempt. "You don't see anything wrong with that?" I searched their eyes for an apology, but I just found them doe-eyed. "The worst part is you didn't trust me enough to tell me. How many times have I asked for more information on our family, or about this greenhouse?

"If I hadn't found out the truth, I would have been locked in here forever with you guys. Bitter and lonely, just like you." I shoved back from the table, standing. "I can't believe I ever trusted you. You were just looking for your ticket out of here." I shook my head and looked down at them. "I know," I said with mock delight. "Here comes the snotty-nosed American brat! We'll sacrifice her to the greenhouse and finally get our freedom!" I dropped my hands and gave them a steely glare.

"Well, too bad for you. I'm not finishing the ceremony. Screw the curse. I don't believe in curses. I don't want anything to do with you or your stupid greenhouse."

"Scout, wait," Effie said, but I was already running to the door, wristlet and phone in hand.

"No, leave me alone!" With a quick look over my shoulder, hand on the rusted, worn-out doorknob, I mustered as much anger and hate as I could pack into one sentence and spat back, "I hate you and your cursed family! Leave me out of your wicked plans." I wrenched open the door and fled into the night.

# 18

# Scout

As I slammed the door, I let a scream rip through me. So much anger had never bubbled up and exploded out of my body. A fierceness churned in my gut and tore through me leaving my skin burning—beyond my control. A shiver coursed through me as my breaths came heavily, though I was relieved to let everything out.

I veered to the left of the house like I'd done many times before, heading toward the sea to blow off some steam.

But the auntie's home wasn't there. The field of seagrass wasn't there. There was no warm sea breeze pestering my hair. Actually, a quick look around had me wondering where I was entirely. I spun in a full circle to get my bearings.

The greenhouse I'd come from was gone.

I was in the middle of the woods.

*No, no, no. This can't be happening. This is a dream. I am in my bed, I will wake up.*

I backed up with the heel of my palms boring into my eyes. I fully expected to wake up staring at the greenhouse ceiling, to find this has just been another vivid dream. At the very least, I expected to back into the door I had just bolted through. But no door caught me, and I stumbled backward over my own feet.

114

A hiccup of fear struck me as I swallowed the gasp from falling. I landed in the soft peat moss on the forest floor. Heat raced away from my fingers, as a nervous thrum of adrenaline began coursing through me. My body shifted into survival mode; all of my nerves were on high alert.

I squeezed my eyes shut again and prayed for this nightmare to end and to wake up in my own bed.

Opening my eyes, I saw the dense forest around me, unmoving. I pushed up from the ground. Dusting off the beautiful red dress, now covered in pine needles and other forest debris. The moon hung low in the sky and a few stars peeked between the treetops. I needed to move. The panic was taking over. If I didn't start flushing the adrenaline out, I'd end up frozen in place.

I shook my hands out and started pacing.

How was I going to get out of this? Where even was *this*? An aggravated scream worked its way up my throat, burning as it left my mouth. It felt like one thing after another was happening to me. First I lost my summer to my aunties, then I lost whatever freedom I'd thought I'd have here in England to work in a stupid greenhouse, only to find out they planned on pressuring me into some bogus ritual. As if being forced to follow in my parents' footsteps at the end of summer wasn't enough.

My thoughts began swirling again, but a rustling in the bushes nearby called me to attention. *Shoot, I shouldn't have screamed. I'm basically begging Bigfoot to come get me.*

I froze. Was I supposed to run, hide, play dead?

The bush shook again and I noticed the branches full of ripe pink berries.

I backed up slowly, glancing over my shoulder so I wouldn't stumble. Working my way over the gnarled tree roots, I retreated into a big pine. Its branches dipped low around me and I hoped it would offer a bit of shelter from whatever animal may launch out of the bushes.

A moment later, the rustling stopped and a rabbit shot out of the bush followed by another. I released a shaky breath. Relief flooded me and a nervous chuckle escaped my lips. I stepped out from under the tree's boughs. I needed to figure out where I was so I could get back to my aunties.

It was eerily quiet. The heaviness of night cloaked the trees around me and made everything feel small and enclosed. The forest grew denser around me, and I could barely make out the moon and glittering stars through the canopy. Trapped under the darkness, the air hummed tight with electricity. It reminded me of summer storms and watching for heat lightning with my mom on the porch. There was a tingle of anticipation just before the snap.

I crept a little farther to see if I could hear running water, something I remembered seeing on those survival shows my dad watched. But only suffocating silence met me, the kind that made me feel like I was being watched. I looked around. Nothing but dark and dense woods surrounded me. Anything could be out there and I'd never know it.

*Well, I can't just stand here waiting for it—whatever it is—to come and get me.*

Pacing a little to the left, then back again to the right, I begged the universe for a sign. Which way was the right way home? My gut said right, so I threw up my hands and—

My phone! It was in my wristlet all along!

I yanked the zipper open and pulled out the phone.

No signal.

Knowing better, but desperate enough to try, I lifted the phone higher.

"C'mon, c'mon," I hissed at the chunk of plastic. I tried dialing the SOS number and the screen just went black. Stabbing at the screen, the reality of the situation began to dawn on me. I didn't know where I was, I had no way of calling for help, and no way of getting home. The panic gripped me and I whipped my phone into the darkness.

Not recognizing anything in sight, a thought occurred to me that sent a different kind of chill over my body. Zelda and Effie were talking about a portal... a portal that I opened, allegedly.

"What if—? No, that's crazy." But a nagging feeling in the pit of my stomach told me I'd stumbled onto the truth. And into another world.

My icy fingers shook as a gust of cool wind breezed around me. It felt like someone leaned in to whisper in my ear. A chill crept down my spine and I regretted throwing my phone. I quickly searched the forest floor in the direction I threw it.

After an agonizing couple minutes, I snatched it from a tuft of pine needles and held it close to my chest. Swiping open the screen, I turned the phone's flashlight on and breathed a sigh of relief. At least I had some light.

A twig snapped behind me and I whirled around only to be met by a towering man with glowing platinum-tinted eyes.

"You're trespassing." His voice boomed.

I let out a whimper in response, dropping my phone and wristlet at my feet in shock. My mouth opened and closed, eyes darted, searching for somewhere to hide. Judging from this man's sheer height and breadth, nothing would shield me from this giant.

"Answer me." It wasn't a question. His voice had a peculiar timbre to it. It didn't sound quite English. Or quite human.

"I—" I didn't even know how to answer that. I didn't know where I was, let alone what I was doing here. The giant bent down to pick up my phone. He peered at it curiously. I wanted to speak, but no sound came.

Around me, men silently approached from behind trees and bushes; a few even dropped down from branches above. A tremble pulsed through me. They had been there the whole time. They were watching me. Somewhere deep in me ached in betrayal.

I knew I should have trusted my instincts.

# Alaric

The pulse of the human stumbling through the portal reverberated within me. My eyes were on Airian, watching for his lead, as he dropped from the trees in a stealthy approach, but my senses were clouded by the girl. Her words, her appearance–her very existence here–was wrong. I could hear her heart racing, her fear rumbling within me, and it unnerved me. Humans contained the worst traits of the Creators; they were arrogant, greedy, dishonest, manipulative, weak, and selfish.

And yet, the thing that sent my heart rate skyrocketing was none of that. The girl felt familiar. *I knew her.*

Airian spoke in the same foreign language as her. It took me a moment to recognize it. English. I had only heard merchants who used the portals speaking English. The people beyond the veil spoke English. Soleil had forced us, a small crew of her guard, to learn enough English to ensure we were never taken advantage of by the foreigners. But it had been many years since I used that tongue. *Of course the humans never bothered to learn MirVis,* I gritted my teeth in ire.

Airian gave the signal for us to move in. As we formed a tight circle around the human, I raked through memories trying to place the girl. When I faintly recognized what she was saying, my eyes on the lips that formed her words, I stumbled on the impossible truth.

She was the girl from my dream.

My mind began whirring. What did it mean for a human to be here right now? They had all been sealed behind the veil during the Great Blackout by the time I broke free from Kilburne. The few experiences I'd had with humans were with greedy merchants who used our portals to broker trade routes to expand their earthly kingdoms.

"Let's go," Airian commanded. We fell into perfect step. Airian's wind energy swept around us and carried us back to camp.

The guys' eyes stayed fixed straight ahead as I knew mine should also be. But I allowed myself to glance at her through my peripheral vision. She had long waved hair and a fixed face of terror. She was smaller by comparison, standing in our midst, and radiated the panic of a caged animal. I was not used to the waves of energy a human could send over us. It took all my focus to resign my features and stay tuned to the task at hand.

We would arrive at camp soon, and I wouldn't dare get caught being weaker than the others. I had more to prove than they did. I had more to lose than they did.

She wiggled between us in terror. *Tough,* I thought. She was going to have to deal with it and the consequences of opening the portal. I found myself wholly irritated by her existence here. We were prepared for a serious threat, an ambush or worse, but instead a weak little human tumbled through. What this the Creators' idea of a joke?

Her writhing caused her to jostle against me. The movement would mean nothing, *should* mean nothing, but that small touch shot a bolt of fire through every last nerve in my body. I almost choked, stumbling on nothing. I covered my movements within the fraction of the second they came. No one would be aware of what consumed me.

The sequence of images that flooded my mind had me careening through a free fall of emotions.

The girl with fire in her eyes, animosity just for me, stirred me. The challenge tugged at the most feral parts of my soul. How could this human also be the girl in my dream who stewarded fire?

Another flash of dream memory pulled at the corners of my mind. The same girl crumpled at the edge of the woods, stowed under trees bowing to the storm around us. Inside, my heart thundered to save her. Bile rose up the back of my throat. Never had I expected to feel mercy for a human.

I wouldn't dare to revisit the memory of the kiss. Being this close to her warm, trembling lips sent shivers down to my toes, and I... I had to stop this train of thought immediately. Human or not, I had no time or interest in a companion.

A new image fluttered to mind—the light draining from her eyes, scarlet red, so much red. Red on her face, on my hands, on the floor. And a voice I swore to never surrender to again. "Well done, my faithful little sentry."

*Soleil.*

# 20

# Scout

"Where are you taking me?" I demanded.

There was no response. Not one of these giant monsters reacted to my existence. Okay, maybe they weren't *giants*, per se. But they were uncomfortably tall by comparison, and broad. *Hello, muscles.*

*Wait, focus Scout. Danger!*

"I haven't done anything wrong! I just got lost. Let me go!" I tried to wiggle, but the guards around me were so close I couldn't budge. The sharp beading of my dress scratched against my bare arms. The panic was rising, clawing at my breath. I was trapped, doomed.

I blinked the tears from my eyes, shoving them away for later. I wished I could take it all back. The fight with my aunties, the misunderstanding. I would rather live out the cursed sentence of being some magic gatekeeper and never see my parents again than be here right now. Fear filled me, splashing images across my mind. Me tied to a chair. Me dangling by my arms chained to the rafters. I blinked. I couldn't let my mind betray me now.

*Breathe, Scout. Breathe.* My lungs burned as if a cannonball was rolling across my chest. The world raced under our feet, and I didn't understand how I hadn't stumbled yet. The whipping wind kept my eyes from focusing on any one thing around me. Looking down, the ground seemed to blur beneath our feet. How were they doing this? It seemed like we were only walking, but everything was speeding around us.

I was so tempted to give in to the panic and the fear. It would be so easy to let it sweep over me and pull me under. Just as the last wave reared back to crash into me, we came to a stop. The wind faded and my cheeks warmed from the lack of breeze. I pushed my hair back and let my eyes focus.

We halted at the edge of a clearing. A short distance away stood a humbly clothed man. Loose white and beige garments draped from him and floated on the wind our escort created. I gazed around him as the leader of our entourage stepped into the clearing, approaching him.

Tents of beige canvas stood on stilted platforms, their openings flapped quietly with the breeze. Beyond the tents were a couple of huts, only visible by the rugged thatched roofs and smoke billowing out from behind them. The remnants of embers cracked in the distance, a forgotten fire left for dead. A short way from me were piles of cut wood and animal skins hanging to dry. It reminded me of the Civil War reenactment camps my parents would cart me to when I was in elementary school for "enrichment".

The guards shifted around me, loosening their stance now that we approached the center of the clearing towards the two men. I stole a glance at the guards. They were all well built, much taller than me, but not nearly as tall as the two men speaking. They spoke a language I'd never heard before. I listened, trying to make out the sounds and syllables, but they whispered low and hushed.

The leader of the guards stood next to the white cloaked guy, who stepped up to us. The leader said a single word, and then men around me snapped to attention and formed a new position, creating a gap around me and an opening for this new man to step into.

Upon closer look, this man's eyes glowed purple. He moved carefully and slowly until he was only an arm's length away. He had a genuine smile on his face and peered at me curiously.

"Josephine? Is that you?"

My skin prickled at the name. A part of me was still freaked out, while another was incredibly relieved to hear someone speak English that sounded more normal! Could he be talking about my great-grandmother?

I looked at the guards around me, but they were statues. Forward facing, unflinching. Where the two men's eyes glowed platinum and purple, the guards' eyes elicited a low light that pulsed. Their faces were arranged in perfect symmetry, giving them a familiar but unrecognizable *je ne sais quoi*. They seemed…otherworldly in their frozen perfection.

"What's it been, a century over there? A millennia here." He chuckled, reaching his arms out wide to me.

I blinked, trying to make sense of what he was saying. His accent tripped me up and made my brain melt as I struggled to understand.

"We've been waiting for you to return, but I suppose you always did take your good 'ol time." He gave me a friendly smile with knowing eyes. He didn't at all seem put off by my deepening scowl.

"Well, come now, tell us where you've been," he urged excitedly, like he expected a riveting bedtime story of swashbuckling pirates.

I was so confused. I opened my mouth and closed it, unable to form words.

"And what are you wearing, Jo? I would have thought you learned your lesson after that one time," he nudged me playfully, pointing at my disheveled, beautiful gown.

A quietness fell over us. Cocking his head sideways, he gave me a peculiar look. He leaned in closer, looking deeply into my eyes, before saying something in another language over his shoulder to the guards' leader. The towering man came to stand beside him and stooped to look into my eyes, too. His platinum orbs glimmered like moonbeams on water.

They conspired in unintelligible whispers, heads drawn together. What if they were planning to torture me? What if they decided to rip my toenails off one by one and then proceeded to rip my hair out strand by strand? My heart racqueted higher with each passing thought. My eyes widened and I attempted to form a coherent thought, but I couldn't get a grasp on it.

The two men righted themselves, and with a dismissive wave, the stoic men on guard fell back. The man with glowing purple eyes turned and simply said over his shoulder, "Follow me."

I was so taken aback by this turn of events that I was stuck in fawn mode. My eyes were wide, and it felt like a trick. I peered over my shoulder to find that the guards had formed a line several paces behind me like a wall so I couldn't turn and run.

The only way was forward.

I looked again around the clearing. The full moon was high in the sky and small sounds from the forest filled the air. I snuck a peek at one of the tents and considered screaming for help. But who would come out of those tents? More men like these guardian sorts? Or were they cannibalistic headhunters? I shuddered and shut that line of thinking down. Not now.

I took a deep breath and steeled myself to take whatever came next, but the leader of the guard interrupted my process. "He'll only ask once."

He didn't look at me, but it seemed like advice rather than an intimidating command.

It put me in gear. I scurried to make up the difference those few seconds of consideration cost me. He strode toward the hut in the corner of the clearing. It was a modest hut, squat and low to the ground, larger than the tents and more sturdy to the elements. The thatched roof hung just a little over the walls to create a small space to huddle against in case of rain.

He walked up to the door and held it open to me.

Everything inside me screamed not to go in there first. *It'll be my death—I'm sure of it.* But as I got closer, I saw an oil lamp lit on the table inside and... It didn't look like a torture chamber. So I stepped in carefully, wide eyes taking in every square inch of the place looking for weapons or guards in hiding.

The man moved around me to a kitchenette and returned with a cup of water. He handed it to me. I looked at the rippling water in my trembling hands then back up at him. He chuckled and shook his head as if to say, *no I did not just poison you.* A light touch at the small of my back gently directed me to the table near the kitchenette.

For how small the hut appeared on the outside, it was much larger inside. And well-furnished. A hut kinda implied "humble means," but this one was beautiful. My aunties' summer home was an old-English-proper-meets-free-spirited-beach-cottage. But then again, that might just be the blend of Zelda and Effie's personalities. This space was relaxed and in order but ornate with designs and vibrant colors, and I wondered if it was also a reflection of his personality.

He sat across from me, and I set my water glass on the table. Thirst left me parched, but I'd be darned if I came this far only to die a slow death by poison.

"So if you're not Josephine, who are you?" He leaned back, crossing his arms over his chest and studied me.

"My name is Scout. I think there's been some misunderstanding." I aimed for diplomacy as I opened and folded my hands on the table, holding his gaze.

"Oh, most certainly." He agreed without hesitation.

"I think I got a little turned around in the woods and wandered too far from home. If you could let me go, I'll just find my way home." I gave my best mock confidence as if I absolutely knew what happened and exactly how to get out of here.

"I don't think I can do that."

Hope plummeted inside me.

"Why not?" I snapped. Just because *I* knew I was afraid didn't mean I'd let *him* know that.

He chuckled to himself and leaned forward, elbows on the table.

"Do you know where you are, Scout?" He called my bluff.

I didn't answer. I *couldn't* answer.

He nodded solemnly. "That's what I was afraid of." He thought for a minute. "Can you tell me how you got here?"

I snorted. "Ask your guards. They all but snatched me from the woods and dragged me here against my will." I sat back and crossed my arms.

He didn't flinch. Instead, he probed further. "Before that. How did you get to the woods?"

It seemed like he knew there was more to it, like he knew more than I did. Or maybe he was fishing for information. I weighed the options of telling him or holding it close to my heart. I was out of my depths here. I looked him up and down.

"I've told you my name, but I don't know yours."

"Khalon. It's a pleasure to meet you." He paused. "Did you know Josie?"

My heart seized in my chest. *Khalon.* Josephine mentioned him in her letters. I took the water glass from the table and sipped it to cover my shock.

"I'm not sure I know who you're talking about," I said finally, looking around the room, anywhere but at him.

He looked down and counted on his fingers. "I think she must have been your great- or great-great-grandmother. And it's amazing because you look just like her."

How was this possible? I thought about the photo I slipped from the family album at the Aunties' house. How Aunt Effie traced Grandma Jo's face with her finger.

Josie.

How did this guy, in the middle of nowhere, know my great-grandmother?

I must have asked some version of this question out loud, too caught up in my thoughts to realize it, because he was already answering me.

"Your great-grandmother was a dear friend of mine. She used to visit us many years ago when she was not much older than you are now." A wan smile touched his lips and he sighed. "When she disappeared, we wondered where she went." He ran a hand over his tired face. "When she never returned, we just assumed she was called home and would come back in her own time. She wasn't the sort you told what to do. I imagine her eyes aren't the only thing you inherited from her." He laughed and gave me a playful wink.

I knew he meant to be charming and disarming, but I found this news unsettling. I stared at this middle-aged, deeply tan man in the lamplight. When my great-grandmother was my age, he shouldn't have been alive...

"Actually, when the guards caught wind you were coming, they thought you were Josephine finally returning to us. Imagine our surprise when our friend had no memory of us or this place." A sadness entered his eyes.

I considered this, not yet able to make heads or tails of how it could all be possible, and chose my words carefully.

"Grandma Jo died a long time ago. I don't know what happened, no one will talk about it." I watched his expression closely as he reacted to this news.

His mouth yawned open in disbelief, he wiped his hand down his face in a slow, tired motion, pulling at the obvious grief he displayed.

"I take it you didn't know?" I hazarded a guess.

"No," he tented his hands to his lips. "Of course, we always knew it was a possibility, Josephine was only human." His gaze darted around erratically, as though he was trying to make sense of this.

"When was the last time you saw her? Did she come here often?" I had to know what she meant in those letters. She said something about a place and going to help Khalon. To me it sounded like he may have been the last person to see her. And I had to know why.

"Gatekeepers weren't technically supposed to use the portal, although I suppose there was no rule against it—not that that would have stopped Josie if there had been. But Josie wasn't like the others. She hungered for more. She wanted a big life and a big story. She would come through with merchants for a little at a time and return home." Khalon paused and looked over his shoulder. "Nearly a millennia ago, something shifted in our political landscape. A place far from here entered into a civil war following a coup. Josie was determined to go help the people caught in the crossfire. Of course, we wouldn't let her and escorted her home. We couldn't risk a gatekeeper being killed here."

"Why? What would have happened?" I was enraptured in his voice, the way he told the story.

He leaned in as though conspiring with me. "It would have destroyed the portals."

Why hadn't the aunties mentioned that in the list of information about the curse? *Felt kinda important!*

"When Josephine disappeared, didn't you consider that maybe she had gone to this place to help, but had been killed?"

"No," he said, utterly emphatic. "Absolutely not, I knew Josie, and she wouldn't have been so careless. Besides, the portals didn't disappear until a while later. One by one they slowly closed, despite other living gatekeepers' attempts to keep them open. Josie's disappearance isn't the only mystery here."

This information settled heavy between us. My eyes raked over Khalon as he sat forward, leaning his elbows on his knees, his beige linen clothes draped around him. He didn't look like a killer. But his pulsating purple eyes reminded me that he wasn't human, *if that was even possible*, and I couldn't trust him yet.

"Where are we?" I whispered, afraid to find out. Or worse, for my request to be denied.

"You mean here," he gestured around the room, "or *here*?" He gestured widely as if to encompass everything. His eyes never left mine. "Tell me how you got here and I'll tell you where you are," he countered just as quietly. His glowing eyes drew me in, but I huffed to refuse the lure.

"If this isn't the same place I'm from... a different world entirely," I could barely believe the words coming out of my mouth, but I pressed on. "Then, how come you know English so well but the other guys were speaking some other language?"

He sighed, his brow dipping in clear exasperation at my segue, and chewed his lip. "All the leaders in Landow are expected to know English, it's the language of trade. Some stewards take up the practice for fun or for a challenge, but no one is forced to. What you heard was the local dialect we speak here, MirVis."

"Ahh." I nodded and looked away. Not a language I'd ever heard of on Earth... but maybe it could be like a made up language, kinda like how cults do it? *No, Scout. Quit jumping to wildly inappropriate conclusions!*

"Come on, Scout, please. Tell me how you got here." He was on the verge of pleading with me, leaning forward even more.

Finally, I caved. "I don't know. I really don't know how I got here. All I know is one minute I was in a fight with my aunties, storming out of the greenhouse, and the next I was in the woods."

He sat up. "Wait a minute, did you say greenhouse?" He said to me, then to himself, "So it's still there."

"Yeah." I looked at him curiously. "My aunties said it's been there forever."

"That's great news. We thought it may have been lost or gone. We might be able to get you home after all."

Relief flooded through me—going home was great news. But something was missing. The *how* seemed important. Here we were, glossing over the fact that I just magically appeared in another world.

"First thing in the morning, we'll take you back to the portal and we'll send you home." He stood up from the table, conversation over.

"Wait, why not tonight?"

"It's dark, my men are tired, and it's late. You don't want to be out in the woods right now. It's not safe."

"But, I—" He turned away, leaving me alone at the table. End of discussion.

I huffed and slumped in my chair. Nearby, a small cot was propped open with a pillow and blanket folded on it. *Was I supposed to sleep there?* If that was the case, I wouldn't be getting much rest.

Before disappearing, the man turned back. "And as for where you are? Welcome to our little corner of Landow. You'll be safe here in the Ruack Valley."

# Alaric

After Khalon took the trespasser to his hut, Airian dismissed us. As we strode back toward the forest, Airian pulled me aside to give me a reprieve for the rest of the night watch. It made me wonder if he knew what I wouldn't let on.

That somehow this human was connected to my worst nightmare.

Before he left, he charged me with a new task. "I don't have a good feeling about this human," by the way his lip curled over the word *human*, I guessed Airian and I finally had one thing in common. "I can't afford to put any of my men on detail for her, so I'll need you to keep a close eye on her." He looked me up and down looking to see if his sting landed. I made sure my face gave nothing away to the rejection I felt being excluded from *his men*. I nodded once. "Report back to me about anything suspicious."

When we parted ways, and I sat by the dwindling fire. It was just coals now, but I needed a safe space to think. Reaching my hands out towards the flame, I sent a blaze into the coals. The warmth ignited my soul, slowly refilling me in a deeper way than the sun ever could.

A quiet swish-swish of wet grass had me turning to see Maël walking toward me with a pail of water. He threw it on the ashes which sizzled and smoked. Instantly, my connection with the flames shattered, and I felt colder within than I did externally. I disguised my huff behind a cough. I didn't want to start something with the only other steward here who didn't hate me. I got up from my place.

Maël tucked the bucket under one arm and stared into the diminishing light. "How did someone like her open the portal?"

"I haven't a clue. I didn't know humans could open the portals." I rubbed roughly at the back of my neck.

"Humans have been gatekeepers in their realm since the portals opened, but they've only been able to guard them."

I heard what he wasn't saying. Humans couldn't create portals or open them once they were closed.

"Maybe she's not human," Maël said simply.

"She's definitely human," I said, a little too quickly, garnering a fierce look from my comrade. "Come on, you were there. Couldn't you hear that human heart beat and feel that fear? What else could she be?"

"All I know is that those portals have been closed for a long time, and very powerful people have been trying to open them ever since. Something big is going on that someone isn't telling us. Either she's the key, or she's part of the problem. But either way, I don't think she's *just a human*. And I don't trust her."

# Scout

Standing in the middle of the forest, the guards positioned themselves at a careful distance from me. Some sported mildly annoyed faces while others looked ready to quit.

"I'm sorry, but I don't know what I'm supposed to do." I shot a fleeting look of exasperation at Khalon, who leaned against a nearby tree, watching me fail. I readjusted the straps of my dress, feeling very overdressed in this evening wear in broad daylight. Compared to their tunics and basic protective coverings, I was more than a little exposed. The weight of their judgmental gazes was a burden I carried intrinsically.

"It's all right, Scout. Just do exactly what you did last time." The look on his face reminded me of the coaches on the outside of the boxing ring when their players were down. His voice was optimistic, but the smile didn't quite reach his eyes.

I threw my hands up. We'd been at this for an hour already.

"That's just it. I didn't do anything."

"You must have," he insisted.

"I don't know what you want me to say. I did nothing out of the ordinary."

"Walk me through it again." He came over to role-play with me. "So you were in the greenhouse." He pantomimed the greenhouse and stepped in. "Then what?"

"Then my aunts and I started arguing, and I just wanted to get away. I grabbed the doorknob—"

"Go through the motions, Scout," he said.

I rolled my eyes but mimed opening the door and walking through it.

"I slammed the door behind me, screaming for them to leave me alone, and when the door closed, it was gone. And I was gone too."

"Just like that?" he queried.

"Just like that."

"And you didn't—"

"I didn't do anything else," I cut him off.

He put a finger to his lips, tapping. He murmured to himself in his native language while pacing. I made a mental note to ask about that later.

While Khalon considered what he knew, I did the same with what I knew. One, I was not in England anymore. Two, Khalon was in charge around here. And three, though no one has said it yet, I was beginning to think this place might be enchanted. The thought scratched through me like nails on a chalkboard, and I recoiled instantly.

"What if we reenact it perfectly? I'll be your aunties, you be you, and we'll try again."

I swear you could hear the collective groan of the guards standing watch around us even stone still.

I caught the eye of one of the guards, and something flickered in his gaze, like bemusement. He looked like he wanted to laugh, but in the span of a breath, his face emptied, and his sharp gaze fixed ahead. It happened so fast that I thought I made it up. I blinked but kept my eyes on him a moment longer. He looked like the others, all sharp features and hard bone structure, but his eyes flickered with pulsing orange bits while the others had green and blue. Something about him seemed familiar.

"What if we take a break?" I asked, moving to sit at the base of a tree—I left my wristlet and phone there, not that it seemed to be of any use. Every time I checked it, the screen read SOS ONLY.

"All right." Khalon nodded to the leader of the guards with platinum eyes. "Airian, come, let us confer."

Airian's voice thundered over us, sharp and authoritative. In response, the men watching guard loosened their postures as others came to take their place. My eyes trailed after them as they all shifted places. The first group of guys went to collect their canteens. Some lounged under the trees; others ran up the side and launched into the branches, settling their haunches above us.

I pulled my knees up to my chest and leaned my head back against the trunk of the tree, eyes closed. The morning sun warmed my face and fought off the chill that panic was introducing to my system.

I wished I could undo everything in the past twenty-four hours. I so regretted the fight with my aunties now and wished I hadn't stormed out the way I did. *They're probably having a heart attack wondering where I am right now. I wonder if they've called my parents yet.* I groaned. That's the last thing I wanted—to ruin their discovery trip. I needed to get home before my mom found out.

The quiet chirps and trills of songbirds and rushing water surrounded us. The forest was still waking up and the strains were light and infrequent. I breathed through the sounds, focusing on them to force out the panic. I was going to figure this out. Surely that door wasn't the only way in and out.

A ray of warm light cascaded through the boughs, blinding me. The pierce of warm light reminded me of the man with orange eyes. My head whipped up, and somehow, I was unwittingly drawn to look for him. Searching the clearing, I came up empty. He was not in my line of vision.

"Actually," a male voice began, then cleared his throat, breaking through my thoughts. From my place at the base of the tree, I gazed up directly into intense fiery eyes. As if my thoughts had called him over, there he was. The man with orange eyes, resting against the tree beside me.

"Until you showed up, we didn't think there was a way into Landow. Or out." His English was rusty and he spoke slowly. His vowels didn't sound like English, and it took me a second to parse out what he said.

And then it hit me like a bowling strike. Every pin of hope I had still standing just blew over.

"What do you mean?"

He crouched down beside me, a shock of dark chestnut hair sweeping across his brow, and picked at twigs. His hand grazed the edge of my arm and my breath caught, leaving my heart hammering within my chest. The heat he exerted wound its way around me, and something restless uncoiled within me.

"I mean, if you didn't make this happen..." He waved indiscriminately at the forest. "And if you can't make it happen again, then..." He trailed off.

It was a kindness to not rub my nose in the situation, to point out just how stuck I really was.

I scanned the clearing we were in, the guards waited in various positions. Some rested, drinking from a canteen, while others pulled dried meat from pouches on their belts. The rest stood at attention while Khalon and Airian conspired in the middle. Khalon was using big gestures and Airian was scrutinizing him, nodding slowly. My stomach churned like fire and molten lava.

"Then what?"

He eased down next to me, leaning against the tree. His eyes raked over me with a slow calculation, as if he was memorizing my every feature. The heat—his intensity was almost too much to handle. But I chose to study his face in a daring response. Minute freckles dotted his cheeks and nose while sweat, in equal measure, speckled his brow. The humidity here was doing us no favors. Whatever this silent standoff was felt dangerous, I had the uncanny feeling that I was playing with fire.

"Then," He pushed off the tree to stand, pausing momentarily, "you're a worthless human just like the rest of your kind."

"Gee, thanks, *buddy*," I scoffed after him.

I groaned, letting my head fall into my hands.

"*No good human*," a voice hissed from over my shoulder.

I jerked my head up and looked around for the sound. Beside me a group of tall angular-faced men stood talking and laughing. A few looked over at me and nodded to the others.

"*What a waste of space*," came again as a hiss over my shoulder.

To my other side, two guards lounged by a tree peeling some fruit with crude knives. I cringed as a muggy bit of air breezed past, sending a strange feeling from the top of my head all the way down my spine. Pins and needles. My head started to feel dizzy and warm. The voices replayed and bounced in my head until one broke through.

"*No one wants you here, leave!*" This time it was more than a hiss, it was a resounding gong.

I was on my feet and frantically searching the faces of these strange men, looking for the culprit. Their faces began to blend and contort as I spun around and around.

"*You worthless piece*—" The voice slammed into me and sent my hands to my head.

"Stop it!" My fingers intertwined in my hair, my palms flat against my ears.

The guy with orange-flecked eyes broke away from the group and approached me with a sneer.

Heat flashed through my body in wave after wave as he reached me. His mouth opened, but I didn't hear the words. The hisses and swirling voices were all around me, making it hard to focus. I smacked my hands against my head again and screamed.

"Make it stop! I just want it to stop!" I was choking on the panic now.

His hand landed on my shoulder and electricity rocketed through me like a shock wave. The force had me staggering backwards. I gritted my teeth against the fire coursing through me. Every nerve alighted with blinding pain. Squeezing my eyes shut, I thought I might die. Fear and anger mixed within me like a shaken bottle of soda. I needed to find some way to expel the pain and craze of what was happening inside.

Commotion kicked up around us. Some men stalked closer with disgust painted on their faces and teeth bared, while others lowered into position to pounce. Khalon held out an arm, signaling for the men to stand down. Airian was next to him, analyzing me.

This sudden vortex of power around me and in me was so new, I was overcome. The voices drowned out all at once. My outstretched hand reached for the man with orange eyes, drawing in all the burning tension collecting in the air around me, and I yanked at something deep within, calling to me. Orange eyes locked with mine and that's when I felt it.

Fire. Passion. Bloodlust.

Around me, a roaring fire kicked up. It separated us from the rest of the guards.

A new wave of energy coursed through me, fueling this power that was as foreign to me as the language they spoke. Orange Eye's grip on my shoulder weakened and he staggered, as my vision blurred.

A small part of me gnawed in worry. Deep in me a still, small voice called, *Scout, stop.*

"All right, that's enough." Airian commanded, bringing his hand up between us. The earth rumbled under my feet. When he sliced his hand down through the air, the fire disappeared. Then the commander opened his hands wide and clapped once; the ground responded with a convulsion, and the sky split, releasing a downpour. Even as these wild displays rippled around us, no one moved.

Except for Khalon, who was at Orange Eye's side, helping him up. My legs wobbled and bowed as they tried to find balance on the rolling ground. Khalon closed his eyes as his hands roved over the man's chest and shoulders. Orange Eyes waved him off with a weak dismissal, but it did nothing to dissuade Khalon's aid.

The first droplets of rain splattered on my forehead and rolled into my eyes. It broke the intense connection that simmered between the man and I. Wiping the rain from my eyes, I looked to Airian, and then the rest of the guard who stood slack-jawed.

What just happened here? I brought my hands up in front of my face, turning them over to inspect them. Did I do that? It couldn't be me, it's them. Then my aunties' words floated back to me: *You've been chosen as the next gatekeeper.* Was this all somehow a part of that?

My thoughts began to swirl, my head grew fuzzy, and my legs began to go numb. Whatever was inside me was now gone, but I sensed the vacuum it left behind. There was a yearning there that I didn't understand. I stumbled as the ground continued to roll under my feet. Airian's gaze, locked on mine, seemed to disrupt whatever I was accidentally doing.

As Khalon stepped back, orange eyes flicked up to mine. The faint orange pulse was replaced by a bright fiery red. It was the last thing I saw as the world pitched sideways.

# 23

# Alaric

"Are you out of your mind?" Mireille hissed at me. She wrung a towel in her hands and glanced out the hut door where the rest of the guard sat.

After Scout's demonstration in the woods, commotion broke out. Airian's reaction was the only one I was prepared for; he was annoyed at the inconvenience it created in his routine. The rest of the guard shared questioning looks that read, *should we be worried?* I couldn't help but wonder the same thing. Despite the unforeseen connection I now shared with this human, I couldn't have anticipated her being able to steward fire. Is this what the one dream was trying to warn me of?

My cheeks flushed at the thought of Khalon coming to my aid. I didn't need help. She wasn't hurting me. He made me look weak and vulnerable in front of Airian's men. The last thing I needed. After Khalon shared healing energy with me to restore the depletion Scout caused, he commanded me to take her to Mireille. She was too far gone for even his abilities. So I carried Scout to the Manter's hut at his behest—the way the others' eyes followed my every move while crossing the open field with an unconscious Scout in my arms was enough to reassure me that they still saw me as the villain. The way their tones hushed as we passed, suspicion coloring their thoughts, left me vexed.

It didn't matter that the whole guard was following me or that Khalon and Airian were leading. Once a villain, always a villain. At least their reaction was predictable.

Scout lay on the table in the center of Mireille's hut where she made quick work of assessing the human girl. Mireille threw blankets over her and placed two poultices on her head and heart to draw out anything that didn't belong.

"What do you want me to say? 'I'm sorry'? How was I supposed to know she had any powers? Let alone was a *channeler*. I wouldn't have touched her if I knew that!" I'd been pacing beside the girl's body, my arms stretched taut behind my head. I struggled to breathe deeply.

"I didn't think channelers were real," I said, more to myself, as I tried to make sense of this anomaly.

"Oh, they're real. You should know better. Or was your training for naught?" She scolded.

"Mireille, something was off here." I dropped my voice to a whisper and rounded the table. "If you could have been there, you'd have seen it. It was like she was seeing and hearing things that weren't there." I flinched at Mireille's reproachful look. "Don't give me that look, if I knew what she was thinking I would already have told you. I was completely cut off. I couldn't hear anything."

Mireille examined her head and murmured. Then she listened to the human's heart and faltered, as though something was wrong. Her eyes flickered up to mine, holding an emotion that made my mouth go dry.

"What's wrong with her?"

Mireille just shook her head. "I don't think she has enough life force to recover on her own," she finally admitted. "I'll need access to the reserve. It will need to be put to a vote."

Just then, a searing, ripping pain flashed across the surface of my chest.

I stole a glance at the girl, her heart beating in rhythm with mine, and mine thundered in response. I held my breath. I couldn't afford to give away the impossible as it happened; as an imprint formed just below my collar.

"You have to save her, Mireille." A crack in my stoic self control had emotion welling up in my throat. Imprints were rare, to lose one would be devastating.

"It isn't up to me, it'll be up to the others."

I spent the next several hours at the Manter's. If anyone asked, I would tell them Airian put me on her detail. It would be reason enough for my dereliction from duty this afternoon after the strange commotion. So long as no one asked too many questions, they'd never suspect the newly forming imprint.

After a while, Mireille kicked me out of her space in preparation for the village's vote. Out back, I started a fire and sat close by it to recharge and think. Looking over my shoulder to make sure I was alone, I pulled back my tunic collar. Exactly what I was afraid of. I ran my fingers over the raised edges and ridges of the new scar that formed.

I'd felt pain before. No man of war was ill-acquainted with it. But this wasn't the pain of injury. I'd felt this only once before. With Mireille. When she bonded me to her.

An imprint.

My fingers caught on the new marred skin just under my collarbone. A perfect oval, a mirror replica of the human girl's fingerprint. How did this happen? I didn't know her apart from the dreams, but I knew in an instant that she was mine.

I'd never heard of a steward imprinting with a human before. I let out a low growl before sinking my head into my hands.

I basked in the healthy glow of the fire and scanned through my dreams once more. Who was this human? Why was she here? With those soft eyes and thundering heart, I had the urge to reach out and slip her long hair behind her ear and pull her close; to calm her heartbeat against mine.

Deep exasperation roiled through me, I would rather run patrol for a week straight with no sleep than be imprinted to a human.

Digging the toe of my animal-skinned boots in the dirt, I let out a frustrated sigh. I didn't ask for this, these new emotions. I knew they only existed because of the imprint, but they felt like a part of me so quickly. The intensity began to cloud my senses. I shook my head. No, I'd been down this road before and it ended in grief.

"Dear boy, what is it?" Mireille floated towards me on silent footsteps.

"I hate it when you do that." I looked around to make sure no one was watching, but the guard had left long ago. I didn't know why I was so protective of our bond, but I couldn't stand the thought of the others ruining it.

Mireille walked around the fire and perched on a nearby log.

"Fine, don't tell me, but I already know a certain arrival has you worked up. More than usual." She picked up a stick to poke the fire.

Mireille had a mysterious way of knowing things, and not just because of our bond. We didn't have Manters in Kilburne. They predated the creation of our factions, and according to legend, they were a gift from the Fates, the Creators. The Manters ruled alongside King Islwyn and were the interim rulers when the united kingdom splintered into many small kingdoms ruled by each faction.

I thought about what that must have been like, eons ago, all factions living united in one kingdom. How had they not split sooner? With the way the other energy stewards reacted to fire-bound stewards now, I wondered how the factions ever got along.

"Do you want to talk about it?" Mireille asked me, her ancient voice doting.

I shook my head and moved inside to sit at Scout's side. Mireille trailed in behind me.

A small lump formed in my throat, emotion I refused to name. I could feel Scout. Not just by proximity, but as though she were a part of me. When Mireille bonded with me, it took me some time to adjust to the new sensations, knowing where Mireille was all the time, having my skin prickle when she was near. I knew on an anatomical level everything there was to know about her. It was comforting to have such a deep platonic bond with someone so caring. It worked the same in reverse, and she always acted out of a loving instinct to look after me.

The only advantage I had over Mireille was that I could hear her thoughts while she couldn't hear mine—a perk of being fire-bound. Mireille took the opportunity often to think loudly in my direction. Like she chose to now—

*Is there something I should know? Something about this human girl that has you glued to her side?*

Avoiding her thoughts, I stared down at Scout's feeble form. There was a new sensation competing with Mireille's connection; another heart that beat alongside mine. The long, slow thumps of a human heart and the low hum of a sleeping mind rattled at the back of my thoughts. I instantly felt a guttural need to take care of her, to protect her. She was mine. Mine to care for, to protect, to die for, if it came to it. It was similar to my affection for Mireille, the loyalty felt the same, but the brilliance of this passion made Mireille's imprint pale in comparison. What was it about her that made the bond stronger? Just because she was a human?

"We're ready." Khalon's voice came from the slightly open doorway. It had taken a few hours for him to round up everyone after getting Mireille's prognosis.

Mireille assessed me. *This conversation isn't over.*

# Alaric

Mireille and I stepped outside her hut together and stood at the back of the gathering, closest to the hut wall. The guard, elders, and other Manters circled around the large fire pit that was constructed for this emergency meeting.

The sun was nearing dusk already. We'd wasted the day waiting and I feared we were almost out of time.

"As most of you are already aware, the portal has been accessed. A young human girl stepped through the portal late last night during the guards' third watch. She was incoherent and confused. We have no idea how she managed to open the portal, or if she was even the one to open it. After today's demonstration, we have reason to believe she is not just an ordinary human, but a *channeler*."

At that, small gasps floated across the air around the circle. Shocked questions popped here and there.

"It doesn't seem she has any knowledge of her gifts, nor has she mastered them. Do not engage her, as she is a liability until we can understand more." Khalon made a few more closing remarks, but I lost interest as a recent image came to mind.

The light drained from her eyes as red poured from her broken body. I searched her gaze for any sign of revival, but my sticky hands just left brutish marks on her delicate face.

Soleil's voice echoed from above me, *Well done, my faithful little sentry. You have no one to blame but yourself.*

As I gazed into the fire, I shut it down. I had done monstrous things in the name of loyalty before, and swore to myself that, after having seen what Soleil was capable of, I would never bend a knee to another so willingly again. I'd had to live with the terrors of innocent screams and mangled bits of flesh haunting my every blink. I shuttered as the memories poured through the tiny opening in my mind.

Soleil had no right to overthrow the fire kingdom like she did. The way she used dark grave energy, to mind-control the stewards, or burn them inside out with just a look, was unlike any warfare I had been a part of before.

Mireille had done her best to help me heal, but I knew this picture was a warning from the Creators. If I didn't stay away from this girl, I would be the death of her.

"Alaric?" Khalon's concerned face came into view.

"Hm?"

"Would you care to vote?"

I clearly missed an important question. My cheek flamed with the heat of embarrassment and I pulsed my fists to keep the fire under control. I glanced around the circle, met by determined faces. Only one or two elders wore a look of contempt.

Mireille whispered an affirmative into my mind.

"Yes, aye." I cleared my throat.

"Then it's settled, majority rules. The Manter will administer the collection of energy from our last harvest party to revive the human for questioning. I'll be contacting our emissaries and sending word to the water territory and wind territory for insight on the portal front. Let's ensure the presence of the human remains confidential until we know more. If anyone has concerns they'd like to discuss in private, my door will be open after dinner."

Mireille shifted her weight next to me and sighed in relief.

As the group scattered, Mireille headed back inside to prepare the energy transfer for Scout. A few disgruntled elders banded together to gripe about the waste it was to use our village's collected energy on a human. The disdain they shared rattled me, reminding me that just a few days ago, I'd have felt the same. If it weren't for this imprint, I would still feel the same. But now, things had shifted, and I had to manually check my rage to keep it from boiling over.

For a moment, my words came back to me. Before Scout had channeled fire from me, the words I spoke to her were harsh and out of order. *You're a worthless human just like the rest of your kind.*

A stab of remorse gutted me. I had meant it at the time, but that was before... I couldn't think of it any longer. I would make it right as soon as she woke.

) ) ) ● ( ( (

I hung around by the fire, storing up energy until the stewards dispersed. Once they were all gone, I stepped to Mireille's door and rapped once. It wouldn't take much for her to sense my presence nearby.

"We're in here," she called me in.

Mireille worked in the kitchen with lit candles strewn about, giving a soft glow to the darkened room. Hovering quietly at her side, I watched as she tended to the poultices on Scout's head and heart. She removed the cloth strands and cleaned the mashed herbs from her body. Taking a mortar and pestle from the shelf, she ground new herbs.

"What are you not telling me, my boy?" Mireille did me the kindness of not looking at me as she spoke.

I scratched at the back of my neck and looked down at Scout. I was sure an imprint had already taken shape somewhere on her delicate skin as it had on mine. I scanned her body, following the shape of her arms to the crease of her neck, letting my thoughts and eyes wander, looking for the location of our new matching scar... If the new wound wasn't tended to before it scarred, Scout would wake with some pain and surely ask questions. Mireille was bound to find it sooner or later.

"It happened again," I said quietly.

Mireille set the mortar and pestle down and turned to me. With her back to the candles, I couldn't make out her expression.

Her amber eyes searched mine in the growing darkness. *Are you alright?* She asked in her gentle way.

"I'm not sure," I admitted unwillingly. "This is different. It doesn't feel like it did with you. In a way, it made sense with you. But she—" We both paused to look over the human girl lying in Mireille's kitchen, the gravity of the situation crashing into me. This was a girl who never should have found a way here. "She's *human*. She's a channeler. This shouldn't be possible."

*You're scared*, she thought to me.

"This shouldn't be happening," I whispered. Mireille came around the table and slipped a thin arm around my waist, pulling me close to her.

"Mireille, I don't know what it means, but I've seen her before. A few night ago, the Creators sent me some dreams of her. But it felt too familiar for it to be the first I've dreamt of her. I'm sure I've seen her before, but I can't recall the dream memories. They must be too old."

Pain pinched my cheeks and my eyes watered without my permission. Something only Mireille had the ability to bring out in me.

Mireille knew about Samirah and what happened with Soleil, she worked it out of me years ago. She claimed it was part of my healing process, but I didn't feel any more healed. If anything, I was more haunted now than ever before.

"What was the dream, what did the Creators say?" She asked, releasing me from the hug.

"Nothing good, it would seem. A destined tragedy, just like—" and I stopped before saying her name. "Agh!" I turned and slapped the counter behind her station. My skin started to boil. I needed to burn off this steam.

I was about to tell Mireille I needed to go for a run when Scout gulped in air, coughing and choking. She sat up on the table.

"*They know you're here. They're coming for you,*" Scout said in an eerie, dissonant tone once she regained her breath. Her eyes clouded and fixed in the distance.

Mireille laid a hand on Scout and pushed the calm of her energy over her to sedate her and she thumped back against the wood of the table. Calming and sedation was a gift the earth-bound energy stewards shared, but only once they reached full maturity.

"What was that?" I hissed in a low whisper. I didn't want to admit I was spooked, but the words were unnerving. All the frustration drained out of me now and a fresh wave of exhaustion hit me.

"I haven't the faintest idea. Let me finish renewing her poultices and find her mark, then I'll have you take her to Moss' tent. Airian thought it would be a good place for her to stay for the time being. Khalon agreed."

I nodded, heading towards the door. I needed to go for a run to clear my mind before paranoia got the best of me.

"We'll watch over her. Moss is a good girl."

She better be, she just became the unofficial guardian of a piece of my soul.

# 25

# Scout

When I sat up, my head began throbbing. I eased myself down into bed and rolled over onto my side. What a strange nightmare. Images flashed through my mind—the greenhouse, slamming the door, being lost in the woods, and a strange man in a hut? The last image that filled my mind was of a man with dark hair and burning red eyes looking at me. Those eyes had me in a trance. When I blinked, I saw them again, almost as if I couldn't look away.

My body reacted viscerally and I startled awake, reaching for my phone. Patting the coarse wool blanket around me, one thing became clear: this was not my bed. There was no stuffed elephant, no wind chimes, or sea breeze. And no matter how much my hand roamed for my phone, it wasn't there. Launching up in bed, I rubbed my eyes. I was on a cot in a canvas tent. This was not in Biddenmore.

My feet swung from bed to the raw wooden floor, another cot sat a few feet from mine. That bed was empty, blanket and pillow neatly folded and stacked at the end.

It wasn't a dream. I closed my eyes and try to will it away, but all I saw were those glowing red eyes piercing my soul. I tried to rub my eyes and blur the image away, but it was worse than sunspots. I couldn't get rid of it. It might as well have been inked on the back of my eyelids.

I pushed the blankets back and got off the cot, but I stumbled. I caught myself against the wooden pole in the center of the tent and eased myself back to bed. What was wrong with me?

Pausing, I took inventory of my body and my senses. My head was throbbing, but I didn't know why. I tried to sit up but couldn't. I puffed out an exhausted and exasperated breath. My fingers and toes prickled on fire, like they'd fallen asleep and were waking up now.

The canvas flap at the front of the tent slid back as someone peered in.

"Oh good, you're awake. I thought you'd *never* wake up." A girl a little younger than me pinned the flap back. The cot squeaked as she sat and rummaged under it. After a moment, and a good yank, she produced a grimy rucksack from under the makeshift bed. She rustled around inside of it and looked up at me.

"I'm Moss." She pushed her thick dark curls behind an ear with the back of her hand. "I guess you're Scout? I've heard all about you. *Everyone* was talking about what you did to Alaric–*you know, the hot fire guy*–and how Airian had to hold you back." She talked a mile a minute and I couldn't keep up. Not only that, but her brightly shining green eyes glowed in our dimly lit tent. Her English sounded better than the others I'd heard so far; her accent wasn't as thick, which was good for my head, but the throbbing reminded me not to think too hard yet. I reached up to hold my head.

"Oh, I should call for the Manters. They'll be able to help." She darted out of the open flap and disappeared.

I groaned and slumped over. A little while later, she returned with an old woman in a shawl, carrying a tray. Moss moved her cot closer to mine and pulled a little stand out of the corner. Moss graciously set it up between the cots so that the Manter could place the tray on the stand.

The old woman eased down onto the foot of my cot and watched me carefully. I looked down at the tray. It carried a tin cup of water, a bowl of what looked like oatmeal and berries, and a small glass jar of powder. The small bowl of flowers on the tray made me wonder if this was the equivalent of a hospital visit.

My stomach growled at the sight of food and water, so I sat up. When Moss read the confusion on my face, not finding a utensil to eat with, she mimicked holding the bowl and slurping. Whatever. I was hungry enough to do anything. I threw caution to the wind. If they were going to kill me, they'd have done it by now. Probably.

I took a long pull from the cup of water, finishing it in seconds. Moss grabbed it and ran out again. The Manter watched me from behind folds of weathered skin for a while and then posed a peculiar question.

"What's the last thing you remember?"

I looked at her over the edge of the bowl I was slurping from. The oatmeal-like substance was a little raw. Maybe steel-cut? But the berries gave it a nice, sweet touch. I lowered the bowl and wiped my mouth on the back of my sleeve. And that's when I realized I wasn't wearing the dress anymore. They traded my aunties' birthday dress for a beige, linen long-sleeve tunic and tights. My eyes widened, and I wondered who undressed me, where my clothes went, and how long I'd been sleeping.

"I remember being in the woods with Khalon and Airian trying to find the greenhouse."

She took a deep breath and slowly let it out. She mused to herself, taking the jar of powder and pouring it over the small bowl of flowers. With the back side of the jar, she pulverized the flowers. Okay, not a gift then.

"Where does it hurt?" she asked, grinding the mixture.

I paused and looked down at my body. Everywhere ached, but a spot below my left clavicle was searing with pain. I didn't know how it hadn't registered sooner. Probably disguised under the pounding headache and the rumbling of my stomach demanding nourishment.

I showed her the spot under my clavicle and she *tsks*. She seemed annoyed, but I must have misread it. The spot on my chest was no bigger than a thumbprint but it smarted wickedly. I faintly wondered how I got the mark, but it was low on my list of questions that needed answered.

She surveyed the spot for a long moment, cocking her head this way and that deep in thought, then her eyes flicked to mine with a question in them for more. I pointed to my head. The pressure and pain was nearly unbearable.

The Manter sat back and dug in a small bowl to get a fist full of her new concoction. Lifting my hair from the back of my neck, she gently applied the new salve she made at the top of my spine and then to the searing spot on my chest. It dried into a cakey film nearly at once. When finished, she let my hair down before holding one hand on my neck and the other on my chest. Eyes closed, her lips moved silently. Was she praying? She opened her eyes with a smile. "How does that feel?"

I took a deep breath to reset. "Better already."

She nodded and wiped off the salve. "You've been asleep for three days."

"Three days?" I squawked in alarm.

"You used powerful energy and depleted your entire being. It was touch and go for a little bit."

"I'm sorry, I what?"

She continued as though I never interrupted her. "Your headache will return, and things will feel different for a couple of days. Other than that, physically, you will be fine."

"And not... physically? How will I be?"

"Oh, child." She patted my hand. "You will be more than fine."

Moss came in again with a new cup of water. I accepted it gratefully and washed down the oatmeal and the shock that came with the Manter's visit. The sage woman rose to leave, but before she did, she turned to Moss.

"Look after her, would you?" She squeezed both of her hands together in hers and left.

Moss took the tray off the stand and slid it under the cot before returning everything to their places and taking a seat to stare at me.

"Sorry, it's just you're all anyone can talk about around camp. Plus, I've never met a human before."

I blinked hard and reached a hand up to my head. *What?* I was trying to wrap my head around all the new things I learned since waking up. For one, apparently, I almost died and was in a coma for three days. Also, at some point during that time, I was moved into this tent and someone changed my clothes and made me a roommate with someone *not quite human.*

Oh, and how could I forget to mention this—apparently I had magic powers now? *What?* My heart spun, and not from pain this time. Magic wasn't real. Other worlds didn't exist. There must be some sort of logical explanation for all of this.

"Are you feeling okay? Should I get one of the Manters?" Moss's green-flecked eyes flickered in worry.

"No, I'm okay. It's just a lot to take in." I smoothed my tunic down and grounded myself off the edge of the cot. "Do you mind if we just slow it down a bit?"

Moss sent me an apologetic look. "I'm so sorry. I can come off a bit strong." She tucked a wild curl behind her ear and bit her lip. "Everyone says so."

"Hey, it's okay. Me too." I gave her a half-hearted smile. "Uh, before I forget... where'd my clothes go?" I searched for my beautiful red dress and wristlet, but found the tent sparse. Moss herself was clothed in loose fitting linen clothes that looked like beige on beige. Macy would gag. *Oh Macy... Danny.* A sudden pang of homesickness hit me. I was going to miss the Last Blast and my shot with Danny.

"I'm pretty sure the Spinners have them. King Khalon asked me to lend you some of mine until the Spinners could make you your own. It should only take a few days."

I nodded, taking it all in. "What about my phone?"

She screwed her mouth up and slowly said, "Phone?"

I realized she had no idea what I was talking about. Judging by the lack of technology here, I wouldn't be surprised if she didn't even know what a phone was.

"I'm sure you have a lot of questions. King Khalon asked me to help while you adjust, so if there's anything you need, just let me know." There it was again. So Khalon was their king? Why didn't he introduce himself that way when I met him?

"Can I ask you a quick question?"

"Of course." She nodded eagerly, folding her legs up under her, settling in.

"Where are we exactly?"

"You're in Landow, the land Beyond the Veil. Some of us fondly refer to it as the Mirrored Kingdom. We're a world just like yours... but different." Her eyes twinkled a little, the green flecks lighting up as she spoke. "King Khalon's camp is in the south, in Ruack Valley. We're not far from the Whispering Winds and the wind-bound steward's territory, Prentiss. It's just over those the Mountains of Anguish." Moss pointed out the tent and in the distance I could register the faint outline of craggy mountain tops.

"And what are you... if you're not human?" I tried to ask as delicately as possible, but of course, had no experience with the concept.

A long finger scratched above her brow as she thought and I held my breath, anticipating that finger to turn on me and cast a spell.

"I guess something *Other*." She beamed.

"Over there is apparently where you entered the Kingdom." Moss gestured to a path in the woods and then stopped in front of a sprawling, well-organized garden. "Which was a breach of our perimeter, by the way. How did you do that?"

My head still throbbed, so I gave her my best pained expression.

"Okay, let me back up," Moss said reading my confused expression. "Since Soleil staged the coup and took over Kilburne—that's the fire territory—she's been trying to sweep up all the other territories, so Khalon had the Manters created a dome to cloak Ruack Valley to keep us safe. I managed to slide in just before they put the walls up. I was on an assignment in Prentiss with some wind stewards. So flighty. You know how they can be." She winked at me.

I couldn't even corral my face to make a polite smile at her incessant chatter.

"*Ooookay*, anyways, since that perimeter has been established, no one has come in since. That makes you," she jabbed me in the shoulder, "an anomaly. Oh my Creators, are you a spy for Soleil? That would be *insane*!" Her jaw dropped as she guffawed at me.

"No, Moss... just, no." I didn't even know how to defend myself. It was like trying to explain to a toddler why the sky wasn't purple.

She squinted at me before laughing, "You're right. That's crazy! Moving along, here is the community's garden. It's where I spend most of my days. Especially since the Khalon gave me the role of overseer. Can you believe it? I barely can." Mystified, she looked at the gardens spread out before us, hand on her chest. I look at it all with her.

The community garden was made up of several raised beds, about nine from my count. Some sported rudimentary trellises, and one had poles at either end with wires between them. Grape vines, I think. I was surprised the king would trust someone so young with it. Moss appeared fifteen years old or so. Although it occurred to me that I had never met an "other" before, so maybe she was older?

Beyond the raised beds, in the center of the clearing, was a line of rough-cut tables, both heaping with vegetables. Moss pointed out that they were for sorting and cleaning. Beside this gathering area was a large mud-red hut. In the daylight, I could tell it was the same thatched roof I took notice of my first night in the clearing.

"This is our community storehouse," Moss said, buzzing with excitement. She skipped in front of me to talk face-to-face while walking backward. "The Manters have several designated huts and this is one of them. There's another in the woods, but that's our infirmary and where Khalon and Airian hold meetings." She gestured behind us.

"Wait, who are the Manters?" All I knew was that they gave off voodoo-medicine-man vibes.

"The Manters are the keepers of life. They are the lynchpin of the village, the ultimate protectors of our tribe. This storehouse is where they guard the food, energy, and keep watch over the village. They're like the most ancient creatures in our world. Rumor has it, they walked with the Fates!" She squealed in an excitement that I couldn't comprehend the relevance of just yet.

My hand trailed to the dried salve on my chest as I thought about this.

"Oh, and they are gifted in healing. Duh," Moss winked at me.

Just then, the storehouse doors opened and a few Manters filed out together. There was something attractive about the women. When they walked, their long robes never jostled. Every movement was fluid. Watching them had me fixated in a moment of peace. I wished I could dally longer with them.

The Manter who helped me this morning led the group of three women, and as if she sensed me staring, she stopped to look directly at me. Her eyes didn't pulse like the others I'd seen; they were a steady glow. It called to something deep in me, but I didn't know what.

Moss toured me all around camp and introduced me to her friends. Niah, a girl with deep blue twinkling eyes who worked in the fields and smelled like flowers. Warrick, who barely reached my shoulders and wore his hair longer than mine, had eyes blue as a spring day. And Rhydian, whose deep espresso-colored skin shone in the midday sun, but it was his lime-colored eyes that struck me the most.

Moss flitted us around the known area and introduced me to what seemed like dozens of people. They were all nice enough to my face but, after we moved on, I heard the telling whispers. I felt like the new kid at school once again.

I cringed internally as we weaved around another group hard at work. They paused their wood-cutting only briefly to look questioningly between Moss and me. As they looked me over, I caught a twitch of disdain and shuddered as the shade from the towering trees bowed over us in iciness.

They were watching like they were wary of me. Of *me*? What did they have to be afraid of? But then the last thing I remembered before waking up slipped into view in my mind. I hadn't had a moment alone to think about everything. A chill raced through me at the memory of me in the woods. I wrapped my arms around myself and rubbed at the goosebumps. I should find the guy and apologize. I can't believe I did that. It's so not like me.

"What did you say that guy's name was?"

"Oh, the one you almost fried?" She chuckled and wiggled her fingers at me. I couldn't help but laugh and roll my eyes at her. "His name is Alaric. And don't worry, happens to all of us as we learn how to steward our gifts."

"Yeah? What's his story? He doesn't seem like the rest of you... guys."

"Alaric came in a few years before me, it was strange how it happened. I guess one of the Manter's poles was glitching and he could see the Manter through the cloaked dome and ran to her for help. Some said it was a miracle, and others balked at that idea, because," and pointed at her eyes and then made a *crazy* sign by her head. "He's the only fire guy in an otherwise anti-fire land. Well, not that we're '*anti-fire*', because Khalon would never stand for that, but he's the only one like that here. The others aren't interested in having someone who used to be so close to Soleil around."

I held my hand up to stop her as she took a big breath to go on. "Do you know where I can find him? I think I probably owe him an apology." I would feel awful if I didn't at least try to say sorry for whatever it was that I did.

"Oh, he's usually at the Manter's this time of day. But, hey," Moss reached to put a hand on my arm, but before making contact, hesitated. The movement stopped me. "Don't get too close, Scout. He isn't like us, the fire stewards get a bad rep for some of their gifts... they can't always be trusted."

"What's that supposed to mean?" I watched as her eyes darkened and she turned away with a shrug, going back to the garden.

"I'm gonna go find him then," I called after her. And then I was going to get the heck out of this place before these rumors of war descended on us.

# Scout

I realized too late the mistake I'd made. The only directions I had to find the Manter's place was a vague hand gesture from Moss, pointing opposite of the garden. I made it across the clearing to the edge of the woods when I found Rhydian, the boy with limes for eyes.

"Hey, Rhydian!" I called out, jogging to catch up to him.

"Hey, Scout, how's it going? Are you lost again already?" he teased.

"Is it that obvious?"

"Only because your humanness is showing." He winked at me, and I had to admit I was a little taken aback. I was not used to guys my age being anything other than awkward. Also his English was really good. I made a mental note to ask him about it later.

"Where are you headed?" he asked.

"Well, I was looking for Alaric. Do you know him? Moss said he's at the Manter's place on the edge of the forest. Do you know where that is?"

He ran his hand up the back of his tight black curls. He winced a little. "Yeah, I know the guy, but... You sure you wanna do that right now?"

"I owe him an apology... for before..." I looked down at my hands.

"Oh no, I know. Trust me, everybody knows what happened." He sneered a little, and I noticed his accent was wholly unique to him. "Hopefully, you took him down a few pegs and he stays there." His comment had me chuckling, but I filed that information away for later. Alaric had a reputation for being cocky.

I cocked my head sideways, "So...?"

"Right, well he's not at the Manter's. I just came from there. Maybe he's out running patrol?" He offered.

"Oh, thanks, I guess I'll just walk around a bit until dinner. See ya 'round." I waved as he turned and headed off across the clearing.

A glance around told me everyone was doing their own thing. This place seemed like a well-oiled machine. There didn't seem to be a system of "work," and yet they all had this unparalleled drive and motivation to get stuff done. I was not even sure I understood the point of it all. But I watched for a few minutes in wonder.

I didn't fit in here. And I didn't want to be here. Thankfully, no one was waiting or looking for me, so this was my shot to really disappear. I retraced my steps back towards the garden, clinging to the forest's tree line so I didn't catch any prying eyes. I passed a few tents and watched all the others working tirelessly. I spied the little path to the woods the guards brought me through the first night here.

I started down the path, not even really sure what I was looking for, and several minutes went by as the trail gave way to dense woods. Thick pine branches scratched against my sleeves as I ducked through them. The path back toward camp disappeared between the trees. Ahead, the trodden footpath gave way to bungled tree roots and the path disappeared. I had no idea how to get to where I was when I first arrived here. I stopped to think back to that first night. My mind fogged. All the trees blended together in my memory, and I couldn't seem to recall anything particularly unique about the spot I dropped into.

A thought started to occur to me. I wondered if the spot really mattered? Maybe I could work some freaky magic and conjure up the greenhouse here and now. I paced a few extra feet away to find a spot with room between the trees, where the ground was level. I bridged my fingers together and apart, cracking knuckles and shaking them out. I had no idea how to warm up to use magic, but this was what boxers did, right?

I jogged in place and rolled my neck. When I felt adequately stupid for warming up without any confidence in its effect, I stopped and decided to just do it. I held my hands out like I was carrying a box and closed my eyes, focused.

"Magic, come!" I whispered to the forest.

I waited.

Nothing happened.

"Pssssst, come!" I peeked one eye open.

Nothing.

*Ugh.* I groaned out loud. This was futile. There's no way I was going to just wish my way home. *Ooh! Maybe that's it*, I thought.

I clicked my heels and wished for home. But I couldn't decide whether England or the United States was the home I was trying to get to, and I decided that my indecision was ultimately what thwarted my attempts.

I groaned some more and kicked the tree sod around. I groaned and groaned until it turned into a yell that displaced the birds from the trees above. I didn't want to be here. I didn't even want to go to England and somehow I fell down my aunties' stupid trap door. I clenched and released my hands, shaking them out to calm down. I took some deep breaths.

"You're not trapped. Everything is fine. We're gonna go home. It's gonna be fine." I barely talked myself down here. I stopped pacing and placed a hand on my stomach. My dad used to always make me stop and take big, fat breaths. He would say, *if you don't look fat, then you're not breathing deep enough.* It made me chuckle then, just like it did now, too. Oh, Dad. Mom. I missed them. I even missed my aunties.

I took a few more stabilizing breaths to stave off the panic and anxiety. But a twig snapped behind me. I whipped around.

"Who's there?" I called. Seriously, if Moss or Alaric were hiding behind the trees watching me whisper *Magic, come* to the forest, I was going to be livid.

Another twig snapped, and a low-hanging bough rustled. Hunkering down, I crept close to the large oak tree and peered around it.

In the thicket, a doe swished its tail as it plucked buds off the oak saplings. I sighed in relief.

*New game plan: figure out where I am, who the others are, and how to use this so-called magic to get home. I think I can handle that.*

I started back towards camp, thankful that I didn't actually enter too far into the woods, or get caught embarrassing myself by anything other than a deer. A breeze whistled through the trees, and the hair on the back of my arms stood up.

My instinct prickled. I didn't see anyone, but I'd learned that doesn't mean they weren't hiding from sight, watching me.

I picked up my pace and felt a strong wind resist against my whole body. A whistle whizzed by my ear. It tickled and I reached up to brush my hair back.

The wind came again, battering me even more. My hair whipped around me, making it hard to see the path I was jogging up. I slowed a bit and heard a whisper.

"Who's there?" I asked roughly, pushing my hair away from my face.

The whisper called again. I stopped to peer through the sunlit trees. It didn't look like the setting of a horror film, yet here my beating heart and I stood. Waiting to get killed, I suppose.

I turned around to start back up the path. The whisper slammed into me.

"*They know you're here.*" It was a howling sort of whisper. The kind that makes you wanna run for your life.

"Who are you?" I said into the wind with as much courage as I could muster.

"*They're coming for you,*" the voice echoed back to me. I whirled around a few times. The voice came from everywhere at once. It was a voice without a body and yet ran into me full-force, like I hit someone.

This was too weird for me. I turned and started running. I looked over my shoulder to see if I could pick up on any movement, but I ran right into a tree.

"Whoa, there," a tree who could talk, apparently, said to me. "I'm pretty sure you've already sustained enough head trauma for the year." A calloused hand reached down to help me up.

# 27

# Alaric

"It's just a hand, not a snake," I said as she grimaced at my outstretched palm.

Around us the wind whistled and I listened closely. Scout's heart beat faster and more furious than a baby bird's wings. I pushed into her thoughts for a moment to register her fear, *they're coming for you*. It was the same phrase she uttered when she awoke from being depleted. I didn't know what it meant, but I had to tell Mireille as soon as possible.

She blinked slowly as realization dawned that she just ran smack into me while I was on my run. A deep blush covered her cheeks as she accepted my hand.

"Wait, what did you just say?" She asked, dusting herself off.

"Nothing," I shrugged, "You were just looking at me as if my hand were a snake about to bite you."

"That's it!" She exclaimed, way too emphatically.

I breathed in her proximity, and the image in her mind floated naturally into mine now. A blurred vision of a viper attacking her, and a voice calling to her in the distance. A small chill lit up my nerves. She's remembering a nightmare. I thought quickly through what it meant, but humans weren't like us. I didn't have any idea if their dreams were as poignant in their symbolism as ours.

"So," I said, coming back to this moment. "Be careful in the woods." It took an annoying amount of strength to push myself away from her when all my instincts said to *stay*. But I wanted to update Mireille about the voice following Scout.

"Wait." The leaves crunched underfoot as she turned.

Despite myself, I was glad for the delay. To stay with her for just a moment longer was more than I could ask for.

"I was hoping we could talk?" Her voice was a frail thing, unsure. A corner of my heart tugged towards her, and I pushed back against it.

"Sure. What is it?" I turned only slightly back toward her, angling away to send her the message to keep it brief. I could sense her emotions growing embarrassed again. She only came up to my shoulder and she was gaping at the muscles crossed over my chest.

I snickered inwardly, flexing instinctively, and cleared my throat.

"I wanted to apologize. For what happened. You know, *before.*"

"Oh." When had a human ever apologized to a steward? I would dwell on her apology later.

"So, I'm sorry."

"It's nothing. Happens to everyone at first. We all short-circuit sometimes." I shrugged, keeping my words clipped. Then remembered my need to apologize. "I am also sorry. I believe I may have incited the incident."

She shrugged, mirroring my stance. "Well, it didn't seem like *nothing*. The way everyone's been treating me..." she trailed off.

"How have they been treating you?" My eyes narrowed.

Her heart hammered inside of mine, running at a much healthier pace than it had when I last saw her lying on the Manter's bare table. She shrugged, looking small. "Nothing, it's fine, they were just concerned is all," she said this audibly, but I could hear her thoughts, N*o one wants me here, they've certainly made that clear.*

That seemed to be one thing we had in common.

I noticed her lip twitched as she re-lived moments from earlier today. After being introduced, the others began speaking in MirVis once her back was turned. My jaw tightened hearing the things they said about her. They had no right. Those ungrateful, inconsequential earth stewards. It was one thing for them to treat me that way, but I wouldn't stand for them treating her that way. A small tinge of relief came from the fact that she couldn't understand MirVis.

She stepped closer to me and I became aware of the energy tingling around us, bouncing off me. I backed up to lean against a tree, maintaining a safe distance from her.

In the fire territory, we were never expected or trained to keep fire locked down. It was our status quo, our badge of honor. Everyone had experience with fire and we could handle it without being burned. But not here. Here, my fire was a threat, a reminder of the war just beyond Ruack Valley's cloaked borders. I had to train harder than everyone, not just how to use my energy gifts, but how to refuse them. It was the most exhausting and unnatural experience, but I had quickly learned my gift could hurt the other stewards if I wasn't careful. I didn't even want to consider what it could do to Scout.

"Concerned, huh? That's probably not the word I'd use to describe the looks and whispers the earth stewards send *my* way." With a scoff, I kicked my foot back and up against the tree as though it was a kick stand. Though I must have used a bit too much force, because the effort shook the limbs over us and sent small white buds down from above, landing in my hair and one on my cheek.

She looked at me with a daring curiosity in her eyes. She reached out to brush a finger across my cheek, but I shifted away and averted my gaze. I silently thanked the fates for self-control and my training. Otherwise, Scout would soon find herself in a dress of flames.

"Sorry. Maybe we can start over—"

"I wouldn't do that if I were you," I cautioned at the same time as she stuttered another apology.

"What do you mean?"

"Do you want a repeat of what happened in the woods?" I bit back without thinking as I shook the buds out of my hair. She was a danger to herself, likely to combust again if she wasn't careful. Someone should be training her. I turned to face her head-on, my hands shifting to loop through my utility belt.

"No," she looked to the ground, "It's just you looked so..." and her gaze swept back up to mine. An electric shock ripped through me as our eyes met. For the first time, I considered that this girl just might be the death of *me*.

A small gasp escaped her parted lips, "Wait, what do you mean *a repeat*? I thought that was a freak one-time accident?"

My eyes were drawn instantly to her perfect cupid's bow. Human or not, she was stunning. It would be so easy to let nature run its course. I groaned inwardly. *Be stronger than this, Alaric.*

In Kilburne, when we did business with the humans, we never struggled with feeling overwhelmed by their emotional states. Why did Scout have this ever-consuming effect on me? Her feelings and thoughts felt like an assault on my psyche. And somehow, for some reason, this energy didn't feel the least bit platonic.

And that scared me.

"Better safe than sorry. I have to go," I said, turning.

*So much for making friends,* she thought.

My heart cracked. I sighed and said over my shoulder, "You should go talk to Khalon, he'll explain everything."

# 28

# Scout

I knocked on Khalon's hut door as the sun hovered just above the tree line. "Khalon, it's Scout. I want to talk to you."

Silence.

"Khalon, please. I need to talk to you." *Bang, bang, bang.*

Nothing.

I walked around his hut towards the back to see if he was outside. There was nothing but forest edged up against his hut. I let out a strangled-sounding huff.

I trotted down the path from Khalon's place along the tree's edge and turned into the clearing. Moss was a ways off kneeling by the garden, and I opted to join her. Maybe I could find out what she loved so much about this garden. I had never gardened much until I got to the aunties' place. They also seemed captivated by the process, but I was still adjusting to the smell and the part where you always have dirt under your nails.

Moss saw me coming and sat on her heels, waving at me with wiggling, mud-caked fingers.

"Hey! Where did you wander off to this morning?" she asked.

"Just getting the lay of the land, you know," I squatted down beside her.

"You were trying to escape, weren't you?" She snickered and knocked elbows with me. Up close, freckles sprinkled Moss' nose and cheekbones. They danced as she giggled at me and it made me laugh too.

"So, what are you doing?"

"We're weeding the carrots and beets. Wanna help?"

"Sure, although I'm not sure how good I'll be since I only just started learning a couple weeks ago."

"It's easy. Look at this sprout here. See how the leaves are thin and almost look like a chicken's foot?"

"Yeah." I nodded, peering into the raised bed.

"That's the carrot sprout. Pluck anything that doesn't look like that."

"Oh, that actually sounds really easy."

"Yeah, it is," she chuckled.

We worked side by side for a bit, and I began to see why she enjoyed it. It was relaxing, mindless work. It gave your fingers something to do so your mind could wander. With my fingers in the cool, damp dirt, I felt grounded and settled. It made me wonder if this place really was enchanted. Even the breeze of the trees soothed me. I almost forgot about the fact that I hadn't seen Khalon since I woke up and I *needed* to talk to him.

Moss's shoulder bumped into mine. "I'll be right back." She nodded to the overflowing pile of weeds in her woven basket.

She strolled across the open area, basket swinging and passed three sorting tables. One table was heaped with dirty fruits and vegetables and random bunches of herbs and wheat. The second and third tables were neatly organized with sorted, cleaned vegetables.

The ground sloped around the tables, evidence of a well-worn path. It was obviously a high-traffic area for the gardeners. Some of the low spots had water pooling as though it had rained recently. I hadn't noticed until now, but I supposed it could have been while I was out for days.

Beyond the tables, near the edge of the trees seemed to be heaps of organic refuse. Several other stewards working the gardens were making trips between the tables and the heaps. Moss dumped her basket and returned, whistling a melodic tune.

"Hey." Her big green eyes looked across the clearing and back to me like she was scanning to see if the coast was clear. When her eyes locked on mine, a small chill traveled down my spine. I was not unsettled by her anymore, but I was still reminded that she was *other* in moments like this as her green eyes pulsed vibrantly.

She leaned in to whisper, "I know something you don't know."

Her voice lilted like wind chimes in a summer breeze. I pulled back to look up at her, curls loose and wild around her face. She ran the back of her dark soil-covered hand across her forehead to push them back.

"Well," I dropped my voice low, "Tell me everything." I giggled, as though I was her co-conspirator. I returned my hands back to the soil, digging around for the roots I had loosened as I waited for her to spill.

"I heard Alaric—" Moss was cut off by a yelp, followed by a crash. Our heads whipped around as we saw movement around the sorting tables that stood several meters from the community garden.

I looked over to the sound, watching as water ran from the table in rivulets that created spots of shimmery mud. It looked like this spot was slippery and partly to blame for the commotion. There was a young guy scrambling on the ground. From the looks of it, he'd slipped and fallen, taking out the leg of the third sorting table. The week's worth of sorted and cleaned vegetables sunk into the mud around him. He hastened to gather them with a twisted look of horror and disappointment on his face.

I squinted at him. It was Rhydian. My heart bruised for him. It was one thing to mess up where no one could see it and quite another to do so in public. Embarrassing, but it was just a harmless mistake.

I turned back to my work when I saw Khalon stride out of his hut—the very same one I knocked on not just a moment ago—and made a beeline for him. His gaze was inscrutable and my heart rate picked up.

"Moss?" I looked over at Rhydian who was racing to get up and put everything back before Khalon got there. My heart ticked up another notch. I had a bad feeling about this. I forced myself to my feet, rubbing the soil from my hands on my tights.

"It's fine, Scout, just go back to work." I looked around the clearing. The others silently left their posts to form a circle around the boy. Something isn't right. I lived through high school with mean girls—I knew what a circle up meant. A brute punishment was sure to follow.

"Something's not right."

I took a few steps when Moss gripped my sleeve.

"Scout," her voice was barely more than a choked whisper. "You cannot interfere."

The crowd grew denser the longer she held me back. I pulled my arm from her grip and ran to cover the distance. I didn't know why, but I just knew I had to get to Rhydian before the Others did.

The closer I got, the more I realized this crowd was a strategic bulwark to keep out anyone uninvited. The younger and stronger men formed the outermost layer of the circle. Mostly guys I recognized from Airian's guard. They linked arm in arm. Silent and unmoving, eyes fixated on nowhere in particular, just ahead.

I pushed against their dark skin, clawing at their shoulders to get through, but at best, I only came up to their elbows. I tried jumping to see between them. The elders formed an even tighter-knit circle around Khalon, and presumably, Rhydian, at the center. But he was completely hidden by this wall of skin and cloth.

Moss reached me by my third leap to see over the men in the back of the circle.

"Scout, I'm serious. You need to go. If they catch you here, you'll be in so much trouble." I didn't listen. She would get him killed if she just stood around.

I started yelling, "Excuse me! Excuse me, Khalon? I just need—" Moss snaked one arm around my waist and one hand over my mouth, yanking me to the ground. She pinned me and kept her hand tight on my mouth. The energy drained from me, pooling away from my center. The ground awoken under my skin conspired against me. Every blade of grass reached up, pulling at me, anchoring me in place. My eyes grew heavy and my jaw slacked.

"Moss," I fought to mumble her name. "That isn't fair... and... you know it."

"I'm sorry, Scout, but if you're not going to honor the village's way of handling things, you aren't going to be allowed to stay. I can't let you interfere. It would be treason." Her green eyes surged with a spark and glow. Energy washes over me in peaceful laps from head to my toes. It was so serene and unlike my explosion of energy earlier. Wave after wave hit me, causing my eyes to droop. I could feel how much power she was exerting over me. It wasn't fair. I had no way to fight back when she called on the earth's energy like that. Under me, I could feel the grass growing, almost like it was re-energized by her exertion. A small line of fire hit my nerve endings, a small tinge of fear rolling in my belly that awakened something within me.

"Promise me you will not interfere and I'll let you up." Her eyes plead with mine. She released her hold on my mouth.

"I..." I swallowed, my eyes flicked sideways casting a glance through the feet before me. Wait a minute.

I turned my head, and Moss's hand hovered just above my mouth, ready to clamp down on me if I screamed. I couldn't believe my eyes. I squinted and shook my head. Moss brought me down hard, and the hit distorted my vision, aggravating my already-injured brain.

Moss lifted off me as she sensed my fight dwindled to moderate confusion and interest. She knelt beside me and turned to see where I was looking. She gave a knowing murmur and resigned herself to sit on her heels by my side, while I watched.

There, just ten feet away, covered in mud was the king sitting with Rhydian. Khalon held his face in his hands, cupping his cheeks. His grip must have been unyielding though because I watched as Rhydian whimpered and continuously tried to pull away. The crease in my brow deepened. What on earth was going on?

There was tension in the air, the same as before, but now I understood it wasn't a violent tension. It was apprehension, like waiting for your teacher to grade a test. Waiting to hear your name in the doctor's office. It was a pregnant pause. Something was indeed happening. But I didn't know what.

I watched intently as I saw the king's lips move silently. At first, Rhydian writhed and wailed in response, and I questioned whether I was making the right choice to lie still. But the longer the king's gaze was locked on his, the more he calmed. I wondered what Khalon could be saying. Was it horrific? Threatening? Kind?

I stole a look at the elders surrounding the king. All their gazes were still fixed forward. It was like they didn't even blink; they didn't dare make eye contact with what was happening. It was the strangest thing.

Soon, Rhydian was still and the tension dissolved as Khalon's hands and gaze dropped. Then, in a swift movement, he lunged forward.

I flinched so hard that a hand flew to my mouth to cover the scream I choked on. I couldn't take my eyes off of them.

I leaned up on one elbow, barely aware that I was also covered in mud, as my jaw went slack again, but of my own volition this time. The immovable circle made a fraction of a shift at the king's gesture.

Khalon embraced the boy and Rhydian wilted into his arms.

I looked at the circle. They all bowed their heads in unison. My eyes darted around to understand the noticeable shift in the atmosphere. I finally pulled my eyes from the happening of it all to find Moss.

Her head was also bowed. I wanted to ask her about it, but the timing was wrong. I would have to wait for sundown, when we'd be back in our tent. So I looked back to Khalon and Rhydian, but there was something so vulnerable about the moment that I felt the need to avert my gaze. It felt like the right thing to do. I waited for nerves to kick in or a tingle of fear to spread ice through my veins, but none came. It was the right thing to do.

Instead, I fixed my gaze on the grass, plucking and twirling it between my fingers. Small blue flowers dotted the grass and I wondered what they were. Without thinking, I rolled it between my fingers, freeing the little bloom and brought it to my nose. It had a lovely fragrance.

Once the commotion passed, Moss and I resumed our duties kneeling beside the raised garden beds.

"What was that?" I dropped my head low to whisper into her ear.

She squirmed away from me. "You wouldn't understand."

"Seriously, is Rhydian going to be okay?"

She sighed a long breath before answering.

"They were exorcising his shame."

# Alaric

When Khalon gestured for the elders and guards to surround him during the exorcism, I stepped back. After I arrived here, fresh from the "scourge of Landow," I didn't try to blend in. I didn't take part in their "practices" or "rituals." I didn't know whether I would be received here very well, and figured it was safer to just keep my distance. Besides, just because Khalon graciously allowed me safe passage didn't mean I was ready to join their "Kumbaya" ways. Sanctuary and commune were not synonymous in my book.

But it had been years now, and I still hovered in the shadows during exorcisms. I thought maybe over time, someone—just *one* of the guys—might beckon me to join, but the invitation never came. The longing soured in my gut. *I was pathetic.*

It was different when I first arrived. I had done evil things. Soleil had formed me into a weapon and used me to sate her unending vengeance until I broke. I deserved their suspicion. I was due the disrespect then. Every sliding glance and curled lip felt like I was paying my penance and I truly believed if I just endured it long enough, it would come to an end eventually. The earth-bound stewards would run out of hostility and their long-lauded ways of hospitality would return. My punishment paid, my dignity restored.

But it never came.

It had been a hundred years and the vile looks they gave me hadn't worn out the same way their cloaks and tunics had.

It would seem it didn't matter whether I served the camp or skipped out entirely on their duties, they looked at me the same. Resentment bubbled under my skin, and my fingertips sparked with heat.

I crossed my arms bitterly to restrain the building fire and watched the group of stewards huddle closer, forming a safe haven for Rhydian. Equal parts of me wished to be him and to be among the circle surrounding him. My lips twitched in disdain at my envy.

Khalon didn't call for exorcisms very often. It had maybe happened thrice since I'd arrived here, and it was incredibly hush-hush. Even after it ended, it was never spoken about. And they were definitely never interrupted. If I hadn't witnessed them with my own eyes, I wouldn't have know that it happened at all.

When I lived in Kilburne, I had never even heard of the earth-bound steward's practice of it. All I could gather after living among them was this: Khalon prized wholeness, compassion, and vulnerability above all else. I cringed internally at the thought of radical vulnerability. If anything threatened the stability of a steward or the tribe, he intervened, ruthlessly addressing what devastated his people. It seemed shame was their biggest enemy.

Under Soleil's reign, she regarded lazy men as threats to her empire. A guard unable to finish torture was deemed spineless, while the ability to lie and deceive were applauded. The more manipulative you were, the higher you climbed in the ranks. Your worthiness was directly tied to your weakness, or lack thereof.

Khalon's style of leadership couldn't be more different. Khalon's version of ruthless-ness was to intimately inquire after your wellbeing. To piously pursue a fervent connection with each man under his rule. A small—very small—part of me admired the great lengths he went to establish trust. Even though I suspect I had lost my ability to trust anyone after Soleil, I imagined if anyone could redeem that broken part of my soul, it might one day be Khalon.

Shrugging out of my utility belt, I squatted against the Manter's storehouse in the center of the clearing. I didn't see what Rhydian did, but it must have been something that bruised his ego deeply for Khalon to strut through the clearing during the sun's peak.

Running a hand over my face, I slicked back the sweat from working the timber yard. It was the only solitary job I could find here. Even nightly patrol runs required a formative grouping experience, one I only participated in because I had to. The guard was the only place I felt alive. On the edge of danger. Even though barely anything had happened in Ruack Valley during my time here—until Scout, that is—there was never the guarantee of safety, and that thrill kept me sane.

I scanned the field. The elders stood around Khalon and the rest of Airian's men wrapped around them at the edges. Tieran and Kallias linked arms with Elys and Maël. It had only been a few minutes, but my fingers twitched as the agitation started to build. Turning my attention to the grime under my nails, I started picking, as I did every time a tinge of jealousy cracked through me.

I'd never had someone care enough about my well-being to stop what they were doing to pick me up. Literally in Rhydian's case, but figuratively nonetheless.

Fire-bound stewards didn't traffic in "encouraging words" or "acts of kindness." Maybe if they had, less of our nation would be in Soleil's chokehold at this very moment.

It's not right.

*It's not right. Something's not right.*

Scout's voice slammed into my head and I wobbled forward, dropping a hand to the ground to catch my balance, reeling from the impact. Standing to search for her, it took only a moment before I felt her and another moment before I saw her. She ran across the field toward the exorcism.

*No.* My feet lurched, fingers twitching at my side. Moss darted after Scout, closing the gap in only two strides. She yanked her back from the group of men.

I rocked back on my heels and watched warily. In moments, Scout struggled loose from Moss and Moss pinned her to the ground.

A guttural growl rumbled up my throat. Watching Scout wiggle against Moss's earth-bound energy tore at me. I wanted to rip her off Scout. The fear emanating from Scout smelled like sulfur. I silently begged Scout to wrangle Moss's energy away from her like she had done to me.

*Fight!* I chanted in my head. *Sap her strength,* I willed Scout to hear me.

Shuffling came from inside Khalon's gathering and the exorcism finished. My breath sounded gravelly, somewhere between a huff and a groan. Trudging back to the timber yard, I kept a care eye on Scout and Moss as they returned to the garden beds, and I resumed work. I leaned down to grab my axe and in one swift movement, brought it down on the chopping block.

I was angry at Khalon for holding these stupid compassionate rituals.

Angry at Rhydian for being somehow worthy of their attention while I was constantly overlooked.

If someone had told me a hundred years ago that I would one day be standing in Ruack Valley, craving the care and attention of others, I'd have incinerated them on the spot. I wrestled with the embarrassment, ashamed of my own longing. The anger doubled within me. I was angry at Moss for drowning Scout in her energy and tiring her almost to the point of sedation, and I was angry at Scout—

Maël clasped me on the shoulder, breaking my train of thought. I paused the axe mid-swing and dropped it at my feet. The muted disdain on his face told me everything I didn't want to hear. *You're supposed to be a part of the exorcisms*, he'd say later at the guard's meeting before patrol. *You can't expect to be treated like one of us if you resist being one of us.*

I hated hearing him think it, and I knew I'd hate hearing the words come from his mouth even more. Would it kill them to ask instead of criticize?

"I know," was all I said to him now. Over his shoulder, I caught a glimpse of movement and veered away from him.

Scout beelined for the water basin on the other side of the manter's hut. I quickly grabbed my utility belt from where I left it in the grass and rounded the corner after her. Grabbing her arm, I tugged her aside.

"Are you okay?" I searched her eyes frantically, the anger I felt earlier melting away seeing she was unharmed.

"I'm fine."

She shrugged out of my grasp, her eyes flared with anger. The moment our energy entwined, I regretted touching her. I backed up to give her space to burn it off.

"Moss shouldn't have done that," I said, voice low. Then silently added, *if she does it again, I'll singe her limbs off.*

"What even was that?" She pointed back to the sorting tables that were now perfectly rearranged in the wake of the exorcism.

I looked around carefully. We weren't supposed to talk about it, and while I didn't mind living on the edge of their collective, I didn't want to put her in jeopardy.

"Can't talk now." I told her as the others began drifting back to their duties. "Meet me at the fire pit in the center of camp after dark. I'll explain."

Scout's eyes, limitless as the sky, twinkled at me as a blush rose to her soft cheeks. I turned a blind eye to her internal reaction. I knew there would be a reckoning for this moment, but I put it off for now.

) ) ) ● ( ( (

Sitting by the fire, I drank in the flames. The tightness in my chest eased a fraction as fresh energy flared in my body, washing me new in the flames' dancing light.

"Hey," Scout stepped over the carved out log and sat next to me.

I didn't have to turn to see her face. Her reflection glinted up at me from the silver pan forgotten in the fire's ring. She smelled like river water and primrose salve.

"What's with the cloak and dagger meet up?" She wiggled her eyebrows at me.

"I have no idea what that means."

She nudged me with her shoulder, "You know, like why are we meeting in secrecy? That whole thing today can't really be that big of a secret." She scoffed, a temper rising. "I mean it happened in broad daylight."

Grabbing a stick to poke the embers with, I used it as a reason to create some space from her. I found myself unreasonably annoyed at the need for distance and equally frustrated for feeling such a way for a *human*.

"Well?" She said.

"What were you thinking running into the fray like that?" I snapped, regretting it immediately. I could trace the flare of anger present in her eyes from our momentary touch.

"Have you ever heard of the bystander effect?" She crossed her arms defensively over her chest. "It's when everyone sees something bad happen and thinks everyone else will do something to help, so no one does anything." She answered. "I refuse to let that happen."

I cleared my throat, managing the creeping burn through my body. She elicited something in me, something I didn't have a word for. First she apologized, and now she was displaying selfless acts of heroism? Maybe she wasn't really human after all.

For a moment, I wished she weren't human. This imprint would be a lot easier to deal with if she were a steward. Not a channeler affected by our every touch, but just another steward. "Exorcisms aren't talked about." I changed the subject, letting her cool down while I tried to get a handle on these unruly feelings. "I think it has to do with Khalon's deep desire for wholeness. Something about dignity and protecting one's honor."

"So...*exorcism*?" Her face twisted up in exaggerated disgust.

"Is there a problem?"

"It's just... that word means something else entirely where I come from."

Now she had my attention. I watched her face as she talked, but I didn't listen to her words. Instead, I focused on the visuals she pulled from. Boxes of moving pictures, horrific scenes of heads turning and people screaming.

"No wonder you're terrified."

She sniffed at that. "Who said I was terrified?"

I laughed, "Well, it's not like that here. Exorcisms are a King Khalon specialty, and they're a good thing."

"Wow, that's convincing," she poked me in the ribs.

I extended my legs and shifted my weight ever so slightly away from her. I needed her to stop touching me, for her sake. Her channeling ability was raw and unharnessed. How many more brief touches could she handle before coming undone again?

"No, they are," I said slowly. "We don't have them where I come from either."

"Ah, so you're an outsider, too? I never would have guessed." A simple joy poured out of her eyes, something so light and freeing, I craved a sip of it.

Our eyes locked and I inhaled quickly before looking away.

"Really? The orange eyes didn't give me away?" I thought about how much to say. "I am from Kilburne, It's—"

"Is it far from here?"

I nodded. "Beyond the Whispering Winds. Maybe you heard about the war Soleil started?" I shuddered imagining what ruthless war games Soleil was a part of now.

"A war? I guess I expected this whole other world to be sunshines and rainbows."

"Sorry, you fell through the wrong portal if that's what you were looking for."

Her laugh was melodious and I found myself wanting it to never end. A sudden craving to make her laugh again stirred me and had me cracking a genuine smile for the first time in decades. *What is this?*

"Well, I can relate. I've felt like an outcast my whole life. My mom's work kept us constantly on the move. Eventually, I just stopped trying to make friends. I was always the new girl, always the shiny new toy, until I wasn't what they wanted me to be."

She offered information easy, despite how it made her heart thump out of rhythm. I didn't have a response. Stewards never opened up willingly me, and I didn't expect a *human* to be the one to break the mold.

"Being what others want you to be is unnecessarily glorified. I stopped trying."

"And how's that working out for you?" She quipped, face radiating a light from within that I envied.

She caught me unaware with the challenge. "Great, can't you tell?" I gestured at all my nonexistent friends, garnering a laugh from those perfect lips. "Well, it's going better here than it was in Kilburne."

"That bad?"

"Bad isn't enough... I don't know the English translation to describe it. Fire-bound stewards used to be stewards of power and honor. But Soleil was greedy, and marred many stewards by bending their will to hers for the sake of vengeance." My shoulders flexed as a breeze sent shivers across my skin. It felt lawless speaking ill of a leader.

"So not all leaders are like Khalon?"

"Sadly, no. But don't tell him I said that." I winked at her.

She laughed again and leaned into me. The way I naturally envisioned snaking my arm around her waist, pulling her closer almost undid me.

"Uh," my breath caught. She was warm and soft.

Competing thoughts vied for my attention. The dream from the Creators, her lips on mine, the familiarity of it. The ache of the imprint on my chest. I knew it was fated.

But the memory of Samirah, her broken body in my arms, and Soleil's mace in the corner of the dungeon ripe with her blood.

If Soleil found me, if Soleil found out about my imprints, she would destroy them. Mireille and Scout both. They'd never be safe.

"You probably shouldn't...I mean, *we* shouldn't..." I trailed off not knowing how to finish the sentence.

Scout went stiff at my side and scanned my face. Her thoughts swam in the direction of anger and embarrassment. She thought I wasn't interested, that she misread me.

I suffocated a groan in my throat. I wanted to ease her mind. I wished that I could tell her it wasn't her. How could she think it's *her*?

"Until we figure out what's going on with you being here, I don't think it's a good idea." It hurt me to say it. But to keep her safe, I had to keep her away from me.

She stood abruptly, and without a word, she stomped back to Moss's tent. However, her thoughts left no question of her opinion of me.

I dropped my chin onto my fist and closed my eyes, exhausted despite the presence of the fire's energy filling me continually.

*Why did you give me an imprint?* I prayed silently to the Creators. *Why would you bond me to a human?*

# Scout

At first light, we rose and walked to the river where empty wooden buckets waited to be filled. I rolled my neck and shoulders, straining against the hold of exhaustion. I got exactly zero sleep last night after that talk with Alaric, and my body ached from tossing and turning.

Moss showed no sign of exhaustion as she prattled on about the Manters and the water supply. Apparently, they also oversaw the water supply, and each morning everyone made a trip to the river and brought back a pail of water after recharging in the vibrant energy of a new day.

*Great.* I yawned.

"We all look after one another," she said to my curious gaze. "I've heard about how humans have these mini tribes called families, and you look after each other. Is that right?"

Taken aback, I tried to consider her question.

"Yes... We have families. You don't have that here?" My eyes grew big, but I was trying not to be rude as I figured out all the ways the others were so different from me.

"No, we only have each other. It's why we're so close and protective of each other."

"So you don't have moms and dads?"

"Wait, I've heard of these." She stopped to pick up the bucket and looked at the sunrise really hard. "They are your Creators right?"

This was beyond my wildest dreams—I couldn't believe she only knows about moms and dads in theory!

"Yeah," I said, and because I was wondering, I asked, "So if you don't have parents, what do you have?"

"You mean who is our Creator?"

I nodded.

She held out her arms and spun around. "It's why we are so serious about taking care of the elements. The faction we're born into is determined by the element we're born from. All designed by the Fates."

My brain was exploding. I couldn't even wrap my mind around this concept. "So you don't have a family?" This actually made me sad. I don't know what I would do without my mom and dad. It would be so lonely.

"Well, not in the human sense of the word. The Creator, or Creators—depending on who you ask, some view the three Fates as One since they work in harmony and are of one mind, but some view them as three separate beings—made us from the elements. But we have our faction and we have our tribe. The two are not the same." She held up two fingers rubbing them together to show their separateness.

"Faction? What's that?"

"Traditionally, our kind are born into factions, the element we were created from. There's water, earth, air, and fire."

I nodded along. At least I was familiar with the elements.

Moss continued, "We are bound by the faction we are born into. So a fire steward can't steward the gifts of the earth."

"Okay, got it. There are only four factions." *Huh, if it was that simple, why didn't Khalon just say that?*

"Well, yes, and sometimes no." Moss hesitated, as if wondering how much I would understand. "Do you remember Airian? The king's commander?"

"I'm not sure, I didn't catch a lot of names."

"Tall with freakishly white eyes?"

I nodded, remembering the giant who found me in the woods.

"He's a hybrid. They're rare, but sometimes two factions merge and the result is... interesting." A dark look passed over Moss's face and I was about to ask her about it when it vanished.

"Okay, so four-*ish* factions. And what are the gifts like?"

Moss looked around and pointed to a girl sitting in the grass. As she played with the grass between her hands, flowers began to grow. "See that's a perfect example of a gift that comes from the earth-bound steward's connection. The Manters have a natural gift for healing, and—have you met Niah yet?—Niah has a gift for stewarding water. Those are all very *natural*." Her emphasis on natural piqued my interest.

"I haven't met Niah... but I understand what you mean. So are there unnatural gifts?"

"There are some gifts that are inherited and some that come by unnatural means. Some are good and some just are."

"Could you be any more vague?" I joked. "Like what?"

Moss' eyes darted around to see who's listening. "I don't think it's a good idea for us to talk about this here." She pulled me closer to the water, away from the other earth stewards. "Soleil, the queen of Kilburne is notoriously obsessed with unnatural gifts and grave energy." A strange emotion clouded Moss's eyes dulling the green there. It took me a moment to recognize it. Fear mixed with hurt.

I realized this was a serious matter, not the time for jokes. A couple stewards jostled me as they walked by, and an immediate craving to get in the river consumed me. At the same time, Moss took my hand and pulled me further down the river bank.

Out of kindness, I changed the subject, "I just can't believe you don't have moms or dads here. No families. Do you guys have love? Do people fall in love here?"

"Oh! It's a long story, but stewards were made to be connected and interwoven in a myriad of ways. We have these imprints. It's a type of bond that can develop between two stewards for platonic reasons or romantic."

"Do you have any imprints?"

She yawned, covering her mouth. "I need to recharge."

"Oh, you were talking about this earlier. What did you say about the new day's energy?"

"Energy is new everyday. We only get enough from the elements for the day ahead. Unlike food and water, you can't store up energy. We need to come down and recharge either in the water, the sun, or pull from the earth or wind." I supposed it was a lot like eating or sleeping. Humans needed to recharge daily, too, so maybe it's not so different.

She giggled as she left me to mull it over. Down by the water, she kicked her feet in the shallow water and dug them into the mud. While it was a lot to consider, I'll admit it was fascinating. Stewards, gifts, and unnatural obsessions with... what did Moss call it? *Grave energy?* I shuddered and put it out of mind.

I paused by the river to drink in the early light, the desire to take a dip lifting. It was early enough that only a few others joined us at the riverbank. Niah and Warrick waded into the water now, standing still. A slow smile breached their sleepy faces.

A few others trickled down by the water, but they stopped to take their sandals off on the bank and sit. I watched as they dug their toes into the dirt and fingers in the grass, grounding themselves, pulling from the earth's reservoir of energy like Moss said they would. I mentally stepped back from it all. You'd think it was just a group of hippies congregating by the water unless you got close enough to feel the heat radiating from them or see the spark and swirl in their effervescent eyes.

And there I stood. I didn't understand this new world I stumbled into, but I knew enough about science and hormones to understand the benefits of sungazing first thing in the morning. So while they did their thing, I would do mine.

With eyes closed, bathing in the sunrise, I heard people shuffling quicker than when they first arrived. A tingle of excitement and warmth bloomed from within my chest. I opened my eyes to see the others picking up their things and clearing out. Two guys quickly thrust their pails into the water, eyes darting to the brooding figure coming through the tree line. I followed their line of sight to Alaric. When his eyes met mine, my heart ricocheted without permission and I blushed at my response. I averted my gaze and watched the harsh ripples on the still lake water as stewards stomped back to camp without lingering to recharge,

I looked over at Alaric who didn't meet my gaze, or anyone else's for that matter. Instead, he pulled his shirt off, exposing a surprisingly well-built and well-tanned form. He sat down in the grass and leaned back with his arms behind his head. I noticed a scar under his right clavicle, and forced myself to look away as heat rose up my neck.

I was still mad at him for sending me mixed signals. It seemed like he liked me and was interested, but every time I got close, he pushed me away. Been there, done that. So high school.

Moss came out of the water and nudged me. She had seen me looking at Alaric. Linking an arm in mine, a cool wave of peace floated over me that I recognized as Moss's energy.

She lowered her voice to speak against my ear, "I know what you're thinking, and don't. Alaric isn't like everyone else here."

"Well, neither am I, Moss," I quipped.

"Rumor has it, he was Queen Soleil's second in command... and yet he claims not to have been affected by her mind control. How does someone *good* serve someone evil if it's not by force?" Moss tilted her head to me with a knowing look. *They don't.* She moved past me to sit among the trees and pull from their energy.

But something about that scenario tickled a thought at the back of my mind. It reminded me of the strange dream I had before coming here... what was it? I thought harder, forcing the recall.

There was a party, and a guy, *Eric, baby,* and his girlfriend Lei... he was stuck between a rock and a hard place. I remembered how real the conversation felt. Like it truly happened, but what did he say?

I stood by idly while the others recharged, my eyes swept around, landing on Alaric.

Without Moss, I wasn't sure what to do, and it left me standing idle watching Alaric. As though he sensed me, he slid open his eyes and held my gaze for a moment. His eyes were dark and vacant. The warmth spread through me again. I wanted to look away but I couldn't. Just then, his eyes kindled and sparkled bits of red. My cheeks heated and I knew they must be bright with color.

I recognized the feeling immediately, it was how I felt in the dream looking into Eric's eyes. *I have made the mistake of caring about people she hates. If I don't do what she says, when she says it, they pay the price.* His words came back to me then.

It was similar... the dilemmas they both had faced, but it was just a coincidence. It was just a dream.

I dodged Alaric's gaze and shuffled to the water's edge. Needing a distraction, I slid out of my sandals as the others who'd come before me had done.

Dipping a toe in was all I could handle this early. I didn't know how the others waded out in this freezing-cold morning water. I shivered but stayed in place until Moss popped up from her spot near the tree line, looking fully recharged with her bright, pulsing eyes. She grabbed two pails and handed me one while dunking the other under.

I took the pail from her and bent low to collect water. As I stood, I could almost swear I felt the prickle of someone's eyes on me, but when I turned around, no one was there. I scanned the bank where Alaric had been lounging, but he was already heading back through the trees. Empty-handed.

Moss spoke from over my shoulder. "Don't get too close, Scout. He isn't like Warrick or Rhydian. He's dangerous."

Before I could tell her not to worry, that I planned to steer clear, she turned away, ending the conversation before it began.

We carried the water back and dropped it off where Moss showed me, just outside the Manter's storehouse. Moss tugged at my sleeve, already pulling me to our station. I let my strides shorten so I could watch her lead us to the gardens. Moss took the responsibility of caring for the gardens seriously as though it was a call to the royal guard. I couldn't remember the last time I worked so hard or diligently on a project that meant so much to me. It was actually kinda cool. Admirable.

We paused at a workbench near the raised beds where Moss gathered some digging tools and seeds. When she turned around, she was practically bouncing on the balls of her feet. A smile broke out and her eyes flashed excitedly.

"Are you ready for this? You're going to love it!" She led me to the third raised bed and pointed to where I could begin. I kneeled down and got started.

We worked in companionable silence until the sun was high and we were famished. I spent the morning thinking over the thousands of unanswered questions I still had for Khalon—if he would ever bother to show up.

Moss tugged me to my feet and I followed her out of the clearing. I quickly learned that Moss was the right person to shadow in the village. She not only knew everyone, but she was beloved. When passing through the clearing, one of the guys broke off some sugar cane for her to snack on. She took it with a wink and a giggle, splitting some off for me to try. We ran through the woods back to the tent and crossed paths with some of the Spinners, and they placed a hand-woven mat in her hands, insisting she use it in the garden. I marveled.

We ate some berries and carrots for lunch next to the fire in the tent circle. The moments where we were moving weren't so bad; it was when we slowed to a stop that the thoughts creeped in.

When we flew to England, I thought the worst thing had already happened: losing my summer of sun, boys, and fun to a dreary British summer with my old aunties. How was I to know that their backyard had some secret garden trap door in it that opened up into an entire *other* world?

As I finished my lunch, I picked at the fraying linen tunic I wore over simple cloth pants. When I stumbled into this place, I was obviously out of place, running through the woods in a satin evening dress. I didn't know whether the *others* were more bewildered by the sight of me or me by them. Rubbing at the fraying string between my fingers, I wondered where my dress was now. I was grateful for Moss' hand-me-downs, but not having my own clothes was weird.

The memory of Airian ending my power surge flashed to mind. The way he used his magic, or whatever, to make it rain had me sopping wet. Even though my dress was probably dry by now, wherever it was, it wouldn't be right to put it back on.

I felt so special when I saw that dress laid out for me. Even more special when I slipped it on and twirled in front of my mirror. Running my fingers over such a gorgeous dress was new to me. My parents didn't place a high value on appearances and never would have bought me something so *frivolous*. I'd never worn anything like it. And now I probably never would again. A lot had changed from that moment to this. A forlorn sadness grew in my heart.

Moss sat nearby with two guys and another girl. They served in other stations, so I hadn't yet met them. Their eyes flickered platinum and steely blue. They chatted in a different language, one that sounded very different from the MirVis I'd gotten used to hearing in passing. I couldn't tell what they were saying, but by the tone, it sounded trivial.

Moss saw me picking at the linen and said, "Are you okay? Do you need to visit the Spinners for a repair? Maybe your new set of clothes are ready?"

I opted to take that as my out. "Yeah, actually, if you don't mind, I'll head over there for the rest of our break and meet you back at the garden." She nodded and resumed her animated discussion with the others.

I took my time walking the path back towards the clearing. A warm breeze floated through the branches, reminding me of my mom. I conjured a picture of her stress-baking in the kitchen at home. How she had a love-hate relationship with our oven. I thought of how she always smoothed her hand over my hair before kissing my forehead. I recalled her eyes and how they turned down on the edges. She had the world's softest eyes... What I wouldn't give to look into a set of non-pulsing, un-glowing, normal eyes for a change.

The wind picked up around me, and I realized I was crying as the gust trailed the tears diagonally down my face.

I thought of my father and how he wrapped my mom and me up in a group hug any time one of us was hugging. He could never stand someone being left out. I thought of how he calmed me with a heavy hand on my shoulder. A paperweight holding ruffled papers in place. He held me in place while my emotions sorted themselves out. I missed that lively glint in his eyes. Before now, his were the only eyes I would consider sparking or pulsing. A wave of grief hit me and I wrapped my arms around my waist.

I'd been surviving here in this foreign place for a few days now, and the weight of put-off anxiety found its voice and began screaming at me. A disembodied growl rumbled around me as a deluge of intrusive thoughts wailed at me. The sky began to darken, like old bruises, and I found my way to the hollow of a tree and slid down into a crouch, holding myself tighter.

I was never going to see my parents again. I was never going to feel understood again, feel loved or seen by my people. I was never going to get out of here. I was going to be trapped here with a strange group of people who considered me a novelty at best. And a blight on the village at worst. A sob choked out of me at the thought. Pain rippled through my stomach as I cried harder from the rejection.

The air was humid and sticky. A frisson of static energy built in the summer air, begging for a storm to shake out the pressure. A howling wind peeled through the trees above me. I was not scared though. It was an adequate representation of what's going on inside of me. A small part of me thought that if I was crumbling, so should everything else. I was satisfied hearing small branches fall from the boughs above.

And then this final thought was what gripped me more than any other. I was stuck here. I would never find my way back, and no one would come for me. I couldn't believe it was just this morning that a potential crush was taking up my thoughts! What had I been thinking? *This isn't a vacation. It's a nightmare. A permanent one.*

My stomach twisted in despair. *This is where I'm going to die. Forgotten. And alone.*

Like a punctuation to this thought, heat lightning cracked through, brightening the darkened storm-clouded sky. I leaned into despair and let the sobs roll through me. I curled over on my side, and bits of bark and dried leaves crunched against my cheek. But I didn't care. I couldn't do this. I didn't want to do this anymore.

I would give anything to go back and do it all over again. I would go to Duke. I would follow in my parents' footsteps. I would follow their scholastic agenda to a T if it just meant I could get out of here.

My sobs hiccuped in time with the thunder, and when a fresh wave of tears hitched up and threatened to pull me under, the lightning cracked, reminding me where I was for a moment. I should probably find my way back to the tent for safety.

*They're coming for you.*

The voice whistled on the wind and slammed into my head. The storm was getting out of control and fear was starting to outweigh the sadness. I had to get out of here.

I righted myself and took a moment to breathe through the tightness in my chest, clearing my airways of tears and crushing pain. I tried to push up from the ground, but the idea of moving utterly exhausted me at once, so I buried my head in my hands and pulled my knees up to my chest. I breathed out and the hollow vacuum inside me ached.

"Scout?"

If I had the energy to be alarmed, I would. But I barely managed to hold my head up to see who called my name. At first, I didn't see anyone through the overcast haze and bending trees.

The leaves rustled a bit to my right. I'd have to twist to see over my shoulder, but *no can do right now*. My hair whipped around me wildly, making it difficult to get a clear picture of who was there. Instead, a pillar of a person, and I do say *person* lightly, moved in front of me. I couldn't hold my head up to see above their knees, but I assumed it was a man. I knew I should have been embarrassed. I should wipe the tears away, make sure my nose wasn't dripping. But this defeat was so heavy.

He must have realized this because he dropped to his knees and cupped my chin in his hand.

"You're going to be okay." Something about the voice tugged at something deep within me, but I couldn't keep my eyes open to find who it belonged to. My eyes were swollen, swallowed up by this emotional outburst. His voice had a lilting tone that reminded me of Moss. The softness nudged against the wall of apathy that filled in where the grief burst forth. My heart beat faster as I felt this unnatural calmness by being close to this man; even the wind abated around us.

He unfolded my arms, and with a firm tug, I was on my feet. Calloused hands scraped my smooth arms and encircled my waist so I was tucked into his side. He was big, and my head nestled in the crook of his arm and chest. As he walked, he carried most of my weight so I was not really walking but rather gliding alongside him.

He began humming as we moved through the woods. It was a haunting tune. It could have been a lullaby if it weren't for his deep register that rumbled through his chest vibrating along my temple. It soothed me. I didn't feel lulled into a coma like I did with the spiraling thoughts. Instead, it cleared away the chaos. It overcame me, this peace, like a shadow.

The wind settled to a whistle, relinquishing the trees from the hold it had on them. The storm within me was calming, too, and the thoughts had stopped assailing me as I slowly regained my strength. I lifted my head to looked around. We were on a different path than I'd been on, and I was being moved toward an outcropping of tents with a small hut with fresh smoke billowing behind it.

He must have caught me stirring, because he quieted his humming and spoke again. But this time I looked up to see his face as he spoke.

Alaric.

"Everything is going to be okay, Scout. I am not going to let you die here, and neither are they." I wanted to ask him how he knew to say that. I wanted to ask him how he found me. But we were already at the hut's wooden plank door. He rapped once and the Manter who tended to me before was standing before us.

# 31

# Scout

"Bring the child in and lay her over there." The sage, old Manter gestured vaguely to a table. Alaric moved to glide me over the threshold, but I had my senses enough about me to realize he basically carried me out of the woods, and the chagrin was catching up with me.

"I got it. I'm fine." I stepped into the space and looked around the room, but everything began slanting sideways much to my dismay. It wasn't until Alaric caught me with a chuckle and a sarcastic "*mhm,*" that I realized I was not fine. He led me to the chair by the table, and much to my embarrassment, helped me to sit.

The Manter mused to herself and rummaged in the makeshift kitchen area. I glanced sideways, unable to trust my ability to move just yet. She pulled at glasses and jars of various organic materials.

"What happened?" she asked, shuffling a few jars off the shelf to reach the ones in the back. The air of her hut smelled faintly of holiday pies, and I wondered if her jars were like the spice jars my grandmother had.

I looked down, too tired and embarrassed to say I got homesick, wandered off the path as a freak storm hit, and had to be rescued.

"Ahhh, you'd rather not say. Well, let's see what we're working with here, then." She turned back.

"Mireille," Alaric said her name as a warning, "go easy on her, will you?"

My lashes blinked rapidly as I tried to relive the past three seconds to see if I subconsciously answered her, but I didn't. I looked over at Alaric. His eyes were trained on Mireille, a wrinkle of concentration in his brow.

Without looking at Alaric, she dismissed him.

"That will be all. Thank you."

But he didn't move. Alaric's pulsing, orange and red eyes slid from Mireille to me. They flecked in intensity, like he was waiting for me to give the okay. I didn't understand why he brought me here or why he was looking at me like that. He'd been so hot and cold with me lately, I couldn't even pretend I knew how to read him.

I shifted my weight uncomfortably in the chair as soft tingles raced along my extremities. The Manter stooped over the table with her arms full of glass jars that tinged and chinked as she set them out. Once the little jars of herbs and powders were arranged on the table, she turned to Alaric.

She drew close and gazed deeply into his eyes. Lifting her hand to cup his cheek, she whispered something in the language I'd heard the others speak. I couldn't tell what she said, but her tone of voice told me it was kind and reassuring. He nodded and spoke urgently back to her in the same language. Before leaving, he glanced back at me with an unreadable burden in his eyes.

Then he was gone.

"Well, aren't you quite the powerful little channeler, dear?" This Manter's accent wasn't quite so thick. She had the same melody in her voice that lifted up at the end. The same one I noticed in Moss and Khalon's, but unlike them, she held out her *o's* in a strong way.

I watched her closely as she mixed two powders into an empty jar, creating a charcoal-looking mixture. It shimmered when she held it up to the light. Her silver hair was wispy and smoothed back in a long braid. Her eyes had the sweetest smile lines all around them. She reminded me of my grandmother on my mom's side, both in the way she looked and how she prepared whatever concoction she had going. My grandmother never used a recipe when cooking. She favored the "little bit of this, dash of that, and a piece of this, too" method.

"Channeler?" I asked, looking up into her amber eyes.

"Mhm, I'm sure you must have questions about what you're going through."

*You don't even have a clue, lady.* There was so much to unpack in that statement.

She asked for my arm. I hesitated to give it to her, but then remembered the deep drawing I had towards her and the other Manters earlier. Deep within me, I knew she was safe.

She took my arm and placed a scoop of the shimmering, black concoction on the smooth side of my forearm. With a sloped stone, she smoothed it out from wrist to elbow and waited. The slight hum of static drew my attention, and we watched as the powder began to separate, forming abstract patterns along my inner arm.

"Just as I suspected," she muttered.

My mouth was poised to ask the question. She picked up a paper and pencil and drew the shapes and symbols. She lifted her head like she was about to call for someone, but Alaric reappeared in the door. My mouth went slack. I thought he was gone, not just within earshot.

She turned to him and said, "Find Khalon."

He nodded and backed towards the door, eyes sliding to me. A tortured expression flickered across his gaze. What was he thinking when he looked at me? Why was he being so protective? I held eye contact with unwavering curiosity, until Mireille cleared her throat. The moment seemed to shatter. His gaze dropped from mine and he disappeared as quickly and silently as he came.

There was something odd about the way they communicated. It seemed intimate and otherworldly. If Moss hadn't told me moms weren't a thing here, I'd think she was his. Maybe he's telepathic. But then I cringed at the thought. I never believed in psychics or mind readers; they were all fake charlatans in my opinion. But the things here didn't have that same ingenuous quality I'd encountered back home. Could all this stuff here be the real deal? I wasn't ready to commit to a stance on it just yet.

After the Manter brushed the powder back into the jar, we waited together quietly. I watched her while she tidied up, returning the jars and glasses back to the shelf along the hut wall.

"What's a channeler?" I cleared my throat. "When you mentioned what I'm going through... What were you referring to?" I spoke up finally, as much to her surprise as my own it would seem. She turned to me and pondered. As time passed, I thought she wasn't going to answer.

"What were you doing before the storm hit?" She walked toward me, her long tunic grazing the dirt floor.

Her eyes were a steady, warm yellow and glowed uninterrupted, absolutely captivating. Peering into the depths of them made me think she already knew the answer. A gentle warmth and familiarity radiated from her. I almost leaned in for a hug, but refrained myself.

"Uh..." I looked down at my hands and pulled my sleeves down into my balled up fists. I squished my eyes shut, not wanting to remember the feeling of despair, but inadvertently calling it back to me anyway. My father's eyes were what broke me. The kindness and distinct humanness about them. And the fact that I might never see them again.

The door creaked as the wind whipped against it. My eyes shot open at the sound. She pursed her lips at me.

"I just really miss my parents. What if I never see them again?" A small whimper escaped my lips. The door continued to rattle under the wind.

"Oh child, time doesn't pass the same here as it does there."

"You know about where I'm from?" A glimmer of hope. Maybe it was naive to grab a hold of it, but I needed something to cling to.

She nodded but said nothing else. Instead, she placed a hand on mine and it sent warmth over my skin. It calmed my heart and regulated my breathing the way a good bath did. The wind dropped outside. She patted my hand before moving to cup my cheek again. She held my gaze until my forehead relaxed, my jaw loosened, and my shoulders dropped. A moment later, the sun peeked through the window and cast rays through the door cracks.

Her kind eyes crinkled, and a soft smile lifted her lips. I trailed her amber eyes as they traveled between mine and the rays dancing on the floor now. "It's fun, isn't it?"

"What is?"

"Our connection with the elements." She said it with such a "duh" flourishing of her hand.

Realization dawned on me. "Wait, you don't think I'm doing this? You couldn't possibly think I have any control over..." At a loss of words, I whirled my arms around gesturing wildly. "This?" My voice was high and tight, giving away my fear.

She moved towards me and I jumped up from my seat. "Oh no, no, no. Don't come any closer. You're changing me. This place is changing me. I don't know if it's in the food or the water or if you're doing some sort of voodoo on me, but no. Don't."

"I can see we better start at the beginning. I have to go stoke the fire if Khalon is going to take his good, sweet time. Come sit with me and we'll talk." She left through the door I came in. I was half-tempted to sit still and not budge. Or run.

But what if she had all the answers I needed?

# Scout

I stood by the fire outside, waiting to be invited to sit. The Manter motioned to the upright log as she stoked the tall bonfire and I took my place.

"You didn't answer my question before. What is a channeler?"

She sighed and waited a long while before responding. I could tell she was deliberating on what to share by the way her jaw flexed under the tension.

"Channelers and stewards are not one and the same. *Stewards* have a portion of energy deposited in them via their faction's source to steward and share before needing to recharge from their original source. *Channelers* can gather energy from any source"—She fixed her eyes on me as her voice took on an ethereal and haunting tone—"of any level, at any time. It's what makes them dangerous."

"*Me*? Dangerous?" My voice hits a high note and breaks.

"Channelers don't need to recharge," she continued as if she didn't hear me. "We'll discuss this more when Khalon gets here."

I kicked at the dry sawdust on the ground around the fire pit and thought through our interaction moments earlier. There was another question she didn't answer.

"So you know about where I'm from?"

She held the poker like a walking stick and leaned on it. Eyes on the fire, she didn't answer me.

"So you know how I can get home then? I don't understand. If you know, why didn't you say something? You can just send me home and I'll get out of your hair." I knew the vulnerability was playing on my face—my cheeks were wet with the start of a meltdown.

"It's not that simple, child." She sighed.

"How is it not simple? We just have to go find that door, and poof, my life will go back to normal." *Or somewhat normal.*

She resumed raking the coals over.

The silence stretched on for another minute while I agonized.

Finally, with a wistful look, she began. "Thousands of years ago, your people and my people used to move among one another seamlessly. There were many doors in many places, and our worlds were amicable allies. We traded and worked alongside one another. There were very few problems. We each had a purpose and honored the treaty. Until Queen Soleil's ambition and greed for power led to our nation's longest running civil war. It's still going on beyond Ruack Valley's ridges. I don't think she'll stop until she has complete power." She moved around the fire now, and her gaze drifted out of my direct line of sight.

I looked toward the horizon, where the sun began to dip, and imagined a war raging. My blood ran cold.

"What caused the war?"

The Manter hummed to herself, deep in thought. "There are many causes for war, child. Ultimately, kingdoms rise and kingdoms fall. King Tarrent wasn't good to female stewards. Based on the rumors I've heard of his style of leadership from Alaric, he could be unnecessarily brutal, and condescending. I assume Soleil felt she'd had enough. And like most broken vessels, once they taste power, they think more will fix everything."

*Dang, that was profound.* I let her words sink in. It didn't sound so different from the wars in our world.

She cleared her throat, changing the subject. "As you may have noticed here, Ruack Valley is comprised of mostly earth-bound energy stewards. Although, we do have a few who possess the inclination for water and wind. The factions are rather well-knit groups who bond and live alongside their own kind. It's for no other reason than because it's practical, and easier to share resources. Some venture out for a time, but most return to their faction in the end."

"How do you know the different factions from one another?"

She considered it. "*The eyes are the window to the soul*, they say where you come from, don't they?" I nodded. "Ah, so it is here. Our eyes give away our source. The color indicates the faction and the pulse indicates strength." She continued around the fire, stoking and raking.

"Now, where was I? Oh, yes. Soleil is a fire-bound energy steward. And boy, is she strong. The fire stewards have many special gifts. They can read minds, influence thoughts and emotions, and if they are very strong..." She paused now to hold my gaze. "They can manipulate your free will."

A chill shot up my spine, sending tingles into my extremities. But not because of what she said about Soleil. There was one boy who came to mind in particular, and I shuddered.

"Soleil wasn't always that strong, but she began crossing treaties and dipping into the grave energy. It's a very dark, very ancient earth energy that was never meant to be stewarded."

"Why did Soleil use it then?" My interest piqued.

The Manter shrugged, but I suspected she knew full well.

"Shortly after, doors began closing. Trade was suspended, and alliances were withdrawn. Word spread that a war was coming if the energy stewards didn't retreat. We cherished our relationship with the human world enough that we heeded the warning.

"Once the doors began disappearing, Soleil went to work. She drilled into the factions, using her newfound dark energy to distort their minds and control their will for her purposes. She multiplied her army overnight, and nearly every single fire bound energy steward was caught in the crossfire. They either swore fealty to her prefecture or were tortured by her army lieges in pillages."

I thought of Alaric. His eyes weren't like Moss' or the others' who stewarded water or earth. I blinked and the image of his fiery eyes burned bright. That image haunted me when I woke up after the incident in the woods.

"So, Alaric has fire magic?"

"He's a fire-bound energy steward," she corrected me, nodding though. "I was wondering if you'd noticed." She gave me a small smile now.

Realization and shame mixed in my belly and goosebumps popped up over my flesh. And the very thing I was worried about—decidedly certain it couldn't be true—just stole my speech away.

"So the doors..." I led.

"They closed. And that's why I cannot simply take you home. Although, I have crossed over once before. When Bertram was the gatekeeper, I believe. Josephine was just a little girl, though, it's unlikely that she remembers me now."

My eyes prickled at the mention of my family. There was this whole other side of them I never knew. I kicked myself to think I could have known about it sooner... then a thought clicked into place. *Did my dad know about all of this?*

"And now?" I asked, still trying to get my head around everything.

"And now, somehow... you are a channeler. You can pull energy from anything and anyone. It takes practice to harness. When not used, it lies dormant. It can surge and be dangerous, as we witnessed earlier this week."

I rubbed at the goosebumps on my arms. "Should I be worried? You said I was dangerous," I couldn't meet her eyes.

She sighed and stabbed the poker in the grass before coming to sit next to me. She took my hand. "Scout, *you* are not dangerous. An *immature gift* is. There's a difference. Let's prioritize your training so you can gain control over your gifts and open the door to head home. Okay?"

I looked up into her soft honeycomb eyes and grumbled, "That sounds like a plan I can get behind."

We shared a smile for a few beats before a rap against the Manter's hut broke our attention.

"You wanted to see me?" Khalon stepped forward and our attention moved to him. Alaric hung behind him.

He gave me a welcoming smile, and I could see that his purple eyes were alight with a steady glow. I had to remind myself to look away. Those glowing eyes saw too much.

"Yes, you should be ashamed of yourself." Mireille stepped right up to him, towering over her. God, he must be almost seven feet tall.

Khalon quirked a brow and smirked down at her finger pointed at his chest. "Is that so?"

"Yes, you just let a channeler free-roam our village without giving her any information about the factions or her own abilities. *Tsk*. You could have put our people in danger." She stalked around him towards the hut. "Good thing she can be taught, or there'd be trouble for you."

The Manter's display of advocacy for me warmed my heart.

"Come inside, I have things I need to show you," she said over her shoulder and she threaded herself through the hut's doorway. Khalon followed her after giving us a small smile.

I poked the fire as I heard the wooden plank door creak shut behind them. That left Alaric and me at the fire alone.

After a long silence, in which I purposefully kept my mind focused on nothing now that I knew he could read my mind, he spoke. "Has the Manter filled your mind with all kinds of exciting tales?"

Alaric leaned against the Manter's fire poker where she had left it sticking out of the ground. If we were back home, I might think he was cute in a rugged, bad-boy sort of way. But in this reality, he was a fire-bound-magic-steward-guy with mind reading abilities.

He chuckled and my eyes shot to him.

"'Bad boy'?"

"So what? You weren't gonna tell the human you could *read minds*?" I fixed him with my most deadly glower. The anger burned up any room I had for embarrassment that he had been reading my thoughts for days without telling me.

"You were already afraid. I didn't want to make it worse." He held his hands up in mock surrender. "Besides," he continued, "there's no 'off' switch." His smile was playful, but I was outraged at the thought of it.

"You've been spying on me, haven't you?" I leapt to my feet.

"Hey! I don't have any say over the gifts I have. Trust me, I don't want to be privy to others' thoughts. I do my best to tune them out. Privacy for them, sanity for me. I'm lucky the guard has been trained to shield their minds. It's one of the only times I get a rest."

I maintained glaring eye contact with him. "Read my mind," I ordered, then thought a message just for him as hard as I could.

He laughed again. "You should see your face. You don't have to try so hard. You're actually incredibly easy to hear. Being human and all."

I huffed, exasperated.

"I promise to respect your privacy. If you want me to pay attention to your thoughts, think my name and I'll listen in. How's that?"

I considered him for a long moment. He seemed sincere. Could he really mean it? Would he really be able to control the thoughts? I guess it's worth a shot.

I nodded before changing the subject. "Hey, I had been meaning to ask you. How did you find me?"

He pushed off the pole and came to stand next to me. I thought about how he stooped to my level when I was crumpled against the tree and cupped my cheek. This supposedly scary, outcast, wildfire dude *comforted* me.

He rubbed his brow like he had a headache. When he pulled his hand away to finally look at me, his eyes drooped. I looked him over. He towered above me, at least six foot four, a giant to my five foot three. He was well-built and broad like a bulldozer.

He chuckled. "Can you stop for a moment? I'm trying to think."

My eyes widened as I remembered that he could hear my surveying thoughts. Another blush swallowed me whole. "Hey, you just broke your promise!"

Holding his hands up in a *calm down* manner, he chuckled before saying, "I heard you."

I looked at him, confused."Yeah, I know, I'm sorry. I'll work on that."

"No." He paused to tap his temple. "I *heard* you. I saw you and the storm before it started. Then it was like following breadcrumbs. I just had to find the center of the storm."

"Ahh, so you also knew I was a 'magic channeler' and didn't tell me, hm?" I used aggressive finger quotes then crossed my arms over my chest and fixed him with a fresh glare.

"Wait." He looked over his shoulder and gestured back to Khalon and the Manter. "Did he tell you?" His brow furrowed in confusion.

*Ha! Serves him right.* I was glad someone other than me was finally confused.

"The Manter did."

"Ah, good ol' Mireille."

"Yeah, so much for thinking we were friends. That whole 'don't want a repeat of the woods,' 'oh better safe than sorry,' that was total baloney. You knew and didn't tell me."

Alaric crossed between me and the fire to sit. For a brief moment, I imagined shoving him in. Would it hurt him if he was made of fire?

"For one, yes, it would hurt." He gave me a disdainful look, sizing me up. "And two, hot as I am, I am not *made of fire*." His sarcasm had a bite to it. It made me wonder if he was flirting with me.

"Don't bury the lead."

"What?"

I stared at him and waited for my thoughts to register.

He nodded. "Okay, I knew. But again, it wasn't my place to say. Your gifts are between you and the Fates. And apparently Khalon and Mireille now."

"Wait, the who?" Now I was actually confused.

"Actually, I think it's better if I show you. Can I take you somewhere?" It was a genuine question, and I took a moment to ponder. Even though he'd lied to me and withheld information, he did save my life. Twice now. And at that, my heart leapt.

"But not right now," he looked at the where the sun sat in the sky. "I have patrol starting soon. Tomorrow morning, after recharging?"

I nodded. Eager for more answers, and maybe a little be thrilled at the idea of spending some more one-on-one time with Alaric.

# Scout

"Where are we going?" I asked Alaric as we strode up the path from the river the next morning. He walked past me in the opposite direction of camp.

"Colling's Cavern. I think you'll recognize it when you see it."

A few minutes later, we were at least a half-mile from camp. Just beyond where I entered their world, Alaric took a sharp turn and veered off course.

I squeaked and jogged to keep up with his long strides. The silence that fell between us reminded me of the silences I shared with Aunt Effie. There was something oddly comforting and easy about him.

"Did you ever meet her?"

"Who?"

"Oh sorry, I assumed you were tuned into my thought's."

"No, I try not to be. Who?" He peered at me over his shoulder.

"My Aunt Effie. Did you meet her? Or my great-grandma Josephine?" I stomped on jagger bushes to create a better path.

"No, I don't think so. If they were here when I first got here, I wasn't in the right mind to build new friendships."

From his confession, I realized how little I knew about Alaric apart from what Moss and the Manter told me. Honestly, I was getting conflicting insights and I wasn't sure who to believe.

"Why is that?" I braved the question, unsure whether he would deflect like usual or give a real answer.

Within a few strides, the forest around us became so dense, it clouded out the morning light above. Alaric's whole demeanor seemed to darken with the atmosphere. He stopped without turning around, without answering me, then stepped from view into the thicket.

Upon closer inspection, the thicket was a covering at the base of a large boulder. I couldn't see it through the trees, and now that I did, I paused to take it in. Following in his footsteps, I studied the familiar trees, the stones, and the gaping chasm in the midst. It all came into view: the vendors, the curtains, the warm lighting, the whimsical music. The farmer's market was so clear in my head that I could almost reach out and touch Aunt Effie as she led me through the glen. But with a few wonder-filled blinks, the market faded into a carved out glen.

The boulder looked exactly the same. Alaric stood off to the side with his arms crossed, watching me.

"How can this be?" I asked, bewildered.

I stepped into the rock-walled corridor and traced the path Aunt Effie took me on inside the glen. Where there were vendors and crowds of people milling about in the sunshine, it was now perfectly empty and quiet. This glen was far less touched than the one in the village by the seaside.

I pressed deeper into the ravine and walked along the coarse-cut stones. Alaric kept his distance but followed me in. He stopped at the beginning of the corridor and made some gestures that looked like he was paying homage to the space. I watched over my shoulder as he kissed his fingers and pressed them to the stone before continuing.

He caught my eye but didn't look away. I made a mental note to ask about it later.

"Does this place look familiar?" he asked me.

"Yes, I've been here before, but on my side." I walked slowly, tracing my finger along the eroded crevices. "But how is that possible?" Abruptly, I stopped and turned to face him, but he was much closer than I anticipated, and I brushed against his chest.

He backed up and said, "The legends say our worlds are mirrored versions, a shadow of the other."

"So this place, right here is... England?"

"Something like that," he said.

"What was that about earlier?" I hitched a thumb back at the entrance and the boulder where he paid homage.

"This place is sacred for us."

I looked around. The way the waterfall up ahead cut into the stone, creating the most elegant display of years in the rock wall, was breathtaking. The stream flowed from it, shining in the sunlight with greens and blues. Moss and vines thrived on every plateau where the sun hit and cascaded down the rock walls.

"I can see why. This place is beautiful."

"That's not why," he said quietly. I waited for him to continue, walking slowly at his elbow.

"This place used to be our home. It's a place of divinity." He continued on ahead until we reached the base of the fall. Here there were rough-hewn steps carved out of the side leading up to and above the waterfall. He stepped up one and leaned against the rock.

I almost chuckled. The sight of Alaric being wistful was too much.

He heard my thoughts and scowled.

"What was it like when it was your home?"

"Oh, it was never *my* home. This was supposedly where The Fates' offspring were born."

I cocked an eyebrow at him.

"Our 'Creators' were the Three Sisters of Fate: Darkness, Justice, and Mercy. As the legend goes, the Fates fought and when they converged to remediate, the result was the creation of their twins: Destiny and Free Will. The Twins... well, *they* had *us*." He pushed off the rock wordlessly, turning to leave.

I followed after him. "Wait! Us who?"

"Us. Humans and stewards."

"Wait, is that it?" I asked his retreating form. "Seriously, you brought me all the way out here for that mysteriously short story? You've gotta give me more than that." I reached up for his arm to pull him back around, then thought better of it. I scurried around him and stepped in his way. A question flashed in his eyes as little flecks of warm honey and blood orange flared in his irises.

"Help me understand, Alaric."

# Alaric

I couldn't help but wonder if Scout knew what she was doing with that pouty face of hers. Fates, this girl was gonna be the death of—the thought choked me as I once again remembered the vile image of her blood spilled.

*No. It would not happen.*

This specialized form of torture must come directly from the Twins. I imagined they were reveling in my suffering. It was one thing to bond me to a channeler—one who could suck my life force at whim—but it was another to bond me to a vulnerable human that I would surely be the death of. A fated tragedy.

"Please, Alaric." Scout stepped closer, her steady heartbeat moving the air around us. Time had a habit of standing still when she was near. To be so close and yet maintain a distance from her was requiring more strength than I had.

The moment felt fragile, and I didn't want to bring the fickle Fates into the conversation. I didn't want them here now, *with us*. Just across the path, a moss-covered rock jutted from the wall, large enough to sit on. I navigated over and leaned back on it.

I should have known that a simple explanation wouldn't be enough for a human. I gazed up, up, and up to the trees lined above on the plateau.

"There are some things you need to know first. For one, just mentioning the Fates invites their attention. It's why people refer to them as the 'Creators.' They say speaking their names can be a blessing or curse, but most know their affections are limited and run colder than the river." I stopped to regard Scout, who was rapt with attention. "Do you wish to continue, knowing that you may invite unfortunate fated whims by doing so?"

"I don't believe in curses. If I did, I'd be cursed just for being here." A bitter laugh echoed between us as she twirled a bit of vine in her hand. "It could be a blessing, though, and not a curse."

I grunted in response and continued.

"Darkness was the first of the three Fates. She was known as the Mother of Night and sprung forth from *Chaos* and *Uncertainty*. The second Fate was Justice, the Mother of Order. They say she came forth from *Need*. You can imagine how they were at odds in the beginning. That was until the third sister came: Mercy, the Mother of Hope. Born of *Humility* and *Truth*, she saved the world before the first two sisters could destroy it. Unfortunately, it didn't last. Mercy wasn't strong enough against Darkness. There was a fight between the elder sisters that created all our hills and valleys. Legend says every crack in the earth came from their anger.

"Then, we had what the Inaras call 'The Great Shaking.' It brought the sisters together in a cosmic collision that resulted in the creation of the Twins. They are called Destiny and Free Will." I sighed heavily, watching her face.

Scout's eyes cast skyward and her pink lips parted, forming an *o*. I had to force myself to look away. She wasn't the only one having trouble forming thoughts in this moment.

"Wait, who are the Inaras?" she asked, drawing my gaze from her lips to the trees above us.

"The Inaras are similar in status to the Manters we have here, except they are the elders of Prentiss. Instead of the Manters' gift of healing, the Inaras have the gift of wisdom and vision. They can see the past and the future."

Scout's eyes slanted in suspicion, she didn't believe in these types of things. It gave me pause. What must it be like to grow up in a world without gifts?

"Okay," She accepted tentatively, "And The Twins?"

"Right, *Them*," I nodded, pursing my lips. *Creator, help us for mentioning them.* "As it is told, your kind, *humans*, were born from Free Will, and we, stewards, were born from Destiny. A rivalry was ignited by the Twins and wars between our kind broke out throughout history. Eventually, the three sisters had enough. They separated us, humans from stewards, but not before binding the Twins together and placing them in a prison world, the In-Between. Since then, your world and mine have only been accessed via the portals on either side of the In-Between. Otherwise, all we're allowed are glimpses of our mirrored existence through dreams and visions."

"Have you seen things in your dreams? Things from my side?"

This was dangerous territory. To tell Scout I've been dreaming of her could mean more than she could handle... at least that's what I told myself.

Edging carefully around the truth, I replied. "I have seen your side before in my dreams. Soleil used to run us ragged so we would sleep deeply, then awaken us to share the visions, in case they could provide intel.

"Not every dream is from the Fates though," *Dear Creators, let that be true,* I thought. "Soleil had an Inara imprisoned that she would haul out of the dungeons to interpret our dreams on command. They were sometimes the only ones who could make sense of those night visions."

Scout seemed to consider this. "I've been having a lot of dreams lately. My dad always taught me that they weren't relevant, just our body's way of processing and recalibrating. But my aunties seemed to think otherwise." She shrugged and stepped around me, gaze dancing around the glen. Wonder was a good look on her. "Maybe there's more to the world, *this world*, than I originally thought..." Her fingers ran along the ferns poking from the crevices of rock layers.

Following her, we trailed slowly back to the opening of the glen. "What are you thinking?" I asked her, rather than invading her thoughts.

She turned to me, still observing the glen around us. "I don't know. This is a lot to take in," she inhaled sharply. "Though I suppose it's not much different than how our world has various religions and different cultures. I didn't grow up in a religious family, so this idea of a *Creator* just feels out of reach. How do you know it's true and not just a myth?"

It was a good question. One I had questioned many times before, particularly after Soleil staged the coup and recruited me for her own purposes. Where were the Fates then? Was that the plan they had for me?

"There isn't *proof*, if that's what you're looking for. It's more a matter for each to decide within themselves. But for stewards, it is all we know. There isn't an alternative. We were with the Fates before we came to be, and we'll be with them after. The gifts we have from them are the closest thing to evidence and presence we have of them. While I haven't always looked on them favorably, I do know my place under their authority, and I recognize new qualities about them after being here."

"What does that mean?"

"The various territories where stewards live, each have their own perspective on the Fate's gifts. In Kilburne, the gifts are something to take, something we are entitled to. It reveals the power of their nature. But here in Ruack Valley, Khalon's revelation of the Fates and their gifts is that they are undeserved favor, and that the imbuing of the gifts is an act of love. One to be reciprocated with our Creators."

"Wow, talk about a culture shock." Scout chuckled, and the sound was enough to make my heart catch fire. I bit my lip to keep the grin from spreading.

"Yes. It has been. But after nearly a century here, I'm beginning to see the value in their perspective." I conceded.

"Hmm... I do have another question though. These gifts from the Fates are meant for stewards, aren't they?"

Before I could answer, I already saw where the line of questions were headed.

"Yes..."

"So then," She started, then stopped. "Why—"

I know I promised not to, but I couldn't stop myself from listening to her thoughts. They wound around and around, folding in on themselves as her mind raced. Worry lines appeared as her brow squished together. I wanted to take her hand, smooth the fear from her face. But to chance a touch, even a chaste one, could result in an unwanted energy transfer.

Then one final thought clicked into place and I heard it clear as the river on a warm day.

*If I'm a human, born of Free Will, and the others are stewards born of Destiny, how can I be a channeler? How can I have gifts like the others?*

I was wondering the same thing.

# Scout

Later that evening, I knocked on Khalon's door. The sun was just about to set, and I yawned, realizing just how tired and sore my body was from another full day of working in the community garden.

After we left the glen, my mind reeled. If everything Alaric said was true, did that mean our history books were completely false? Where was the evidence of anything he said? I mean, this place existed... Was that evidence enough? Now, more than ever, I needed answers about this place and what was happening to me.

Yesterday afternoon was the lowest I'd felt in a long time, and that scared me. Something Alaric said to me during the storm echoed in my mind.

Maybe I imagined it, but it sounded like he said, *I'm not going to let you die here and neither are they.* My heart fluttered at the thought. I didn't know then how he could know to say that. But now I did. Something warm flooded my chest and I tumbled those words around inside my head over and over again. Maybe there was more to Alaric than what he let everyone see.

My thoughts halted when Khalon's rugged door swung open. He towered at the threshold.

"I suppose we're overdue for a conversation." Khalon extended his arm and welcomed me in.

As I followed Khalon through the open living space, I noticed everything was re-arranged. The patterns shifted from vibrant and blocky to detailed, intricate dark hues. I nodded in acceptance. I didn't know what it meant, but it was interesting.

"So, I reckon you've got some questions." Khalon sat at the kitchen table and gestured at the seat across from him.

"Oh, I reckon you've got some explaining to do." I walked around his little living room, poking ferociously at painted clay jars.

"Sit. I'll make you some tea." His kindness in response to my sarcasm was suspicious.

"Oh, you have that here?" I fired back, unable to release my snark just yet.

"Jo, we might not be human, but we're not barbarians," he said playfully.

I stuttered. He turned to the kitchenette and put a metal kettle on a small fire.

"You just called me Jo," I pointed out.

"Did I? I suppose sometimes you remind me so much of her. You are the spitting image of your great-grandmother in every way." He smiled faintly. "I had such a similar experience with her when she first came. She was every bit a fighter as you are today. Boy, she gave us a rude awakening."

I wanted to chuckle, but I was not ready to share cute memories with him of my *missing, and presumed-dead,* great-grandmother just yet.

He met me at the table and sat. "What is it you'd like to know?"

"I want to know everything. I deserve to understand what's happening to me here." I jabbed a finger into the table for emphasis.

"Well, then you'll be standing for an awfully long time. Please sit and let us talk like civilized beings. Surely, we can hold space for one another despite our differences?" Amicable as ever. I looked at him closely, still not sure if it was a facade.

I huffed, realizing he was right. So I resigned myself to sitting at the table.

"Thank you." He nodded gracefully.

"So, what happened? Start at the beginning. Please."

He got up and gathered two cups from the shelf and shook some leaves into them.

"In the woods?" he clarified over his shoulder, pouring water into the small ceramic mugs. "Well, it would be my guess that something animated your energy, perhaps a certain young man evoked an emotional reaction." He gave me a wink. I blushed deeply and took the cup he set before me to avert my gaze.

"Most energy-bound stewards experience some surges in their gifts when they first learn how to use them. We were hoping that as part of your trial and error, you might have opened the portal during a surge."

"Boy, that was risky."

He shrugged, "It was a calculated risk, but Alaric was never in danger, not with Airian and myself present. We wouldn't have let anything happen to anyone, Scout."

I pursed my lips. I had trouble believing that. "Yeah, but how did I do that? I've never had any abilities before. I don't understand how I could have opened the portal or used magic. I don't even know anyone who does."

His eyes sparkled. "Are you sure about that?"

"What do you mean? Of course I'm sure." I didn't like feeling challenged. I wouldn't let him make me doubt myself.

"Perhaps because you are Josephine's great-granddaughter, you inherited unique abilities. It's my understanding that none of her other children or grandchildren ever did show a sign of possessing gifts. It's rare among humans, but not impossible. Gifts can lie dormant for years before being activated." He leaned forward and twirled the cup in his hands, avoiding my gaze.

"Can someone lose their gift?" I hedged carefully.

His eyes snapped up to mine. "Absolutely not. The gifts are irrevocable."

My heart sank. So I was stuck like this? I must've been visibly disturbed because he leaned forward to rub my hand on the table.

"I know this must be hard for you to understand, but everything will be alright. We'll help you understand your gifts. You're in a safe place to practice them." He was too pragmatic, too political sounding. I bet it was just a line to make the problem child go away.

I nodded with a sniff and slid my hand out from under his.

"You said when you came through the portal, you had just been in the greenhouse, yes?" He got up and crossed to the wash bin on the counter, rinsing tea leaves from his fingers.

"Yes..." I rolled the ceramic mug in my hands.

"And what were you doing in the greenhouse before you accessed the portal?" He turned and leaned against the counter, arms crossed.

I bit my bottom lip, remembering the birthday party my aunties threw for me. The bond acceptance ritual they said they were performing. Was this a direct cause because of all that?

"If looks can be true, I'd say you are the same age Jo was when she first came. Newly eighteen?" he guessed.

I gasped. "You know about that?"

"Of course. Before Jo came, there was her father, Bertram, and before him was his father, Emrys. Every so many years, a new gatekeeper gets curious enough to come visit. We're used to new visitors, but"—He paused and ran a hand slowly down his face—"your being here after the portals closed in addition to your recent display of powers is... unusual, to say the least."

"But I didn't complete the ritual. They started it, but I didn't let them finish. I don't want to be a 'gatekeeper'. I just wanted to live a normal life."

"So." Khalon's eyes locked on mine, and I could see the gears turning in his mind. "You didn't accept the bond ritual? That might explain everything then..." He quietly mused to himself. "Well, not *everything*, but most everything."

"Are you saying *I* did this?"

*I didn't ask for this. I tried to get away from it!* I groaned. Maybe my parents were right—I should have just shut up and studied biology like they asked. I bet Duke didn't have a wacky portal that students fell into.

"Now, Scout, I am not saying anything of the sort." He looked out the window, eyes fixed on the setting sun. "I have to go soon. We have a meeting just after sundown."

"No way. I am not going anywhere with you. Last time I did, I ended up in a coma for days, and who knows what you all did to me!"

His brows knit together in a pained expression. "Scout," he said softly, "peace and compassion are our highest values. We would never hurt you."

"Then what happened while I was asleep? Who put me in a coma? Was it you? Or Airian?"

"No one put you in a coma, Scout. You are young and new to experiencing the power of energy. You are limited. The energy you used completely depleted you to dangerous levels and it cost your body a lot to rejuvenate those resources. We had round-the-clock care for you; the Manters rotated in and out to keep you company and watch over you. When you were close to waking, they had you moved into the tent with Moss."

It was disorienting, the loss of time, waking up somewhere foreign with strangers staring at me. My experience didn't feel quite my own; my gut soured in distrust.

My eyes roved around the space, landing on some whittling tools sitting on a dresser. I made a mental note that he was a woodworker, and pictured him holding a small wooden bird. I'm not sure where the mental picture came from, but I tucked it away for later. It reminded me of Moss and her exuberance about working with her hands in the garden.

"Oh! Speaking of Moss, she said you made her overseer of the community garden? I know this is not my business, but, doesn't she seem kinda young for that?"

He laughed. "Young? How old do you think she is?"

"Well, she looks about fifteen and talks like she's on speed, so I'm gonna guess a teenager?"

He laughed out loud. "Pardon me, no, it's not funny, it's just... I forget you're not accustomed to our people yet." He cleared his throat. "Moss is just a little over two hundred years old. Although she is one of the youngest here." He mused. "She has shown remarkable control over her gift set. Airian thought it would be best to give her space to *work her magic*," he said with finger quotes. It would seem bad jokes aren't just a human dad thing. I groaned and chuckled.

But another thought began to form as I drummed my fingers on the ceramic tea cup.

Moss was two hundred years old? But how can that be?

"Time doesn't move the same here as it does there. A hundred years for you is a millennium for us."

Worry churned in my gut.

"Does that mean everyone I love is going to be dead by the time I get back?"

"No, no, quite the opposite. They probably won't even know you're missing. While it's been a week for us here, in your realm it's only been minutes." Khalon pushed off the counter and crossed to the door. "Now, if you please, we have a meeting to attend." He held the door open for me.

I grumbled as I got to my feet and walked through the open door.

As we walked, I trudged slowly and tried to piece together what he'd been telling me.

"So I have *magic*?" I squinted up at him—even saying the word made me wince. I never believed in magic growing up, not with having two science-based professionals as parents.

"Well, I think that's the slang term humans use. But here we just call it gifts. They come from the Fates, through the energy around us. It's a beautiful thing." We turned down the path towards a different Manter's hut.

"Okay, so this 'gift' I have..." I pause to use finger quotes. "What is it? I mean, what does it do? I can open worlds... I make fire out of thin air... Is there a limit to it? Can everyone do this?"

"Hmm, you ask some great questions. How can I put this simply..." He held a branch back for me as we stepped into the clearing around the hut. "Yes, yes, yes, and no."

I shook my head in disbelief. "Elaborate, please?"

"As a channeler, theoretically, you can manifest all of the Fates' gifts. You can steward, fire—which we've seen—earth, water, and air."

"So—"

But there is no time right now for more questions," Khalon cut me off. "Come, there is a meeting starting soon."

# 36

# Scout

As Khalon and I walked into the small clearing around the Manter's hut, the group that had already begun to form turned to watch us enter. A hush fell over their conversations, and I scanned the crowd for a friendly face. I spotted Moss sitting on an upright log near a ring of fire with a few other water stewards.

I crossed from Khalon's side around the fire to sit with her. As I did, I couldn't help but notice the eyes that followed my every move. My skin prickled with an uneasy chill.

"Hey," I said to Moss. The two water stewards beside her, Warrick and another girl I hadn't met yet, slid their eyes to the ground and mumbled a quick goodbye to her as I plopped onto the log beside hers. A small sting of rejection swelled in my belly.

"Hey, what are you doing here?" Moss gave me a wan smile, her eyes shooting over my shoulder to Airian.

"Am I getting the feeling that I shouldn't be here or something?" I crossed my legs and tucked my hands between them.

Moss's eyes stayed fixed over my shoulder as she answered.

"No, no, you're fine. It's just..." She lowered her voice and slid her eyes over me. "I don't think a human has ever sat in on a stewardship meeting before."

"Well, Khalon brought me. If I wasn't supposed to be here, I think he'd have mentioned it." Her passive aggressive dig and the mild rejection left me feeling raw.

I snuck a glance around the clearing before the Manter's hut. Khalon and Airian stood at the center, holding court with other stewards gathered around. Interested, I watched as Khalon whispered in Airian's ear then laughed. It was a small, intimate moment that reminded me these were real people who had real lives before I ever showed up. And after I left, their lives would continue the same without me.

It made me feel small. Insignificant. My eyes flitted around the circle; small pockets of stewards stood closed-off and angled away from where we sat. I caught a few eyes as they darted away from me.

Ahh… Yet again, I was unwanted here. I groaned inwardly. I guessed it was mutual. Maybe they'd come up with a way to get me the heck out of here.

The meeting at the Manter's hut began as Khalon cleared his throat with a kind smile. He stood at the head of the group. I watched through the flames of the fire as he stepped forward into the smattering of stewards. The men closest to him looked familiar. I scrutinized their faces as they were engrossed in conversation with him. They were dressed in dark clothes, tunics over tights with cloth belts at their waists. If I didn't know any better, I'd think I was at a medieval knights' festival watching a blacksmithing expo.

Khalon opened his mouth and a thunderous phrase came out. The men in dark clothes dropped to their knees in response. Moss sat with her head bowed and a fist clasped over her chest. The group repeated the unknown phrase back to him in a reverent whisper. The collection of voices was haunting, and the united melody of their voices sent a shiver racing from my toes to my hairline.

It was only now that it dawned on me I had no idea what this meeting would entail. This sudden show of patriotism—if I can even call it that—had me questioning if this was a cloak-and-dagger meeting. Was this where they decided to off me? The images from the other night raced through my mind again. Me tied to a chair, gagged. Me hanging from chains pinned to warped beams in the Manter's hut.

Khalon continued in English and opened the meeting, if he did it for my benefit, no one else seemed to notice. I attempted to breathe through the stirring anxiety and tried to distract myself. I poked Moss.

"Hey, what language was that?" I whispered.

She looked almost annoyed to be distracted from Khalon's speaking. Her youthful, smooth brow wrinkled in dismay. I didn't think her perfect face could fold in any emotion except glee. I was momentarily caught off guard. But she blinked hard and answered with a curt smile.

"The earth-bound stewards that are native to this tribe speak MirVis. But you'll notice members from other factions have filtered into this camp." She gestured over to the water stewards who were sitting with her before. "They all speak various languages native to their tribes: Saattar, Nuchul, Etnyre, et cetera. So when we're together, we speak English or Gaelic, since that's geographically close to where we are and the majority know it for trading purposes."

That made sense. "What kind of trading?"

"Shh," she hushed me as Airian stepped into the place where Khalon once stood. I frowned, seeing I had missed whatever he said.

"King Khalon has gotten word back from several emissaries throughout Landow. There have been no new developments regarding the portals in their territories. It would seem that for some reason"—Airian's pulsing platinum eyes landed on me and narrowed— "the portal that opened just outside Ruack Valley's perimeter was an exception to the portals' closures. There do not seem to be signs of a resurgence. At least not any time soon."

His gaze slipped over the crowd, weaving until it landed on three Manters standing stoic at the back. "The Manter's will rotate watch at the dome's perimeter. My men will continue their patrol as usual. But there are some things that have come to light. The Inaras have been tracing the stars and all open consciences to find the insight we've been looking for. From their observatory in Prentiss, they have figured out how Soleil garnered enough of the forbidden grave energy to steward against the people of Landow. It would seem she came into possession of 'The King's Book'."

A choked gasp floated around the fire, my own screeching inhale among them. My arms flailed out to the side, knocking Moss back. She teetered on the stump before steadying herself.

"What's your problem?" she grumbled under her breath at me.

I shot her a disturbed side eye. What had gotten into her? She didn't seem like the same Moss as this morning. I wished *that* Moss would come back. I could use her soothing presence right about now.

"Nothing," I said too quickly and looked across the fire. Many stewards spoke up now asking questions.

*The King's Book.* The name punched through me, grasping at memories. I squeezed my eyes closed, and the memory of Josephine's letters came to mind. They mentioned Emrys' book and the importance of it not falling into the wrong hands...

Khalon said the portals' closing was a mystery, that it couldn't be because of Josephine's death. But could it be because 'The King's Book' fell into the wrong hands? I had thought the book was tucked away in the aunties' locked pantry. But maybe I was wrong.

I tried to breathe evenly, as my thoughts raced to make sense of the overlapping insights. It felt like the answer was right there, but I just couldn't quite see it yet. With my eyes closed, I conjured the image of great-grandma Jo I had seen in the family album. Her soft round cheeks and crinkled almond eyes. I got a niggling sense of worry that there was more to Josephine's story than we all thought there was.

My eyelids fluttered open, landing on Alaric. He sat between Airian's men, slanted away from them, towards the fire. His gaze flooded me with intensity when my eyes locked on his. The pulsing orange glow of his irises reached out to me like a warm embrace. My heart fluttered like bubbling champagne. Delicious, but dangerous. I smiled at him, knowing full well that a blush had crept over my cheeks.

A sudden burning sensation in my chest pulled my eyes away from his.

I tugged at the neck of my tunic and tried to peer down my shirt in the darkness. There was nothing there but the scar the Manter tended to when I first awoke. Brushing my hair over my shoulder, I tried to shake off the tingling electricity I felt when Alaric looked at me. *Focus, Scout. Now is not the time for a random hookup, regardless of how hot he is.*

"After the Manter's assessment, it has also come to our attention," Airian's voice boomed closer this time. My attention slid from Alaric and my scar to Airian, who stood between me and Khalon. "That Scout never completed the bond ritual to become a gatekeeper. And this is why her gift has been... erratic."

A worrisome gasp collected around the fire. The shame morphed and deepened. It was one thing to get caught staring at a hot guy, but quite another to be called out in front of everyone. My eyes prickled with heat and betrayal, but I refused to let the tears slide down my face. Crying in public was a slippery slope from sad girl to desperate freak.

"It is my assertion that Scout should be detained until she completes the ritual, thereby releasing whatever unfortunate and meager hold she has over the portals' powers. All those who in favor?"

An aggressive chorus of "Aye" popcorned around the clearing. My chest thrummed in painful wallops.

*I have to get out of here.*

I was about to make a break for it when I looked towards Alaric, a pitiful goodbye on my lips, and saw Khalon standing behind him. His knuckles were white with strength as he gripped Alaric's shoulders.

Khalon raised a hand to the angry mob. "Peace, my friends."

Trailing my glare lower, I caught Alaric's attention, and his eyes incinerated me. My face burned so bright with chagrin, but before I could turn away, Khalon gestured for me to step aside with him and Alaric. I followed Alaric around the side of the Manter's hut while Khalon dismissed the meeting.

# Alaric

"I am not letting you turn me into some gatekeeping freak!" Scout spat after whirling on us once we were safely tucked at the back of the Manter's hut, away from prying eyes. Her thoughts spiraled in panic, and with a front row seat to it, I pinched the bridge of my nose to suppress a display of concern.

"What do you know?" Khalon asked Scout, disregarding her outrage.

"Give her a moment," I snapped under my breath, momentarily forgetting my place both as a man under authority and as the only one in camp who could read minds.

Scout scowled up at us both, fingers twitching in an angry dance at her side.

"It's clear you've heard of 'The King's Book', given your reaction," Khalon prompted directly.

She crossed her arms, swaying closer to me, and I breathed in her scent. Fear, mixed with a sheen of sweat. I tapped into the energy around her and listened for her heartbeat. It thrummed loudly in my ears. Her voice was a cacophony of hurt, betrayal, and suspicion. But along the edges, as though hidden behind a closed door, was a spark of fire. *That* got my interest.

"Scout, I know this is a lot, and you're probably scared to trust us."

Her eyes searched my face, anger glaring at me, but then gave way to a more dubious look.

Khalon must've understood the situation because he added, "But I promise we are as worried about Josephine as you are. We want to help you figure out what's happening with you and how to get you home."

"You expect me to play patsy? Just do exactly as you say? I don't think so. You could get me killed for all I know!"

"Play patsy? I don't know who or what that is, Scout, but please, just consider completing the ritual. The likelihood of your powers balancing once the bond is accepted is very high. You want to go home, don't you?" Khalon softened his stance, leaning toward her.

I saw the moment defeat washed over her face. She reached up to pick at the dry skin on her chapped lips.

"But first, we need a little help from you. I think you know more than you're saying," Khalon prompted.

She scanned the woods around us, but finding no way out, she divulged: "My Aunt Effie told me Emrys had a book called 'The King's Book'. She said it drove him mad. I don't know if it's the same book though. My aunt said his book was about mythology and poetry or something."

"Do you know what happened to this book? Does Efrata have it?" Khalon continued.

"No, I—Wait, I never called her that. Do you know my Aunt Effie, too?"

"Of course," he breathed out, "She's been over a time or two visiting. Now, focus, please. Does Efrata have the book?"

"I don't know. The night I arrived here, they had a big book in the greenhouse that they were going to read from. But..." Scout trailed off, looking over my shoulder.

"But what? Please, Scout. The truth," Khalon insisted.

"But," she drew it out, as though still deciding whether or not to fess up. "Remember how I asked you if she could have disobeyed your orders and gone to Kilburne anyway to help the casualties? You said she wouldn't have." She looked up into Khalon's face, who'd gone still as a boulder. "But I found hidden letters that my aunts never saw that say otherwise. In one she talked about the war in Kilburne and said you needed her help and that she had to go. In that letter, she told Effie to protect her granddad's book and not let anyone have it." Khalon's mouth hung open. "And in the other, she said that if everything worked out according to plan, then Effie wouldn't become the next gatekeeper."

This news left us all a little shaken. I didn't know Effie or Josephine personally, but I'd heard Khalon's stories. Josephine was a staple around here long before I arrived. My mind wandered, and I considered if I could have met her as she was tending to casualties in Kilburne. After I broke away from Soleil's regime, I stayed for a little while to tend to the fallen. It wasn't long before Soleil realized she could control even the fallen ones to do her bidding. I got out not long after—

"So she could have had the book in Kilburne... and Soleil could have gotten her hands on it. Oh, Josephine, what have you done?" Khalon grieved, dropping his head into his hands.

A look of panic crossed Scout's face before her eyes glazed over.

An icy wind pulsed around us, though there was nothing to see, an unnatural swarm of stinging energy electrified my skin. I pushed my energy out over Khalon to see if he registered the change, but his gaze was fixed on Scout's face.

Khalon could be a little intense, but his loyalty and sense of responsibility to and for his people was what inevitably endeared me to him. I knew he was a good guy, but I was worried he'd scare Scout with his consuming passion for figuring this out.

I cleared my throat, and Khalon looked at me sharply. I lifted my brows and gestured around.

"What was that?" He straightened up. "Get Mireille."

I closed my eyes and reached out for the energy around the fire. Khalon shifted meetings from daybreak to evening so that I could have a small opportunity to recharge my energy. Small things like that reminded me he wasn't the leader I once had. He was far superior in every way.

When I made contact with the energy swirling around the fire, I invited it to swirl through me and reached for the bond with Mireille. Giving it a tug was enough to let Mireille know I needed her presence.

She responded immediately, *Coming*.

Within moments Mireille was beside me, a familiar presence at my side.

"Do you sense that?" I asked her.

Mireille extended a hand out to take Scout's. Mireille closed her eyes and cocked her head to the side, like an animal listening for a sound only they could hear.

"*They know you're here. They're coming for you.*" I repeated the voice I heard in her mind. My eyes wide and fixed on Mireille.

"There's an assignment against her. A curse." At that, Scout snatched her hand back. "It's an ancient one, and it's channeling the Whispering Winds against her."

# Scout

"This has been going on for *how long*?" Khalon's voice climbed as he whirled back on me. We had moved inside the Manter's hut and Mireille and I sat while Khalon stood at the counter. He totally flipped out at the mention of the "Winter Winds" or whatever and how long I had been hearing them.

"It started in a nightmare I had a few days before I got here." *Just a nightmare*, I wanted to say. But a curse, Mireille said? It seemed to be a recurring theme. First Aunts Effie and Zelda declared our family cursed, then Alaric was worried that talking about the Fates and their Twins would curse us, and now this. There couldn't be any weight to this idea. It was ridiculous.

"You heard it... over there?"

"Yes? Am I in trouble?"

"Are you in—yes! No. I mean—it just would have been helpful information for us, Scout. Please be more forthcoming with information in the future." Khalon sputtered and began pacing the floor.

"Has this ever happened before?" Alaric asked from his spot leaning against the doorjamb, causing Khalon's pacing to stutter. "Could it be a message?"

Khalon began pacing again, more determined.

"I don't want you walking the woods by yourself anymore. From now on, you'll stay at the Manter's from sun up to sun down. You'll be escorted by Alaric from your tent to the river and down to the Manter's and back again.

"The others put it to a vote, and they want you detained—Now, I know, Scout." He gave me a pointed look, countering my rebuttal before the words left my mouth. "I won't be detaining you, but you will always be accompanied. If not by Alaric then another in the guard. It's the only way to protect you, and satisfy the vote. Are we clear?"

I wanted to fight him on it, but I saw his kindness and protection through the circumstances, and it reminded me of my dad. It was annoying, but also very sweet.

I rolled my eyes in response.

"Scout, I am being serious." Khalon placed his hands on his hips and stood in front of where I was sitting at the Manter's kitchen table. The spot where she did all her usual *voodoo* on me. I sniffed the air and the warm spices still lingered in the air.

"I don't need a babysitter. I can handle the winds, it's just a little mental warfare. Everyone in America has anxiety in case you hadn't noticed. It's not like this is any different."

"Scout!" Khalon slammed his open palmed hand on the table. "For the love of the Twins and all that is Fated, you don't know what we're up against here! This is beyond your wildest nightmares."

Like a petulant two year old, my lip turned out in a fierce pout and my arms found their spot, instinctively wrapped around my chest. I was not budging on this.

A pair of eyes drilled into me. Turning slightly, I found the origin of the intensity. Alaric. His gaze swept from mine to Khalon and seemed to darken. Whoa, I thought he liked Khalon?

Khalon turned on his feet and looked desperately at Alaric. Would Alaric incinerate him because of some previous dispute? Surely, it wasn't me that he was worked up about.

Alaric's shoulders rolled back and he pull his lip in to chew in thought. Some sort of understanding passed between them, and I knew what they were doing. This was the good-cop, bad-cop hand-off.

"So, you know how you 'fried' me?" Alaric asked me, wiggling his fingers in my face.

To my embarrassment, I snorted in laughter at the memory.

"Okay, listen. Imagine if you didn't do that every time you touched someone here?" He winked at me, and his sarcasm loosened my resolve. "Mireille wants to train you, and besides, she is probably the only one we could trust with you. Her being the most ancient and powerful being in our midst. Given your faulty energy surges, she's the safest person to put your fire out, if needed." He winked again, and I was a total goner.

"Okay, okay, but I am not accepting the bond ritual. I'll let her train me so I don't hurt anyone, but that's it. I swear. I am doing this on my terms."

"We'll take it." Khalon slid back in. "You start tomorrow morning."

Before Alaric escorted me back to the tent, he stepped aside with Khalon to speak for a moment. Their voices were low, and they spoke in MirVis; I didn't stand a chance of eavesdropping, despite my sly efforts. Whatever Alaric shared had Khalon's face contorting in concern. I caught his vivid violet gaze as he glanced over at me before nodding solemnly at Alaric.

I wonder what that was about?

The next morning, I crawled off the cot and dressed for the day in the same clothes I wore everyday. Especially considering I kept forgetting to visit the Spinner's for new clothes. Strange. If I were at home, wearing the same clothes would be taboo, but here, everyone wore the same simple clothes. Life here was about so much more than what everyone was wearing. It was refreshing, and I caught myself smiling about life here.

The moment I flicked our tent's flap back, Alaric stepped up to the base and flashed me a grin.

I narrowed my eyes at him. "What's got you so chipper?"

"Nothing like a beautiful day, reporting for beauty." He bowed and opened his arm out wide in an *after-you* gesture.

"You mean *duty*?" I scrutinized him. *Was that a Freudian slip? Or is his English still rusty?*

Nudging around him, I headed to the river, like I had gotten into the routine of doing with Moss. Having an official escort didn't mean I was going to do anything differently.

Once at the river, I kicked off my sandals and lowered myself to the grassy bank.

"Hey, some weather we had yesterday, huh?" Moss said, coming up from the river. She left before dawn this morning, so I hadn't had the chance to fill her in. "Niah said a tree fell on the path to the tents and the guys spent all day yesterday clearing it." Moss gave me a worried look. "Did you manage to get somewhere safe during the freak storm?"

It was nice to see Moss was back to being herself again, but I couldn't bring myself to look her in the eyes. How could I tell her that I caused the storm when I was still unwilling to admit it to myself?

"She was with me helping the Manters," Alaric answered for me.

I shot him a dagger-filled glance and thought loudly in his direction, *I can answer my own questions, thank you.*

Moss smiled, ignoring the interaction. "Oh, what with? The upcoming Harvest?"

"Yes, lots to do." He lied so smoothly that it gave me a check.

"Yes, though no one has explained it to me yet." I stared pointedly at Alaric before shooting Moss a saccharine sweet smile.

"At the end of every month, we have a Harvest Party. It's a big fire and lots of food. I think it's Khalon's way of keeping everyone united and encouraged. It's always really fun."

"Am I sensing there's a catch?" I dug into the grass, ripping it out by the root.

"Well, participation is mandatory and everyone is supposed to bring an offering for the community." Moss said.

"A what?" I stopped to look at her. This had better not be some kind of ritual where the white chick dies. I'd seen too many horror films to know this doesn't bode well for the unwanted visitor.

"Well, you know how we are all stewards of the energy around us? The community offering is an opportunity for us to share our gift with the tribe for the greater good."

"I'm not following." *Where's the part where you people thread me up on a stake and watch the human fireworks show?* I wanted to say, but I figured it wasn't the best idea to start down that rabbit hole.

"I'm sure they won't make you do it, you know, since you're new here, and..." Her eyes darted to Alaric, making me even more suspicious.

"And what, Moss?" I prompted her.

"And... because of what happened with Alaric."

What did Alaric have to do with anything? He coughed at my side. She must have seen me trying to puzzle the pieces together because she continued.

"I mean, everyone understands that your being here is an accident, it's not like they hold you responsible for what happened." Her backtracking and dancing around the proverbial bush was starting to get to me.

"What is it, Moss? Just spit it out," I snapped, and she went quiet.

"The others are scared of you. They don't trust you." She didn't pick her eyes up to meet mine until the quiet grew taut. Alaric stiffened next to me. I managed to contain my thoughts.

I let out a shaky laugh. "Are you kidding me?"

This wasn't fair. I tumbled through a door into a new world of magical creatures and strange happenings that kept threatening *me*, and *they* were the ones who were afraid of me? I shook my head.

"Listen, I'm not scared of you. It's just that... We haven't had a human here in a long time. A lot of the stories we hear about your kind are the evil sort. About how your people are destroying the earth and killing one another. Then you show up here after a century of being unable to traverse between our worlds, you said you have no power, but then you go on to have some of the most powerful surges and displays of energy we've seen from one individual."

"That's enough Moss," Alaric said with an air of finality.

Moss's jaw snapped shut and she scuttled to her feet and grabbed her overflowing pail.

No, no. I shook my head harder in disbelief. I didn't believe what she was saying. *They* were the ones *I* should be afraid of. They're hundreds of years old with limitless access to power that they're literally born to steward. How can it even be a question? There's no comparison.

"There's one more thing you should know." If I was anxious before, now I was on the on ramp to a full-blown panic attack.

I cocked an eyebrow at her in response. I didn't trust my voice not to break.

"Some of the others found out you were the recipient of last month's energy harvest, and they're not happy."

"Moss," Alaric growled in warning.

"I don't even know what that means, Moss." I just gave her a deadpan look. She took a deep breath to explain, but I held up a hand to pause her. "Don't beat around the bush again."

"When you were depleted, the Manters had to pull from the energy to heal you from somewhere—"

"That's enough." Alaric stood.

"Stop, I want to hear this." I clamored to my feet too.

"She deserves to know, Alaric."

I gulped.

"Khalon has the Manters keep a reservoir, you know?" Moss locked eyes with me. "It's where the energy harvest goes each month. They only use it in case of emergencies, and well... you were going to die if they didn't. It has created some tension in the camp."

The news detonated within me like a bomb. My insides were vibrating and anxiety ticked up my heart rate. Blood pulsed through my ears so I heard *whoosh, whoosh* instead of the wind around us. Alaric inched closer and his finger grazed mine, feather light.

I thought back to the first day when Moss gave me a tour around the village. Everybody was staring at me. Most waited until I walked away to whisper in their native language, but some outright turned from me. I assumed it was just because of the fact I was human and unlike them. I had no idea it was because Khalon and the Manters pulled from the village's special energy reservoir to heal me.

*I'm not just an anomaly. I am a burden to them. They aren't just unsettled by me. They are angry with me for stealing from them. They all know it, too.* I was intentionally kept out of the loop. I couldn't breathe.

"I'm sorry for bringing this up. I just didn't want you to be caught off guard." She reached out to put a hand on my shoulder, but I recoiled. "When they go around the circle and everyone shares their energy, they'll just skip over you. They don't want to create another incident or set off an unpredictable surge of power that you can't control. Especially since we'll all be gathered together." She looked down and wrung her hands out. "It would be extremely dangerous."

"That is the most absurd thing I've ever heard, Moss. The scariest thing about me is my sarcasm." I gave her a weak side eye.

But even as I said the words, I didn't believe them. What if she was right? What if they all were? The vacuum opened up inside me and a hunger growled. It was only slightly dampened by the pain of rejection weighing on my heart.

"It's time to go. Mireille needs our help." Alaric slipped his hand in mine and tugged me away from the river. Leaving Moss behind, I let him lead me down the path towards the small hut, momentarily enjoying the feeling of his fingers around mine before sparks began to ignite.

Once we were out of earshot, he spoke again.

"Don't believe those lies. Moss doesn't know what she's talking about."

I dropped his hand and stopped following. How could he say that about the only friend I had here?

"She's looking out for me. Sometimes it seems like she's the only one. I can't believe everyone kept such a huge secret from me. Do you know how that makes me feel? How it makes me look to the others? No wonder they hate me. They should! I seem like a privileged, ungrateful—"

"Stop! You can't speak about yourself this way." His hands raised to quiet me.

"Then don't listen," I ground out with a snarl and turned on my heel.

"Scout!"

"No, I'm tired of this—" I gestured all around, "I need a break, some space to think."

His face hardened as he read my thoughts, and a moment too late, I realized I left them unguarded. I hadn't just meant *this* place, *those* people. I meant him, too.

"Alright," he resigned. "I'll make sure you're safe. Do what you need to do."

When he turned and stalked away, I thought I heard him quietly add, *If you need me, just think of me.* But when I turned back around, he was gone. Must have just been a whisper on the wind.

# Scout

Three days had passed and I hadn't seen Alaric once. In his place, Rhydian accompanied me to and from the Manter's hut and back to the tent. He didn't explain, and I didn't ask. Alaric had been so hot and cold lately, that honestly, a break from his gloomy shadow was for the best.

The Manter pushed a warm ceramic mug into my hands that reeked of mushrooms and root rot. "Drink."

I pushed it away, scrunching my nose. "What is it?"

"It's a tea blend that will dampen your strength and clarify your mind. Drink." She knuckled it toward me across the table. Alaric left only five minutes ago and she was already trying to poison me.

"Thank you for your honesty. But I will *not* be drinking that." I began to push up from the table ready to leave. The past few days we tried to train without needing the drink, but each time some small catastrophe struck. If I wasn't setting random things on fire, or dousing myself in spontaneous gushes of water, then I was accidentally causing earthquakes like Airian did that day in the forest.

She lowered herself into the seat opposite me at the table in her hut. "Sit a moment and talk with me. Then we'll train."

I watched her warily and lowered myself to sit as well.

"What is this really about? Surely, you're a smart girl. You see we mean you no harm. Tell me what's really bothering you."

The Manter's tone was low, sweet and inviting. Like honey dissolving in warm milk. It disarmed me. I shrugged my shoulders, realizing they were full of tension.

"Everywhere I go, people are telling me what to do."

She nodded, her intentional, kind amber eyes on me. I saw a glimpse of my mother in her, and a small tear slipped loose.

"If it's not you, it's Khalon. If it's not him, it's my aunties. It's been that way my whole life. I have good parents, don't get me wrong. They love me and all, but I am realizing they never really ask me what I want. My life has been a series of obedient moves. I'm getting tired of just being told what to do."

"I see." She lifted herself from the seat. "Let's see if we can remedy that."

Outside the Manter's hut, the sun poured over us in radiant afternoon waves. She took me to the side of the hut, where the forest was nearest and most dense. She stepped in and I followed her. From that first day, I felt such a peace being near her. I couldn't explain it, but in an almost animalistic sense, I knew she was good. Safe. Right.

She stopped a few yards from her hut and began pacing. "Scout, it's true that your kind doesn't belong here, just like ours doesn't truly belong in your world either. But somehow, for some reason, you carry our gifts and have certain... features, we'll say, that only our kind have. Right now, I am afraid if you don't learn your gifts and how to steward them, you will hurt more people than you'll help." She paused and turned to me. "What do you think, Scout?"

It was the first time someone asked me what I thought. And in this exact moment, every thought I had leading up to this point had entirely vanished.

"I don't know what I think. I feel so tossed around and confused. I didn't know my family kept a portal to another world in their backyard, let alone that I would develop the powers of that place and fall into their world. I'm trying to reorient myself, but I don't know what to think."

"Thank you for your candor." She paced a few steps away and back again. "Let's begin with some warm-ups and see how you feel. Okay?"

Aside from healing and tea brewing, I hadn't seen the Manter use any gifts, so I wasn't really sure what to expect.

She raised her hands and a warm breeze blew between us. As she lifted her hands higher, the wind picked up speed until my hair whipped into my eyes, blurring my sight.

"Come and take my hand," she said over the wind.

Hesitantly, I walked to her side. Looking down at her hand, it was pale and wrinkled from the ages I knew nothing of. My heart beat quicker. My mind questioned my instinct to trust her. Was this really a good idea?

I looked around. What other option was there?

I took her hand and felt the spark of electricity in my fingertips. Like touching an electric fence. The electric slowly zapped through me and every ounce of exhaustion melted away, replaced by blinding light that disheveled my thoughts.

*Whoa.*

I let out a startled squeak. Thoughts, feelings, and pictures all flooded my mind, vying for my attention. I stumbled backwards, and a hurricane of wind followed me. The gust pulled at my clothes and hair.

"Make it stop!" I yelled.

"It's all you."

I swiped through the wind like it was a solid force against me and fought to order my thoughts. It was exactly like it was with Alaric. Completely overwhelming as powers coursed in undulating waves through my veins.

A thought struck fear to my core—*I don't want to die like this.*

Sucking breaths in so large my nostrils hurt as they expanded, I found a balance. The power surged through me in chaotic bursts as my chest burned with the pressure of a held breath. I puckered my lips as I exhaled, forcing the energy out of me.

The power slipped away, and as it went, the wind stopped and the exhaustion returned.

Looking up, I found the Manter watching me.

"I'll take that drink now."

"Mmm, I thought so." She walked right past me back to the hut.

Inside her hut, we sat side by side at the table.

"All right, so I guess you made your point." I hugged the reheated mug to my chest and sipped the herbal remedy. Despite its off-putting smell, it had a faint taste of licorice. It wasn't too bad.

"It'll get easier," she sighed. "At least, I hope it will. Stewards start training the moment they come into being, and grow their gifts with their maturity. We've not had a channeler in"—She paused to consider this—"a *very* long time."

"So there are others like me?" I asked, blowing on my steaming cup.

"Not quite. There have been, but I doubt they're still alive now. Of course there could be, and we just haven't heard about them. Channelers tend to stay away from others. As you've seen, the gift is not for the faint of heart."

"Mireille," I said carefully, testing out her first name. "Can I ask you something?"

Mireille's face was placid, serene. I imagined nothing could ruffle those ageless features.

"You said I was cursed by the Whispering Winds last night. What does that mean? I thought it was a place, according to Moss."

She sat back and crossed a leg under her floor-length linen dress.

"Ah, I was wondering when we might have this conversation. The Whispering Winds is a sentient place."

I spurted the tea back in the mug. "Excuse me?"

"The Whispering Winds is just outside Prentiss, somewhere between the edge of Ruack Valley and the Mountain of Anguish. It's been a long time since I've been outside Ruack Valley, and the exact location changes with the winds.

"Thousands of years ago, when Landow was united under King Islwyn, he had the Inaras impart their gift of wisdom to the woods. Over time, the nation split and the factions broke apart. The Inaras stayed in Prentiss to support the energy they poured back into the woods, but the split damaged the nature of their gift. The division darkened the land's energy and distorted the wisdom. It became suspicion, accusations, and paranoia."

"Didn't you say something about an assignment? What's that? How can someone make a forest be against me?" I ran a finger around the uneven edge of the mug, pondering the logistics.

"Well, it's not that simple. The forest is sentient. It has a mind of its own. And it isn't contained to one place. It would seem as though the energy of the forest is either drawn to you, or it's been sent. Let's hope it's the former."

"But what if it's been sent? What does that mean?"

Mireille leaned over now to peer into my mug. "Finish that, and we'll go again."

I wouldn't forget that she didn't answer my question, just like I wouldn't forget the look in her eye. A flash of fear. If looks could be trusted, the Manter didn't think the forest was attracted to me. She knew it had been sent against me. I just needed to figure out why and how to get away from it.

Half an hour later, we stood in the same spot in the woods just outside her hut. The Manter opened her hands as before and the wind began. She lifted them higher and the vortex spun between us, separating us.

"Come." She gestured to me, extending a hand.

I had a smidge more confidence this time, now that I knew what was going to happen, although I wasn't fully convinced a cup of tea could magically make me a channeling guru. But, oh well...

Her hand was warm in mine, despite the dusk-chilled wind. This time, though, her fingers' zap was less like the electric fence and more like the subtle shock that came from static electricity. The energy worked its way slowly up my arms and buzzed warmly in my chest. If I didn't know any better, I'd have thought I was sinking in sludge. It was a thick and slow sensation encompassing me, mostly pleasant. Almost enjoyable.

No thoughts or feelings vied for my attention; I could see the Manter clearly and the vortex spun around us, allowing me in. She dropped her hand and instructed me.

"Imagine the wind slowing, wrapping through the trees and allowing some leaves to fall."

I did as she said. I could see it in my mind first before it happened, and when I opened my eyes it was just so. The breeze felt like an exhale, warm and content. It stirred the tall trees around us, and they swished in a melody recognizant of spring. Transfixed, I stared at the evidence of the wind. *What would my parents say if they knew I had energy powers like these?* A small yellowing green leaf floated down from above and into my opened hand. A sense of pride bloomed within me.

*I did it.*

I cherished the leaf, making note of the intricate gold-like patterns along the stem.

"Very good," Mireille said with a proud smile. "Now, we just have to get you there without a cuppa."

When we finished training for the day, my brain hurt and my shoulders were sore from trying so hard. Much to my surprise, Rhydian was waiting for me outside the hut.

"Still no Alaric?" I asked.

"Trying to get rid of me already?" He jested, citrus eyes flashing at me.

"Me? Never."

"Alaric will be back in a few days. Airian sent him and few others on a reconnaissance mission."

"Oooh, sounds dangerous."

"Only if they're lucky." He winked, jostling my shoulder with his. I noticed the point of connection felt remarkably different than when Alaric and I bumped into each other. While his was often a quick jolt of fire and anger, Rhydian's presence seeped out waves of peace and stillness. I felt like I could breathe a lot better next to him.

"So, a recon mission? What are they hoping to find out?"

"Not sure, it's *privileged* information." He rolled his eyes. "Airian said it was on a need-to-know basis. Guess we don't need to know."

I laughed with him. "Alright, then what's next for us?"

"Well," he gestured at the dying light, "I believe it's time for you to go to bed and rest up those super-charged channeler muscles. And then it's time for me to report for patrol duty."

"Boooo! You're so lame. Is that all anyone ever does here? Work and sleep and recharge?"

He laughed. "Yeah, pretty much. What did you expect?"

"I don't know. We're in this fantastical world and you all have these magic powers... you don't do anything fun with it all?"

"Well, it's not that we don't do anything fun, but it's more about the fact that these are gifts from our Creators that come with a specific purpose." He meandered closer to me as we ducked under a low-hanging branch on the path to the clearing.

"Which is? Not fun?" I guessed, luring him to take the bait.

"Our gifts help others and the way we steward them honor the Creators. We don't want to take advantage of the gifts and grieve the Creators."

"So... not fun, got it."

"Scout!" He elbowed me with a snort. "What did you have in mind? If you could do something 'fun' with your ability, what would you do?"

"I don't know, maybe like build a rock climbing wall out of vines and plants to climb all over? Or create a giant castle of ice and star gaze from the top." I looked across the empty clearing now imagining it.

"I'll admit, those do sound fun." He tapped his chin, mock considering it.

"See! Maybe I could be good for you stewards after all."

"Oh, I'm sure." He stopped a few feet from my tent. "Alright, it's been a pleasure, but I must leave you here and join the crew."

I saluted him goodbye and chuckled as I ducked into the tent. Another full day of training in the books. Maybe soon the others would believe that I was not such a danger to them and their community. Maybe they would see me like Rhydian did. *If only,* I thought as I drifted into a dreamless sleep.

# Alaric

After returning from the recon, I was tired and ready for a dip in the river, but a whistle from Maël had me turning around. He hitched a thumb at Airian's domicile, a tent outside the clearing. Together, we reported to Airian's. I hadn't been sleeping much since Scout arrived. Normally, I'd nap in the afternoon, when the heat was most sweltering—the familiar warmth reminded me of Kilburne's desert climate and lulled me right to sleep—but with the extra patrols, escorting Scout, and this latest mission, my mind and body were aching for sleep.

Tieran and Kallias shoulder-checked me one after the other as they walked past me to the head of the entourage. Tieran snickered as he muttered a slur for fire-bound stewards. It roughly translated to *ash head*. Definitely not the most inspired of insults, but then again, Tieran really wasn't one of the most inspired stewards I'd met here.

My fists clenched, and warmth spiraled from my head down my arms. But before it reached my hands where the fire could burst forth, a new thought took shape. Guys like him reminded me that there were stewards who lived absolutely normal lives and didn't face the gravity of war daily. Tieran didn't know what it meant to be broken and rebuilt.

And for that, I pitied him.

The anger diffused in the wake of this new perspective, and I turned my head to face west. Catching the last glimmers of the setting sun, I stifled a yawn.

"Alaric!" The commander's voice rang out from the head of the group. "Front and center, if you please."

I weaved between stewards. No one parted for me, making me work just a bit harder than necessary to reach Airian. When I stepped up to him, his platinum eyes razed over me.

"Sir?" I expected him to demand a report on the mission, and prepared my thoughts to give an analytical breakdown of what we had learned.

"I want you to spar with Tieran and Kallias." He glanced toward them and they responded by stepping forth, smirking.

Tieran and Kallias were both water-bound stewards. Aside from our drills and running patrol, I steered clear of them. They'd made it clear over the years that friendship was not an option.

The stewards spread out and formed a circle, the demarcation of our sparring ring. I looked between Tieran and Kallias, locking down deep the exhaustion I truly felt. "Who wants to spar first?"

Airian chuckled humorlessly. "Oh, did I say you'd be sparring one at a time? Oh no, I meant both of them. *At the same time.*" His wicked grin ate me alive. "Well, what are you waiting for? Boys!"

Tieran and Kallias orbited me slowly. I was careful not to turn my back to either one. Tieran surged forward, a jab aimed for my gut, but I danced around it. Kallias skirted behind Tieran and got ready to attack. Kallias's ice-blue eyes drilled coldly into me. His fist shot for my jaw. I ducked under it, but Tieran was already low, sweeping his leg out to knock me off my feet.

I rolled back and thrust myself forward onto my feet, ready to go on the offense. The two spread wider now, making it harder for me to keep both in view. Tieran charged me and threw jab after jab. My frustration was building, though I kept it at bay. Sparring was not meant to be energy training, but physical exertion. Airian didn't want his men relying on energy.

Kallias slipped behind me as Tieran gained ground with his incessant jabs. I dodged them skillfully, but it distracted me from what Kallias was up to behind my back. I dipped under Kieran's latest throw and drove my shoulder into his gut, tackling him to the ground. Just as I righted myself, straddling him, a cold plunge of water enveloped my head.

I shook my head to get the water to drain off, but it didn't. I blinked, and the water was held, contained just to my head. I slid off Tieran and beat at the water surrounding my face. Tieran began to pummel me; kicks to my stomach had my breath running short. I feared taking a breath.

Thoughts were far from me, and panic clawed at my chest, burning its way through me. The only thought circulating my head was if Airian wanted us to play dirty, he could count me in.

The panic converted to rage in my fist and fire enveloped me, turning the water around my head into a sizzling mist. I gasped for air. Water droplets coated my throat and I choked. Fists like hammers beat at my back as I turned over on all fours to catch my breath.

I slammed a fist into the ground and turned the dry forest floor into a pool of fire. The stewards jumped back. Some of the guys clamored around Airian, cheering my opponents on, while a few others stood a ways off with bland disdain coloring their thoughts. I noticed Maël was not found among them. Kallias snickered, emboldened by the attention, and sprayed water everywhere my fire leapt up.

High above us, the pine trees' boughs were heavy with cones, and an idea sprung to mind. Pushing off the ground with my legs, I shot up to grab the branch above me. It was just low enough that I could swing myself up and over. Perched over a knot in the tree, I collected several pine cones and stored them in the length of my tunic. In moments I had a sizable amount, despite the intolerable slurs the men called out from below as they shot streams of water into the tree ineffectively. Before hopping down, I tore off the bottom of my shirt and wrapped strips around the plucked cones. I gave them a tight squeeze to pull the resin from within and lit them on fire before hurling them to the forest floor, where they popped and sparked, igniting several spots around Kallias and Tiernan.

As they tried putting out the fires, I created more. If I couldn't match their energy, I would wear them down. The flaming cones they delayed to extinguish exploded with bursts of hot sap, singeing their clothes and hair, much to my pleasure. When I ran out of missiles, I launched from my perch and called the energy of the remaining fires to me, siphoning them into one massive flame that began to swirl around the sparring area.

The men around us bolted from the immediate area as the firestorm grew and began sucking oxygen from the air. Kallias fell to his knees before me, grasping at his throat.

Tieran shot a rush of water out from both hands, causing billows of white smoke to engulf us.

The smoke clouded my vision long enough for me to lose sight of Tieran.

Just then, he hopped onto my back and began to strangle me with a rope of water. Kallias got in my face, taunting.

"Just say the word and we'll quit. We're built different, built better than you." His grin reminded me of a viper revealing its fangs.

I shook my head, refusing to accept defeat to such a woeful opponent. If I failed—*if* I had to tap out—it would be with dignity.

Tieran leaned forward and whispered in my ear, "Whatever will happen to your pet human when we're through with you?"

A blaze consumed me from the inside out, "Touch her and I'll torch you."

"I'd like to see you try." Kallias snickered, flipping his wrist, and water filled my peripheral, blurring my vision. I took a gulping deep breath as he plunged me once more under a helmet of water. This time though, it was frozen. The water clouded and my eyes burned, frozen open. My nostrils pricked, and I already knew I'd come out of this with a terrible nose bleed.

I reached out to implore my fire to ravage his body, but he snatched my wrists and weaved them into an ice block. Airian stood close by, watching everything unfold. His gaze penetrated me deeply, and humiliation prickled at my spine. The last of my breath was burning in my chest, the suffocation of the ice making my mind hazy. Reaching out for my fire once more, I pushed it forth, begging it to be enough. I couldn't feel how thick the ice was or if he was simply adding more after each layer defrosted, but I finally resorted to pounding my head against a rock to chip off bigger pieces of ice.

Each ram left my head feeling woozy, but the need to survive drove me. To save Scout from these malignant scourges.

"This is pathetic. I'm not going to watch him kill himself," Airian groaned. "I wanted a fight, and you gave me a desperate attempt at surviving. Enough." A vibration rocked me off my feet. The ice around my hands and head broke up. A crack opened near my nostril and fresh air rushed in as hot breath escaped me. My chest heaved from a mix of relief and panic.

Calling to the energy around me, it came slower now, as if the Creators turned their back on me like Airian had. I let the flicker of warmth defrost my hands until the feeling returned to them.

The gathering of stewards dispersed to their regular drills, leaving me alone on the ground. This wasn't the first time I'd seen Airian-approved hazing in the guard. But something about this time felt like mortal combat. It wasn't just roughhousing—the guys were toeing the line of life and death. The thought turned my stomach, and I rolled over to dry heave into the bushes.

) ) ) ● ( ( (

"You want to talk about it this time?" Mireille found me staring into the coals of a fire long gone.

I shook my head, water still dripping from my damp hair.

Silence hugged us close, a welcome reprieve for my pounding headache. Mireille's presence was a gift. Just her quiet nearness offered my weariness a home. I let my mind drift away from Airian and this place. Away from Soleil and the memories. Away from the Fates and their nightmares.

Khalon's hut door opened, and his silhouette stretched long in the sliver of light. A Manter left with a bow, and Khalon hovered at the threshold before deciding to close the door behind him. I thought he'd gone inside until he nestled in on the other side of us.

We three sat and watched the dying coals fizzle out. A comfortable stillness settled in, and my thoughts turned to Scout, as they often did these days.

"You don't really believe the forest is 'attracted' to her, do you?" I said, turning to Khalon.

I could tell it was the last thing he expected me to bring up, as his eyebrows leapt to his hairline. He cleared his throat to answer, but Mireille responded first. I swiveled to her.

"No. I think Scout was either being harassed or hunted."

The thought of the Whispering Winds being used as an assignment against Scout was an interesting concept, but something wasn't right.

"Perhaps she is just a messenger? Wouldn't that be brilliant?" Khalon said, his head teetering on his closed fist. "For someone to use a channeler to steward the Winds' suspicion?"

"What if you're both right? What if it was a message, but from the Creators. What if someone was coming for her or for us and they know we're here—" A chill caressed me as I recalled the past few days Maël and I spent trekking through the Whispering Winds.

"In spite of the cloaked dome? I don't think so," Mireille interrupted.

"I know, but what if it *is* a warning?" I countered.

"Why would the Fates, who never intervene, decide to do so now?" Khalon said thoughtfully, caught up in his own mind.

"I don't know. Why would someone harass a *human* girl?" I said.

"A *channeling* human girl," Mireille corrected me.

"What would they want with a *channeler*?" I said disdainfully.

"I can think of a few things... There are some grave energy rituals that require a special sacrifice. It's part of the reason the Twins got sent to the In-Between. Everyone knew they were rivals, but more than that, they pitted humans and stewards against one another, and to increase their power over one another, the Twins took part in heinous rituals that required them to sacrifice hybrids and channelers. They drove them to the brink of extinction." Mireille spoke with haunted eyes.

We all knew the Manters were ancient, having been around for Fates knew how long, but no one ever pushed the letter with them. Either no one had the courage to know the truth, or no one had the gall to question an ancient being like the Manters on matters this dire.

"I thought channelers weren't around because they chose to go into hiding for the sake of their sanity?" Khalon asked, equally surprised by this new information.

She shook her head grimly. "It's better for everyone if the others think that."

"Okay, so who would do this?" Khalon pondered more to himself than us.

I didn't even have to think to know the answer.

*Soleil.*

There wasn't a line she wouldn't cross to get what she wanted: power and control. The Manter gave me a pained look before speaking the name that'd already been haunting me.

"So what do we do?" I said, resigned to moving forward. I couldn't even stand to give her an inch of space in my mind, let alone my life.

"Soleil?" Khalon backtracked. "You think the message is from *Soleil*? For her to figure out how to control humans and send them into our midst..." He scratched his chin. "We would be none the wiser—offering refuge to her, while she cleans us out from within... it's diabolical."

"No, I don't think Scout is a messenger, or spy, for Soleil. I think she's being hunted." Mireille intoned sagely.

A chill wiggled its way through my mind, bringing me all the way back to Samirah. Soleil hunted for someone close to me once before, and I knew exactly how that turned out.

"I think Soleil is after her to complete a ritual." Mireille said with an air of finality.

"And the Whispering Winds?" Khalon rubbed his head.

"I think Alaric may be right. Perhaps it's a warning."

A double-edged silence pierced the air around us, uncomfortable and gutting.

"So what do we do." I ground out between bared teeth. The idea of Soleil's terror reigning in this place of peace made me sick.

"We strengthen our reserves, tighten the patrols, double check the dome and reinforce it if necessary. And we go about our business. There is no way Soleil could have found us. I don't think Soleil even has the resources to open a random portal, throw the exact right human girl through, and use her as a spy among us anyways. It's impossible. If Scout is her target, then she'll be safe here. The dome will keep her safe," Khalon determined.

*We mustn't underestimate her.* Mireille's eyes slid to mine, and I knew exactly what she was saying.

)  )  )  ●  (  (  (

I jolted awake in bed, heart hammering. The feeling of eyes on me prickled the back of my neck. As I sat up from my cot, sweat wicked down my chest and back in slow streams before pooling. I rubbed my eyes and tried to make sense of the waning darkness. Rhydian's quiet snores were the only sounds I heard. But something woke me, I was sure of it.

Making as little noise as possible, I eased off the old cot and shuffled out the tent, down the platform's stairs. The air had a bite to it—the nip of seasons changing. I scanned the clearing around our tents, standing stone still as I listened, really listened. When I was certain there were no movements, I closed my eyes and extended the reserve of energy I had to sense any wakeful thoughts moving about camp.

At the very corner of my mind, an errant thought scraped by. Whomever it belonged to was too far for me to connect with. I stalked towards it in a deliberate circle to ascertain which direction it was moving.

*...it won't be enough. They need more.*

A frantic thought appeared with more clarity. I continued to move in the direction it came from. The main clearing.

*I need to see him. It has been too long... If I don't make it back soon, I'll be too late.*

Contrary to what non-fire stewards believed, hearing the thoughts of others was more complicated. Aside from our imprint bonds, we couldn't tell who was thinking what most of the time. Without proper training, we would never know a single thought apart from our own. Most fire stewards skipped the training and let the noise fade to the background. Only specialized training helped them decipher a thought and identify its source.

However, if I saw the person in the middle of the night, it wouldn't be hard to tell.

I was nearly down the path when another thought fragment flashed through my mind. This one, more menacing in its tone.

*No one's going to miss her when she's gone. She's just a human.*

At the mention of a human, I knew exactly what they were after. There was only one human in Ruack Valley.

I raced toward her tent at the edge of the clearing, praying to the Fates that I made it in time. I begged my legs to carry me faster. They groaned, thick with exhaustion. My muscles ached, having been pushed to their limits as of late.

I was only a short distance from Moss and Scout's tent, appearing exactly the same as the other four in their row. But creeping along the side of their tent was a dark shadow. Straining ahead, I used what was left of my energy to welcome fire into my hands. The shadow turned, and in the faint glow of the roaring flames in my hands, I saw a figure shrouded in darkened linen clothes. Seeing me, they darted away.

*No, no, no. I was so close.*

The attacker's anguish made my steps falter. But I pressed forward. They tore off into the darkness of the woods behind the tents. I chased after them with all I had. The trees blurred past me as I raced after the figure. They turned once, then twice to glance over their shoulder.

The third time the hooded trespasser turned, he threw something. Something *hot*.

A new bead of sweat streamed down my body, chilling me at the sight. He'd thrown fire.

*A fire steward?* No, I'm the only fire steward in Ruack Valley. At least, that's what I'd been told.

I almost stumbled from the pure shock of it, but quickly regained my steps and dashed after them. With fire still in my hands, the shadows of passing trees whipped around me, making me think I was seeing more than what was there. I quickly lost sight of the figure and pulled up short to listen for them.

The forest was eerily quiet. Scanning the ground, I silently begged the Creators for a clue, anything to indicate who the trespasser was. A gentle thrumming in the earth was all that I could sense. Dejected, I committed the entire experience to memory and turned to begin the long walk back to the clearing. Out of the corner of my eye, something caught my attention.

A set of footprints trampled down the grass. But they were small. Much smaller than any of the men I'd seen around camp.

Upon closer look, a set of bluish flowers appeared to have been budding before getting crushed. I rolled my eyes at myself. *You're grasping at smoke. There's nothing here.*

Emerging from the woods, Scout's tent stood still and untouched as before. A craving deep inside me had me itching to step up to her platform and pull the flap back, just so I could watch her chest rise and fall with breath. I needed to know she was okay.

I approached her and Moss's tent, quietly so as not to disturb their slumber, and as soon as I was within range, I heard the familiarity of her thoughts and heartbeat. A medicine balm to my worried heart. Sleep pulled at my eyes, and they burned, refusing to stay open any longer. If I stayed a minute more, I was certain to fall over—asleep—here and now. I entertained the thought only a moment, considering it the safest option for Scout, but a crueler image took its place. No one could know about the bond. If she were in danger now, it would only double her worth—and leverage against me—to an attacker for them to find she was not just a human, but the recipient of an imprint.

I ambled back to my tent and fell into bed, sleep catching me up in its arms once more.

# Scout

"Where are we going today?" I asked, lunging over a fallen tree. Alaric stepped over it as if it were a puddle. I followed him through the woods in a direction I hadn't been before. All the trees blurred together, and most of the wood looked the same. We didn't walk a path, so it wasn't clear where we were going.

"Mireille wants to train you by the water today, so we're heading south to Ruack Valley's Lake Hollow," he said over his shoulder.

We went on for a while in the quiet early hours, not talking. Alaric hummed intermittently, as birds chirped to life in the boughs above. If I weren't trapped in a foreign world, I'd think it was a perfect morning.

The days were beginning to blur together. Without my phone or any clocks in the valley, I had no real way of identifying the passing of time. The image of prisoners carving tallies into their cement cell walls came to mind, and I wanted to bop my forehead. *Why didn't I think of that?*

However long it had been—three or four days maybe?—had been spent training incessantly with the Manter to get this gift under control. I had finally managed to achieve a sense of control, and with only half a cuppa needed.

"You're quieter than usual," I said between breaths. Keeping up with Alaric was like running triple time for each of his long strides.

"Didn't sleep well," he mumbled.

"Oh, sorry to hear that. Nightmares?"

He nods one sharp bob, eyes ahead.

"I've been having nightmares too."

Alaric began humming again as the lake came into view. Blue so deep it looked black stretched on forever. In the far distance, mountains pierced the sky, snow spots scattered across their tops.

The air felt crisper, cleaner. I took a deep breath and let it fill my lungs. A few yards away, a dark-haired girl broke through the tree line. The Manter glided in behind her. I looked up at Alaric to see his reaction, but all I noticed were the bags under his eyes.

*Those nightmares must really be taking a toll on you, huh?* I asked him, mind to mind.

His eyes glazed over, bored, as if he didn't hear me, although I knew he did.

*That's fine, you can pretend to ignore me,* I thought at him.

"Who are they?" I asked him.

"Scout, right?" a voice called.

I looked over my shoulder to see the dark-haired girl. She was beautiful in a strong, tom-boyish way with pulsating blue eyes that matched the color of the river water in the morning. I turned towards her and instinctively crossed my arms over my chest.

"Yes?" I looked her up and down, trying to place her face from among the numerous stewards I'd met since being here.

"Niah," she said, raising her chin in a quick jut.

"I see you've met Niah, Scout." The Manter drew close, leaning in to kiss Alaric's cheek in a greeting, then came to stand by me. She placed a hand on my shoulder and squeezed.

"Today, we're going to find your faction. While I could theoretically test you for all of them, I thought it would be nice for you to see how the others interact with the element they're bound to. Take it away, Niah. We'll be over here if you need us."

"I'm guessing we're training water first then?"

"I'm sorry, did you have something else in mind?" Niah's eyes rippled in waves of dark blue, and she gestured obviously to the lake.

I stuttered. She was bold and sassy. Reminded me of my gym teacher at school. I smiled a little. I could handle someone pushing me around a little, but learning to use energy was not the same as learning kickball. I thought about the first time I learned to swing a bat or serve a volleyball. Those all seemed foreign until I learned how. Maybe this would be the same.

I gave her a half-hearted smile and acquiesced.

"From what the Manter told me, I've gathered that you're a channeler who's faction-less. So we're gonna find your faction."

"Uh, I think we're gonna have a problem with that."

"Why's that?" She crossed her arms in noticeable annoyance.

"Well, we not only don't have energy where I come from, but we also don't have factions."

"Duh, I knew that. You're *human*. What, do you think I'm stupid?" She rolled her eyes.

"I don't really know what you are." I meant it as simply and innocently as possible, but the moment it escaped my lips, it reeked with snark. My eyes widened, and I started to backtrack, but she just stared at me.

But before the anxiety could strike me down, her boisterous laugh lifted the heavy silence. I sighed in relief. It was nice to speak so freely.

"Okay, you're hilarious." She flicked me a leather tie for my hair. "And that's fair. Let me explain what I do know about you *humans*." She tied her long hair back in a ponytail and kicked off her shoes, so I did the same.

"While you're not born into factions, you can still access factioned energy. We,"—She motioned to herself and over her shoulder towards where Alaric and Mireille sat at the tree line watching us—"are limited because we are born into factions. You —" She paused to motion to me—"are not limited by the same constraints because you are born outside of the faction's reach. Channeling Stewards are usually born into a faction and it's their default, though unlike other stewards, they can access all the factioned energy. Here's where you're unique. You aren't a steward and you weren't born into a faction... but maybe you have a default still. So far, though, you've only accessed energy by touching others, correct?"

"Yes..." I thought I was following.

"I'm gonna try to show you how to pull from the energy source itself. It'll be tougher than just touching someone, but it'll pay off in the long run." She began wading into the water.

I nodded, following her into the lake. "Can all humans steward energy?"

She paused to think, and I appreciated the moment to adjust to the cool water.

"Yes and no. The energy is the same in both our worlds, but it doesn't demand our attention. It calls to all of us and yearns to be stewarded. But only those who accept its call end up stewarding it."

I tried to piece this together. "I don't remember hearing the call or accepting it though?"

She shrugged. "I don't know. You're sure you never heard a whisper on the wind or felt water heal you? Never had a fire churn inside you and reveal the thoughts of others nearby or touch something and see an image flit to mind? You might not have realized it was the call at the time." She dove in head first without waiting for a reply.

"Well when you put it like that..." My mind drifted back to when I worked alongside Aunt Effie in the greenhouse. Before she told me about her time in there, with her sisters sleeping over, I saw it play out. A daydream, I assumed at the time. But maybe it wasn't just a fluke?

I waited for her to surface before telling her about it.

"Aha, so see. That's the call. And somewhere along the line, you accepted it and gave it room to fill you. So it did. And now you're here. So we've got work to do." She said each sentence so matter-of-factly. She punctuated the last sentence with a clap of her hands. Water sprayed the air. I swam out to her, and we treaded water at a leisurly pace.

"First thing you gotta do if you're going to steward factioned energy without touching someone: you have to learn to recognize energy."

My face fell and I looked at her like she had an egg on her face.

"Why are you looking at me like that?"

"Do you know how ridiculous that sounds? '*Learn to recognize the energy*'? How am I supposed to do that?"

She swatted at me. "Well you're never gonna learn if you don't shut up and listen. Also, you gotta learn to chill. You think you can do that?" She leveled me with a feisty look.

"Are you sure you don't channel fire? 'Cause..." I trailed off under my breath, scratching the back of my neck. I flipped my hair around and said to her instead, "Uh, yeah. I think I can manage that."

"I know this is stretching, Scout." It was the first sensible thing she said, and it got my attention.

I looked at her and took a deep breath. "All right, what do I do?"

"I want you to be still and take some deep breaths. Practice clearing your mind so it's empty. Let all your other thoughts flow in and back out until they're all gone."

She turned to float on her back, and I did the same. I closed my eyes and took a deep breath. I released the thoughts that'd been plaguing me. The thought that no one really wanted me here stung as it passed through, but I let it go. I heard the Manter's voice telling me I was dangerous and Khalon's scolding me, but I let them both run their course and fade from my mind. I thought of my mom and dad and the grief that threatened to swallow me whole, and I pushed it away with a deep exhale.

"Good. Feel yourself being held by the water, feel the waves beneath you. Take inventory of your body and how you feel. Pay attention to any tension in your body."

I breathed in and searched my body for pain or tension. The pain in my head from the previous day was nearly gone and unnoticeable. I rolled my neck and shoulders, checking in with my muscles, and realized they were stiff. I made a mental note to stretch before bed tonight, but I let it go. I also noticed a small burning below my collarbone where the Manter put some salve that drew my attention, but I let it go as well.

"When you find things, acknowledge it, and then release it. If you don't find anything, just focus on your breath."

I gave a slight nod to acknowledge her and breathed some more. My head cleared and a gentle warmth crept through my body. The sun had begun its climb in the sky and the brightness caused starbursts behind my lidded eyes. My hair floated out around me, tickling my shoulders and neck.

"Scout, now I want you to focus on what you hear around you. Listen with your ears."

I cocked my head sideways at what I thought was an unnecessary clarifier. But I listened to things around me. The quiet lapping of lake water against the shore. The tickle of leaves in the trees as the wind shuffles by. It was melodic. It reminded me of home.

A knot formed in my throat.

"Release it," Niah whispered, her voice coming from over my shoulder.

I tried to breathe through the wobbling fist in my throat. *Release, Scout,* I told myself. I reminded myself that I would go home. I breathed and released it.

"Good, you're doing great, Scout. Now I want you to turn your ears inward and listen intently to the calling inside you. Listen for what it wants, what it's asking from you, for you. It may take some time to find it and hear it. Give yourself time to discover it."

It was the weirdest request, but I was the most relaxed I'd been since getting here, so I couldn't even make a fuss about it. I just settled in deeper.

My chest rose and fell with the gentle waves, and I focused on my breathing again like Niah instructed. I imagined my breathing like a spiral staircase, and I descended deeper and deeper. Each breath deepened and slowed. My heart rate slowed to a restful pace. I thought of the vacuum inside me that Alaric incited that first day. It roared to life when he goaded me. I looked for the pit at the bottom of the staircase in my mind.

Everything else faded away in that moment. I could no longer hear the wind in the trees or the waves' rhythmic *slush-slush*. It was just me and this staircase, hunting for the deep cavity within. I was searching within me so intently that it felt like my eyes were wide open though I knew they were shut tight. I didn't hear anything, but I sensed a pulse of warmth under my finger tips. The hunger stirred deep within me. I shuddered as a chill traced up my neck. The chill left me exhilarated. My nerves were alive and every sense was full of electricity.

Niah exclaimed in her native tongue something that sounded like a curse, and it pulled me out of the depths.

"What is it?" I looked at her and saw what she saw now that my eyes were open.

All around me, water droplets hovered just above the lake, suspended in mid-air. Light cascaded through them casting prisms of colors all around us. A fog of rainbows surrounded us.

"You did it! You channeled water without touching anyone, Scout."

I marveled at Niah first, then at the droplets around us. "What does this mean?"

"Well, it means we're off to a good start..." Niah's calloused fingers lifted to extract a drop from the air. "You might just be a water-bound steward after all."

# Scout

We laughed together, I more out of disbelief, and in the distance I heard clapping. I swiveled in the water to see Alaric and the Manter with smiles at the shore.

"This is crazy!"

I recognized a twinge of pride in the Manter's eyes.

*And I did it without a cuppa, Mireille!*

It was the same look my Dad gave me when I mastered riding a bike, breaking up with boys, and nailing my jump shot on the basketball court in our driveway.

The droplets hung like diamonds all around us. I reached out to touch one, and it fell. A ripple swirled around us, and I turned to smile at Niah.

*I could get used to this,* I thought as I floated on my belly in lazy circles under the weightless chandelier of water droplets. *I finally have control over my gift. Maybe I would finally be able to go home after all.* I sighed deeply and contentedly.

But... Maybe being here with these people wasn't so bad after all. At least it was gorgeous in Ruack Valley. The forest felt like a safe place to me, and this lake and the river were idyllic spots. If I got over the struggles, the fear, and completely forgot about how trapped I felt in a strange world, surrounded by stewards with indispensable magic at their fingertips, who were being hunted by an evil fire queen—

My breathing sped up, and my muscles tensed as my legs fell beneath the water, slowly sinking beneath me. All the water droplets fell from the air, hitting the water like canons. I was out in the depths, unable to touch or see the lake's bottom, and panic began to claw at me. What if the water turned on me? What if I drowned? The waves from the ripples began to churn towards me. Swirling faster, they created a whirlpool, sucking me in. My muscles burned as I clawed against the current.

"Stop!" Niah grabbed me and held me in place. We spun in the tide of the water. "What happened?"

"I don't know, make it stop. Please!" My voice was high and tight; even I could register the panic.

Niah just laughed. "It can't hurt you because you are stewarding the energy. It's not yours. It's just passing through you. It's the same for all of us." She leaned back and drifted away, letting it spin her out.

I stared at her, my jaw hanging wide open. "What do I do with this?" I slapped the water, and droplets flew in my eyes.

"That'll be for our next lesson." She chuckled again. "For now, you need to learn to open yourself to the energy around you and close it off when it's time. Your emotions play a key role in how the energy moves through you. Self-control is the most important lesson. We spend most of our lives practicing it."

"All right, so how do I turn it down or off?" I fought against the waves while she just rolled over them as if this were natural.

"The same way you let it in. Gently show it the way out." When I stared at her, trying to make sense of what sounded like astrophysics, she huffed. "Close your eyes."

I closed my eyes and fought the adrenaline telling me to stay alert to the danger that sloshed my body around in circular turns right now.

"Take a deep breath. You need to relax, Scout."

I wanted to laugh and say, *Easy for you to say—you're not at risk of drowning*, but I bit my tongue. I took a deep breath. Followed by another. And another.

"Right now, energy is coursing through you. Imagine it like a bowl of yarn unraveling. Grab the ball of yarn and gently tug it back in and wrap it up. Focus on pulling in inside and putting it away."

I tried to hone in on the coolness of the water lapping against my skin, the energy of a rhythmic heartbeat. The energy flowed freely out of me. I retraced my steps in my mind, quieting the noises around me by listening deeply. It was easier now that I'd already forged a way.

I retreated back to the staircase in my mind and pictured myself pulling the yarn with me, tugging it back inside, deeper and deeper, until I reached the bottom of the staircase and placed the ball of yarn in front of me. The sounds around me began to take shape again as I resurfaced from the depths of this vacuum inside. A satisfaction replaced the cavern where the hunger was. My mind was clear, awake, and at peace. Just like it was last time with Alaric when he found me in the woods.

The moment crystallized in my memory. *Could fire be my default faction?* I wondered. *What if I wasn't like channeling stewards and this was all for nothing?*

My eyes fluttered open, and I found Niah beaming at me. The lake stilled and all around us the sun glinted off the top of the water. Niah swam to shore and I followed after her, grateful for a moment when no one could see my face. I couldn't stop grinning. I couldn't believe I did that. I channeled *and* regained control when I started spiraling.

"How do you know all this?" I asked as we lay ourselves out to dry in the sun.

"I'm a good listener." She winked at me.

What a peculiar non-answer. I stared at her and tried to picture who she'd been listening to in order to learn all this. Maybe the Manters?

"I think you're ready," she said, surveying me.

"For what?" Alaric asked, coming to join us, the Manter in tow.

"To accept the bond." Niah sat up on her elbows and pulled a hand over her brow as she squinted up at Alaric.

A seed of dread dropped into my belly.

"No, no, no." I groaned.

"Why not?" She squinted from Alaric to me and smiled.

"Why should I?" I countered, sitting up and crossing my arms over my chest.

"You want to stay limited in your abilities? Be a perpetual risk to everyone's wellbeing? Not to mention put our entire world in jeopardy of imbalance and destruction just because you won't man the gate according to your birthright? Sounds kinda selfish if you ask me." She wrung out her wet ponytail and shook the excess water from her hands.

*Ouch.* I didn't have an answer for her. She could be right. Maybe I was being selfish. But I had the right to be selfish. Accepting the role of gatekeeper would mean I'd have to live the rest of my natural life in Biddenmore, *in England.* Ugh! I wanted to get out of my parent's shadow, bust out of their constricting will for my life. Signing up to be the protector of some portal was the exact opposite of that.

Alaric eased down beside me. Energy radiated off him like a furnace. The droplets of water that clung to my top and skin began to evaporate. I caught myself shifting closer to feel more of his warmth and drying effect. As I did, a red hot poker of anger stirred in my belly. I recognized this clearly as my channeling gift, and closed myself off to it. Slowly, I was beginning to differentiate the gifts of others from my own emotions. It made me thrilled, and so proud of myself.

I let my mind wander. What if I did accept the bond ritual? What if, like Josephine and Effie, I used the portal and came to visit sometimes? A small spark kindled at the idea of seeing Alaric again.

"So the energy harvest is coming up," Niah said innocuously.

Just hearing the words made my stomach sour, and *poof!* there went the daydream. Now all I could think about was how Moss told me the Manter's used last month's collection to save me. I couldn't bear the thought of showing my face there.

"I'm not sure it's a good idea," Alaric said, casually picking up my thoughts.

He shifted closer to me, his arm brushing against mine. The anger that was previously stoked by his nearness reappeared as intensity. It was just a seed until he scratched his knee, knuckles grazing my leg, then it unfurled into something more. It took all of my self control not to press my skin against his. A blush raced up my face. I was embarrassed by my sudden craving for his touch. I distinctly shifted myself away from him and tried to wrangle my thoughts away from his prying senses.

"Scout can totally handle it, if that's what you're worried about," Niah said coolly.

Alaric chuckled, and my skin flamed hot, registering the feeling of his eyes on me. It was more intense than it should have been for this conversation and I knew he didn't miss the racing thoughts I struggled to banish.

"Scout, listen. If you can do that," she said to me, pointing out at the lake, "you can share in the energy harvest."

*If only that was what I was worried about.* I chewed my lip as she hopped up to shake off the excess water and trotted back to camp.

Walking back from Lake Hollow, Alaric didn't mention what happened earlier. I counted my lucky stars. It was enough to suffer embarrassment once; I didn't need to relive it again. It was moments like these that I really hated the fact that he could hear my thoughts.

"What do you think I should do?" I asked, changing my line of thought before it could get sidetracked.

"Why are you asking me?"

"I don't know. You seem like you've got a pretty good handle on how things work around here."

He barked out a humorless laugh. "Do I?"

"And I don't know, I trust you for some reason."

"You shouldn't," he said gruffly, the distance between us growing.

"Why do you do that?" I stopped.

He turned slowly, eyebrows arched over empty, distant eyes.

I gestured between us. "This."

He stepped closer, eyes shimmering back to life and searched my face.

"Every time we start to get close, you pull away. I mean, I get it if you're not interested, but..." I trailed off, not wanting to be blunt.

"If only it were that simple." He shuffled over to a tree along the path and leaned against it.

"Why can't it be?"

"It's dangerous. *I'm* dangerous," he said, looking up through the tree's leaves, head lolled against its bark. "Haven't you heard?"

I took a step closer.

"You can't seem to touch me without getting incinerated with anger or fire. You think I want that for you?" The pained look in his eyes flickered through so quickly that I barely caught a glimpse of it. But I did. I saw it.

I took another step closer, only an arm's length apart now. I could reach out and touch his face, as I've caught myself dreaming of doing a time or two.

"Don't. It'll be worse for you if we start something." He pushed off the tree.

"I want to try something—" I caught his arm as he turned away.

He tried to slip out of my grasp, but I latched on.

"Please, Alaric." When I felt myself losing, I added, "It's for training purposes."

He huffed and turned to me, lips pursed, and crossed his arms over his chest. His left eyebrow quirked up in response.

"Every time I touch someone powerful, I get flares of their gift, right?"

Alaric didn't say anything in response, waiting for me to go on.

"So, what if I could control that? And before you say anything—no. This doesn't have anything to do with you. This is about me trying to find a semblance of ownership for these abilities that have been thrust upon me for God knows what reason. Okay?" I attempted my most confident stance and withering glare.

His eyes roved over me for a long beat until finally he nodded and stepped back in concession. "All right, let's see what you got."

*All right*, I think to myself. *This is happening.*

I shook my hands out and gave my neck a roll. The energy didn't require me to do this, but something about this physical warm up made me feel more ready to go. To a regular steward I must have looked so stupid, but I was owning this now.

After what happened with Niah and seeing how my training was progressing with the Manter, there was no denying that this gift wasn't going anywhere. I could fight it, but to what point? Niah was right. I was being selfish if I didn't get it under control.

All this time I was waiting for a way out of the plan my parents had for me, some cataclysmic event that derailed the duke train. Well, *this* was it. Being a channeler, being in Landow.

Living with my aunties in their cottage forever as a gatekeeper didn't feel quite right, and I wasn't completely sold on the idea of completing the bond ritual. This, however, being a channeler, training with the Manters, being with Alaric... *This* felt right. *This* made sense.

I took another deep breath and let the weight of the moment fill me. The peace that surrounded me felt light and airy, a sweet sensation. I recognized that as the earth's energy. Welcoming it in to recharge me for a moment, I stepped closer to Alaric, who stood in place, scrutinizing me. I recognized the change in the air. The sweetness dropped away and the intensity of energy that sparked from him was loud, aggressive, attention-seeking. My thoughts bent and formed to it, and I retreated before I lost control over it.

Closing my eyes, I willed myself to shut down the outside stimuli, to build a wall to keep it out. I imagined the wall being built. Strong, sturdy stones stacked like bricks. I reinforced the wall in my mind with putty between the stones, leaving no crevices for the energy to seep through. Once the bulwark was built, I stepped closer to Alaric to test it out.

We were only a few feet apart, bathed in the forest's greenery. I lingered there, but didn't feel the sensation of his energy. A twig snapped beneath my foot as I shifted closer, closing the gap. Alaric was within arm's reach, and somewhere deep inside my chest was an ache to feel his skin. A tingle raced across my chest, dancing over my collarbones. I reached out to him, my knuckles brushing the outer form of his arm.

I was keenly aware of how close we were. A frisson of energy sparked between us, breaking my focus. For a moment, I was a mere human girl... did I smell okay? Did my hair look combed, and—*That's enough. Focus.*

That's when I realized it! Before, when I came in contact with Alaric's energy, there was no time for outside thoughts or my own, because his energy, the fire, was such a commanding presence that I couldn't do anything but entertain it.

"It worked!"

My eyes popped open and I beamed up at Alaric. A smirk flashed quickly before his face crumpled.

"What's wrong?"

His eyes, pulsating bright reds and oranges, glowed in a way that warmed my soul. The yearning in my chest tugged me closer to him. I wrapped a hand around his bicep and felt his strength. His hand landed gently at my waist, tentative at first. My body fanned to flame, beginning just over my heart, under my collarbone.

He wasn't breathing, as his head bowed toward mine. His gaze utterly consumed me. His grip tightened on my waist.

I dropped the barrier between us, craving not just the feel of his skin, but of his presence and power.

His hand cupped my cheek softly and I leaned into his warm palm.

The lines in his face deepened into grooves, and the sorrow in his eyes almost broke my heart.

"I can't." He pulled back, dropping his hands from my waist and face. He skirted around me, careful not to jostle me.

Instantly, I missed his warmth. Left breathless in his wake, I felt more alive and frustrated than before. We were so close. I could feel him, *really* feel him. I was finally able to let him in, and not be absorbed by the fire energy. The disappointment had me reeling.

The rest of our walk back to camp passed in silence, several meters apart in the forest. Alaric glanced back every so often, making sure that I didn't lose sight of him, but far enough to get some space from my thoughts, I imagined.

# Alaric

As evening fell, Khalon greeted us to begin our weekly meeting at Mireille's hut. Despite the current goings-on that completely reshaped life as we knew it, he wanted us to focus on something normal: the harvest party.

Despite his best efforts, the harvest party was the furthest thing from my mind. I kept trying to replay the moment we shared in the woods, but the vicious dream interrupted my thoughts now just as it had ruined our moment. Maybe I should be grateful. The terrible dream memory stopped me from doing something we'd both regret. It was the perfect reminder of what was at stake.

"This month's harvest party just so happens to coincide with All Fates Day." Khalon's eyes roved over the group, waiting for them to quiet down. "It is our annual celebration in honor of the Fates in hopes that we shall receive their blessings in the coming year. It's the one time of year where our moon separates as a mirror image and resets—the Twin Moons, a symbol of the divine Twins. It's believed to be the most powerful night of the year. A time for a divine realignment... It used to be a time when all the portals were accessible by both sides." Khalon smiled around the gathering. A smattering of his leaders and Airian's guard joined us for the meeting.

"Recite with me the ancient oracle of the Inaras: *All things hidden come to light, all things withheld are made right, while all things fated are found and what's left bated is bound.*"

Mireille, an ethereal, ever still presence at my side, leaned close to whisper. "Remember, if you don't tell her by All Fates Day, the Fates will do it for you. The truth will come out." She slid her gaze up to me in an *I told you so* sort of way.

"So they say," I grumbled back.

Airian stepped up beside Khalon, chest puffed out, asking for more attention than he was worth. I bit my tongue.

"Our emissary in Prentiss has sent an update. The Inaras believe this year's Twin Moons event will surpass each one that has come before it. If the observations are to be believed, the energy surge that will come from this lunar cleaving will be enough to power our village for decades." Khalon unfolded the message written on thick paper, something we didn't have access to here in Ruack Valley. My fingers twitched remembering the feel of fibrous papers of hand bound books. The pleasure of Khalon's camp was found in its simplicity, how removed it was from the progressive—and sometimes aggressive—nature of the cities in Kilburne and Prentiss.

"What about the channeler? Are we in jeopardy?" Before Khalon could continue reading the remarks from the emissary, he was interrupted by a voice from within our midst.

"Yeah, has she done the ritual yet?" another hastily added.

A montage of grumbles rose around the circle.

"The channeler has been contained. She is being closely watched and guarded for the safety of everyone here. We intend to leverage the lunar episode during tomorrow night's festival to complete her bond acceptance ritual." Airian said, the smugness of his tone wasn't lost on me.

As they talked about her, my skin crawled. A fierce need to protect her spread like a forest fire in my chest. I wouldn't let them force her hand.

"We are working with the gatekeeper to prepare her and train her," Khalon said amicably. Rustling the paper in his hands, he returned his attention to it. "The emissary sent a warning, 'During the Inaras' preparations for All Fates Day, a Tembi broke into the Temple.'" A few gasps sounded around the group, and my fingers flew to the bridge of my nose, pushing back against the throb that formed in my head.

Tembis were an enormous nuisance. Their ethereal, non-corporeal bodies made them well-suited to espionage, and their slimy ambition and tendency to favor manipulation made them valued assets to Soleil. While under her reign, I had run into my fair share of Tembis. While they could gather intel proficiently, reporting back to Soleil in real time through her Well of Sight, they weren't an apex predator. I hadn't come across any Tembis who had serious potential to harm.

"'After giving the Inaras a scare, the Tembi left without a word. The Tembi was then spotted roaming the border of Prentiss and Ruack Valley. Be on high alert.' It seems the Tembi is after something specific," Khalon folded the paper as a grave expression clouded his usually jovial features. "And he didn't find it in Prentiss."

Khalon's eyes met mine across the fire. *He's after Scout.*

*That's fine,* I wanted to say, *Soleil's Tembi would have to go through me before ever laying eyes on Scout.*

### ) ) ) ● ( ( (

After the meeting was concluded, I waited for the guard and leaders to disperse before approaching Mireille. "I need to speak with you."

"Ah, well this is a first. Usually, I have to pry it out of you." Mireille poked at the fire and looked up at me, eyes alight. "How have the nightmares been? Any more dreams from the Creators?" She sat with me at the fire now that everyone was gone.

"Yes, but that's not what I wanted to talk to you about." A recent dream came to mind, one I hadn't made sense of yet. Scout stood before a vault, organizing the treasures and distributing them. It didn't make much sense, especially since most of my dreams of her lately had been blood-tinged and laden with my screams. But Mireille couldn't help me with the interpretation. Only the Creators knew the truth and would reveal it in time.

She shifted her weight to really look at me. "She's resisting the bond, isn't she?"

I sighed. "Also not what I wanted to talk to you about."

She squinted. For a Manter, she had untapped wisdom, but as an imprinted bond of mine, her bias gave her a blindspot.

"I heard someone the other night. Their thoughts were—" I shuddered. "They were hunting for Scout. They wanted to hurt her, take her."

Her lips formed a question, but she refrained. If I were anyone else, she would ask: *How do you know that? Are you sure?* But as the only mind reader here in camp, it made it hard to misunderstand people. Even those who tended to be a bit slimy, hoping to hide behind the subtle lies of a misconception. Even they couldn't escape the lie detection I was cursed with. It's a lonely existence, I'll admit.

"You're sure?" she said anyway, for lack of knowing what else to say, I assumed.

"It couldn't have been anything else. But that's not all. When I chased them, I saw them steward fire." I paused to let that sink in. Another fire steward in our midst. How could we have missed it? How could one have snuck in?

Mireille didn't reply as she thought through all possible scenarios.

"I ended up losing them in the thick woods behind her and Moss's tent."

"Did you tell Khalon?"

I shook my head. As far as leading a community, he was great. But I was a man of war. I didn't need someone to tell me what to do when there was a threat. My body was primed for action. It itched for the adrenaline some days. *Curse Soleil for making me this way. Curse the Fates for making this bond the impetus of a threat against Scout...* And yet, it was also the very thing that generated my need to protect her.

"Who do you think it was?"

"I'm not sure. I've been trying to identify them on my own, but either they aren't among us or they are *very* good at shielding their thoughts." *Too good not to have formal training,* I thought. "It was someone small in stature. Quick too. They left a footprint, and some small blue flowers sprung up from within it. Could someone from outside have gotten in?"

"A hybrid?" She paused to think of the possibility before dismissing it in disdain. "No, you heard Khalon and Airian. These past weeks, our defenses have been doubled. It would be nearly impossible for someone to get in undetected."

"So it had to be someone already inside Ruack Valley?" The revelation chilled me from the inside out.

*I don't want to think about that possibility.*

She paused and I heard her thoughts unfold as she processed the information, tripping over the blue flowers. Various images of flowers flashed through her mind before I recognized it.

"That's the one," I interrupted her flow of thought.

"Gravebloom." Mireille's eyes flashed to mine, full of fear. "That's a very poisonous plant, one that is not native to Ruack Valley."

An ominous silence fell between us, and I schooled my fear-filled thoughts into stoic obedience.

"We can talk about something else," Mireille said with an air of compassion. "So, she's resisting the bond? You couldn't turn on your natural charm to woo her?" Mireille jested.

My lungs deflated in a heavy sigh. Not the topic I hoped to switch to, but certainly one capable of distracting me. Mireille had no idea of the real struggle. Turning away from Scout hurt me deeply. Not emotionally, but physically; the imprint begged to be acknowledged. It was tortuous as a steward to deny one. Mireille never had to deny one. Few stewards had the pleasure of receiving an imprint, and even fewer would dare deny one.

*I'm not sure how much longer I can stay away from her.* My muscles ached for exertion, but it would be morning before I was schedule for a patrol run.

"Wooing her is the furthest thing from my mind. Keeping her alive is my only priority." Grumbling, I stalked off to chop some wood.

# 44

# Scout

"I really don't want to go to this thing."

It had been a couple days since Alaric and I had shared a moment in the woods, and he was most definitely avoiding me since then. Again. In his place, Maël had walked me around camp. He was more stoic and severe than Alaric. After working in the garden each morning with Moss, Maël would retrieve me with a grunt and take me to the Manter's, where I spent the rest of my day training. But just training. I definitely wasn't waiting around hoping Alaric would stop by.

"Too bad!" Niah said. She had a death grip on my arm as she yanked me up the wooded trail toward the clearing. The afternoon sun kissed us goodbye with waning warmth, and a breeze caught my hair, blowing it over my shoulder, and whistled through the thinning leaves. The air was crisp, as if fall was on its way, but welcome after working all day in the garden with Moss.

"Come on!" Niah tugged me again, causing me to stumble over my feet. Alaric never yanked me. But it seemed he had better things to do than escort me to this festival, so I'd have to deal with Niah in his place.

"Hey, Scout! Hey, Niah!" Rhydian appeared beside us, dressed in the usual primitive fabrics everyone around here wore. Although, upon closer inspection, I saw gleaming threads woven throughout, as though this was a special tunic. When we passed the trail's junction near the guys' tent circle, he fell in step beside us. "I bet it's gonna be a good one tonight." He wiggled his eyebrows at Niah and me. It was the first time I could get a good look at him since what happened in the clearing. His exorcism.

"Ugh, what are you guys planning?" Niah moaned playfully. I studied their interaction. Rhydian didn't seem worse for wear; he actually seemed more relaxed. Less like he was striving or pretending, more free to be himself.

"Oh, you'll see!" Rhydian winked again at me then raced ahead.

"What was that about?" I asked, watching Rhydian disappear around the thicket.

"Oh, every month the guys do something crazy for the Harvest party. You know, typical guy stuff."

I lifted my eyebrows and nodded, though I had no idea what the stewards would consider as "typical guy stuff." If I were back home, I would have expected pranks, belching contests, or other stupid games devised to make the guys look macho. But here? Where the guys weren't human and had powerful energy at their fingertips? I wasn't sure whether to be amused or afraid.

We broke through the bush that overgrew the path to the river and stepped into the clearing. The sorting tables that used to be covered in piles of dirty vegetables were now cleaned. The tables were covered in lavish-looking flowers and vines with chopped vegetables and dried fruits and meats arranged delicately.

"The Harvest Table," Moss said with a flourish of her hand. She stood on the other side of it from us, where she was meticulously laying out fresh flowers around plates, adorning the table with fragrant herbs that complemented the food.

There were fire-lit torches on poles around the table, and a few taller ones marked out around the clearing to see in the dark. Off beyond the community garden was a massive bonfire. There were whole sections of tree trunks lying carved out as seating around the fire. It almost looked cozy, like an elevated kegger in the woods. I made a mental note in case I ever got home to my friends. They would love something like this. My heart sank. *Would I ever see Macy and Danny again?* Not likely.

"What are you smirking about?" Moss joined us now.

"Oh, it's nothing. This all looks really great," I told her.

"Yeah, you guys did a great job, Moz." Niah gave her a light push, and Moss blushed at the compliment.

"Awe, thanks, guys! I couldn't have done it without all the help." She gestured to the crowd of others, all milling around the clearing.

As we got closer to the bonfire, I saw a pig roasting over it. A charred carcass hung from the spit. I had to admit, it smelled much better than it looked. My stomach growled as I realized it had been a while since we had eaten meat. I glanced through the crowd, taking it all in, when Moss crooned over my shoulder, "Looking for someone?"

Turning to swat her, I breathed through the heavy blush. "No, I was just looking at everything."

Niah was already off chatting with some other blue-eyed stewards, and Rhydian was nowhere to be found. Moss moved across the fire to sit with a couple of other green-eyed girls while I sat on the carved-out tree trunk and took it all in. The sky was pitch black, no moon. Stars studded the atmosphere, giving the faintest impression of freckles. I breathed in the night air, held it, and relished it. It smelled like smoky, earthy goodness.

When I breathed it out and opened my eyes, I saw Alaric on the other side of the bonfire, his eyes on mine. I didn't even have a moment to think before he backed into the shadows and was gone.

I was more than a little surprised at both the fact that he turned away from me and the amount of rejection that surfaced. The last time I was this hung up on the interactions of a guy was with Danny.

*Danny.* I couldn't believe I had forgotten all about him. There was a time when I could have sworn I was in love with him. The tousled brown hair and bright blue eyes had me a goner. But being in Landow, I felt a thousand light-years away. Any high school crush I harbored grew stale the moment I passed through the portal and entered survival mode. Thinking of him now made me miss him.

"Ahem," a throat cleared behind me.

I nearly jumped out of my skin after being so wrapped up in my thoughts. I turned to see Alaric standing beside me. I stood so he wasn't towering quite so far above my line of sight.

"So who's *Danny*?" His irises pulsed blood red. "And do I need to be worried about him?"

"Well, that's forward." I laughed to cover my complete embarrassment. *Time for a subject change.* "Where have you been lately?"

Just then, a large group of young-looking stewards poured into the bonfire area, bottlenecking between the logs. They jostled against Alaric and me, shoving us together. His arms wrapped around me, stabilizing me.

Everywhere his body touched mine lit up with surprising warmth and pleasure. I expected him to pull back immediately, the way he always seemed to, but he didn't. The familiar sensation of Alaric's energy kindled in my body, and the pit in my being yawned open in response. It began to suck the energy from him, but I paused and breathed. Allowing my eyelids to shutter closed, I folded in on myself. I imagined the barrier surrounding my heart and the cavernous place where this gift dwelt within me. The hunger lashed out against the barrier, but couldn't cross it. Likewise, Alaric's energy licked at the gate, but I didn't feel consumed by it.

I opened my eyes and looked up into his. Alaric's gaze was hotter than the bonfire, and the reds and deeper burgundies smoldered into me. A heat burned through me, but it had nothing to do with the energy he was emanating. A pained expression flickered across his face, and I wondered what it meant. He looked tortured every time he touched me.

"Airian had me on an assignment. I hope Maël was..." He trailed off, seemingly at a loss for how to finish the sentence. I assume he knew exactly how Maël was. Professional and grumpy. I had missed him while he was gone.

His eyes raked over me in mirth, picking out the thought, and I realized he still hadn't let go. For a moment, I was tempted to question his interest in me. But as I grew up, my dad instilled a confidence in me that I wouldn't waste, not even for a boy.

I tilted my chin up just a fraction and let my gaze wander down to his lips, longing to pick up where we left off before. My thoughts were clear and inviting—there could be no misunderstanding of the idea I was entertaining about him.

"Not here." His voice was a low, husky whisper. He leaned in to place his lips to my ear, and a chill dripped down my spine. "Airian has me running patrol this evening, but if you need me, just think of me and I'll be there."

He pulled back from me, his hand cupping the side of my face, and I leaned into it. *This feels right.* A prickle at my collarbone piqued my attention. I rubbed my fingers across the cloth tunic.

"I'll be back," he said again in a low tone and disappeared into the crowd.

I turned back to look at the majority of stewards, all dancing and enjoying the fresh food. It dawned on me that I hadn't really tried to make friends here. Everyone I'd met had been forced on me or me on them since arriving here. *Show yourself friendly, Scout.* My mother's voice chided in the back of my mind. It worked with Niah. What's the worst that could happen?

I stood up and hovered just behind the bonfire and the benches, looking for someone to talk to. As I peered across the field, my shoulder jostled.

"Oh, sorry 'bout that."

I turned to see a pale girl with platinum eyes. Her voice was a lower register and heavily accented. She was obliviously caught up in a conversation with a shorter guy with long blond hair before she bumped into me. She returned to the conversation after excusing herself.

"Hey." I reached out to slow her. "I'm Scout. No worries, by the way."

She paused to look me over. The warmth on my body receded as I waited for a backlash of rejection. I held my breath. Maybe she didn't speak any English, and the interaction would be over painlessly...

"Elodie," she said, then jerked a thumb over her shoulder to the blonde guy. "This is Warrick."

My lungs deflated. I smiled. "Cool. Nice to meet you guys. Actually, I think we met on my first day here?" I gestured to Warrick.

Warrick nodded briefly, then cast his gaze around the fire, already bored.

"So..." And then I realized that's all I've got. *What I'd trade to get home again, to be surrounded by my friends who I didn't have to work so hard to create conversations with.*

"So," Elodie picked up, "that weather the other day?" Then she gave me a wink.

Did she know I caused the storm? Did *everyone* know I caused the storm?

"Yeah," I chuckled nervously, then coughed to cover it up. "Moss said it was a freak storm."

Elodie's eyes sparked, the platinum glowing brighter. They were the same as Airian's; maybe she could make little earthquakes too.

"I think we both know the term 'freak accident' was used to cover up a misuse of energy," Warrick snickered. "Remember when the guys tried to make a whirlpool in the river but ended up flooding the whole camp? Yeah, that was a..." He paused to raise his hands and made air quotes dramatically. "*Freak accident.*"

We all three laughed. Warrick knocked my shoulder. "Don't sweat it. We all flub it up from time to time. Emotions get high, bad days happen, you know." He shrugged, wobbled his hands, and let them float on into the invisible horizon.

I groaned. "So I'm guessing everyone knows I was the 'freak accident'?" I used the air quotes like Warrick did.

"Sorta." Elodie scrunched her face up as her pitch got high, and I realized immediately she was the worst liar. So I laughed.

"I appreciate the attempt, but it's fine. I'm a big girl. I gotta learn eventually I guess."

"So how weird is it being here right now?" She turned towards me and crossed her arms over her chest.

I took the opportunity to look at her and Warrick. Elodie had pale hair, pale skin, and pale, platinum eyes. If I met her in my world, I'd think she was albino. Warrick, on the other hand, looked like a Californian surfer bro. He was tan with long, blond hair and ocean eyes.

"Beyond weird," I said. "It's like every day there's something new to come along and wreck my sense of life as I knew it."

"Yeah, I bet. Finding out you're a channeler is no joke," Elodie said, eyes lowered.

Warrick whistled as if to say, *that's a doozy.*

"It's been... what?" Elodie started.

"A *long* time since we've had a channeler in Landow." Warrick ran a hand through his blond hair and shot Elodie an alarming look.

"What do you–"

Elodie cleared her throat, "Did they prepare you for the merging twin moons—"

Someone whistled loudly and pierced the joyful chatter.

I gritted my teeth. I only needed a moment longer to learn what Elodie was going to share.

"Can everyone gather around?"

# Scout

"Excuse me! Can everyone gather around?" Airian's voice wasn't as commanding as the previous times I'd heard it, and there was a small smile on the corners of his lips. He was giving off-duty teacher vibes. *You know, when you see your teacher on vacation and you realize they have a first name?*

Everyone moseyed towards the bonfire. A few stragglers remained at the harvest table, enjoying the literal fruit of their labor. I looked around and watched as small groups congregated together. I was left standing alone after Warrick and Elodie moved to sit with other platinum-eyed stewards. I moved back towards the bonfire and took a new seat on the hollowed-out tree trunk.

Khalon stepped up in the light of the fire. The tall flames flicked across his face and stretched his profile in lengthy shadows behind him. Khalon was smiling, each of his movements laden with energy and flair. He gestured widely to welcome everyone.

"I am so thankful to have thrived through another lunar cycle with you all." He brought his hands to his heart and looked lovingly on the people. I could see why they loved him—he was an emotional and jovial leader.

"I want to personally thank everyone for the good harvest we've had thus far this season. I know the hours are long and the days are short. We have worked fearlessly and tirelessly to provide for our community and to right the injustice of imbalance in our world."

I glanced around the circle. The crowd was at least ten-deep in some places and every face was enraptured by their king's voice.

"Let us take a moment of silence to honor the Fates that have provided for us so richly and give thanks for the abundant harvest." Everyone bowed their heads and closed their eyes.

His phrasing instantly reminded me of how Aunt Zelda used to start dinner each night. Maybe there was more to the idea of my great-grandmother being here. Suddenly, the idea of my great-grandmother experiencing this ceremony, living in this camp, and taking all her knowledge back to her daughters flickered through my head. I wanted to focus on the moment of nostalgia, of connection to a more familiar time.

But my mind whirled at a thousand thoughts per second, and I couldn't close my eyes. So I settled my gaze into my lap and waited to hear the others shuffling around me.

"We owe our lives to the sun, the earth, the wind, and the water. Without these factions, we would be empty vessels. But what's more, without the Fates and their Twins, we would not exist. So let us give thanks and rejoice for the wonderful power of these elements and the Fates that look after us every day."

Everyone broke into shouts, whistles, and clapping. The spirit was contagious and I found myself grinning in surprise. I spotted Moss, and she, too, was beaming and clapping, her green eyes alight with love for her source.

"It is with great honor that I introduce one of our most beloved elders, Xylina." He turned to make way for an older woman to step into the firelight. She looked like the Manters, old and wrinkled by the passing of time. I wondered how old she was—she must be in her eighties, but then I remembered what Khalon said about Moss. This elder was old compared to a two-hundred-year-old Moss, who appeared as a teenager. I didn't even want to know how old Xylina was. My head would actually explode.

"Xylina will lead us in our energy harvest. Please give her your rapt attention and begin grounding yourselves for the offering."

The elder stepped into full view as Khalon bowed and retreated behind her, next to Airian and the guards. When she began speaking, her voice haunted over us in a melancholy melody.

"Several ages ago, a chasm opened in our world. It took time and a lot of energy to close the gap. We were not prepared for such a rift, and because we were ill-prepared, it cost us many lives, and we forfeited much of our sacred ancestry's power. Since that time, we have utilized our community gatherings as a most anointed time for energy pulling. You have all come to know it as the energy harvest. For some of you young stewards, let me explain."

She settled herself on an upright log as a stool. "Each lunar cycle dictates to us how the sowing, reaping, and harvesting will go. And each new moon, we gather together to celebrate and bless the elements for providing for us. We sing, we dance, and we feast!" She raised a fist in huzzah, and others laughed and cheered with her.

"But what we often overlook is the cost of this harvest. The powers of our world are finite. Age after age, there are new demands and challenges we are presented with. We are the keepers and stewards of what has been entrusted to us. Let us not go on another night forsaking the memory of our ancestors and what they have fought for us to take for granted." She gazed around the circle, making pointed eye contact with some of the young-looking ones in our midst. Finally her eyes rested on me. And fear struck my core. I was not ready to be seen by her or anyone right now. I blinked rapidly and ducked my head to break eye contact.

"Tonight's energy harvest is unlike all others before it. Once a year, our moons splits in two, a divine reminder that we are to honor the Fates and their Twins. As we enter into the harvest this evening, the new moon will be reborn as twins, and once all have completed their offering, we will bathe in its light and be restored."

She continued. "Tonight, Airian, Khalon, Alaric, and the Manters will stand together and prepare the fire before us. Each of you will recognize the call of energy to come and give of your gift. None of us will know how much you are called to deposit nor how much you will surrender. That is between you and the Fates. May the fire find you honest or you will reap discord. For you cannot mock the call or the source. If you do, it will cost you your life."

She stood and bowed as her exit. Her speech was much more haunting and serious in tone than that of Khalon's. One would say she was a real bummer, man.

Khalon stepped back up and clapped broadly and with great invigoration. "Remember the common good we serve by sharing in the energy harvest. There have been times through the ages when our own have needed help beyond what one mere Manter can do. There have been lives saved and chasms closed by the power in our energy reservoir. We are all born for a purpose, and now is the time to take part in something bigger than yourselves."

I blushed, knowing I was one of those people who had benefited from the reservoir. Heat crept up the back of my neck. Everyone knew.

He clapped in closing, drawing my attention again. He gestured to Airian and the Manter, who took up places directly behind him. He looked for Alaric around the fire. He must have spotted him and he gestured for him to come now.

The four of them stepped up to the fire and a gentle hush was laid over the crowd. No one spoke. Only the sounds of fire crackling, birds conferring in the trees, and wind blowing gently around us. The four began making shapes with their hands in the air, and the fire wobbled and expanded in front of us. They slashed their hands through the air, murmuring in their native tongue in sync like chanting a spell.

This was definitely the most "magic-y" thing I'd seen since being here. Aside from what happened at the lake... and everyone's glowing eyes... and okay, who was I kidding? It had all been *very* magic-y for me. So I stole another look at the others around me and noticed no one else was very surprised. Looked like their regular old Tuesday faces.

But it didn't sound like a regular Tuesday ritual.

They finished and stepped back.

Khalon spoke in a subdued voice. "Let the Fates call to you. Come when they call."

And silence fell over us.

The first to step up to the fire was a woman who looked middle-aged. She stood before the fire and gazed into the flames; she had glowing green eyes and they swirled for a few seconds before stopping. She backed up and nodded to Khalon who bowed his head and mouthed, "thank you" to her.

The next to come up was a green-eyed man, who did the same. Several people came up one after the other. Each only took about five to ten seconds before stepping back. Some eyes swirled faster, brighter, or slower. I didn't know how that translated to the passing of energy or the "surrender," as Xylina called it.

As I watched others come and go, the deep vacuum stretched out inside me like waking up from a nap. *Oh no.* This was not the time or place for a light show. I gripped my hands into fists and willed it away. It gnawed for attention on the outskirts of my mind.

I bore my eyes into the logs on fire in front of me. I counted the lapping waves of smoke. But there was no ignoring this awakened beast of hunger inside me. Niah told me to learn to recognize the energy around me. But it didn't take a stirring inside me to recognize the energy when stewards were lining up to *steward it* right in front of me. The energy was fairly blatant.

But I reminded myself that I could build the wall around it, a barrier to protect myself. *I can do this. I just have to focus.*

I tried to turn and back away from my front row seat at the energy harvest, but the crowd was pressed in so closely that there was no getting out. My breathing quickened, I needed to find a quieter place before the panic got to me.

Fluttering my eyes to refocus my gaze, I saw only the fire in front of me. Only heard the logs popping and sizzling. *This is good, Scout, focus.* Slow shuffles echoed through the grass as one after the other, stewards came forth to surrender a measure of energy.

The energy surged and begged for my attention—it burned through me. I couldn't let it out though. I began to sweat from the wrestle. My fists flexed and my nails gripped into my palms. *I'm not sure I can do this on my own. Alaric?*

His gaze swept to mine across the fire. His eyes, usually alight with a warm glow felt cold as steel as he pursed his lips and gave a slight shake of his head.

Before I knew it, my feet were gliding me to the ring around the fire. Whispers gasped around me and my cheeks burned in embarrassment. I had no intention of doing this. I cursed my body, my feet, this thing inside that betrayed me.

I gazed into the fire and had no control. I wanted to speak, to quietly apologize or beg for help.

There was so much inside me that I wanted to say to them: *You don't have to be afraid of me! I would never hurt you, never hurt anyone!* But there weren't any words. There was only this dire feeling inside me that I had to get out.

My chest throbbed, and the blood rushed through me, its warmth oozing from the inside out.

"Focus, Scout. Take a deep breath." Niah's voice cut through every other sound. She appeared beside me and held my hand. Her calming presence was a gift in that moment.

I heeded her advice and closed my eyes to take a deep breath. I tried to focus on the energy, but it was all around me. It poked in at me, asking for attention from all sides. It overstimulated my senses. I tried to find the barrier I built before, but I couldn't get my thoughts straightened out long enough to find it.

A fear streaked through me. *I am going to lose control again.*

A whisper in the wind hurled words at me. *You don't know what you're doing. You can't do this.*

"Hold on, Scout." Niah's voice was strained. "Ground it out and release it slow like a breath."

I did as she said and the growling pit in my stomach closed. Satisfied. I sighed with relief. That was close. The fire was mixed with all the colors and burned brighter and bigger than before. I looked up for Alaric, expecting to see his smile, but he wasn't there.

A hesitant smattering of applause followed. They were as unsure about this as I was.

As the next hour passed, I enjoyed watching the stewards approach, one by one, taking their turns to make their surrender. Once everyone had gone, the feasting resumed.

Someone was singing a lively jig, a few clapped and stomped, beating on random things as makeshift drums. While a few other stewards danced, I took in the view. The night was crisp and felt like anything could happen. Their joy in the festival was reckless and contagious. My body wanted to move, to dance, to be caught up in the celebration of it.

Above us, the black sky began to carve out space for the Twin Moons to make their debut. Looking around for Moss, I spied her lying in the grass watching the moons take shape. I joined her. At first, it was a rapid evolution from new moon to full moon. Then the full moon split and morphed as its twin moon hovered next to it in the sky.

Xylina's haunting voice beckoned us back to the fire. "It's time."

# Scout

We slowly crowded around the glorious, enchanted fire, and as we did, I lost sight of Moss. There was something even more magical about it, knowing we all had a part in creating it. Even me, with this capricious new channeling power. I did something good to help others with my gift!

The fulfillment of it buzzed within me. I looked for Alaric, thinking how nice it would be to share this joy with him. But I hadn't seen him since earlier.

Xylina repeated her earlier sentiments about the Twin Moons event and invited everyone to form a series of lines in front of the Manters where they were stationed at the harvest table. She instructed us to take and drink from the cups in the Manters' hands before going to lie down in the moonbeam.

I floated into line behind Elodie and Warrick.

"Hey," I said, "no one mentioned this." I pointed ahead of us to the Manters with golden goblets. "I was always taught not to drink the *Koolaid*." I elbowed Elodie, and let her know it's a joke with a wink.

Her brows dipped in confusion and she chuckled before turning back to her conversation with Warrick.

As we reached the front of the line, Airian came to whisper in the ear of a Manter I'd never seen before. It was Elodie's turn. She sipped from her goblet and bowed low in deference before going to join the other stewards lying in the grass. I followed suit and stepped up to the Manter, but she gestured for me to move out of line. She led me to the harvest table at the edge of the clearing, far enough away that the sound of the stewards was a faint din. There she handed me a different goblet and urged me to drink. It was cold and sweet enough to make my jaw ache. The overwhelming taste of licorice flooded my mouth. But the after taste was an earthy, rotten thing. It reminded me of the Mireille's concoction.

Airian returned with a few things in his hands, and a knot began to form in my stomach.

"Turns out our ritual isn't safe for channelers," he said without looking at me. Instead, Airian lowered his arms to the table and spread out the items. A bowl, some stones, and a jar of dark shimmering powder.

"One of the Manters informed us on how to prepare your specific gift to receive from the Twin Moon. According to her, we need to cleanse you under the full moon." He glanced up and saw the moon full in all its beaming glory. Its separation wasn't complete yet. "We should hurry."

He grabbed a decanter of water from the table and used it to fill his bowl. He spoke in his native language over it and lifted it under the moonlight. When he returned it to the table, he took my hands and placed them in the bowl. Next, he took the shimmering black powder and began to dust it up my arms.

A hot tingle lit up my spine and spread out across my body. Something deep in my gut told me this wasn't right.

When he pulled the small pouch from his pocket, dread unfurled in my chest. I knew that pouch would contain polished stones. He upended the pouch in a smooth motion, and into his palm, gemstones clinked. My mind raced back to the moment in the greenhouse with my aunts. When they submerged my hands and lined gemstones up my arms. The fear was hot and glanced through me, quick as panic. I ended up disrupting their conniving that time.

And I was about to do it again. I would not let him force me to complete the gatekeeper's bond acceptance ritual. This was my choice, and mine alone.

*Alaric!* I screamed in my mind, hoping he was listening.

"Actually, I really need to use the bathroom before we get started. I'll be right back." I attempted to shake off the stones.

Airian's eyes flashed to mine, the platinum around his pupil vibrant. Everything began to vibrate—the ground, the table, the stones in his hands. Airian snatched my hands and clamped them to the bowl with a death grip.

"I'm afraid I can't let you go now. You see, once we begin the ritual and you drink the elixir, we have to finish it or you'll die."

I clutched at my throat and stared down at the unique glass goblet. It didn't look like any of the other Manters' goblets. And that licorice taste reminded me of the Manter's tea that dulled my channeling gifts. A panic bubbled up from within and I yanked my hands back, but they were frozen in place. My eyes searched Airian's face and found a stony cold, impenetrable sickness there.

*How could Khalon trust a man like this?*

I wiggled, but it was futile. Airian was too strong.

*ALARIC! Help!* I screamed for him again.

"Mir—" I called for the Manter, but my voice was choked, and only a weak whimper came out.

"Ah, ah, ah, I don't think so. Can't have you ruining this opportunity. It's the only one of its kind."

He quickly placed the stones back on my arms and spoke over them in his language. As he did, I yanked with all my strength, but my arms were like a statue. Tingling seeped up my arms, freezing more and more of me in place. I tried to turn or kick at the table, but even my feet were held in place. Slivers of ice pierced my skin. Everything was so cold.

Only a soft groan escaped my throat when I screamed. Inward, I beckoned to the sleeping giant inside me. Maybe I could pull the energy from whatever he was doing and redirect it. I searched for my staircase to descend, but there was nothing there. I poked at the cavern inside me that I tucked neatly behind a barrier. But it slept, unfazed by what was happening. I begged it to wake up.

If I could just get Airian to touch me, I think it would awaken.

"Uh, my nose itches. Could you get it?"

He didn't even deign to look at me.

"Are these stones supposed to be slipping? I think they're falling off."

That got his attention, and he quickly looked down and reoriented them. When he did, his fingertips grazed my skin, and the beast yawned awake inside of me.

*Yes! Yes. Yes! Thank you, Fates, whoever you are!*

The familiar pull and hunger churned within and spread throughout my body. I searched for Airian's unique energy signature. It was faint, but it was there. A cold, rough chill blew through my cavern, and I knew it was Airian. I imagined his energy was like the anchor rope on a ship, and I was heaving it up. Heavy, as though the anchor was an anvil, it took all my focus and what little energy I could muster. As I pulled for the thread connecting me to his energy, a bright light arced through the camp, blinding me.

Airian was momentarily disabled, and his hold over me waned. I took my opportunity and bolted. I didn't know where I was going, but I shouted for Khalon, Mireille, Moss, or Alaric. Anyone who could help me.

My foot connected with a log, and I stumbled, careening head over heels. When I tumbled to the ground, I was alarmed to find it wasn't a log I tripped over but a steward who was now in a trance under the moon's effect. It was the closest thing to a dead body I'd ever seen, and it thoroughly freaked me out.

I pushed to my feet and raced out from the clearing toward the tree line.

The space inside me where my gift resided felt starved and demanding of energy. With a backward glance, I saw the clearing was filled with rays from the moon, and every steward was under its spell. I gasped for air, my chest constricting with panic and fear.

*Alaric! Where are you? I am in the woods, please help!*

I darted through the woods, unsure where I could be safe to hide. Another voice slammed into me, into my mind.

*They know you're here.*

*You can't do this.*

*They're coming for you.*

*No one wants you here.*

All at once, the voices were all around me, crowding my mind. I couldn't see straight or hear anything but the dissonant voices screeching within me. I lowered myself to the ground and curled up into the fetal position, begging it to stop.

I didn't know how much time had passed, but the moons' beams dissipated, and the voices in my head slithered away. I roused myself from the ground and peered through the trees. I was a long way from the clearing, but I could still see the fire from here. I waited quietly and watched for movement. Eventually, people arose, and their sounds carried through the trees.

I had barely managed to breathe in relief when I was suddenly yanked by the armpits into a standing position. Two large men in dark tunics manhandled me back to the clearing. I fought and kicked and screamed against them, but their size made me no match.

At the edge of the clearing, far from the fire, they threw me on the ground at Airian's feet. A sob, barely refrained, choked out of me. One turned back and landed a kick to my gut.

"Shut up. I don't want to hear your pathetic cries, *human*," he grumbled before spitting on me.

*I just wanna go home. I don't wanna do this anymore.*

"I don't think you were listening earlier." Airian crouched down low for me to see his face. "When I said if you didn't complete the ritual, you'd die. I meant it. Ruack Valley can't have a channeler running around ruining all that we worked so hard for. So if you won't accept the bond and return to where you came from"—he leaned in close to whisper in the most menacing way possible—"then I guess I'll just have to end you myself."

I jerked backwards and looked up at Airian in utter horror.

"Oh, you thought I meant that the elixir would kill you? Now where's the fun in that?" He laughed and got to his feet. The two guards next to him smirked in disgust at me.

The hunger inside me panged, reminding me how insatiable it was. The sensation of energy building in me, ready to burst forth, mingled with a dire need for more. It swirled within and without, blurring my vision. What I felt at the fire was only a fraction of this. My head pounded as blood coursed through me, its heat consuming me. I reached out to feel for the energy around me. Airian's, the moons' beams. *It might just be enough to create a little explosion, enough to give me a fighting chance.*

Before he could silence me again, I let out the most blood-curdling scream I could muster. I shut my eyes tight and let the hunger take over. All at once, it burst out of me into the air around me and sucked everything it came into contact with back into me. My back arched and my teeth grit together. It took all I had not to let a sob loose. Tightening my fist, my nails carved half moons on my palms.

I channeled all of that collected energy back outwards again. Every bit of life inside me was pouring out at full force despite the concentrated elixir. Pops and screams came from various spots in the clearing. I sucked in air faster than I could convert it to carbon dioxide. The screams got louder, and now I willfully kept my eyes shut. I couldn't bear to see what happened. What I'd done.

The anxiety and the panic built, the hunger burning through me. I was a live wire. My eyes shot open, and I looked for help, begging to find someone to take it all away. But no one was coming. Airian and the two men scattered.

When I heard a tearing coming from above me, I squeezed my eyes shut. Loud booms and guttural cries echoed in the clearing. *Alaric? Alaric! I need you.*

The sobs came quickly now. And in the space of one breath to the next, my fist was uncurled only to be curled around another hand. The hand gripped mine tighter, and their energy flowed into me, seeking out my empty vacuum and filling it. It was familiar and inviting. They exuded confidence, and their resolve not to back down despite the sheer amount of energy surrounding us filled me.

Then I was lifted into arms, strong and warm. They were carrying me away. It was Alaric, finally coming for me. Saving me like he did before in the woods. I relaxed into his arms and looked up.

Purple glowing irises took up my whole field of vision. Khalon's hands tightened around me, and the dampening effect of his energy was instantaneous.

"I'm sorry, Scout," he whispered.

And then the pain stole my breath, shutting me into a world of darkness.

# 47

# Alaric

Screams ripped through the foggy forest, causing my pace to falter. I harkened to the screams. Were the shrill shrieks an indication of a party gone well? When I had left the fire, all was well, and Scout was still conscious. I had spoken with Khalon after Airian made a show of bullying Scout into accepting the gatekeepers' bond, and he agreed they wouldn't do anything untoward, only "appeal to her good sense," he said. Trust didn't come easy for me, but Khalon had earned mine. I believed him.

Deep, guttural screams chased the wind. Was I wrong to believe his word? If anything happened to Scout...

I ran toward the voices, deserting my patrol course. My run had taken me nearly around Lake Hollow this evening—a run I was grateful to take since fire-bound stewards traditionally didn't celebrate holidays for the Fates. I'd only helped create the fire to receive the harvest because they needed a steward from each faction represented for balance, or whatever Khalon said the reason was when I first arrived.

My footfalls pounded the ground, and my mind turned toward the camp. Airian said he wanted a wide course covered just in case any outside forces were going to use this evening's event as an opportunity to take advantage of our people.

He was right.

*How could I miss them? If anything happens to Scout, I'll never forgive myself.*

In my mind, I searched for Scout's voice, waiting for her thoughts to beckon me near. But I heard nothing from her, only the dim but frantic buzz from random stewards. I wound my way back to camp, cutting through the bushes and reeds that stood between the edge of the lake and camp. Rather than taking the path through the woods, I darted between the thick trees. My breath came in huffs, sweat wicking from my brow into my eyes.

That's when I heard it.

Just before breaking into the clearing, an electrical shock vibrated through the air and splintered in a million directions. The sky above, once black aside from the dueling moons, was now streaked through with white hot light.

*The dome.*

Casting my senses out wide, I felt for Mireille and once more for Scout. I registered Mireille near the harvest table in the center of the clearing. But Scout's presence was eerily quiet. For a moment fear gripped my heart, and I tripped on a tree root, imagining the worst.

Letting the anxiety propel me forward, I was by Mireille's side in moments, scanning her from head to toe for injury. She was shaking from fear, and before I could wrap her in my arms and carry her to safety, she pulled up an arm and pointed a bony finger to the edge of the clearing.

My eyes followed her direction, and what I saw knocked the wind out of me quicker than a punch to the gut.

Khalon was moving toward us quickly with Scout in his arms. She hung limp and lifeless, her head arched back at an unnatural angle. The same guttural cries I heard before made their way up and out of my throat as I stormed to Khalon.

"Who did this? What happened?" I growled.

"I don't know. There's been an accident." Khalon handed Scout to me and I tucked her close to my chest. Ignoring Khalon's eyes on me, I checked Scout for bodily harm. My breathing shuddered the moment her heart beat against me. *She's alive. Thank the Fates.*

"Where's Airian? We need to get this under control before more people get hurt." Mireille wrung her hands together.

"I thought he was with you," Khalon replied, fear not yet steeping into his tone.

"I haven't seen him since before the moon bathing communion was distributed," Mireille added.

Khalon looked around, his face hardening. The leader and commander attributes of the king were emerging, my respect for him doubled. As he charged into the midst of the chaos like a general into battle, I turned to Mireille.

"Explain," I gritted through clenched teeth, unable to restrain my blinding rage and panic as I held my unconscious mate.

Her eyes fell to Scout's face. In her mind's eye, she showed me where she was just before the pandemonium. Handing out the elixir to the stewards in line. Crossing to the field herself to lie under the moon's rays with the other Manters. Screams filled the air as the ritual ended and she rose from the ground.

"Where was Scout in all this?" I demanded.

She thought back and let me in, privy to her memories. She watched Scout step into a line, but the crowd of steward obscured her view. Mireille looked away as she led other stewards to sip and lie down. Once more, she saw Scout at the harvest table with Airian; he placed her hands in water, but the line of stewards shifted and she could see them no longer. Her attention was pulled once more to the line in front of her.

As she herself went to lie down, she noticed a girl running into the forest. *Could that have been Scout?*

"We need to find Airian and figure out what they know," Mireille said.

"No." I was not going anywhere apart from Scout. I would not leave her again. "She needs to be treated."

Mireille understood. "Let's take her to Khalon's hut. It's closer and I can examine her there."

Once Scout and Mireille were safe in Khalon's living space—Mireille scrambling for the ingredients she needed to assess and treat, Scout still unconscious, but now stretched out on a cot—I stepped into the cool night air to breathe and recenter myself so I wouldn't add to the chaos. Khalon would find Airian, and once they got everything under control, I would ask him about what Mireille had seen.

Leaning my head back against the doorframe that opened to the back of the clearing, I stared into the night. Anger was a coiled serpent in my chest, seething and waiting to strike. I needed to be moving, finding out who did this to Scout and making them pay. But I also needed to be right here with Scout. If I left and something happened—

"Alaric?" Mireille's voice carried across the space to me, interrupting my wrestle. "I'm going to need some space to think and work through the treatment with Scout."

I trusted Mireille with my life. Could I trust her with Scout's? I was going to find out. The simmering heat I tried to repress sprung forth and singed the doorframe. As a waft of smoke rose from the wood burning, Mireille's eyes met mine, and a look of knowing compassion met me there. "Go," she breathed before diving back into her work.

I stepped from the hut into the frenzy. Stewards were running in opposite directions, tables were flipped over and the fire roared, stretching beyond the pit that contained it. I kept my eye on the fire that leapt outside its ring onto the grass and stalked towards it. I reached out and absorbed as much of its energy as I could, bringing it back into a normal range. Grateful for the boost, I knew I would need all the strength I could get tonight. I used the extra energy to create a locked fortress around my mind. I won't be able to function if the chaotic thoughts of everyone crowded my mind. I left room for Scout's and Mireille's bonds, and the thoughts of Khalon, but no more.

A surge of energy tore through the sky. Streaks of lightning ripped through the night, combining to make a web of ecstatic light. I didn't know what it meant, but based on the horrified screams of the others, it surely wasn't good.

Two guards were trying to put the new fires out. One scrambled to fill a pail with water, while the other stretched his hands toward the ground, pulling water up from below to extinguish the flames. A few others tried to gather those who were on the fringe of camp. A crack of energy screeched above us and the others screamed in response. I looked up in time to see something like the sky falling. *The dome is failing.* Crouching, I covered my head awaiting impact, but it fizzled out in midair. Without the dome in place, we were vulnerable. The only reason we had lasted so long against Soleil's war efforts was because she couldn't find us. This was catastrophic. Standing, I heard shouting. Khalon's commands bounced off the Manters' storehouse in the clearing. I ran to him.

"All right, everyone. Gather around and listen to me carefully. We may be under attack at any moment. Without our dome cloaking us and warding off the powers and thrones outside of our community, we are at risk of being found. Now is not the time for questions. Now is the time to unite and fight to survive. Alaric, take the guards and form a secure perimeter. No one gets in or out until we can establish an equilibrium. Everyone, stay together and wait for further commands."

Outside the storehouse, a gathering of Manters formed around him. I listened as He gave clear instructions for half of them to go and fortify the dome and its protective shield over us. The other half he instructed to go to Colling's Cavern and prepare a place for the stewards to hide.

*Just in case,* he added silently, glancing towards me.

"Do we know how that happened yet?" I cocked my chin to the holes spawning quickly in the dome.

*One guess.*

Even if I couldn't read his mind, I'd know what he was thinking.

"No. Scout couldn't have done that on her own." I refused to believe it. We'd get to the bottom of this and see it wasn't her.

"No matter. There are more pressing things. I still can't find Airian. I need you to step in and help the stewards get to safety. Find Maël, he'll assist you. Once a proper perimeter is established and we have everyone, then have them gather an overnight rucksack and lead them to the glen. We're not taking any chances. Dispatch the rest of the inactive guard to escort them. Take a headcount while you're at it. We can't be too safe." With a curt nod, he backed into the fray to find the injured.

# Alaric

As I gathered the guards, my mind was fixed on Scout and the Manter who tended to her. I would rather be sitting at her side, doing anything Mireille asked of me than standing here, the image of composure and strength. It was the facade I wore most often, but I never felt the crippling weight of the mask until now.

But with Scout in capable hands, I had to lock my worry away and got to work. I went through the motions, my body sharpened to obey on autopilot.

The guards received the update from Khalon without a word. They must all have been in shock, because they listened and obeyed the outcast they had spent an age criticizing and rejecting. They retreated to their positions in the perimeter. Each man knew his place. Even though I didn't get along with them, it didn't mean I couldn't see their skill. Questionable methods aside, Airian had sharpened these men. When we finally found him, I would put our differences aside and shake his hand.

I found Maël next; he secured the storehouse from panicked stewards who were trying to loot it. We broke up the fights and calmed the stewards. Gathering them together by the water pump, I tried to be kind with them. But it was exhausting. *How did Khalon do this?* Defaulting to orders, I instructed vagrant stewards back to their tents for their belongings before reconvening in the cavern. As they ambled back tired and afraid, I heard their whimpers and cries. My heart softened a fraction.

The war in Kilburne started out like this. The chaos, panicked stewards racing around, waves of flames engulfing every dry and barren inch of our land. The only striking difference was we knew who the enemy was then. Soleil was everywhere. She was in our minds, our thoughts, our dreams—nightmares, really. She haunted us and made sure she was the only sun our bleak lives orbited.

While Soleil could be at the edge of our lands waiting to pounce, I doubted it. She had a knack for making an entrance. She never left anything to chance. If this was her doing, she would have struck the final blow in the dome and swooped in, leaving carnage in her wake. Killing was a sport to her. A sick and dangerous game.

Bolts of fire flashed across the sky. Drawing me back to the moment, watching the stewards scurry to their tents. Next on Khalon's list was a head count. I got Maël to help me.

After we ran our immediate patrol course—around the clearing, habitable tent area, the Manters' meeting place, and the river—we returned to conspire. So far a handful of earth stewards were missing, one of them being Moss. Airian and two guards, Tieran and Kallias, were also unaccounted for.

Wracking my mind, I tried to think of various reasons why Airian would sequester a small group of stewards. Maybe for their safety? A company to aid him in reconnaissance? No. None of that made sense.

Maël took the returning stewards with the other half of the Manters to the glen. I reported back to Khalon with the updates.

Something wasn't sitting right with me, I needed to do a larger loop. Quickly, I vocalized my concerns to Khalon who shared the same unease as I. He agreed to let me search for others if I took another with me. Rhydian came to mind.

Before I tracked him down to run the long loop with me, I paused at Khalon's hut to check on Mireille and Scout. Straightaway, I shared my suspicions with Mireille. She neither comforted me nor counseled me. All her attention was focused on Scout. For that I was grateful.

Time slowed down as I stood at Scout's head where she lay. I took in every bit of her face. The pink in her cheeks. The freckles across her nose. The long lashes that fluttered when she was embarrassed.

I needed her to wake up and be okay.

Something wasn't right here. Somewhere deep in my bones, the energy was off. She didn't feel the same as she did before. This wasn't Scout's doing, even if Khalon didn't believe me. I'd find a way to prove it.

Outside, I spotted Rhydian. He was still putting out the fires that spread outside the ring.

"Some people are still missing. Run a wide course with me?"

"Of course." He emptied his pail on the smoldering coals and limbered up. I pulled from the flames until they extinguished, and rolled my neck around, enjoying the refreshment.

We kept a steady pace as we easily covered the distance from camp to Lake Hollow where I had left off on my earlier run.

Across the lake, something glimmered in the broken moon light. The twin moons shook in the lake's reflection. Vibrations pulsated from the dome's edge.

*Soleil's invading.*

We picked up our pace and raced to the point of the vibrations origin.

We slowed as we reached the boundary, only to find a few Manters repairing the boundary that anchored our protective dome. I wasn't thinking clearly. Of course it wasn't Soleil. Everything with Scout had me shaken in a way I'd never been before.

I didn't like it.

Gritting my teeth, I surveyed the stewards. I recognized a few of them, but didn't know them well, not having spent much time with any Manters besides Mireille and Xylina.

"Rhona, what happened here?" Rhydian asked.

We stood in the forest, beyond the far side of the Lake, where Ruack Valley's territory ended and Prentiss began. The protector poles were bent at crude angles, clearly broken, and the hip-high rock wall fence that fortified the boundary all around the territory lay in a heaping pile of debris.

Rhona spun to me. "We are definitely under attack. And we have no idea how long the enemy has been walking among us." Rhona shared the ancient amber eyes of Mireille, but their resemblance ended there. Where Mireille had graying long hair, Rhona's was a sleek black. Where Mireille's face aged with grace and tiny beauty spots, Rhona's complexion was clear and sharp as glass. She unnerved me in every way that Mireille comforted me.

"How long will it take you to repair the breach?" I questioned.

"A breach this large... It will take us an hour or more. Why?"

"I'd like to do a quick sweep on the other side. Can you wait to close it until we are back if we don't come before the hour is up?"

"You better be quick."

# Alaric

Rhydian and I moved through the rubble over the boundary, and we noticed a tangible difference in the air. I was instantly brought back to what it was like escaping Kilburne. The last leg of the journey to Ruack Valley was brutal. The Valley of Anguish and the Whispering Winds were what separated this territory from the others, and they tormented me with my deepest fears and exploited my gravest secrets. I shook away those niggling memories.

"Let's make this quick." I was not excited to step out of Khalon's covering, but something drew me here and I wouldn't be able to sleep unless we turned over every stone looking for those who were missing. A yawn tugged at the corners of my mouth, but I swallowed it down with the rest of my unease.

Rhydian followed my lead and we ran along the territory. It was easy to follow the boundary line; the closer we stayed to it, the easier the air was to breathe. Not noticing anything amiss, we routed back to our entry point and carved a wider course. The terrain was more sparse here, rugged and hilly compared to our lush and densely wooded areas.

Ahead, there was a patch of towering timber cloaked in heavy mist that was barely noticeable in the dark. As we approached, an icy wind blew through.

*"They're here, they're here! They're going to get you!"* The chilling whisper on the wind encircled us.

Rhydian's eyes widened, but he remained silent, due largely in part to his training. He swatted the air around his ears. It would be my guess he hadn't encountered the Whispering Winds before.

I gestured to Rhydian to slow down and get low. If anything or anyone was here, I didn't want to give away our location. We crouched low in the tall field grass and weaved towards the trees.

Mireille had said Scout had an assignment against her. In all my time serving King Tarrent, then Soleil, I had never heard of someone willing the winds against someone. Even now as they spoke to us, I was unsure what to believe about them. Did they speak the unspeakable? Or were they corrupted as the Inaras said?

The wind began to howl as we broke into the small forest. I could see through it out the other side, thanks to the moons above. It wasn't very large, but the areas cloaked in mist made navigating near impossible.

We spread out to quickly clear the woods. We had almost made it to the base of the foothills, when a raven above released a startling caw. Rhydian tumbled in response and I choked back a laugh. It wasn't funny, but with everything that happened tonight, my nerves were on edge. I was one incident from losing my mind, and that almost did it.

"You good?" I whispered, turning to find his green eyes in the dark.

When I didn't see them, I spun on my heel to search for him. *Don't play with me, boy.*

"Rhydian?" I called, listening for his thoughts, letting the wall I built in my head down for a moment.

There's no reply. I was about to light up the forest with churning waves of flames so that whatever enemy we were dealing with—

"Alaric, I need some help," a grunt came from several meters behind me.

I didn't question how he got there. I just rushed to the sound of his voice. Rhydian lay on the ground, splayed out over a prone object, a felled tree by the look. He just took a tumble and was too embarrassed.

I leaned down to offer him a hand up, but when he rolled over, he was covered in a dark, viscous liquid. I dropped to my knee and searched him for wounds.

"The blood—" his voice trembled as it eked out, "It isn't mine."

I hauled him up and over, about a yard, and turned back to the log. It's—

"Moss," he whispered.

"Help me with her." Dropping to my knees, I scanned Moss's body. I listened for a heartbeat that never came, and felt for her energy that had already seeped back into the earth.

"I can't—" Rhydian choked out the two syllables between ragged breaths.

Before I could ask why not, I saw his thoughts reveal what happened when one earth-bound steward touched a dead steward. In his words, he would become "unclean." Death tainted his ability, darkened it. If an earth steward came in contact with too many dead things, they could possess the energy of death itself and participate in dark works.

I had no idea. I logged that information away to process at another time.

I took a deep breath and gathered Moss in my arms. As I stood to begin the trek back to camp, I couldn't help but notice the small blue flowers that grew up around where her body lay. I lingered for only a moment, trying to remember why those flowers felt so familiar.

# 50

# Scout

I was falling again, the jolt of being shoved over the edge left me gasping. I plummeted through the air, grappling for something to hold onto. My heart was in my throat, pounding viciously, nauseatingly. I braced for impact and slammed through the ground.

I blinked. The sun filtering through the open tent flap blinded me.

I leaned up on one elbow and looked around. I was on the cot in the tent I shared with Moss. Very 'day one' deja vu. It should have been strange that I was yet again waking up with no memory of how I got to bed, but it was becoming more familiar.

The throbbing in my head told me I was dehydrated and probably hungry. I wondered how many days I had been out this time. I rolled out of bed, stabilized myself, and waited to see if a Manter was going to appear with a tray of oatmeal-ish food and water. When no such thing transpired, I got dressed, taking note that at least this time, no one had disrobed me from what I wore to the harvest party.

Who should I go see first—the Manter or Khalon? I weighed my options. Who could I trust right now?

I stopped in the clearing at the water pump and gathered some in cupped hands to drink. The clearing around me was empty, the tables from the harvest party upended and charred. Must have been some party if they still hadn't come to clear it up yet.

I splashed cold fistfuls of water on my face. There was a dense mist that hung in the morning air, making the clearing look smaller than it was. The air around me moved slowly and felt thick like honey. I knew was in Khalon's camp despite the fact that I couldn't see anyone, nor hear the usual chipper work chatter. But why was the air so stagnant and thick? Something was off.

Across the clearing, a muted voice crowed, "They should have let you die!"

My head whipped around in the direction the sound came from, but I didn't see anyone. I turned back to the water and drank once more before shutting it off.

Another faint voice croaked, "He should have killed you!"

This wasn't the sound of someone yelling across the clearing. The sound came from above, within, and all around. A chill ran across my shoulders as dread rooted in my stomach.

The words conjured a faint image: a golden goblet flashed in moonlight with the sound of crystals clinking. But no other pictures formed. It felt important, like there was something I was forgetting.

A crow's caw screeched just above me; it circled and began to fly toward the woods. An eerie feeling told me I should follow the bird. A glance back around the clearing revealed what I'd been remiss in noticing before. I hadn't seen a single soul anywhere. It was utterly abandoned.

I'd been left behind.

Ducking under the low-hanging branches at the tree line, I entered the forest. The mist had claimed much of the woods. It hung low on the forest floor, obscuring my steps. It spiraled upward around trees and through branches, dimming the sunshine and casting a woeful shadow over everything.

The raven called once more from ahead. I couldn't see the bird, but I followed his incessant noise until the toe of my shoe struck something solid. I caught myself on a nearby tree and tried to step over whatever tripped me. My foot landed on something soft and sturdy. As I planted my foot to heave over it, it gave, and I heard a disgusting crack and leapt back.

The raven sat above me on a branch high above, squawking. It irritated me how urgent it sounded, pesky and demanding attention.

"What do you want?" I barked.

The ugly black bird glided down to a branch at eye level. Its head dipped as though pointing to the ground. The mist was obscene in its full coverage. I clawed at the air and fanned the mist away. Slowly, it dissipated, revealing a prone body draped in white cloth. The way the mist hugged the body felt like an otherworldly goodbye.

Tremors raced through my body. I couldn't look. I wanted to turn and dart back to camp. The raven shrieked in protest. Gulping, I knelt next to the body. My hand outstretched, trembling. The linen was damp from the mist and resisted being pulled back.

The cold seeped into my bones and chilled me further. My nose prickled like it did just before I cried or threw up, and I tried to hold my breath. The linen gave, and beautiful brown curls spilled out the top. I yanked my hand back and muffled a cry.

*No, no, no. It can't be.*

Resolved to see the truth no matter how much it would hurt, I snuck my wavering fingers out once more and yanked the covering back.

It was Moss.

A hush fell over the forest, and I took in Moss's solemn face. I had never seen her look so serious. Her sweet freckles looked wilted now, splayed out across her expressionless face. Those bouncing brown curls were limp from the mist, as lifeless as the soul who grew them. My friend was gone. Time froze around us as I leaned over her and cried. Even though I hadn't known her for long, she was my first friend here. The bond and connection we shared was that of sisters. I'd miss her endless chatter and easy excitement over the garden. The garden. *Her garden.* Who would tend it now?

I dropped my head to her chest and cried.

I'd never lost someone close to me before.

This hurt.

More than I thought it ever could.

My eyes swelled with tears, and I couldn't cry them out fast enough. The raven began to chirp, a gentle caw, as if respectfully interrupting my grieving.

Through blurred eyes, I watched the raven jump down from the branch and perch on a large stone at Moss's feet. He pecked at the linen. I didn't understand—what did it want me to do? The raven shook out his wings and plucked again, ripping at the linen. I swatted the stupid bird away.

"Leave my friend alone!" I cried.

It scuffled away and returned to her side, pulling at the linen where I had left it folded down. I thought I understood now. He wanted to uncover her.

I gulped at a wave of nausea. I didn't want to see her dead body, but it felt like I must. Slowly, I peeled back the cover. Her clothes were shredded, and carved in the flesh of her belly was a name. *Airian*. And below it, a set of charred graphic markings. I didn't understand.

I startled backwards.

My mind began to swim with the memories of the harvest party and the twin moons event. Airian had me locked in place, forced me to complete the bond ritual. I ran, but he had me hunted down like a wounded deer. His henchmen dragged me back to him and beat me.

I retraced the last several weeks here. How did we miss this? Airian was the bad guy? Was that who the Whispering Winds were warning me about? It had to be. I would help Alaric and Khalon find him. We would make him pay for what he did. Not just to me, but sweet Moss.

The raven cawed and broke me out of my revenge plotting. I looked down where it scurried at Moss's side. In her bawled up fist was a crumpled paper.

A note.

Scrawled in beautifully girly handwriting was the following: *I am sorry, Scout. I never should have trusted him. I hope I wasn't too late. Please find E'rykr and tell him I love him. And please, don't waste your imprint like I did.*

Holding the note in my hands, it felt insubstantial, like it could turn to ash any moment and crumble away. Just like my friend did. Gone forever. I held it tightly and reread it three times over. Who was she talking about? Airian? And who was E'rykr? *My imprint*? What was Moss talking about? Were these helpful parting words or the ramblings of a dying woman?

The fact that I would never be able to ask her ripped me apart. I tucked my knees to my chest and sobbed.

# Alaric

"Scout? Scout!" The Manter shook Scout's shoulders. "Wake up. It's just a bad dream."

Scout shook as sobs ripped through her. She lied tucked on a cot in Khalon's hut. Mireille had been watching over her while I'd been leading in Airian's stead.

Scout sprang forward in awoken fright.

"*They're here. They found us.*" She looked around, and I could hear her heart hammering. Then she began to whimper, her bottom lips turning out. "He killed her. Alaric?" She looked around frantically for me.

I crouched beside her, taking her hand, the need to comfort her unrelenting. "I'm right here, Scout." I searched her eyes. "Who killed who?"

She gripped my hand with a surprising amount of strength and snarled, "Airian killed Moss. I saw it."

Mireille and I exchanged glances.

While I hadn't been an advocate of Airian's leadership, claiming a steward murdered another was a serious accusation. We didn't declare these things lightly.

In my heart, I wanted to trust Scout, wanted to stand beside her and insist she would never suffer again, but was it possible her human memories could be misunderstanding? I searched Mireille's face and saw her questioning the same thing.

*It could be true. But... how would she know?* Mireille thought.

"What's the last thing you remember?" I asked Scout as she eased up into a sitting position. She pushed to her feet and took inventory of her surroundings. Instinctively, I reached a hand out to steady her as she swayed

"I remember everything. From that snake trying to force me into the bond ritual under the moonlight to him killing Moss. He had his goonies abduct me and beat me until Khalon found me." She paced, carving a vicious groove in the floor. "He's going to pay. I'll make sure of it."

Mireille's eyebrows shot up in alarm. *I think you may need to step back. She isn't strong enough right now to resist your fire. Go check in with Khalon. Let him know she's awake.*

I nodded, though leaving her now felt wrong. "Scout, I have to go check on something with Khalon, Mireille will be here with you." Gesturing aside, Mireille followed me to the door. Lowering my voice, and switching to MirVis I asked her, "How come I couldn't hear Scout when she needed me? I've never had problems with distance when a bond was involved."

Mireille's gaze swept the room before she replied silently, *Whatever Airian gave her to neutralize her gifts also dulled her bond.*

My eyebrows lifted in surprise. Nothing of that nature had been used to my knowledge before. "How did he find the means to concoct an elixir like that?"

*There's been rumors that Soleil had an apprentice who created various tinctures and poisons for torture and coercion... Perhaps he had connections we weren't aware of.*

Grinding my teeth, I ended the conversation before my fire could light. I needed to pursue this further, but not here. Not now.

"If you need me, just think of me." I said to Scout as goodbye and found myself stepping closer to kiss her forehead, but she whirled on me.

"If I need you? I needed you last night and you were nowhere to be found. I almost died with your name on my lips." She seethed. "You're not really there for me. You left me to die."

I winced at her words. She was right. I failed her. All the breath left my lungs as the old memories resurfaced. I'd fought so hard to leave Samirah's death behind me, to make peace with it, and move on. I determined to never love again so as not to risk another innocent life. Until the Fates bonded me to Scout. I'd lost sight of what I vowed, what I stood to lose. How could I do that again?

I would protect her at all costs, but I would wall off my heart.

She was right. I couldn't protect her. I closed my eyes and saw her spilled blood, my hands sticky with the viscous substance. I wouldn't let it happen. I wouldn't lose sight ever again. Fates be warned, I wouldn't play their bonding games. If it meant Scout could live, I'd never love again. So be it.

I fell back from Scout. Her angry eyes cut me to the core, willing me, daring me to speak again. I resisted the urge to say goodbye and left the hut.

) ) ) ● ( ( (

After a brief check in with Khalon, I moved through the clearing, watching the moons set. Most of the stewards were able to find shelter with the Manters and the guard. Those who stayed back were still asleep, so I used this as an opportunity to stalk down to the river. I ripped the shirt off my back and kicked out my shoes and launched into the river. The water was cool against my boiling skin. As I waded in, the water sizzled and evaporated as it first touched me. I needed to submerge myself or I would detonate.

As the water embraced me, my mind drifted back to the only other time I was so strongly emanating fire. It was shortly after Soleil staged the coup that purged Kilburne of King Tarrent. Though he was lustfully unsatiated and a vile example of a man, he was an exceptional, militant-minded general. Serving under him in the army was to me as religion was to many others. We had our practices, our routines, and there was something sacred in it for me. I had a sworn duty to uphold, and it came naturally, this passion I had for justice.

Soleil had deposed the king in front of the whole nation and set to work destroying everything that had any mark of the king. From the castle to the marketplace's coin to the military. She changed our purpose. She didn't just want justice and protection for all. She wanted able bodies at her disposal. She weaponized the entire legion in months and made them a mindless extension of her right arm through the collective dark energy she accumulated.

She'd turned what used to be objective-focused training sessions into impossible obstacles meant to destroy our bodies and morale. After one particularly excruciating afternoon when she sent me out to dig graves for the entire brigade I lived with—a tool of psychological warfare, I thought—I was returning to our bunk, dirty and depleted, when I saw *them*. Several yards before I reached the bunks, my entire battalion was strewn up, headless, on poles around the training field.

I threw up immediately, and then the incinerator began. First, it was just a rumble. I thought I could contain, but it morphed and grew. I don't remember screaming, or the feeling of the tears as they fell, but when I had calmed, every body was charred. I fell to my knees as the wind blew through the barren valley and stirred the ashes from the poles, carrying my comrades away.

When Soleil had her fill of watching from a distance, she strutted out across the field and stood before me. She drew a sword and placed the tip below my chin, drawing my head up to meet her gaze.

"That's what happens when you disobey me. People die. You have no one to blame but yourself." Pure evil had glinted in her eyes as she pushed out her bottom lip into a reviling pout. My skin began to crawl as she baby-talked me. "They all surrendered like good little boys and girls, and look what had to happen to these innocent people. All because poor little Alaric couldn't figure out how to surrender his will to me."

It was the first time I truly hated myself for what I was. She made me feel defective and dirty for having the extra gift I never asked for. The ability to resist other stewards' gifts. If I hadn't been created the way I was, my comrades would still be alive. With my self-esteem in ruins, Soleil exploited me. She might not have had my will on a leash like she had the others, but she made up for it with the leash she kept on my body. I had nothing left to live for, to fight for. She had ruined everything. I lived that way for a long time.

Until Samirah.

But I couldn't think of her now. I shook my thoughts of her away. I looked back on that day on the training field with Soleil as a different man now. That was the day the final straw broke. I decided to destroy Soleil or die trying. I would not be the reason more people died at the hands of Soleil. I didn't know how she'd found me cloaked in Ruack Valley, or how she learned about Scout and the imprint, but I would stop at nothing to end this.

I took a final deep breath before plunging myself to the bottom of the river. The water warmed around me, but the pressure of forcing myself deeper gave me the reassurance I needed that I wouldn't explode and destroy anyone. At least not yet.

) ) ) ● ( ( (

Coming out of the river, more stewards lingered on the bank, recharging in the new day's energy. As I used my shirt to towel dry, a movement at the corner of my eye had me flinching for my knife.

"Relax, it's just me." Khalon held his hands up innocently. "I thought I might need to check in with you. We've learned some things. Could you join me at the Manter's hut? At your earliest convenience, of course."

I tossed my shirt over my shoulder and gathered my things to follow Khalon through the winding paths to Mireille's place. He circled around the back of her hut, which I was grateful for. It felt disrespectful to enter Mireille's home when she was not with us.

He checked around the edges of the fire as though to see if the coast was clear.

"It's just us, so I want you to speak freely with me," he began. "Airian is still missing, and so is Tiernan and Kallias." He scrutinized my face, looking for something. But what? "Do those names mean anything to you?"

I thought back to Airian's "hazing ritual" as bile rose in the my throat.

"They're in the guard with me, but our commonalities cease there."

He gave me a generous pause as he looked over me.

"Their living spaces have been cleared out. Both Airian's and the boys' tents are empty. It would seem they left in a hurry during the harvest party. Right about the time of Moss's death." He circled around the cold and empty fire pit, hands casually woven behind his back. "Under normal circumstances, we wouldn't mind for stewards to come and go from our collective. But when the leader of our armed guard disappears the night our protective dome goes down, we begin to ask questions. Do you understand what I am getting at?"

I thought over Scout's words this morning. She said Airian was the one who killed Moss, that he left behind a message. Mireille and I initially dismissed it as stress. A nightmare possibly.

"Could she be right?" I asked aloud.

Khalon somehow knew exactly what I meant because he responded softly, "I've been asking myself the same thing."

When Airian commanded me to run patrol, I assumed it was partially because he was a jerk, and partly because fire stewards didn't believe in celebrating the Fates or their Twins.

What I thought could be kindness was actually a setup. He wanted me as far from his thoughts as possible, leaving Scout to fend for herself.

"If you know anything," Khalon added, before I could let that thought take up any more space in my mind, "or have any suspicions, or *hear* of any, can you please alert me at once. I would like to not be blindsided again."

Now I understood his reason for asking me here. It was not *me* he wanted, just my *gift.*

"In the meantime," he continued, pacing back toward me now, "with Airian gone, I need a new commander. Would you do me the honors?" He stood before me with bright amethyst eyes that softened at the edges. I saw the stains of grief left hidden in the folds around his eyes.

"It would be my honor, sir." I bowed slightly in deference. "Will there be anything else?"

"Yes, just one more thing. As my new acting commander, I need your utmost discretion with the following information." He leaned close and lowered his voice. "I had Xylina perform the burial examinations and rituals on Moss's body and some very unsettling things came to light. Her body was carved and charred. Someone burnt a message into her. *The truth will come out.*"

A chill rushed through my body. *How fitting for All Fates Day,* I thought.

"That's not all. When Xylina completed her routine exam, she noted some strange charms attached to Moss's body. When she removed them for burial, it seems a glamour broke."

A glamour?

Khalon's voice took on a gravelly rasp, "Moss wasn't who we thought she was. She was a hybrid fire and earth-bound steward glamoured to appear as a mere earth steward."

I thought back to that night when I chased the intruder from Scout's tent. Those blue flowers were left in their wake, the same blue flowers that grew up under Moss's body. The realization dawned on me, and I shamed myself for not piecing it together sooner.

I didn't know what troubled me more, the fact that she betrayed us all or the fact that there was another fire-bound steward right under my nose and I hadn't been the one to expose her. Were there more? Distrust itched through my veins.

And what of Airian? The traitorous wind-bound steward... Could he have been in league with Soleil? Could he have been orchestrating the Whispering Winds against

Scout? I shook my head. Running our guard, ruining its framework from within. It was an option we never dared to consider.

It took all my strength to pull my thoughts back from the edge to the present moment, where Khalon was waiting for my response to a question I had missed.

"Have you ever come across a glamoured steward before?" He repeated.

"No." I replied. "Before I left, Soleil was searching for someone powerful enough with grave energy to weave a glamour, but to my knowledge she never found anyone."

"Either Soleil found someone after you left and had Moss glamoured, or we're dealing with someone else. Someone much more powerful than Soleil." A foreboding hush swept through the trees around us. "For all our sake's, I hope Soleil found her grave master."

# Scout

"I understand you're angry. You have every right to be," Mireille said to me after Alaric left.

I wasn't sure whether I was truly mad at him or if his energy just got the better of me this time, but I couldn't simmer down. My body felt different. Tingles raced along my spine, like I was a shaken can of soda, and my mind buzzed constantly with acute awareness of every little thing. And even though I was angry with Alaric, I couldn't seem to get him off my mind.

"I don't know what I feel. I feel... everything." And I realized it scared me. I tried inhaling deeply and was met with the familiar scent of Mireille's warm, woodsy herbs. My eyes connected with hers and she sighed.

She pulled her shawl closer around her shoulders and sat at Khalon's table, inviting me to join her.

"After thorough examination, it would appear that your bond ritual was nearly completed...." I heard nothing else.

"W-w-what?" I stuttered. *No, no, no. I stopped Airian. I got away before he could finish the ritual, didn't I?*

"I said: Airian botched the ritual under the lunar event. This may account for the changes you're experiencing, as he came very close to finishing it. While I've tended to a few gatekeepers in my time, I've certainly never had to tend to a *channeling* gatekeeper."

"What does it mean?" Uncertainty swirled in my mind. This was the very thing I had been running from ever since my birthday. And now that felt like ages ago. What do you do when what you're avoiding catches up with you? I thought the world might explode, literally this time. But it was painfully still intact; I was the one imploding.

"I'm not quite certain, but I suppose that means your training now will be even more vital. You'll need to understand your gift and practice it, work on not absorbing or expelling too much at once..."

Regret appeared on the Manter's face.

"What is it?"

"How much do you remember about last night?"

"Just what I told you. Why, did something else happen?"

"It's probably better I show you." She reached out to take my hand, and she held it, palm up. She pulled a glass shard from the folds of her cloak and dug it into my skin. I flinched at first, but there was a warmth in my gut that urged me to trust her.

I looked away for a moment, and she whisked away to grab something from a shelf behind her. She came back and placed a quartz stone in my palm, and what happened next was beyond my comprehension.

I squeezed my eyes so tightly I saw white. A searing pain tripped through my head, the worst migraine I'd ever had. I ground the heel of my palm into my brow bone, willing the pain to stop. At once, the pain stopped, and chaos filled my mind. I heard screaming and rushing around. I opened my eyes, and I was no longer in Khalon's hut. I was outside at the fire ring the night of the Harvest Party, standing behind Khalon. He was charging forward, and I looked around him and saw Alaric holding a lifeless version of me.

I gasped and wrapped my arms around my waist, but my hands wafted through me like a ghost. I looked around and began to realize what the Manter did. She showed me what happened that night through her eyes. Emboldened with a new fervor, I pressed into the shared vision.

Khalon and Alaric spoke too quickly for me to understand. Alaric tucked me into his chest and carried me to Khalon's hut. My lips trembled as I watched helplessly what had already happened.

Flames were spreading out from the fire pit and slowly consuming patches throughout the camp. A blaze of shimmering light sprayed near the Manter's hut in the center of the clearing where the community's pantry was. It was only a moment later that it was engulfed in fresh fire. Overhead, there was a surge and crackle of what looked like lightning or electricity tracing through the sky.

Khalon gathered stewards and spoke to them with urgent reassurance. Alaric rejoined the throng and stood at attention. Khalon turned to him, whispering instructions privately, before informing me in Mireille's place to get the other Manters.

I moved with her through her memories, riding the tail of her billowing shawl. She scampered swiftly back to her hut and grabbed many things that I couldn't make sense of yet. She placed them all into a rucksack and gave the hut a glance around before pressing a kiss from her fingers to the doorpost. We left without turning back. I watched through her eyes as she gathered the other Manters with matching honey-tinted eyes. They also prepared a rucksack, and together we retreated into the woods.

I watched as the other Manters gathered around and collaborated. Some were orchestrating something; I was not sure what, but they were gathering rocks and building small towers of stacked stones. I watched as they created these little, well-looking stone structures. Round and round they stacked the stones, forming tight little circles. They each returned to their rucksack, took out jars, and sprinkled the powder out into the little cistern things they'd made.

Each Manter stood behind the new structure they'd created. Each one paced a few yards apart. They raised their hands toward the sky, and things fell quiet. They were reaching for the energy, checking where it was, just like Niah taught me. The energy was alive and always moving; you couldn't just take it without asking.

I stared up at the sky and watched as their chants and songs rose like incense to the stars. The fragments of the sky above glimmered holographically. I let my eyes trail along the sky's edge and realized it was a dome. The sky wasn't fragmented—the dome above us was.

A shred of terror ripped through me now as I realized what happened. My own memories of that night flashed to mind. The pull of the fire calling to me to offer a measure of the energy pulsing through me. Then Airian forcing the bond ritual on me during the twin moon event. I thought he was going to kill me. I... I... I remembered the strain of life pouring out of me and the thunder... followed by the screams. I did this. I ripped a hole in their world. And now it was falling apart.

I choked on a scream. I wanted out of the Manter's head. I didn't want to see this. I couldn't stand this. I knew I should have let Khalon strip the energy away from me while he could. I stifled a sob. And my hands started shaking. I just wanted out of here. I couldn't believe I ever thought this place would be my home. I didn't belong here.

The Manters continued chanting, the sound rising above my flailing thoughts. They spoke in a tongue I was unfamiliar with, but it pulled me from my spiral and had a deeply comforting effect on me. Energy tingled around us. It was like they were speaking life into the air around us. A semblance of peace began to surround us, and a warm haze cloaked us.

The Manter's words floated up and began to seal the cracks in the shining, glimmering veil above.

Flaming arrows began to penetrate through the fragmented openings. A screaming pierced the night, and we could hear the guards' voices loud and abrupt, giving commands. I wanted to pull away from the Manters and see what was happening, but I was tied only to the memories of Mireille. I couldn't see what she didn't see. So I watched and waited.

The Manters began chanting with more fervor, their enunciations even more clear and succinct as they picked out energy from the elements around us and weaved it together for the sake of the others. My heart was beating out of my chest. What had I done? A hot tear trailed down the inside of my eye. It tasted bitter. I couldn't fathom the pain I'd caused these people in such a short time. I'd used up their previous month's energy storage, then destroyed this month's and effectively blown up their protective dome, causing who-knew-what injuries. If only I had done the ritual at my aunties like they wanted. If only I'd understood what they were doing. Why did I have to be so stubborn?

I closed my eyes and crouched down in the Manter's mind, holding myself tight, even though I was ethereal and incorporeal.

Sometime later, I looked up at the sky and saw the intricate woven energies above. The dome veiling us looked like a broken vase that a child glued back together.

# Scout

"Scout! Scout!" Someone called my name from a ways off. The pain rippled through my body, rolling from my head down my spine. It burned everywhere. My heart skipped a few beats and grappled for reality.

"Scout, listen to me. Open your eyes." A cold hand slapped across my face, and I jolted upright.

I was on the floor of Khalon's hut.

"Scout, what did you see? What did you hear?"

I pulled my knees to my chest and gripped my hands into fists so tightly that my nails created little half moons on my palm. I focused on that singular pain until my breath evened.

"I saw everything. The harvest party, the sky falling, and—" My voice broke and I buried my head in my arms. A sob leapt from the depth of my being and I couldn't stop it. "It's all my fault! None of this would have happened if it weren't for me. Moss would still be alive if it weren't for me."

The Manter took me into her arms and held me against her, rubbing large circles on my back. She cooed into my hair as snot dripped down my face onto her cloak. A thought struck me.

"I need to see her." I pulled back and wiped my nose on my sleeve. "Can I see her?"

Pain glinted in her eyes as she mulled it over.

"I need to say goodbye."

"I think that can be arranged."

) ) ) ● ( ( (

Moss had already been buried; I wouldn't be able to see her. The thought niggled at me that maybe, just maybe, that dream was divine. Not just a dream manufactured by chemical dumping and hormones regulating in the body during sleep. I thought the dream was real. As graphic and horrible as it was, I think I got to say goodbye to her there, but I still craved a tangible goodbye.

I stood before her marked gravesite where fresh flowers had been replanted as a makeshift headstone. She'd turned into her own garden. I knew this was something she would have wanted. Despite her betrayal, they showed her this kindness and it broke my heart that everything played out the way it did. A few tears glided over my cheek and into the dimple near my mouth. I tasted the salty sorrow. It overshadowed my anger for now, dampening it in an exhausting way.

Closing my eyes, I said goodbye. Like I did in the dream. Goodbye to the overly energetic girl who introduced me to this world. Goodbye to the patient friend who explained this world and the nature of gifts to me. Goodbye to the roommate whose steady breathing at night gave me an anchor when I was scared I'd drift away.

"Goodbye, Moss." *I hope you find peace,* I added as my heavy lids fell closed. A sweet silence fell around us as I imagined the Fates coming and whisking her away.

"Wait!" My eyes bulged open, remembering something from the dream. "The note! Did you guys find the note?" I whipped around to Mireille, who'd been giving me quiet space. She startled and stepped close to me.

"What note?"

"In the dream, Moss had a note in her hand. Oh, Scout, come on, think!" I slapped my forehead trying to remember the note. I could see the paper. Her girlish handwriting. But what were the words?

"It said something about how she was sorry for trusting him. And that she was too late. Oh! And something about an imprint? She said I had one. But that's not right. I don't know." I deflated. It felt like the dream was significant, but maybe it wasn't, especially if I couldn't remember what felt like the most important part.

Mireille eyed me carefully.

"Oh, Eric, or Riker? Was that his name? I think she loved someone or wanted me to tell someone she loved them? Did *Moss* have a bond? Maybe that was it." I moaned in agonizing frustration. If only I could remember!

"It's okay, child. Dreams have a way of working themselves into our consciousness if given the space to do so. Let's gather your things. Khalon is moving everyone to Colling's Cavern for added precaution."

As we made our way through camp, I noticed everything had a vacant quality to it now. Void of life, like a ghost town. A chill ran through me, and I thought again about how this was all my fault. None of this should be happening right now. Moss wouldn't be gone if it weren't for my cursed stubbornness.

A few stragglers were left behind, boarding up camp and putting out fires. I watched as one earth-bound steward tossed a pail of cold water over the fire. It sizzled and reminded me of the moments Alaric and I shared before everything happened.

Standing by the fire, as his skin touched mine, a spark bloomed in me. It hurt to think about how he didn't show up for me when I needed him the most, especially after we shared a sweet moment. Was it just me, or did we almost kiss?

I was lost in this thought when I failed to walk in a straight line and knocked right into someone.

"It seems we have an odd way of meeting like this." I'd know that voice anywhere. It was the one I hated most right now, the one I resented myself for yearning to hear.

Alaric.

"I was just escorting Scout to her tent for her belongings. We need to get back to the glen."

"Why don't I escort her." His eyes searched the Manter's, and I could tell they were communicating in the way only the two of them seemed to understand. "We'll see you at the glen." He kissed Mireille's cheek in farewell and turned us toward my tent.

"I—"

I was about to say I didn't need an escort, but one look at Alaric's eyes had my jaw snapping shut.

He ducked his head, leaned in, and looked into my eyes. I watched his pupils fan out as red flames danced in his irises. There was passion just behind his cool veil of matter-of-factness. "I am truly sorry for not being there for you when you needed me most. Can you find it in your heart to forgive me?"

His apology struck me speechless. A very small part of me wanted to forgive him, but I was still furious. He kept breaking his promises, not to read my mind, to be there for me... It felt like the ground was swept out from under my feet. Just like it did every time my mom came home and announced we were moving. I could forgive Alaric, but I wasn't sure I could trust him.

Unwilling to shed more tears, I swallowed the lump in my throat and the feelings down with it. We had work to get through; there was still much to do after last night.

Allowing the coolness of resignation to wash over me, I nodded. "I should apologize, too. How I spoke to you was wrong. I got worked up and I lashed out at you. It was uncalled for."

He hesitated like he didn't expect me to forgive him so easily. With eyebrows crooked upward ever so slightly, Alaric said, "I can empathize with not being able to trust people." The corner of his lip slipped behind his teeth, like he'd wanted to say more that he just couldn't.

*Please, don't waste your imprint like I did.* The thought rolled around in my head, and I scratched at the scar on my chest subconsciously.

As we approached my tent, Alaric hesitated. "I need to grab some things left behind for Khalon. Will you be okay for a few moments?"

I nodded, and he strode away, before getting too far, though, he turned back to glance over his shoulder. "Grab Moss's canteen, we'll fill it up on our way to the glen."

I didn't know what to make of the odd expression that crossed his face. I stepped up into my tent, pinning the flap back, and I realized only now that I came here with nothing and I had nothing to take. I opted to grab a spare change of clothes from Moss's folded pile under her cot. I pulled her warm brown tunic to my face and breathed in deeply. She'd smelled like the garden and fresh mint leaves. I wanted to remember that.

I stuffed the clothes into my rucksack and searched for the canteen. Despite our tent being so bare, I had trouble finding it. Then something matte black caught my eye under the tarp where her cot was. I folded on the ground and reached under the cot, grasping until I clasped cold plastic.

My phone. *What is this doing here? And why is it under Moss's bed?*

I quickly thought through how it could have ended up here accidentally, but it was wedged in between the platform and where the tarp fastened. A chill descended my spine. My mind raced back to that first day here. Moss swore she had no clue what a phone was. But why would she lie about that?

I tried to power the phone on, but it came up black. Just a worthless chunk of plastic in this world. I tucked it into my rucksack anyway. Hopefully, when I made it home, it'd still charge.

I stood up and surveyed the tent a final time. This was goodbye. The little tent had become a small home away from home. It reminded me of the time I went to Girl Scouts when I was in elementary school. I'd bunked with the leader's daughter, who had a superiority complex and made my week miserable. Even though that camping trip was awful, it was still formative. And leaving the campsite at the end of the week, having survived my first trip away from my parents, was monumental. The same sentiment washed over me here and now.

My first trip away...away from the States, to a literal whole new world. Wild. I shook my head in disbelief.

Alaric appeared in the fold of the tent and beckoned me out. "We gotta move."

# 54

# Scout

We ran through the woods. Okay, Alaric ran, at what I imagined was a comfortable pace for him, while I was a battering ram bulldozing through the woods at my highest speed. My short legs tried to keep up with him while simultaneously dodging rocks and tree roots. I was not having a good time.

Alaric slowed a few meters away from the boulder covering the entrance to the glen. He stooped, making a show of re-lacing his animal skin boots, but I knew he was really allowing me to catch my breath. I dropped my rucksack at his feet and turned to pace away from him so he didn't hear me gasping for air. The forest was still and quiet. No bird song to fill the breeze or rustle of bunnies through the bushes. Even the creatures knew to take cover.

As I paced back to him, Niah emerged from the glen, wringing her hands. I lifted a hand to wave at her, but Alaric's gaze shifted to me and subtly shook his head.

*What, it's just Niah, isn't it?*

"Hey, guys..." As Niah approached, I couldn't help but notice the look of apprehension shadowing her usual confidence.

"What's wrong?" I asked.

Niah looked over my head to the empty trees. "So the stewards aren't okay with you relocating with us..."

My eyes shot to Alaric, his jaw ticked in anger as a flood of icy water rushed over me. "W-what does that mean? Where am I supposed to go?"

"However," Niah's voice overlapped with mine. "Khalon was able to offer up a compromise that the majority agreed on..."

Khalon and a few Manters stepped from the glen to greet us just then. Alaric straightened and protectively angled his body in front of mine.

*It's just Khalon?* I thought to Alaric. What was there to worry about? Niah faded back behind Khalon and let him speak.

"I'm sorry, Scout, but we're going to have to restrain your energy in order for you to join us. I am sure you'll understand. Our people are very afraid of you after the harvest party and what came of it." He gestured to the puzzle-pieced dome above. Behind him, the Manters held up two thick, woven cords. My *restraints*, I was guessing. "At least until you have a proper bond acceptance ritual, that is. Of course, that is a choice for you to make. We will not force you like Airian attempted to do. If you decide not to join us, you are free to go."

He made it sound like an option, but where could I go? I didn't really have a choice. My breathing quickened. Yet another home I had to leave. Just when I thought I had finally found my place, it turned out they didn't really want me.

"I can't believe you would do this without talking to me." Alaric's body shielded me, obscuring my view of Khalon entirely.

"This doesn't concern you," Khalon said in his least aggressive voice. It didn't match what he was trying to do, though. It made me feel unsteady. How was this kindness?

"Absolutely, it does," Alaric argued.

"And why, pray tell, would it?"

I peeked around Alaric and saw Khalon standing with crossed arms, challenging Alaric.

"Because she's my—" And he stopped.

I knew I held my breath, waiting for him to finish the sentence, but in the silence, I heard no other breath drawn and realized we were all waiting.

*My what? Alaric?* I pressed him to answer me.

"She doesn't know?" Khalon stepped aside, bringing him back into my view, and looked between Alaric and me.

"What doesn't she know?" I asked, overemphasizing each word. The scar on my chest burned anew with a vigor that demanded my attention. I scratched and rubbed at it to no avail. Eventually, I tugged the collar of my shirt down to see the scar the Manter had covered when I had first arrived. It glimmered faintly.

My mouth dropped open.

"Is that my—? Why is my scar glowing? And are those..." Peering closer, I saw the scar had formed ridges. "Is there a thumbprint on my chest?" Even from the awkward angle I had to tilt my head, the swirl of bumps sure looked like a finger was imprinted on my... wait... *imprint*?

Alaric went rigid in front of me. I yanked at his sleeve to get him to turn and look at me, but he didn't budge.

"I don't think you're going to like this answer." All the fire in his voice from moments ago was washed away and replaced by exhaustion.

"I can see you two have some things to discuss. We'll give you a moment, but please be quick." Khalon and the Manters discreetly retreated within the glen.

"Alaric, I need to know." A slight tremor worked its way through me as I faced him.

"You don't need to be afraid—it's not scary. It's just... permanent."

"Permanent?" My eyes bulged, but in my gut, I knew something wasn't adding up. "No, it's just a scar. Scars *fade*, Alaric." I watched him closely, anxiety tripling in my core as I waited for what I knew he was going to say next.

"The Fates gave us a way to leave our mark on someone or be marked by someone who's had great significance on us. Since we don't have mothers and fathers or family as humans do, this is the closest thing to a family bond as we get."

I inhaled sharply. *Does this mean...* I couldn't even finish the thought.

But he waited for me to choose what I wanted to say.

"Do you have a mark too? Because of me?"

"Yes." He loosened the strings at the neck of his tunic and flopped back one side of the collar to reveal a matching imprint in the same place. A mirror image of mine, only daintier, as though it were my actual fingerprint.

"And is it the only mark you have?" I held my breath.

"No."

Oh. My breath escaped me, and the pain was a searing betrayal. It was completely irrational for me to be having these feelings, but I found myself blinking back tears, looking away.

I turned and looked toward the glen opening, thinking I'd rather fair my chances with the stewards who voted me out than stand here a moment longer. But Alaric got in front of me, holding his hands up to stop me.

"It's not like that."

"Said every guy ever." I brushed around him.

"Imprints aren't only for romantic partners. These are our family bonds, Scout." The way he stressed the word *family* with his accented voice, choked with emotion, stopped me. I turned back to him.

I swallowed hard, willing to hear him. To know him despite the yo-yoing he'd put my heart through.

"Don't make this so difficult, Scout. You don't know what I go through daily here. I understand you think you feel more than I do, and not just because I can hear you," he said, tapping his forehead.

"I am the only fire-bound steward in all of Landow right now who is not under the influence of Queen Soleil. Do you know what that makes me? The target of untethered suspicion. Do you know anyone who trusts me? I have two people in this whole world who have given me the benefit of the doubt." He ticked them off on his fingers. "Khalon and Mireille."

"Mireille?" I asked, dumbfounded.

"She is what I suppose you could consider my mother. She is the only other bond I have."

"Aside from me?"

"Aside from you, yes."

"So, if Mireille's scar makes her like your mom, then what does mine make me?"

Alaric pursed his lips and turned a shade pinker.

"I need a minute." My thoughts had me trudging ahead of him to get some space, but trying to make sense of this was like moving through a dense fog. How did this happen? What did it mean? But then a thought hit me, so I whirled back around to face him.

"When did this happen?" I reached up to touch my mark and tried to remember when I first noticed it. Mireille had covered mine after that morning in the woods with Khalon when I had fried Alaric.

If he was surprised, he recovered quickly. I watched as he weighed the option of telling me or giving me another half-answer.

"When you first channeled my fire."

My eyes grew wide. "You weren't going to tell me?" I swatted his arm and remembered a moment too late that my guard was down. The dark hunger within opened wide, hungry for his energy.

"Didn't I have a right to know that I'd been permanently bonded to you?" Small flames lit at the end of my fingertips and I placed my hands on his chest and shoved. When he stepped back, little singed marks glittered his shirt.

"Scout, stop, breathe. I will explain."

I channeled more of his energy, and the flickering candle lights grew into flames the size of golf balls, my gut churning with bitter rage. I was sick of being the butt of everyone's joke. As I pulled back a hand to let the fire fly, a cord wrapped around my wrist.

I yanked in reflex, but it didn't move. Whoever held my arm was stronger. I quickly turned, feeling the *whoosh* of energy leaving me, but as I did, my other wrist was wrapped and cinched. Two tight-fitting cord bracelets were my new accessory.

"You've given us no choice, Scout. If you will not honor our energy and learn to treat it with respect, you will be forced to learn or leave. What will it be?" Khalon spoke gently, hands leaving my wrists as I looked up at him, his purple eyes aglow.

Now that the energy had been dampened, my resolve to fight had burned out. A wave of humiliation washed over me. I wanted to sob, grovel.

"I'd like to stay, please."

# Scout

The afternoon sun shone down over the waterfall and ran off. I was plopped in a corner, shaded from the heat. My wrists ached from the tight binds, or rather, from me trying to wrestle them off.

I groaned. They were probably magic. At least they were like hands cuffs, I had use of my hands still, just no access to the energy I had begun to understand and enjoy.

After Khalon had my "energy receptors" blocked, he insisted Alaric and I spend some time apart. I couldn't blame him. I often wanted to be away from Alaric. But then just thinking of him had the imprint tingling and I found myself craving his proximity. Did he feel it too?

"Hello, my friends." Khalon's voice echoed off the walls of the glen and over our heads, reverberating into the sky. "I know many of you have questions and are concerned. Let me put your woes at ease promptly. We are safe here now. Alaric and the guards are manning a new perimeter and the Manters have set up a new protective covering. It will take a few days to reinforce it to the degree of shielding we had previously, but at this point, we are covered and will not be found." The crowd murmured their relief in response.

"What happened at the harvest party was a devastation. I know we are all feeling the loss of one of our own and the loss of what we once knew as our home. But home was never about a place; home is about the people you're with and the purpose we all serve. Together, we will find a way back to ourselves.

"Unfortunately, we will be staying put here until any external threat can be evaluated and put to rest. We don't know how long that will take, so we advise you all to set up a more permanent camp."

The group responded in a collection of dissatisfied grunts.

"I know." He quieted them with a gentle hand raised. "We will figure this out, but for now, we need to work together. This evening, the elders and Manters will meet and we'll have more information for you. Until then, look after one another, sharpen your gifts, and stay alert."

When Khalon concluded his speech, he dismissed us to help the Manters finish preparing the glen to be our home. Some stewards worked to convert an alcove into a new storage house, while others carried firewood in from outside. A mound of pails sat untouched and I grabbed two and headed toward the stream. I might not be very useful in terms of energy or strength, but I remembered how to fetch a pail of water.

I crouched low next to the stream and pressed one bucket at a time under the water. I made three trips before perching on a rock to take a break. I was far enough away from the waterfall to hear its roar and gaze at its remarkable beauty, but not close enough to get sprayed.

The sun was just past its peak, but it felt so much later. My mind was overwhelmed and weary with grief. My normally upturned face couldn't find the strength to lift. I wanted to sleep and cry forever. Leaning forward, I dipped my fingers into a shallow, slow-moving part of the stream. I muddled the water and watched it resettle. That's exactly how my life had always felt. Like someone stuck their fingers in and muddled everything up just to watch me settle it. Over and over. Every time we moved for my mom's work, it was a new school, a new house, new friends, new routines. Eventually, I got so used to it that I never really settled. I stopped expecting the next place to be home, stopped expecting the next school to accept me. Until Pickins County, I didn't think I'd ever find a good group of friends.

But I did. I'd found them, and they loved me. It was surreal. The big, bad shadow of graduation loomed over us, though, and with its treacherous teeth, it was going to split us up. I was going to lose the only real friends I made in years. But of course, it would seem my parents' surprise trip to Scandinavia did it before college and the demands of *adulting* could.

I plunged my hand back under the water, fingers splayed out rigid, and shook it. All the flecks of algae and moss on the stones swirled in the clean water. Destroying the perfect calm that had been once restored.

And then I dared to think I could find a semblance of home in my aunties' place. I didn't want to go, didn't want to like them. I wanted to hold them at a distance. But stupid Effie and her stupid dancing under the moonlight and wretched gleeful disposition snookered me. She made me hope.

I yanked my hand out of the water and wiped my freezing fingers on my pants.

Now I was trapped with more questions than answers. I thought I knew my family, knew their history. I thought I had begun to figure out the mysteries, but with each new piece of the puzzle came more questions, more confusion. I reminded myself that this place wasn't home either. It was something completely different. There was a time when I had begun to think that this place could become home, but I realized that would never happen. No amount of time or encouragement would make me feel safe here, like I belonged here. I would always be *the human*.

I sank my head into my hands, twisting my fingers through my loose hair. I gave it a frustrated tug.

I'd had to come to terms with so many things in the short time I'd been here.

If I were to make a list: I was the descendent of gatekeepers who protected a secret portal to another world. I was the next in line to inherit the position and be tied to the portal's gate until I died or another descendant reached their eighteenth birthday. I was a channeler with magical abilities that terrified everyone else.

And, oh, who could forget?

I had an imprint with a fire-stewarding guy. I didn't even know the proper terminology. But apparently the bond was permanent, so I guess there would be time to figure it out.

My mom raised me to believe women were strong. That I was capable. No matter the assignment, drama, or conflict, she'd tell me the same thing: *Your strength doesn't come from what you can do, but simply from who you are, Scout.*

But right now, whoever I'd become here... I didn't feel strong anymore. Tears poked from my eyes. This was all just too much. More than this version of myself was capable of handling.

Glancing down at the rough twine around my wrists, I remembered. I was strong enough that these people—magical people—were afraid of me. This version of me wasn't weaker for being far away. I *was* capable. This Scout could handle anything.

*I'm not going to let you die here, and neither are they.*

It almost shocked me upright, the memory of Alaric's voice slid into my mind. It felt so real, like I was reliving the moment again. I blinked back the tears as I remembered him carrying me through the forest, humming a sweet song, and ushering a blanket of peace over my mind.

Lifting my head, I cleared my throat and pushed away the tremble of defeat and self-pity. Across the glen, Alaric was helping build a fire for a few older-looking stewards. I watched as he moved quickly and deftly. He placed each log with care, building a strong base before extending his hands as one would to warm them. A slow burn began at the base, and smoke swirled up. Smiles crept onto the others' faces with sincere gratitude.

It was the first time I ever saw Alaric use his gift, and I realized I never took the time to appreciate it. I'd been so caught up in my life-changing series of events that I hadn't really considered Alaric for more than a glancing thought. Of course he was hot and made my heart do gymnastics, and a small part of me felt drawn to his moody outcast vibe, but I thought I was actually starting to feel something more for him.

He chose that moment, still crouched, gently coaxing the fire to life, to turn and look back at me. A question in his eyes. Subconsciously, I lifted a hand and rubbed at the imprint on my chest.

*Maybe I need to give him a chance...* My heart thrummed in response, and the imprint on my chest tightened. I knew if I looked down I would find a small glow, but instead, I held his gaze until he looked away first.

*Don't waste your imprint like I did,* Moss's note said. Now I understood. Somehow she knew of my imprint with Alaric before I did. Did she see it when the Manter was changing the dressings?

*If not for me, for Moss—*

My thoughts were interrupted by a shifting wind around me.

*Scout, help! Please hurry!* The voice was unfamiliar. It wasn't the same taunting voice that often disturbed me before.

I jumped to my feet, dusting off the butt of my pants and looked around. Who said that? It wasn't like the other times the Whispering Winds spoke to me. When their whispers came, they were haunting, and almost always hurtful. This sounded like a cry for help.

The cavern within me creaked open begging for freedom— the part of me I'd finally begun to make peace with before I destroyed everything. My eyes shuttered closed and I sensed the movement of energy around me. Something intangible pulled me towards the waterfall. The voice echoed in my mind, my heart thrumming in response.

Trekking up the path towards the waterfall, I let my hand trace the layers in the rock. Colling's Cavern was so similar to the glen where Effie took me that I could fully envision the wild pastry man yelling at clients to take his goodies. When Alaric brought me here and told me about our mirrored worlds, I couldn't believe it. Even being here now was strange, like the gap between our worlds didn't exist. Who's to say I was neither here nor there right now? How would I really know if I was in my world or theirs in a moment like this where it was a near replica of my own?

*Scout, please, we're running out of time.*

The voice was distinctly female, and her words trembled in a panicked whisper. I had an inexplicable feeling that told me she was trying not to get caught. I could feel her fear course through my body, cooling me to the bone.

But where was I supposed to go? I scanned the waterfall, my eyes rising up, up, up. At the top, the cavern walls splayed out, a whole new world up above us. In my mind, I remembered the shack Aunt Effie brought me to but never took me inside, and I felt this urge to get to it. Who were those people she had wanted me to meet?

I climbed the stone steps carved into the side of the cavern wall. They were wet with fresh spray and slippery under these handmade slipper shoes. The stairs grew steeper and the cacophony of gushing water slamming into rocks was nearly deafening now. Ahead, the path disappeared as the waterfall descended over it. I huffed and looked back the way I'd come. How did people make it to the top? I tiptoed closer and saw that the path continued behind the waterfall. I paused to let the spray refresh my sweat-beaded face from the climb.

*Hurry.*

I kept going. Over jagged, uneven rocks until breaking through the top. I shielded my eyes from the blinding sun. After being inside the cavern, and in the shadow of the waterfall, my eyes had to adjust. Blinking, I looked around.

On my side of the veil, I remembered feeling alive in the midst of the moment, looking down into the glen and seeing for miles around. There were tall trees that reached down for me, or maybe that was just in my head. But here, on this side, it was even more breathtaking. The trees are taller, the boughs fuller and more bright with shades of green I'd never seen before. Birds flew and chirped all around. The trees rustled with lively movement.

I let my eyes close gently and checked in with the energy around me. It pulsed and surged, and I found it without needing to look for it. It rushed up to greet me and bound around me, touching every inch of my skin. Opening my eyes, I searched the corner of the plateau for the small shack. The forest was much denser here.

As I looked, there came a tap on my shoulder. I turned to find Alaric's gaze locked on me.

"Hey, what are you doing up here?"

"I heard someone." I gestured in the direction of where the shack would be if I were in England. "I need to see what it is."

I got closer to the tree line and reached out to touch the bark of the tree. I just wanted to run my hands over it—somehow I knew it would ground me and ease the wrestle of emotions in my stomach. As I breezed past it, I was flung backwards.

"Scout! Don't. Touch. Anything." Alaric was immediately at my side with a hand on my arm, pulling me back from the forest. I looked at him with a question in my eyes, but he held up one finger to his lips. Quiet.

I listened. Everything had gone still. No rustling of birds in branches or crickets chirping. Even the wind had died down and was holding off.

In a flash, Alaric was in front of me, and the pulse of orange in his eyes was radiating angrily.

"Wh—" I was quickly cut off by the guttural noise Alaric made. The air shifted around us and cooled. He crouched in front of me, ready to fight, swaying slightly to take up more space. He backed us away from the tree line and towards the stairs.

I didn't see danger, but I trusted his instincts in this world better than mine. I tried to reach out to the energy around me to prepare to channel it if needed, but there was a blockage. I looked down at the bonds on my wrists and tried to pull free from them.

I checked over Alaric's shoulder, waiting to see what he already sensed. The air in front of us warped slightly and rippled, the way water did when a stone was tossed in. If I had blinked, I would have missed it.

"What are you doing here, Tembi?" Alaric growled in a low voice. "What do you want?"

An ancient voice chimed on the wind toward us. "Your time is up. Soleil wants what belongs to her." It sounded like it was coming from everywhere and nowhere at once. The hair on the back of my neck stood on end.

"You're not allowed to be here. You are breaching the boundary. Get out." He reached around, pulling me closer to his back.

I reached for him as well. There was nothing I could do. A thought struck me defenseless. Alaric said it wasn't supposed to be here. How did it get in?

Me. I caused the hole in the protective dome that allowed who-knew-what into Ruack Valley. This was all my fault. Again. The urge within shook me from my deafening remorse, and demanded I get to the shack. I had to find it.

Hidden behind Alaric, I looked for a way out. A copse of trees to my left offered coverage. As Alaric threw a gust of flames at the Tembi, I inched my way backwards before diving under a fallen tree to hide.

Alaric's hands rose as he passed great waves of fire between his hands until a spiral formed. The fire tornado was unlike anything I'd ever seen before. A gasp escaped my lips as he launched it at the Tembi. The inferno gained speed and circumference, consuming everything in its path, including the Tembi.

With the Tembi waylaid, Alaric ran to me, holding out a hand. The look in his eyes told me he was asking for more than just my hand.

Could I trust him?

Even after he had hidden the bond from me?

Even after playing hot and cold with my heart?

Despite it all, I trusted him. I couldn't shake it, the way I felt so close to him so fast. Maybe it was just the imprint or bond, or whatever, but when I looked in his eyes, I never wanted to look away.

I lifted my hand and his calloused fingers enclosed around mine, causing a heat to rise from my chest up my neck.

"That Tembi won't be down for long, we'll need to get to safety. The Tembi is a spy for Soleil, which means if it's found us, then Soleil knows right where we are. She watches through their forms. They are her eyes that roam the continent."

A chill crept down my spine and left me speechless.

Alaric tugged my hand and pulled me towards the stairs once more.

"I can't," I stopped. "The voice, I have to find it."

"It's Soleil, I know it. The assignment against you from the Whispering Winds, It was her." The pleading in his eyes almost swayed me. "*This is a trap*, Scout. We have to *go*." His voice was gentler, not commanding. I wanted to go with him, I wanted to try to go back to the way things were before the lunar event. But I couldn't.

"It's not *her*. It's not the same as the whispering winds. I'll admit, it's probably too much of a coincidence to not be her, but something in my gut is telling me the voice I'm hearing *isn't* her."

Heat pooled in my belly as Alaric's pulsing gaze roved over my face. His jaw ticked, brow furrowed in consternation. He gave a curt nod and squeezed my hand.

Just then, a high-pitched screech filled the air. The Tembi was awake.

Alaric whipped his head around at me with terror in his eyes and screamed, "Run!"

# 56

# Scout

I didn't think twice. I bolted for the woods in the opposite direction, reaching the edge of the woods as a thunderous boom shook the earth. As I stepped into the shade of the forest, I stole a look behind me. Alaric had been thrown into the trunk of a tree across the plateau from me, causing it to snap and fold.

I gasped and shrieked. But his fiery eyes found mine, and he screamed at me to go. I forced myself farther into the woods, slipping on damp peat moss. I righted my steps and rushed ahead, searching for the shack that I knew must be here. The drive within me urged me onward. I was bending under a fallen tree when I saw it. The air before me warped again like a mirage, heat rising on the desert. I didn't know what it was, but I knew this was bad. And it was getting closer.

I cowered into a crouch. I was not sure if I could go through it or what would happen. Alaric crashed through the forest behind me. He was loud enough that I wouldn't be surprised if a few trees were crushed in his wake.

My eyes scanned the area, looking for a way out. To my left ran the edge of the cavern's wall and a straight drop down into the glen... *Splat*. I quickly scanned the woods ahead, hoping to see the small leaning shack, but no. Fear was a ravenous beast inside me, consuming me in large gulps. I was so frustrated I could sob.

I considered what power I had at the ready, despite the dampening effects of the bracelets, but something about being in a blind panic prevented me from quieting my mind to find the energy within. Alaric was getting closer now, only a few feet away, but what was he going to do? This mirage had thrown him into a tree.

And that's when I felt it—a surge of heat growing from the ground up, up, up, my legs into my hips, and shoulders. I shuddered. I looked behind me to find what looked to be Alaric but was a pillar of fire. He was in the midst of flames; they were all around him, spiraling from him. The flames trailed from him to me. They grew more intense with each second.

Encased in his glow, I felt protected. Like the fire of Alaric was a barrier between me and whatever this was. Alaric was here. The beginning of relief set in. He would figure something out. He would know how to get out of this.

A blast-like scream bursted forth from the mirage. If a mirage could be sentient, this one was furious. The Tembi grew, morphing into a thick gray smoke. I watched, horrified, as it expanded and formed into a contained globe around us. Smoke took shape, solidifying like it hit a glass ceiling.

I gasped for a fresh breath, but between the smothering heat and the smoke filling the space around me, clean air was gone. Then, disguised behind my coughs, I felt the yank. The tug at the edge of my mind. And my thought train was gone. Any hope I had of channeling, gone with it.

"Your time in Ruack Valley is over, you wretched channeler. Soleil lays claim to your soul!" Another burst of angry, smoke gusted at my face, pushing my hair back. It smelled like stale cigarettes and made my eyes water. Its voice, haunting and ethereal, echoed in the magically contained space, and my heart dropped further with each rendition of the echo I heard.

"I wonder what the queen will do with you." The voice turned taunting, playful. "I'm sure she won't mind if I have some fun with you first."

Alaric doubled over with a gasp, trying to get between me and the disembodied voice. The thumbprint on my chest blazed and a new thought bloomed in my mind.

Alaric was trapped in here with me. I whirled on him and held out my wrists.

*Can you burn these off? I have an idea.* I thought, hoping the Tembi couldn't read thoughts.

Alaric gave me a dubious look.

He took my hands, cupping his palms over the binds, careful not to touch my skin. Heat tingled as sweat formed below his grasp. The smell of charring twine filled the air.

*Is it working?* I twisted my arms to take a peek.

"Hold still." He grunted.

The smoke continued to fill the air around us, charges like electricity glimmering in the darkening orb.

"It's no use, your time is up!" The Tembi jeered.

*Hurry, Alaric,* I whispered to him. My throat constricted with smoke inhalation and I choked on a cough.

I closed my eyes and tried to calm my speeding heart, focusing on my breathing like Mireille and Niah taught me. I blocked out the smells and forced my mind to ignore this invisible monster's taunts.

It was working. My gift of channeling stretched out and uncurled within me. It rose up to greet me and I reached back, welcoming it to move through me.

I glanced down and had the confirmation I needed. Alaric had burned the twines from my wrists. I shook out my hands and the remnants fell to the ground.

The Tembi sprang forward, grabbing from the energy surrounding us. I searched the globe for the mirage, the source of this attack. I extended my hands, sweeping around the confined space. There was no way out, but If I could channel enough energy and quickly, perhaps I could rupture the vault it had created.

Pulling from the charge in the air and the waves of energy emanating from Alaric's body, I extended a hand into the smoke. The Tembi screeched, and when I opened my eyes, I saw a ripple of his figure around us. I let out a frustrated yell before dissolving into a coughing fit. This was impossible. The confinement was slowly killing us.

*Maybe if I can just connect with it,* I thought, *I can use its powers against it. That should generate enough force to blow it apart.*

"Don't. Use me instead," Alaric choked out as a response to my thoughts. And just then, without needing to read his thoughts, I knew Alaric was thinking the same thing. We needed more energy. I needed more fuel. With determination glinting in his eyes, he grabbed my face, and the moment his skin touched mine, the fire started. His eyes were sharp and clear as diamonds. I watched his pupils blow out largely and red flames danced in his eyes. His gaze trailed down to my lips.

A deep connection surged between us. A wanting on a deeper level than I could explain. His arms wrapped around me as my temperature spiked, and I became very aware of the heat radiating from him. Despite how angry he made me and the ache of betrayal I'd felt because of him, somehow he felt like home.

He stooped lower, hair falling into his eyes... his lips were only a heartbeat away. I lifted my chin until his hot breath met my skin. His energy pulsated a thrumming beat between us before his lips touched mine. The moment he did, I was swept up in the fury and the flame.

My knees weakened, and as he pulled away, a soft moan left my lips. I was tempted to be embarrassed, but that kiss stole my senses, and it would take a lot to un-swoon me now.

Opening my eyes felt impossible. They were heavy with longing for more. More of this moment, this feeling outside of time, this feeling of *home*. The scar under my clavicle burned to life. It itched and made my skin crawl. I pulled back the neck of my tunic and saw it glow.

Alaric mirrored my action, pulling back his tunic on the opposite shoulder to reveal his imprint glowing a brilliant red. I ran my fingers over it and felt the minute ridges crest and fall. It was a perfect replica of my fingerprint. I let my index finger rest in the grooves for a moment. It felt extraordinary. The connection fueled the hunger in me.

Alaric trailed his hand down my arm and interlocked his fingers with mine. "Use as much of me as you need," he whispered into my ear.

I remembered the barrier in my mind that I had created before. I pictured it now, opting to allow only his strength and force in, funneling the rage elsewhere. I gave way to the energy. It surged forward, and I itched to release it, but held it in. I wanted it to build like it did the night of the harvest party. Though this time, I was sure I could manage it better and wouldn't blow a hole in their new dome.

The energy pulsed under my fingertips; my heart thrummed wildly, the blood sloshing in my ears. Together, we lifted our hands toward the edge of our confinement.

Every bit of power I could conjure, I released in one steady stream, directing it at the invisible barrier. A gut-wrenching bellow erupted from somewhere deep in me. I let everything go. Alaric's hand pulverized mine as he raged fire at the barrier alongside me. A fissure formed and began to spiderweb out like broken glass. A stab to my gut reminded me that the dome looked the same last night. But I pushed the memory away and focused on this present evil. We pressed in, relentless until the barrier gave out and the smoke whooshed free, dropping to the ground as a covering.

The mirage glimmered before me, rippling through the air like tiny shock waves on a still lake. I lunged toward it hoping for a quick boost of energy. The motion was quick enough to connect with its power, but an electrical current unlike anything I've ever felt coursed through me. Doubling over, I hollered in pain.

"Ah, ah, ah, not such a good idea, my dear," its guiling voice chimed, making my skin crawl.

I reached for Alaric and dropped the barrier in my mind, letting the intensity swirl and intermingle with the electricity in me. His touch was an open match dropped in a barrel of oil. The ignite came just before a kaboom. My back arched, and my teeth gritted together. Every ounce of power inside me burst forth at full force. A shock wave rippled around us, knocking everything backwards, including the Tembi. I couldn't see it as it flew, but I saw the crunch left in the bark of a tree trunk where it collided.

I didn't know whether it was dead or alive, if it even could die, but I turned to find Alaric. He was dazed, but conscious. I grabbed his hand, and we ran.

"I have to find the shack!" I told him as we sprinted through the woods. "You don't have to go with me if you don't want to, but whatever this is calling to me, it needs to get to the shack. Something is waiting for me... or some*one*."

I paused long enough to pant and search his eyes. I saw his questions, but he nodded once.

"I'm with you."

And we ran.

# Alaric

As we barreled through the woods, leaping over fallen trunks and dodging thorn bushes, the frost over my heart thawed. I had never felt this way for another person. Searching Scout's eyes, I saw my future. The deepest yearning I had ever felt burned through me the moment my lips met hers. The dreams the Fates gave me couldn't compare with this. I wished I could hold onto this moment forever.

I wished it had happened under different circumstances.

The imprint on my chest burned greedily, craving more connection, a deeper entwinement. I never had a romantic imprint before. I'd only ever heard stories from jaded men in war rooms and stolen whispers at the bunkhouse. What I felt for Scout didn't compare to even their accounts. I wanted to mull on this, but there wasn't time. I forced my mind to sharpen, to focus.

The Tembi was disengaged for now. Tembis didn't like to get their hands dirty. They were conniving little spy orbs that Soleil used to track her enemies. I had worked with them briefly during Soleil's reign. Despicable creatures, but they didn't fight well. It would be nursing whatever wound or depletion Scout caused for weeks, and likely wouldn't come after us again anytime soon. I just needed to get her to safety.

"I think it's this way." Scout tugged my hand in a new direction.

In her mind, I could see the image of the one she was looking for—a squat wooden shanty. My eyes flicked quickly through the forest, but I saw nothing. I had a bad feeling about this.

"Wait, I feel it. It's close." Scout stopped and reached her hand out. Before us was a small clearing in the dense woods, covered in the shade from the towering pines. The grass flattened, like something used to be here.

Scout stretched out a hand and it stopped abruptly as though pressed against glass. The containment of the Tembi we had just escaped flashed to mind for a moment. After a brief assessment, I came to the conclusion that this was not the same situation. Something was cloaked here in the woods. That realization brought no consolation. Hidden things, after all, were not often meant to be found

A metallic jiggling, her hand cupped and turned around a knob. She crept forward on the balls of her feet, the creak of an ancient door echoing in the still woods. My chest hammered and I grabbed her arm before she could disappear.

Scout's eyes questioned me as her steps faltered in the invisible doorway, and a dark feeling brewed in my gut.

"I don't think this is a good idea, Scout. We need to go to Khalon now. We don't know whose place this is. It might not be sa—"

"Scout?" A distorted woman's voice warbled through the space around us.

Recognition dawned on Scout's face, but her mind was a blur of all the faces of women she knew, trying to place the voice. But I had a feeling that Soleil had laid this trap for us both, and if we didn't leave, we'd be doomed.

"Hurry, please, before it's too late," the woman's voice wobbled in a low whisper, broken by despair.

"Scout, let's *go*." I tugged her hand away from the shack once more, but she didn't budge. Her eyes glazed over as she peered into something I couldn't see.

"What do I do?" Scout whispered. The fear radiated from her, a tangible tremor.

But in her mind, I could see she'd already decided. She was going to go after the woman.

"If you do, I am going with you."

"No, Alaric, I don't think you can." She shook her head without looking at me.

Before she could disappear, a torturous feeling I'd never felt rose in my gut. *Was this anxiety?* I whispered my fears. "Not every portal from the other side leads back to Landow, Scout."

She squeezed my hand, but kept the other on the knob. As her mind began to form a question, I spat out my answer. "Because I can't lose you." I realized it was true as the words left my lips.

With one foot in the invisible door opening, she reached a hand out to my face. Her typical nervousness had made its way into my body somehow, and I felt an emotion too strong to push away. Scout leaned her forehead against mine and, eyes closed, I fought every instinct to drag her back to safety with me. Then her lips against mine sent a tremor of strength through me again. Strength to let her go.

"Everything'll be okay, Alaric. Have a little faith." Her breath felt warm against my ear.

Before I could say anything more, she rushed forward into the shack through the doorway.

"No! Scout!" I roared. Chills ached through me.

I placed one hand gingerly on the door and found it solid. I reared back to drive my fist through it, but stopped. If this shack was a portal, or contained one, it was my only way to get to Scout. I couldn't break it. I needed to keep it intact so I could find her again. I placed my other hand on the doorpost and leaned my forehead against it. Careful, ever so careful.

"No, Scout," I whispered. A small tremor tripped through me, and the shack began shaking. A surging energy pulled from the doorway, and I jumped back from the threshold. Clearing it just in time, my suspicions confirmed. The shack itself wasn't a portal, but contained one. Wherever this door led—wherever it took Scout—I was too late. Scout was gone.

A searing pain stole my breath away. I dropped to my knees, my hands went to my chest, and I groaned deeply. After a moment, I pulled my hands back, expecting to find blood but saw none, just a lifeless imprint. A darkness bloomed in my chest where a pulsating bond once was. My connection to Scout was gone from this world, along with her.

"I will find you, Scout. I promise."

# 58

# Scout

My chest thrummed as I rushed through the door, stumbling on the uneven threshold. A protective cloak, like the one over our Ruack Valley, must have been shielding the shack, making it invisible to the outside world. The shimmer of it cascaded over the door behind me, sealing me within. I gazed back at the door, considering all I was leaving behind. Niah and Rhydian, a group of friends who had begun to accept me, Mireille, who had become so much more than a mentor, a place where I was beginning to find my purpose, and Alaric... Oh, Alaric.

Tears began to pool in the corners of my eyes, but I wouldn't let them spill over. Not yet. For a moment, I could still feel the tenderness of Alaric's lips against mine, and I lifted a hand to cherish the memory. A single tear slid down my cheek. It was all I could allow, or I would come undone.

Tearing my eyes from the door, I pressed inward before I lost my nerve. I wasn't doing this for me, but for all the people I had come to love in Landow. Whatever had come after us wasn't going to stop. It was after me. Staying here, I was putting Alaric and all of Khalon's people in danger. It was my presence that brought foul play upon Moss. I wasn't sure how I would ever live with myself after that realization, but if there was any way to prevent further damage, I had to try.

Staggering from the threshold, I peered around the shack. Dust motes lingered, suspended in the stagnant air, making this space look untouched and outside of time. My eyes scanned the room, looking for the portal, some other entrance, or an exit. I felt a surge of power from touching the door; it reminded me of the explosion I experienced with the greenhouse and with Alaric in the woods. I was coming to realize portals had an unmistakable energy signature. I shook the nerves out of my hands. *I have no idea where this one will lead, but I'm in the right place. I have to be.*

In the corner of the room sat a cot with the frame rusted out in the middle. Upon it was a sagging, threadbare blanket. Beside the cot, a side table separated it from a bucket of brackish water. Dust covered every exposed surface. I was afraid to breathe in the disgusting particles. On the far wall, a mirror stood out from among the dilapidated furniture. Light from an open window poured in, lighting the mirror. It was perfectly clean with a glimmering sheen that drew the eye.

Peering into the mirror, I saw nothing, not even my face. I thought about rubbing it—surely there was something over the glass preventing a reflection—but a voice stopped me.

"*Ah, ah, ah,* I wouldn't touch that if I were you. That's a powerful portal I don't think you're ready to use just yet." It was the same voice that called for me from outside, but it was crystal clear and no longer burdened by fear.

I spun on my heel and found a young woman perched on the edge of the cot. My jaw went slack. My mind whirled trying to piece together the connections. Her thin frame, the piercing blue eyes that crinkled at the edges.

*There's no way...*

"Wondering how it is you missed me, dear? The cottage isn't the only thing cloaked in protection." She lifted her hand and the shack transformed from crumbling and decrepit to pristine. The floorboards were swept bare and shined with polish. The bed became a stunning four-poster king-size with matching classy side tables and dressers. The whole shanty became a glamorous cottage, even expanding in size.

The wonder of it all shook me to my core. *How is this even possible? I've never seen energy do something like this before...*

As though answering my thoughts, the woman stood and approached me. A playful smile tugged at the edge of her lips.

"I know you must have a million questions, Scout, and I promise to answer them eventually, but right now, we are very short on time. I have been waiting for you for many, many years." The voice carried authority like Aunt Zelda's, but was the same sweet timbre as Aunt Effie's. The similarities between them was obvious.

Up close, the woman's features came into stunning clarity. She looked exactly like the photographs in the family album... exactly like me. She'd barely aged a day. It was Josephine. A *young* Josephine.

"How am I here right now? Why am I here? Have you been the one leading me to the shack?"

"Yes—"

"Has it been you all along? The messages about something coming after me? Has it all be you?" I had to know.

"No, I only just found a way to tap into the Whispering Winds... but listen to me. Queen Soleil has imprisoned me, and she's after you now. She won't stop until our line is blotted out and she has control over all of Landow. You have to get out now. You have to go home and complete the bond ritual. You don't stand a chance if you don't accept. The curse will seek you out and destroy you, love. It's the only way. I'm so sorry, Scout... I never should have brought you here."

"Wait, what do you mean? You brought me here?" My mouth went dry as I thought back to the night of my birthday, running out of the greenhouse straight into Ruack Valley. I thought of how Khalon had me surrounded in the forest the next morning replaying each step. I tried and failed to recreate the moment I accessed the portal, but what I told them was true: I didn't do anything...

*Was it all Josephine?*

"Of course. With the greenhouse disabled, I had to do it all myself. I thought if I could reopen the portal, and get you here, maybe—just maybe—you would find me and together we could find our way home together. Foolish," her voice tapered off and she swept a hand across her brow in regret.

My chest deflated. Somehow this singular thought robbed me of all the confidence I'd built up around my gift as a channeler. If I didn't open the portal... was I even a channeler at all? Had we been operating under a false assumption? And now she was demanding I complete the ritual as well. What if it was my destiny—being a gatekeeper—and I had been too stubborn to see it?

"But why? Why bring me here if you knew it was dangerous?" This place I had come to love was slowly being taken away from me. A pain I couldn't explain slowly filled me and made me feel heavy.

"I'm sorry, Scout. I'll explain everything later." She moved toward the mirror, dismissing my questions. Before she removed the cloak, it was a small mirror over a dresser with a rusted frame, but now it was a floor-to-ceiling, gold-embossed, ornate mirror.

"But wait, the greenhouse? You 'disabled' it? Is that why nothing would grow? Also, you know that your whole family thinks you're dead, right?"

A conflicted look caused her confident features to waver. "It was a necessary evil. I couldn't have them come after me where I was going." Her words were clipped and void of emotion. It made me think there was more she wasn't saying.

"I found your letters. You told them you were going to Kilburne. What happened?"

She paused, then gave me a cunning look. "You didn't tell them about the letters." It wasn't a question. "Why?"

I shrugged. "They already lost you once. They didn't need to lose you again."

Nodding curtly, she seemed to accept this response. "I am using a great deal of energy to be here right now to save you. Can we get on with this?" She gestured to the mirror. "No one can know you saw me, and no one can know that I helped you. I'm afraid my power over the gates is waning and you need to be prepared. I will lead you through the portal, but you must go and you must remain at Biddenmore."

Even as she said it, asking me to promise to stay at Biddenmore, I already knew I would be lying if I agreed. I would find my way back here one day.

"What about you? Where are you imprisoned? Where is Soleil keeping you?"

The look she gave said, *daft girl.* "Somewhere no one could ever reach me. The In-Between."

I racked my brain for the familiar phrase. The In-Between. Where had I heard that? Didn't the Fates create it?

"You're with The Twins?" Shock caused the question to lurch ungracefully from my mouth.

Josephine's eyes slanted at me. "What do you know about The Twins?"

"Not much. Just that they tried to destroy humanity and cause a war between the Others and us, so The Fates put them in an otherworldly prison."

Her face softened, remembering as though she was there for it. "Enough, it's time to go."

"But, Josephine. I can't do this. I—" I think about tugging down my tunic to show her my imprint, but instead, my fingers glazed over the fabric. I closed my eyes. Leaving Alaric would likely shred my heart to pieces, but if I wanted to keep him safe and everyone else I cared about here... I had to do this. I had to follow her.

"You fell in love," She paused, eyes assessing me, seeing far more than I was comfortable with, "with this place. Like I did, didn't you?" She reached out to me, but like a ghost, her hand faded right through me. The thought of her touch was comforting.

I nodded as another tear slid down my cheek. "It's the only way, isn't it?"

"If you don't, the curse will claim your love." She heaved a sigh.

*My love?* I wondered, my fingers trailing to my lips, remembering the kiss with Alaric. The imprint on my chest burned faintly, reminding me of our connection. If great-grandma Jo was to be believed, if I didn't go home and complete the ritual, I would lose Alaric. Was it worth it? I'd only known him for a short time. I couldn't unwaveringly say I was *in love* with him, could I?

"Why can't I complete the bond ritual here?" I knew it was futile to ask; completing the bond here wouldn't protect the others, but we could find a way, couldn't we?

"Airian is a fool, always has been. And much too zealous for his own good. But I fear he went too far this time. A gatekeeper's bond ritual cannot be done in any world but their own, it never would have worked, no matter what he did."

Somehow that didn't make me feel better... neither the fact that my great-grandmother knew Airian, nor the fact that I was never really in jeopardy of losing the battle of wills.

In a small voice, I resigned to my fate. "What am I supposed to do?"

"Take a deep breath and get ready. I'll try to send you home, but I'm not sure where exactly you'll end up. It isn't an exact science. When you get home, my sweet Efrata and Griselda will guide you." A wistfulness filled her eyes, sheening over them, as though she wished it were her passing through the portal and not me.

Josephine inched closer to the mirror, pressing a finger to the glass, causing a ripple effect that seemed to activate the portal in a way. Stealing a glance behind me toward the door, I murmured a goodbye to Alaric and everything we could have been. In the quiet of my heart, I made a promise to myself that I would see him again.

A shaky breath rumbled through my chest as I pressed into the mirror—and hopeful-ly—into my world.

# Scout

Electricity zapped and burned through me. Squeezing my eyes against the vibrating pain, I fought to right myself but pitched sideways in dizziness.

As I got my bearings, I opened my eyes and found myself standing in the middle of another forest. Bright moon beams shone from above while the stars twinkled faintly, paling in comparison to the looming giant. Wherever I had ended up seemed to be in a different time zone. *Did different realms have measurable time zones?* I wondered. A shiver down my spine detailed the train of thought. The sunny glen of Colling's Cavern had warmed my skin and left me unprepared for this sudden temperature drop. Rubbing my arms with vigor, I whirled around calling for Josephine.

The only response was the dull echo of my own voice against the trees. "Where are you?"

*No, no, no, no. This can't be happening. Where am I?* This was not Ruack Valley, and it didn't look like home either. I spun in a circle, looking for anything familiar. My heartbeat kicked into gear as the reality of being in yet another new world dawned on me. The pounding in my chest robbed me of breath. I could be anywhere. I had to find my way home *now*.

I swerved through the trees aimlessly, but adrenaline buzzed through my body and I couldn't stand still. Fear gripped my heart, catapulting me forward. What if the mirror Josephine used was the wrong portal? What if this place was actually full of hungry headhunting cannibals who loved to eat young girls for dinner? *Ugh, that puts a whole new, disgusting meaning behind girl dinner.* I tried to stave off my spiraling thoughts.

My legs protested under me as I raced through the trees. A clearing appeared up ahead and I bolted for it. As I entered the dell, I hoped to see the overflowing community garden with beautiful arrangements of flowers along the edges. I hoped to see the Manters' storehouse standing like a beacon of hope in the middle of the camp, but a quick scan of the area crushed my hopes.

What I did see up ahead was a grassy hill and small light coming from beyond it. I gathered my strength to run along the tree line to the knoll. The path was less direct, but I could remain hidden that way. I hurried to the base of the hill, crouching to catch my breath. It was too dark to make out any shapes. But there weren't any noises except for the *swish-swish* of my tights and tunic as I ran.

Forging the hill while staying low to the ground was a workout I didn't expect. Tall grass filled the area and gave me the cover I needed to uncurl my spine and let my burning thighs rest. Ahead, there seemed to be a shed with a dim light. Maybe I could get help. Maybe they had phones in this world? As I gunned towards the light, I heard it. The sound of water. But it wasn't the sound of the river I'd grown accustomed to. It was a constant lapping of waves on a shore, on a rough, pebbled shore. My chest heaved. I knew that sound. I had found solace within it everyday this summer at my aunties.

The anxiety in my heart turned to desperation as I realized that faint light that glimmered above the knoll was the light in the greenhouse.

As I ran, a warm mix of relief and nostalgia I didn't expect filled each foot-strike upon the earth. The greenhouse came into view, and off behind it, the patio with string lights winked in the wind. The sea breeze tasted like salt in my mouth, and I breathed it in as deeply as I could while running.

Thanking Josephine, *as if she could hear me*, I reached for the knob on the green glass door, and I heard it. The familiar sound of women bickering that could only mean one thing: *I was home.* A warmth rushed over me as the thought clicked into place in my heart and resounded as truth. No matter where I ended up, no matter what came next,

I wouldn't be alone. I stroked the imprint on my chest. Landow changed me for good. I would never be purposeless again.

Without a moment to waste, I threw open the door, albeit a tad recklessly. It buffeted off the wall, rattling the old glass and succinctly interrupting my aunties' bickering. The sound was music to my ears.

"Scout!"

"Where have you been?"

"What are you wearing?" Their voices overlapped.

I was greeted with a rush of hands on my arms and face. They pushed me back to look me over before pulling me back into an embrace. I stood bewildered as Aunt Zelda fawned over me. It was the first true moment of sentiment and affection she'd shown me, and it cracked my heart wide open. This was my family. This was where I belonged; all that was missing was my Mom and Dad.

"Wait, what day is it?"

My aunties' faces came into full view as they released me from their worried grips. Apprehension creased their brows as they shared a knowing look.

"It's your birthday," Zelda began, before Effie swooped me up in another hug.

"Don't worry, Poppet, you're home now. You're finally home!"

# epilogue

# Soleil

Pacing the adjunct chamber, my skirt skittered on the smudged obsidian floor, picking up streaks of red. My gaze darted to the empty fountain in the corner of the room.

How much longer until that cursed Tembi reported back? The fountain should have been full by now with his updates. I spun on my heel, throwing my dress back and out of my way as I stalked up to the fountain's edge. With a snarl, I brought my fist down on the edge of the black glossy bowl.

A young servant at the door sneezed, catching my attention, and a small burst of flames popped out of his fingers. It singed the black leather of his suit and left a foul odor in the air.

I fixed him with a gaze that could curdle blood. "Enough!" I pointed to the smudges of blood on the floor, where the last guards had held a sparring match. "Clean this up and get out of my sight."

The victor, if he was still alive, would be in his cell enjoying two portions of rations as a prize for winning his fight. The loser, reduced to mere ashes... Well, he wouldn't be missing his share of the rations, would he? The tradition was wicked fun until they ruined my floor with so much blood; now it was all over me and this room. *Disgusting*.

My throne beckoned to me, and the small ache in my low back begged me to accept the seat. I hated this body—it was failing too soon. Stewards didn't age. I wasn't supposed to be aging.

I ran a black-tipped nail along my jaw, snagging on the weak skin and pinched. Shuddering, I dropped my hand and silently threatened the Fates to hurry up. I watched with disinterest as the young steward stooped low to clean the floor. A rag in each hand, he worked them in circles until the floor shone. I could see his reflection from several yards away.

His vigor disgusted me. It had been too long since I'd properly punished one of my guards. If only his work were sloppier... My fingers twitched at the urge to grapple with a weapon. Instead, I looked away as the sound I had been desperate for broke the silence.

The fountain gurgled to life, water spouting out of the top and raining down, filling the basin with sparkling bubbles. When the fountain stopped moments later, I waited for it to still.

A second guard manning the dais began to cough. Without hesitation, I whirled on him and sent a streak of blazing fire into his mouth. "Silence!"

The fountain's water had my attention before I heard his body thud to the floor. With a curt wave of my hand, the servant disposed of the guard. More rations for the next sparring victor. Finally, the water stilled enough for my reflection to morph into another image entirely, only broken up once as the scene focused. I held my breath.

Through the Tembi's perspective, I could see two stewards, a tall, broad man and a woman with long blonde hair. *No, wait...* The last of the ripples ebbed and I saw clearly. It was Josephine and a man with glowing orange eyes... Alaric.

*Nooo!* I held the scream inside, unwilling to tarnish the image I waited so long for. I had searched for Alaric, his whereabouts unknown, for more than a hundred years, and all along he was with *her*? That couldn't be possible.

The Tembi trapped the two in a siphon orb. Glee filled my chest knowing how this was about to end. I sent out our most decorated Tembi to finish the task after hearing the reports of a portal opening in Ruack Valley. The Tembis assigned to watch the area monitored its opening despite Khalon's shrewd attempts at camouflage.

The siphon orb worked; the two were slowly drained, and my body heated in response, watching the light slowly fade from Alaric's eyes. *About time*, I thought. He deserved every ounce of torture coming his way for the way he disobeyed me and loosed my captives.

But just as I relished the moment, it ended abruptly. Josephine turned toward Alaric, her face coming into clear view, but it wasn't Josephine. It was a girl who looked just like her. The Tembi surged toward her to withdraw her energy, and the unthinkable happened. The Tembi's view shuttered as though he'd been hit. Frantically, I searched for a way to still the waters when I realized I was helpless to change it.

The girl surged with more power, her face flushing. Leaning in, my nose skimmed the top of the water. And that's when I saw it. This Josephine look-a-like was a *channeler*.

I turned away briefly and bit my knuckle, stifling the fire within and suffocating the yell building up in my chest. A quick glance into the basin told me things had gone from bad to worse. The Tembi's gaze on the girl fractured into mirrored fragments. Something was wrong.

My knuckles turned white, gripping the rim, a stark contrast from its bottomless black gloss.

*No, no, no. This can't be happening. This was supposed to be a simple operation, a done deal.*

In the final moments of clarity, the woman latched onto Alaric and brought his mouth crushing down upon hers.

That was *my property* she was defiling.

A flash of light radiated from them and the Tembi's view dissolved into nothingness. With the scene gone, I slashed my hand through the water. It sizzled against my feverish skin.

"I almost had him!" I bellowed out. My gut churned and a strange feeling overtook me... a deep part of me felt fragile. It was a despicable feeling, one I'd fought to never feel. I wouldn't let them make a mockery of me or my operatives.

I might not know who that girl was, but I wouldn't rest until I found her and wore her teeth as charms around my neck.

A sweet memory floated to mind—Alaric's last beloved in chains in my dungeon. The sound of his cries were a symphony to my ears. I would make his blood sing again, if it was the last thing I ever did.

# Acknowledgments

First and foremost, I want to thank God, the Author of life itself. Without Him and His inspiration I wouldn't have told this story.

Secondly, I am eternally grateful for my husband's support—for every cup of water you refilled, and every insane theory you listened to. Your belief and cheer carried me through on more than one occasion.

A wonderful thank you to all the editors who worked on this manuscript. Leah, for taking the first draft and giving me the most brutal and fruitful feedback, and for taking the second and third drafts and making them what they could be today! Shira, for coming in clutch and polishing the book!

Huge thanks to: Jessie Cunniffe at Book Blurb Magic for auditing the book's blurb, making it sing; Megan at Lamplighter Literary for making my candle dreams come true; Amanda at Story Crumbs for bringing my troubled Alaric to life in cookie form; and McKenzie from Bloomery for creating an incredible launch strategy and helping me see this story through launch month!

To my early readers: my mom, the saint who listened to me read for countless hours; my best friend Dustie for taking a chance on my story in the early days; to my critique partners Dana, Gina, Elisa, and Jordan who provided the first bits of feedback; and my beta readers Makinsey, Stephanie, Kelsey, and Nicole your comments both delighted me and challenged me in the best way possible!

To the artist and dear friend who poured her creativity into this book: Kathryn, I quite literally couldn't have done this without you!

And to all my ARC readers and street team members: you guys are the best. Thank you for hyping this book up. You all hold a special place in my heart!

# About the Author

Katie Zeliger is the founder of Meraki Press and a seasoned storyteller whose career has spanned the publication of more than two dozen books. After years of helping other authors find their voice, she is now sharing her own.

Her eight years of missionary work across sixteen countries infuse her writing with global perspective, daring adventures, and a deep empathy for the human journey. She has been featured in *Novelists in November,* a Christian short story anthology from Wild Blue Wonder Press.

In her Christian young adult fiction, Katie blends humor, heart, and hope as she explores identity, purpose, and light amid the darkness.

Outside the writing world, she enjoys cooking, deep conversations, slow walks, crafting, and time spent with her family.